PRAISE FOR MEGHANN FOYE'S *METERNITY*!

"A fresh, contemporary take on love and work, marriage and motherhood, *Meternity* is guaranteed to surprise and delight!"
—Emily Giffin, #1 *New York Times* bestselling author of *Something Borrowed* and *First Comes Love*

"Funny, real and painfully true at times, *Meternity* tackles the bumpy road from singledom to modern motherhood with clever crafting and plenty of heart."
—Jane Green, *New York Times* bestselling author of *Summer Secrets* and *The Beach House*

"A character so lovable, a predicament so fantastic, I could not wait to find out what happens next!"
—Nicola Kraus, #1 *New York Times* bestselling co-author of *The Nanny Diaries*

"A witty and wonderful look at the challenges of being a woman today. Foye's mixture of humor mixed with honesty and satire will have you laughing out loud one minute and seriously pondering the state of the modern world the next."
—Lucy Sykes and Jo Piazza, authors of *The Knockoff*

"If Bridget Jones had a modern-day BFF who worked at a New York magazine, was faking a pregnancy, and was struggling with post-30 singledom, this laugh-out-loud debut would be her book!"
—Kristin Harmel, international bestselling author of *The Life Intended* and *The Sweetness of Forgetting*

METERNITY

Meghann Foye

ISBN-13: 978-0-7783-1930-6

33614059718816

Recycling programs
for this product may
not exist in your area.

Meternity

To my mother

METERNITY

Conception

Nothing compares with the miracle and magic of pregnancy. It's your chance to be involved with life's creative process.

—*Your Pregnancy Week by Week*

May

One

Spoken like a woman without kids.

I turn the article I'm working on over and tuck it under the latest issue of the magazine—I don't want anyone in the office to see the ocean of red marks my top editor has left all over it—especially this one. Not that anyone is likely to walk by, since we're all headed to the conference room for Pippa's shower—one of many baby showers we've already had since January. Smoothing my gypsy top over my jeans, I attempt to take a deep cleansing breath in the five-second walk. In my twenties, this kind of copy note was understandable— funny even, since I could roll my eyes and say, "Yep, no kids and thank God." But now, not so much. Now after ten years, it's begun to sting. Still, I paste on a smile.

"Everyone! Quick, quick! Come in!" shrieks Caitlyn, our shared editorial assistant slash Instagram editor slash "sassy millennial," or so proclaim all her social media profiles. She waves the *Paddy Cakes* staff in for our little Friday afternoon party and urges us to load up on Honey Cup cupcakes while taking it upon herself to raise our collectively dragging energy to #babyshowervibes.

I fight my way through the tangle of white and gold helium balloon ribbons toward the blond-wood table, hoarding a Honey Cup as if it wasn't an ever-present fixture, and *damn it*, manage to somehow get some sparkles from the bunting on me yet again. I'm *so* not in the mood for this—I've got way too much to do. But I still take a moment to appreciate the calm as I tuck in. Quiet. A little space to think. Summoning up sincere joy for Pippa. But from the other side of the party, there she is. The bearer of the red-lined comments. Alix.

My nemesis walks toward me in careful, measured steps in her black patent Tod's with a high-ply camel cashmere cardigan hanging from her pilates-sculpted shoulders. It's a fashion affectation adopted long before it came back into vogue, her expensively highlighted, long blond hair pulled into a perfect low ponytail. Alix consciously careens past the plate of cupcakes, pressing her bowed lips together in silent protest. A holdover from coming up around heroin chic, eating in plain sight is for *other people*—as is doing any sort of work deemed at an assistant level, such as expense accounts, making edits on-screen and more worryingly for me these days, any of her actual work. You know, old-school.

As everyone huddles in, the moms on staff transition over to the usual mommy banter. Talia, our fashion director, is complaining about her twins' inability to detach from various screens. Chloe, our usually impeccable beauty editor, is wearing haphazardly applied fake lashes, the only apparent sign of new-mom sleep deprivation.

Though I try casually to pull the balloons into a showery shield in front of me, the strings form no barrier from Alix's sharp presence edging toward me.

"Liz," she says, finding me in the corner. "Where are we with bottle-shaming? I really need to see it by three. I'm leaving early and I need to read it before I go."

"It's coming...just waiting for Sandy's publicist to confirm 'she'd sooner chew off her own daughter's earlobe than use formula' as you suggested on the edit," I reply.

"And what about '5 Ways to Avoid Narcissistic Kids'?" she demands, now reapplying ballet-pink gloss to her lips in the reflection of the glass wall of the conference room.

"On its way."

"Okaaaay." She draws her eyes up finally. "And what about August's 'Alternative Chinese Dialects for Kindergartners' story... I really need to see that one. It might be getting bumped up."

"I was going to get to that one once I'm back from my trip," I tell Alix. She's asked for a particularly tricky replacement quote, and I was holding off calling Tracey, our tiger mom in La Jolla.

"Well," she reprimands, "you should have told me if you couldn't get to it. I expect you to prioritize yourself."

I would have if you hadn't dropped it on my desk at 5 p.m. as you were leaving to take Tyler to the Baby Whisperer, I think. My eye begins to twitch. I rub my temples and down my cold brew iced coffee as if it were the last squeeze of the canteen on a lifeboat. What was I just reading in the tiger mom story? Hard work equals excellence equals reward? The virtuous circle. Yes, okay. Only after ten years at *Paddy Cakes*, it hasn't exactly worked out that way for me. Not after Alix was hired along with the changeover and claimed the deputy title that was promised to me, a long overdue bump up from articles editor.

Still, at least I've got Paris. Five full days strolling the Seine and the Musée Picasso, five days of café crème, five days of croissants. And five days free of the relentless swarm of Alix's emails asking for more research on the latest baby controversy du jour, treating me like I'm her secretary, and trapping me at the office well past midnight most nights.

Nope. What I've learned the hard way, postrecession "mediapocalypse," as assistant ranks have been traded for tech solutions, is this: having a child is really the only excuse a woman can use to work regular work hours or leave early. Single women don't have the same luxury, and therefore must take on the extra work, little cleanup projects and finishing up when the moms on staff have a hard stop. No baby—no excuse not to stay late.

"Everyone, everyone, *shh*! I'm going to make the call," says Caitlyn above the growing din. She picks up the phone and fights to hold back a giggle. "Pippa, Cynthia needs to see you in the conference room—NOW."

We've played this trick countless times at *Paddy Cakes*, or *The Baby Magazine for Moms and All Their Little Neuroses* as Jules, my work BFF and the only other mid-leveler on staff, and I call it. As we wait, I fiddle with my old cracked iPhone 4—the one corporate refuses to upgrade—and try to switch off the alerts for the FitBaby app our web editor is having me test out for a story. It's the one that supposedly monitors vital signs for your pregnancy, tracking miles walked, nutrition, sleep and the pièce de résistance: an ominous meter that calculates the totals into "Baby Smiles" using a patented and secret—albeit slightly random—algorithm. For "millennial moms who are *dissatisfied* with the typical pregnancy conversation and are looking for a more fun—and fit—experience," read the press release, which I've already thrown in the trash. It won't stop alerting me with "Push ☺ Notifications" that I need to "push it harder" to bring up my Baby Smiles score for the story.

"To do list?" pokes Jules, sensing my Mach-10 distractibility.

"It's getting there," I flat out lie.

Jules winces. "Then I hate to tell you, but I heard Alix talking to Tamara. The Marigold Matthews cover has dropped out—due to 'exhaustion.'"

"Diet pills and a botched mummy tuck, you mean."

Jules rolls her eyes, yes.

"Great..." I tug my blousy top down over my dirty little secret—my pair of size eight maternity jeans pilfered from the office giveaway table. Thanks to my midnight feedings as of late: cereal, some hummus scooped from the container with my finger because I forgot to buy carrots again, followed by a new brand of vegan cashew-milk ice cream/numbing agent. Jules is too quick not to notice, eyeing me.

"Do not even *try* to maternity-jean shame me," I tell her.

"*Liz.*" My overly practical office BFF from age twenty-two has only to say my name to trigger me.

"They're just so...*comfortable*," I say.

Arghhh! I wince as I see the time on my phone. It's 2:27 p.m. I've got exactly three hours and thirty-three minutes to finish my work before rushing home to pick up my suitcase, then head to the airport for my 10 p.m. flight. But now with the threat of the cover dropping out, I start to sweat. More coffee needed sends a signal from my temple. And sugar. My ever-present fantasy arises again: quitting to freelance travel write, my secret back-of-the-mind dream for what feels like months now. Maybe I won't get on the return flight.

I quickly check my account. I have $405 to make it through until next pay period. *Phew.* That should be enough while I'm in Paris on the press trip, and virtually all meals and activities will be covered. Then another alert. My credit card balance needs exactly $425 for the next payment due tomorrow. My throat begins to dry up...

"*Shh!* Everyone, *shh*! She's coming!" Caitlyn hushes us all again giddily even though the walls of the conference rooms are all glass.

Everyone giggles as Pippa spots the balloons. She softens into a huge smile and rubs her large belly as her eyes light up at the sight of the $1,789 Bugaboo Madaleen stroller we all had to chip in for, raised up on the conference table like a biblical golden calf.

"Liz!" says Chloe, touching her eye where her false lash is askew. "So how are you and JR doing? Heading off to Paris, I hear!"

I look down. I guess Jules hasn't said anything to our co-workers. "No, it's a press trip for Bourjois-Jolie, actually. JR and I broke up."

"Oh, Liz," she says, offering me a sympathetic look. "Are you okay? What happened?"

"We just weren't getting along," I say, embarrassed.

"It's okay, Liz. What are you, thirty? You've still got time."

"Thirty-one. But it's fine."

Talia joins in. In her early forties and married with twin two-year-old girls, I can tell she can't help herself. "You broke up with JR? After four years? Wasn't he about to pop the question?"

"Um, sort of. But that's okay," I respond, another attempt at brightness.

"Well, don't waste *too* much time. You don't want to miss your *window*."

"Uh, thanks."

"It's just so *haarrrd* out there right now to be single, isn't it?" says Chloe, her own skating-rink-sized rock gleaming like a searchlight from her left hand.

"No, it's fine." What I really want to say is, "If by hard, you mean searching for the unicorn of Tinder while spend-ing weekends under a duvet, ordering Seamless and watching endless rom-coms on Netflix, starting with *The Back-up Plan* and ending with *Under the Tuscan Sun* as a sort of 'final option,' than yes, maybe, a little."

Chloe then turns to Talia. "So, how are the girls?"

"Oh, you know how it is, new motherhood…"

"I *know*, we're sleep training now. Weissbluth." She cocks a brow conspiratorially.

"We did Weissbluth, Sears *and* Ferber, and finally the girls are *mostly* getting through the night. But you know who ends up being the one to put them back to sleep when they wake up at 3 a.m.?" says Talia pointing at herself. *"Moi!"*

"Exactly," responds Chloe.

The whole room joins in now, as they debate the merits of the latest types of sleep training as if their value as women depended on it. Ground zero for competitive parenting, we've battled our way through Mommy Wars, Tiger Parenting, French Parenting, Elephant Parenting, Amish Parenting, Leaning In, Opting Out, Attachment and Co-sleeping, Anti-Vaxx, Free Range, '70s-style, Gluten-Free Gooping, Paleo Parenting, KonMari Parenting (only do things that spark joy!)…not to mention "She who shall not be named" (*shh*… Jenny McCarthy). The rise of the "mommy" culture has turned modern motherhood into a marketing concept—a business to run—and our magazine has led the charge. Your child is no longer merely your offspring, a conception born out of love and fate, but your *product* to be programmed and perfected.

With the consensus that the baby should be further along, Chloe adds nervously, "We're thinking of trying the sleep consultant we featured in the January issue."

"Before you do that, you might want to think about that baby nutritionist—removing dairy and gluten can make a *huge* difference. Really helped my girls," tosses back Talia.

"But Poppy's six months old—she's just on breast milk," says Chloe.

"Oh, right. Well, maybe try seeing if she can clean up your own diet? Elimination diets are really the only thing that work," says Talia, looking self-satisfied.

Chloe dims.

What happened to just being happy? I wonder.

"I was just reading the American Academy of Sleep Medicine's new study," I muster, attempting to help Chloe out. "It's a fifteen-year longitudinal study involving sets of brothers that shows babies do equally well sleep-trained or not. It has more to do with the constellation of love and support they receive from their fam—"

"Spoken like a woman without a child." The familiar refrain sears into me again from the other side of the room. As if I haven't worked at a baby magazine for the past *ten years*. As if I don't know this stuff *cold*.

"*Everyone* knows *full* cry-it-out is best. A *disciplined* approach is the only thing that gets results. If you can't hack it, then get a night nanny," Alix says, purposefully folding her arms and looking at me directly. Message received: until you have a baby and become a *mom*, your opinions don't count. Or, more accurately, *you* don't count.

"How are things with you, Jules?" says Chloe, chirpily breaking through the awkward silence, which sets everyone off again into chitchat.

"Oh, we're good. Working on business school applications for Henry. Which is a big pain in my ass because I have to do them all, of course."

"Ha-ha," giggles Chloe. "Good luck with that. I should go check in with Pam about the 'Get Your Pre-Baby Face Back' story. Talk to you guys later!"

My shoulders slump.

Jules gives me a stern look. "Liz, listen, I know it's been hard dealing with what happened with JR this past winter, but you've got to get over it."

"I'm trying," I sigh. After years of canceling plans with JR because of work crises, I'd agreed without thinking to attend the *Paddy Cakes* Best of Babies Gala instead of JR's annual sales recognition dinner for P&G's East Coast reps. Ironically, I'd hoped that going to the gala would clinch my promotion to deputy editor, which would make all these years of hard work at the magazine all worth it, get me some assistant help and free me up to devote more time to my relationship. But when I told JR my plan, he walked out.

Jules sniffs. "Lizzie, he treated you like a fifties housewife, expecting you to act like some kind of WAG, not a woman with a job that keeps you at the office late most nights. Plus he secretly watched Fox News. He was not the guy for you. You were just settling and you know it."

"I know," I concede. "But he was *ready*. It's a certified fact that no man under forty who is sane, has a job and is fairly attractive wants to settle down in New York City."

Jules gives me a firm look. "Henry did."

"You met him straight out of college. That's not fair!"

Jules and Henry's story is straight out of a romance novel— in reverse. Fresh-faced and right on the heels of our first jobs at the magazine, Jules had been on her way home one night and recognized the cute boy walking toward her. Henry had been a senior when she was a freshman at Emory. Now both were living in the same Brooklyn neighborhood, and they literally bumped into one another—or so Henry claims. Jules told me she spotted him fifty feet away and planned the whole thing. After their "fateful run-in," he wooed her with his slow-cooked Carolina pulled-pork dinners and "power-cuddling," as Jules joked. They moved in together after only six months, then spent the rest of their twenties having fun, going to hear live music and traveling all over the world before getting married last year—one of the lucky ones, but to her credit, she *never* rubs it in.

"It's just, Talia's right—there's no time to waste. Just get back out there."

"Like with this guy, you mean?" I hold up my latest attempt at turning a Tinder convo into a date. Want 2B scummy with me 2nite? reads the opening line from a sweet-looking Williamsburg man with a scruffy beard.

"Oh, jeez," says Jules. "Just block him!"

"But he's wearing a suit! That means he has a job at least!" I pretend to sniff, looking down. "Or was invited to a wedding..."

The next man that comes up has long, brown stringy hair, a mustache and is holding a poodle in his lap. I like it doggy-style, reads his profile. Shuddering, I click the app closed.

"Just keep pounding the rock," nudges Jules. "One day it will crack."

"I know," I sigh, thinking, *or I will*.

I lean back onto the outer wall thwacking the cold glass with a loud bang as the sad realization hits me: unlike the twentysomething "little blonde girls" or LBGs I see husband-hunting around the East and West Villages, secretly quoting that Princeton Mom, I've been toting dog-eared *Eat Pray Love* and *Lean In* and actually *believing* the two rules my old editor in chief Patricia told me the first day I arrived as an intern at *Paddy Cakes*: *do one thing a day toward your goal and don't give up and eventually success will be yours*. But now it seems like that Princeton Mom was right all along. I've been a total fool. Beyond a certain age (i.e. thirty), women still have no legitimacy unless they're married, have kids and are running a household. We are *still* living in Austen-era England.

I should have been spending my twentysomething nights sweating my ass off at PowerCycle, not powering through stories on attachment parenting styles.

PUSH! ☺ Notification! Pregnancy is one of life's prime examples of letting go of control and allowing nature to take its course. You'll find that your body has a wisdom all its own. Relax and listen to its messages.

That's dark, I think, trying to figure out how to shut the app off.

Then, before I notice it, our new editor in chief Cynthia walks in and announces, "Sorry to cut this joyous affair short, but I need you, Alix." Then Cynthia turns her steely gaze on me. "And you, too, Liz. Now."

Me? Without a word, I leap up, ignoring the stares as I trail after Cynthia and Alix. They burn a path down the hallway to Alix's office.

The second we're inside, Cynthia immediately turns to Alix.

"Did you find those Asian couple options yet? We are going to rework the 'Alternative Chinese Dialects' story and go with the *harder-hitting*-themed issue you suggested— 'Tiger Moms Vs French Moms: The Battle Royale Heats Up.' We'll use that family with the Caucasian mom and Chinese-American dad on the cover along with their mixed-race baby. The press will eat it up!"

Alix looks over at me. "The revise is almost done..."

"When am I to see it?"

"Immediately after this. Right, Liz?" Alix's eyes shoot daggers through me.

"Yes."

Satisfied, Cynthia turns and walks out. Alix motions for

me to stay. The pit in my stomach tells me what's coming next.

"We have just about everything we need, correct? Did you incorporate all my notes? The revised draft was still a bit sloppy. Did you address my question about finding a more *inflammatory* quote from that one mom from California?"

"Yes, I went back to Tracey a few times but I don't know if we'll be able to get more examples of punishment. She's okay with representing herself as a disciplinarian, but not in the more extreme way we, uh, would like her to."

I preempt Alix's next question. "I did ask her if she ever resorted to physical punishment. She said a few light spankings, but that's all."

Her brow creases. "What word did she use *exactly*?"

I know where she's going with this. Yet again, I'll have to get a source to sign off on a quote by assuring her that by tweaking the wording, we are doing them a service. I hear my inner voice say, *This is wrong.*

"She said 'spanking.' That's it."

I tried. But we're not going to use the word Alix wants: *beating*.

"I'm sure we can substitute a word here or there," Alix says quickly. "Since it's broader than spanking, and it means virtually the same thing. Just run it by her."

I swallow hard, and then I hear myself say, "No."

"No, what?"

"I can't."

"Why not?"

"She doesn't *beat* her children, Alix."

"Liz, I know we can get her to agree to that line," Alix says. "Otherwise the story won't work for a cover line, and we have no time for a replacement."

Stomach clenching, I realize it will be a race to the finish line to make it to JFK on time tonight, and most likely I'll be working on the plane and through the rest of my trip.

"Always finding problems, never the solutions," Alix says out of the corner of her mouth.

I catch it, dropping my shoulders. "I'll call her and see what I can get her to say."

"Good," says Alix just as Jeffry Clark, our new executive managing editor hired by Cynthia out of a digital media agency, strolls in. MacBook Air in one hand, his other is in his jeans' pocket, male entitlement emanating off of him with every unhurried step. His Bushwick beard and inked sleeves read carefully studied hipster, but in the past few months his consulting-driven management style has meant he's anything but relaxed, constantly on us to find new "efficiencies," just like his annoyingly foreshortened name.

"Alix, Liz. Have you figured out who's writing this story yet?"

"Liz will do the first draft and I'll top-edit the Monday after next when it's done," says Alix before I'm even able to respond. "Liz, you speak French, right? You can track down the French moms living in the States."

"We're going to need to make sure the subjects are available to shoot next week. Who's prepping?" asks Jeffry.

"I'm out next week," says Alix. "Turks and Caicos, remember?"

"Well, someone's got to be here to manage the shoot. The assistants can't handle it."

No... NO, I think simply as images of my Parisian trip come tumbling down. Alix points her gaze directly at me. "Liz can handle it, I'm sure," she says.

"I'm out, too, next week. Remember the press trip you wanted me to go on? What if I find American mothers living in France?"

"That won't work." Alix shakes her head no. "They need to be based here."

"Sorry, Liz, you're going to have to cancel the trip," he says. "Alix has a family reunion in the Caribbean she can't miss. You can go to Paris anytime. We need coverage here. I'll let the PR firm running the trip know."

I can't quite think what to say with the two of them staring at me. Refuse them and I'll be fired and probably blacklisted from the entire industry. I flash to my shameful $7,897 of credit card debt, courtesy of a stream of bridesmaid-related expenses over the past few years, my rent check, the upcoming $505 reoccurring student loans payment reminding me every month that I chose the priciest liberal arts education so I could make the very connections landing me here.

"Alix, please, is there another way?"

"I'm sorry, Liz. It's not my job to clean up your mess. You could have handled it if you were more efficient with your time."

"But I always have to take on the workload of other staffers out on maternity leave on top of my own. You *know* that."

"You always seem to have excuses," Alix says. "If you had children, I'd understand, but tell me why is it such a big deal to stay late a few nights a month when you have no real responsibilities otherwise?"

All of a sudden, my face feels hot. I had always figured hard work would be rewarded, but apparently the joke is on me. If I were a mother and in the right "box," I'd have a legitimate excuse. But I haven't been able to make that happen yet. And until I do, no matter how hard I work, I won't count. *Fuck it.*

"No."

"What?" Alix says.

"I can't," I respond, simply.

Alix's eyes narrow. "Liz, your attitude has been holding us back for too long. I need to talk to Cynthia." As she turns to leave, I inhale a whiff of her noxious, old-school perfume and I gag. Doubling over, I begin to dry heave.

"Liz, are you okay?" asks Jeffry. He and Alix rush to my side, as they tell me to breathe. Finally, I straighten up. "I'm sorry, I, uh, I don't know what happened. I've been feeling a little off lately," I stammer. Just then, an eerie giggle lets out from my old phone.

PUSH! ☺ Notification! Week 16: Congratulations! Your baby is now the size of a kumquat! Time to start some squats! Baby Smiles: 0!

I fumble to mute the sound and click the screen closed, but it's too late. "Oh, God. Not you, too," Jeffry whispers.

"Are those *maternity* jeans?" gasps Alix.

I go completely blank, and then I hear words coming out of my mouth I don't recognize as my own. "Yes. Me, too."

Jeffry's attention is riveted on me now.

Did I really just say that?

For a few seconds, they are speechless. "Wait, Liz, are you pregnant?" Alix jumps in.

With my eyes fixed on the floor, my whole body freezes. I don't say yes, but I don't say no. A few seconds pass. There's a spasm in the pit of my stomach.

"Well, then, that settles it. We can't do anything now. Jesus," says Jeffry.

"When are you due?" Alix says.

I look down at the app. "October 20."

"Huh," says Jeffry, confused. "I didn't know you…had a boyfriend…a partner."

"Because it's none of anyone's business," I say. *Where is this confident Liz coming from?* "By the way, Jeffry," I add, "Alix asked me to alter one of the tiger mom's quotes to make it say that she beats her children, but it's not true."

Alix's and Jeffry's faces both display a look of shock.

And then I lean over and throw up the contents of Pippa's baby shower into Alix's wastebasket.

Two

Guys, I did something stupid. Need help!!!! I text Addison and Brie with hands so shaky I can barely type. Loose papers are sent flying across my desk as I attempt to grab what I need. I have to get out of here—*fast*. Finally I spot what I'm looking for—my dog-eared copy of *What to Expect*. I stuff it into my bag, then race toward the elevators and out the lobby.

A text from Cynthia! *She's heard*. Set up an appointment for first thing Monday morning. You are coming in, aren't you?

Yes, of course. I will, thank you!!! I type with way too many exclamations. *Shit*.

Finally, just as I'm making my way toward the subway, Addison texts back. Can you come here? She's at a client meeting at Soho House in the Meatpacking District.

On my way too, texts Brie, who's coming from Core Fusion in the Flatiron.

Thank God. I decide to hop in a cab heading downtown from the Bird Cage, our nickname for our publisher Halpren-Davies's beautiful turn-of-the-century Beaux Arts building right below Times Square, as waves of adrenaline flood my system. Did I really just let my bosses think that I'm pregnant? Am I having a psychotic break? This must be some sort of deranged, baby-fever-induced psychosis that *Paddy Cakes* will surely one day cover in its pages.

As the taxi cruises down Ninth Avenue, I start to panic. When Cynthia finds out the truth, I will be fired and never work in the magazine industry again. *Jezebel* and *The Cut* will have a field day mocking "the editor who cried pregnant."

Oh, how I wish I had the guts to just quit on the spot like Addison did. After forgetting to do her boss's expenses in favor of taking on more writing assignments, she'd been put on probation until she could "prove her value."

"I don't need a month," she'd told them in typical Addison fashion. "I already know my value. Consider this my notice."

That afternoon in 2008 she and I sat in Bryant Park sipping smoothies and in the span of an hour, she'd decided that instead of looking for a new job, she was going to launch her own fashion blog. It has now grown to a collection of more than one thousand fashion writers, bloggers and YouTube personalities. In the past eight years, she's transformed herself into a *Forbes* 30 Under 30 "content-preneur" whose influencer machine called *The Couture Collective* has started to pay off, earning her a smooth 15 percent commission on each piece of content written exclusively for boutique fashion brands. These days she's completely obsessed with building out her own proprietary platform so she can "scale"—and meeting hot angel investors to fund it.

I nervously check my texts. Nothing more from Cynthia. I find myself in a mad Googling frenzy. "Faking pregnancy" leads to "workplace pregnancy rights," leads to "criminal time served for health insurance fraud," leads to me almost throwing my phone out the window right then and there. I finally realize there *is* someone else I can call to reassure me. Someone who knows all the players and *exactly* what to do.

Ford. My former work husband, ten years my senior and the one who showed me the ropes when I first arrived at *Paddy Cakes*, now managing editor at our men's publication *Basics*. I text him, and get an immediate response back, I'm there.

When I arrive at Soho House and give the concierge Addison's name, they send me up to the sixth floor parlor. The glamorous lounge is heating up, and I spot more than a few tables of successful-looking men with slim-cut suits chatting up decades-younger girls with stomach-revealing tops—LBG-ism is in full effect. I spot Addison at a center table clacking away at her laptop. Thankfully Brie arrives a few minutes later. Then Ford.

When I tell them what happened and why I am not on my way to Paris, I expect them to be horrified. Instead they're angry *for* me.

"Good for you!" says Addison, sweeping her bayalaged-blond locks into a ponytail. "I've had enough of these elite dinosaurs abusing women for their entire twenties with the false promise of a move up the masthead, only to leave them surviving on cupcakes, caffeine and cocktails and living in cramped Queens Craigslist shares with roommates they can't stand and cockroaches circling their bedroom door! It's torture, plain and simple. They've traumatized you! I say, screw 'em!"

"Addison's right, Lizzie," says Brie, putting a hand on my arm. "You haven't been yourself for a while. When you started out, you had a glow. But lately, you've lost your sparkle. You *had* to do something."

Brie should know. A recent graduate of Life-Wise, a health and wellness digital entrepreneur program, she rebranded herself from marketing associate to "disruptive" innovation consultant. She's now making six figures for regular project work on global health nonprofits, thanks to her sleek Power-

Points that feature emerging social media logos and have titles like, "What Is Change?" But her trendy, chocolate half bun and hot-red lipstick don't fool me. My pint-size friend is still on the same quest to find her soul mate that she's been on since she was twenty-one.

"This is even more entertaining than the male models at the Prabal Gurung event I was at last night," says Ford, tugging at his black cashmere cardigan to try to cover up a tiny pudge by his waistline as he comes up upon our table. When we worked together we'd nicknamed him Ford—as in Tom Ford—because his square jaw and flinty blue eyes could get him just about any male model he pleased. He'd even had a hot and heavy summer fling with that EGOT winner/sitcom star John Paul Harding that he'd let go to his head. In the past few years, though, a magazine-induced designer-foodie habit had caught up with him—probably to cover up the heartbreak he'd never let on about—and now he's more ginger bear than Beckham.

While Addison grills me on the details, Brie nods reassuringly as Ford can't stop himself from laughing, and I keep my fingers crossed no one from *Paddy Cakes* shows up.

"I'm sure it's burnout. I've got this amazing homeopath I've been seeing. It might just be a question of unblocking your gallbladder merid—" Brie starts in as I explain everything that happened.

"I think she needs more than a homeopath…she needs a baby daddy," jokes Ford.

"Well, before that, she needs to start having some sex," replies Addison.

"Guys! Stay focused! What am I going to do? I'm going to be fired. And blacklisted and have to move home to my mom's couch."

"Liz, don't catastrophize. I'm sure there's a solution," responds Addison.

The four of us are silent as we look around, thinking.

There, sitting to the right of us is a towheaded blonde, talking loudly to her laptop's phone feature, seeming to be working on her motherhood lifestyle blog. From her flower-child Coachella style, I'm guessing she's probably from LA. And all of about twenty-five.

"I mean...it's fine," she says, rolling out a succession of whiny calls. "Annie Leibovitz is cool, but you know, we could be doing five of these in a day in LA and getting, like, a major beauty brand to sponsor. Yeah, seriously. Yeah, you know what the trick is? Breast-feeding shots—the followers *live* for them. Virginal maiden thing. It's totally faked, though... Oh, wait, sorry, it's my manager—well, my mom, well, you know—same thing. Ha. Lols. Hi, Mom. Yeah, okay, a shoot in Aspen. Great. When?" Her face changes in a blink. "They *aren't* flying out my nanny? Then I don't wannaaaaa. That means we have to get up at the crack of dawn. Like, 9 a.m.!!!"

Addison looks lit up. "Wait a second... I think Ms. Coachella could be on to something. Why don't we fake it? We're always doing that at shoots. Maybe it could work? At least for a little while."

"Hmm. That's not bad," says Brie, lighting up at the idea.

"Do you think she can handle it?" Ford asks, referring to me in third person as if I'm a mental patient.

"Not helping..." I butt in.

"Look, Lizzie, I think it's your only option. You can fake for one month—until June 6—and use your time to line up enough freelance writing gigs to get a running start. And your first bump will be tiny. No one will have to know besides the key players."

"Ooh, I've got the perfect solution. I'll ask this guy I've been wanting to hook up with to see if he wants to help you create your so-called bump. He's a stylist at the *Naomi Marx Show*. Plus, it'll give me a reason to see him. He's young, hot, kind of a douche. You know, just my type." Ford grins.

"What if I get caught?"

"You can do it, Lizzie. You've been practically breathing babies since you were twenty-two. You know this stuff cold," says Addison firmly.

"If I slip up, I'll be fired."

"You'll be fine!" says Addison. "I'll happily help you screw with that company. They're my biggest competitor!"

"What if word gets back to *Paddy Cakes* that I'm looking for freelance?"

"It's not like travel editors really know parenting ones—they're like full-fat lattes and Alix—they don't mix," says Ford.

"Listen, Lizzie, you've got this," says Addison confidently. "Quick, what are the first set of tests called and what's their function?"

"Standard blood tests—make sure you're healthy," I rattle off.

"When will you know the sex?"

"Easy, as early as the first blood test. Ten weeks."

"What are the first physical signs of pregnancy?"

"Morning sickness, indigestion, loosening of the pelvis and ligaments—and boobs! Bigger boobs!" I look down at my own size-Cs...the lucky inheritance from my mom's French-Canadian side, along with absolutely no thigh gap.

The girls keep quizzing me and the answers leap out of me on their own, rapid-fire, like a baby-knowledge-spewing semi. It's as if I've been waiting my whole life for this day.

"How much sleep did you get last night?" quizzes Brie, now having fun.

"Ha, trick question. Not enough."

"Who's the daddy?" riles Ford.

"Let's just say immaculate conception for now..."

"Perfect, since as we know, motherhood is the ultimate way to deify yourself," says Addison.

"One more. How many weeks are you right now?"

"I don't know?" I freeze. I look down at the app. Since "weeks" start on Mondays, I'm at the tail end of sixteen weeks. Just a little over five months until October 20. My "due date," I realize with strange solemnity. My eyes sweep around the room, feeling my brain abuzz with activity. The coffee grinder whirring combines with the sounds of clinking wineglasses as the lounge begins to heat up. Everywhere, the sights and sounds of possibility are brewing. Maybe more is out there than I've let myself realize. Maybe my friends are *right*.

I sit back in my chair and allow the idea of a "*meternity* leave"—time off for *me* to really figure out what I want to do with my life—to take hold... Could this be it?

A long-suppressed vision of myself begins to resurface. I picture trading my monochromatic office formulas for sunny tanks and sarongs and sipping strong Indonesian coffee while finishing up an article for *Travel + Leisure* from a beach in Bali. Maybe I'll even be spotted by a handsome importer/exporter, who will knock me up for real...

A power surge unblocks something inside me that has been bound up for ages. Looking at my friends, I realize they're right. I have to see this through—it really is my only option. I place my hands on the table firmly.

"So I'm keeping this baby, is what you're saying?"

"Yes." Addison looks me dead in the eye.

"Yes." Brie wraps an arm around my shoulder.

"Yes," says Ford, nodding up and down like a puppy dog.

"Okay, then." I gulp. "I feel sick."

"You're supposed to," giggles Brie.

Meternity, here I come.

Three

By 11:15 p.m. we've slugged back some vodka sodas, and somehow my friends have managed to convince me to join them at a packed karaoke bar on St. Mark's Place. Addison begins to make inroads with a table in the back full of fashion bloggers, model bookers and extremely skinny models from Balkan countries while I try to keep Brie away from checking her phone every three minutes.

At this point, Brie knows not to expect anything besides a friends-with-benefits situation from her forty-four-year-old former ad exec colleague, Baxter. He's made himself clear about not wanting a "romantic attachment," as he icily put it one night at Babbo when she mistakenly assumed ample making out might mean he was interested in something romantic. But still she wonders if she's putting out the wrong "vibe" to the universe if she allows their relationship to continue, since she's not even sure she'd want him if he actually were into her, as like a potential husband. Ever more ironic is that all she's been thinking about since turning thirty is finding a PH (potential husband), as she's started calling every available man with a job.

After text number six, I give her the stink eye.

"I sweeaaaar to you, Lizzie. After tonight, it's plan Secret-4-the-One."

"WTF is that?" I respond as Addison goes up for her song.

"It's new—something I devised at a recent mastermind session. A combination mix of *The Secret*, *The 4-Hour Work Week* and *Outliers*. Basically I'm going to set an intention for the perfect guy, then outsource my flirting on every available dating app to reach my goal of ten thousand hours. I'll attain dating mastery while using up all available 'Love RAM,' so Baxter can't even take up a kilobyte."

To me it sounds about as exhausting as faking a pregnancy, but she seems enthused so I go with it, smiling and nodding as she takes her turn on the mic. Inside, though, I'm panic-stricken. This feeling must be what all our younger editors talk about, I think, fighting off waves of anxiety so intense it's as if the room is swaying. All these years, I'd somehow managed to sidestep the Dark Side that so many editors fall into as a means of coping with the pressure: anorexic bouts, Adderall addictions, the occasional bump of coke. I'd never seen the point to all that—or maybe it was my Catholic good-girl upbringing—but now I think I feel what this new kind of terror is all about. I try to fight through it by gulping more of my gasoline-like vodka soda while panning the room we've been to countless times.

Addison grabs the songbook away from me and hands back a microphone. "You're up, my friend. NO MORE wallowing. I can't take it."

"No, absolutely not. Not tonight." I shake my head. Karaoke has never been my strong suit—ever since the "You Oughta Know" debacle of '02, our freshman year of college when every single guy in the room shuffled out, giving me a first impression that sealed my star-crossed romantic fate all throughout college and a lasting new nickname: Ballbuster.

But then I hear the familiar dance party hit "Hotstepper." Thankfully it saves me. The '90s rap rhythm is followed by "Everybody Dance Now." I turn on my heel, and a very cute, thirtiesish-looking guy makes his way to the stage from right behind us, looking strangely confident. He proceeds to take the mic, and launch into a perfectly punctuated rap, sending us into a round of laughs.

"He's good," says Brie.

"I know," I say, impressed.

"I might have told him my friend was having the worst day of her life, and a little '90s medley would cheer her up."

"Oh, God, you didn't, *Addison*."

"Someone had to give you a push." She smirks.

Next it's "I'm Too Sexy," then "Don't Go Chasing Waterfalls." From the get-go, he's totally got it, nailing every single low-voiced guy part. Halfway through "Crazy," he pushes a hand through his light brown wavy hair as he uses the other to do some sort of complex Steven Tyler move. He's got on those light-wash Gap jeans all the soccer players used to wear in college. He's so into it and so making fun of himself at the same time, I can't stop laughing. By the time Chumbawamba's "I Get Knocked Down" comes on, the entire crowd is cheering him on as he attempts the grand finale—the running man to "Poison."

"He's got balls." Addison nods approvingly.

"He's cute," says Brie.

"I think I know him," I say. "How do I know him?"

Brie surfaces a sticky sweet lemon drop shot. I down it, thinking to myself, *Why not?* Clearing my throat, I turn toward the teleprompter, cursing as I see my name. Addison and Brie, those little cheeks, can't hide their giggles when the traumatically familiar chorus begins to play. As always, every last face in the bar is cringing as I screech out the first few verses. Pretty soon, I'm belting it out, battling my way through the lyrics as if my life depended on it. It feels good. *I'm a woman without a box, and I don't care anymore, damn it.*

"You...you...you oughtta know," I sing out at full volume, just as the song stops sooner than I expect. My voice fills the void with a shriek, followed by silence. Finally I look up. Addison and Brie fight to contain their giggles. A slow, perfunctory applause emerges from the crowd. I notice Gap Jeans Guy is clapping jokily, too. *God.* Head down in shame, I beeline off the stage. Needing another drink, I walk over to the bar, red-faced.

"One vodka soda, splash of cran," I say to the bartender.

"That will be sixteen dollars," he responds. *Ouch.*

"I'll get you a drink," a weird guy with fluttery eyes says as he reaches for his man purse. "Malibu?"

"Uh, no thanks," I say, trying to be polite, searching around in my oversize bag for my wallet. I balance my huge hobo carryall on the edge of the counter to get a better look. Then something heavy inside shifts the center of balance, and all of the contents spill out on the floor.

"Um, can I help you with that?" It's Gap Jeans Guy. He's coming over to the bar. I feel myself growing flustered as we both reach down toward the floor and he hands over my copy of *What to Expect When You're Expecting.*

"That's not, er, mine, well it is, but I'm not...you know... I work at a baby magazine." He looks as if he's biting his lip, trying not to laugh.

"Wait, are you Liz Buckley? Deputy editor at *Paddy Cakes*? I thought you looked familiar up there. It's Ryan—from the Discovery Channel."

That's right, I remember now. He recently turned thirty-seven, which I'd noted when he'd friended me on Facebook. I'd helped handle some details on a *Paddy Cakes* story they'd brought to air on mega multiples.

Before I can correct him on my title, the music comes on. "Oh shoot, my next song's up." And with that, he gets up on stage, as Pearl Jam's "Better Man" starts up. I can't believe how good Ryan is. Well, not exactly perfect, but strong, confident. As I stare at him, I notice his ability to let go. It's sweet. So different from the zombified Patrick Batemen psychos I'm used to dealing with on Tinder. He's actually got a beating heart. Once he's through, he comes back to the bar to join me.

"My buddies made me get up there on a losing bet. My team, Liverpool, lost today."

"Seems like you've been practicing," I tease. It's his turn to grow red.

"Hey, I'm thinking of hitting the ramen spot for some takeout on my way home now. Wanna join me? You look like a girl who could use some soup."

"Why not," I say as I laugh to myself. Brie is in the middle of an overemotive power ballad, making me feel like the night will soon be over anyway, and this is only a preamble to a Baxter hookup.

I signal to Addison that I'm leaving and she waves me off, indicating that she's got Brie-watch covered. I notice her venture capitalist du jour Brady has also shown up.

Ryan and I work our way through the crowded street to a spot down the block called Soju Ramen. There's a line out the door. In front of us, five twentysomething guys in flannels debate the merits of a few ramen shops in Flushing. I secretly love this talk, I think, feeling better. We finally arrive at the head of the line and the server asks us what we want.

"I'll take the pork belly, please."

"Nice. Make that two, please," pipes up Ryan. "Five sriracha in mine."

"Woah, you like it hot, huh?"

"You know it." Ryan readjusts his worn-in baseball cap. "So deputy editor Liz Buckley... Are you going to watch the mega-multiples special next week?"

"Yes, but I'm not deputy. Alix is."

"Aren't you the one doing all the work on the tie-in?"

It took tons of my time—but Alix got the credit as always. "Yes, well, you know how it is...".

The woman at the counter eyes us, making us realize others are trying to order. Ryan guides me toward the side, gently touching my arm. "Do you live around here?"

"Uh, no, Upper West Side."

"Oh, cool. Uptown, fancy. Only the best for Deputy Editor Liz," he teases.

"Ha. Not quite." I think of the same small, rent-stabilized studio apartment I've been living in for the past four years handed down to me from my former editor at *Paddy Cakes*.

"Me neither. I'm on First and A."

"Party central," I tease back. It comes easily, like I don't even have to try.

"No—I live with my brother—he got a great deal a few years back and it's close to the bar where I watch the Premier League games." He looks down at his feet. "Let's figure out a plan to meet up and discuss some new ideas soon."

"Sure," I say, trying to play it cool. "That would be great."

"I, uh, should get your number, just in case," he says, strangely serious all of a sudden.

I'm not expecting this at all. I give him the same 917 number I've had since college.

"To stay or to go?" calls out the woman at the counter. Ryan looks at me, expectantly. I would like to stay and hear more about his job, his love of British soccer and the exact origins of his Gap jeans, but the weight of today's events added to the lemon drop and the vodka-cran have sent me crashing and I don't feel confident about what might come out of my mouth next.

"Ugh, to go, I guess," I tell the woman.

"Make mine to go, too," Ryan says.

"That will be twenty-four dollars," says the woman.

"Oh, they must have combined our orders—" I start fumbling for cash.

"That's okay, I've got this," says Ryan, waving away my attempt.

"No, I don't mean to make you feel sorry for me."

"I've got it," he pushes. "Anyway, I don't feel sorry for you, Liz. I know you're going places. Soup's on you next time."

He grins and takes off down the street.

I notice my stomach has grown warm feeling and it's not just the soup.

Four

PUSH! ☺ Notification! Week 17: Think of every pound gained as a sign of a healthy, happy baby. Of course you don't want to gain too much. So stop and give us 40. Lolz. J.K. Baby Smiles: 15!

"Aren't *you* in desperate need of a makeover?" says Hudson, Ford's just-a-touch-judgmental friend, as he's sizing me up through his Mr. Rogers black-rimmed glasses in an empty makeup room at the *Naomi Marx Show*. At 9 a.m. on Monday morning the dressing room is quiet. None of the other production assistants are in yet, but all around me are racks of jewel-toned dresses, five-inch stilettos, scary-looking hair pieces, and big blown-up posters of Naomi staring back at me, with her signature Cleopatra-like closed-mouth smile.

"I haven't had time," I say in a daze. I need coffee.

"I was thinking we could do one size for each month, since your clothes will cover it. I already have months four through six from the time when Naomi was doing that series on 'Teen-Mom Boot Camp.' I'll have to take your measurements now and then get you the rest of the months later," he says, wrapping the tape around my waist, hips and bust.

I'm thinking I'll just need the one, but then again no harm being measured.

"Now, if you're really going to do this right, you have to wear the bump, cover it with Spanx, then a thin slip. Leave *no* lines. Think you can do that?" says Hudson, snapping the measuring tape off my waist.

"Yes, of course." I sneer and grab the largest of the bumps out of his hands, walk behind a changing screen and slip it over my head. After wriggling it down so it sits right over my pooch, I fit my empire-waist dress over it and come back out to look in the mirror.

"Looks real," says Ford with an eye raise. "Totally real."

"I know," says Hudson. "I'm really good at this."

"Weird," I say, almost in a trance. Staring back at me in the mirror is a six-months pregnant Liz. The bump makes my roundish cheeks look thinner than usual (or is the bump creating an optical illusion?) and my ice-blue eyes have a watery gleam to them. Even in my old peacock-blue jersey dress, my five-foot-five frame looks, well, not bad. My thinnish medium-length "brond" hair seems to fall differently—fuller and wavier.

"At least you're well-proportioned—nice legs, square shoulders—so as long as you don't mess up the application, the bumps should sit perfectly."

I feel the taut orb. It seems to be made of a foam rubber that is slightly firmer than usual, not unlike a half a Nerf football, sitting perfectly over my lower abdomen.

Hudson eyes me. "Memory foam."

"Tempur-Pedic?" I respond.

"Yep—but slightly different—not as squishy. I have a supplier in Sweden."

"Wow," I say, grateful for this little bit of luck on a Monday morning. I thank Hudson, pack up the first little eighteen-week belly and make plans to get the rest later—if I should even need them. Despite the extreme terror I feel as I walk out of the midtown sound studio, I'm buoyed. Could this actually work? But my reverie fades as soon as I walk into the office around ten fifteen.

"Liz, come here," says Jeffry, signaling me over to the spot outside his own corner office. "Alix says she's been emailing you questions all morning about the cover story research and you haven't gotten back to her. You know we're on a tight schedule." He proceeds to tap away at his computer calendar, looking down at my stomach conspicuously. I reach to wrap my arms around myself instinctively.

"I emailed Alix that I had a doctor's appointment this morning."

"Well, you can't take time off just because of your *situation*," he says, which makes me feel both mad and seriously guilty. "By the way I've forwarded you our Family and Medical Leave Act paperwork. Make sure to have it back to me by end of the week. Otherwise, you might jeapordize your maternity leave benefits. And you also need to figure out how you plan to use vacation in addition to the six weeks paid."

Jules and I had taken issue in theory with the fact that the medical leave act FMLA essentially likened pregnancy to a disability, but now I was finding it downright disturbing. Just six weeks paid leave? Maybe the moms in the office don't have it as easy as I thought they did.

Just then, the UPS guy brings over an enormous package. It's from Giggle, the high-end baby store we're forever mentioning in our pages. "Alix emailed us the great news! Congrats, mama-to-be!" says the card inside from Carly, the PR contact I've worked with for years. *Shit!* Hoping no one sees the display, I paw through the box, instantly feeling a wave of complex emotions—guilt, and glee—that Carly now thinks I'm pregnant.

Inside the tissue, there's everything I could ever want or need—maternity sports bras, softer-than-soft pajama tops. There's even a pillow to put between my knees while I'm sleeping. Beneath it are gift certificates for the Nuna swing, the Keekaroo changing pad and even the Silver Cross pram, the mythical stroller of the gods that all the royals use—it's like three thousand dollars. I stuff the package under my desk into a corner to get to work lining up French moms, almost thankful I can take my mind off things.

By midday, group emails about the tiger/French moms story sits stalled on the screen while I make up my profile on BabyCenter.com. As a joke, I send the link to Jules. I've been terrified to tell her what I decided, but I figure now is about as good a time as any.

"Are you on crack?" She practically leaps over the desk partition.

"No, why?" I say innocently.

"I said keep pounding the rock, not jump off the ledge!" Her whispers have a hard edge as she eyes around the office floor. Jules motions for us to go into the only semiprivate conference room. "Aren't you worried about how you're going to pull this whole thing off? I mean, you're not hooking up with anyone right now. Don't you think everyone's going to wonder who the father is?" she asks.

"I have some time to figure it out."

Jules still looks at me like I've got two heads. "But what about your paycheck, future career prospects, your dignity? You can't *pretend* to be pregnant for five months. People are going to know you're lying. You work in an office full of people who are fully aware of every nuance of pregnancy."

"True," I say, trying to hold my ground. "But so do I."

"You mean to tell me the first time someone starts quizzing you about the tests, the names, the schools, the doctors, whatever, you're not going to 'pull a Liz' and go completely blank. The jig will be up before you can even start to show."

"I'll work it out somehow." I'm not sure why I feel such a great urge to push back at her on this. Then I see Alix wending her way over to my cube, armed with a bunch of file folders. Wait—what is she doing here! The least she could do was TAKE HER VACATION!

Without saying a word, she drops something on my desk, allowing the contents to scatter over my already-disheveled pile system. Jules and I head back, and I sit down. Rather than the tiger moms/French moms revise, she's given me the "Stages of Newborn Spit-up" story I'd helped her with over two weeks ago. It must be back from Cynthia with edits.

"Thanks for that," she says, nodding at the story covered in Cynthia's red pen. "Tyler developed a fever and Marisol couldn't get him to sleep, so I had to cancel my trip, after all. I'll need you to be on call just in case he gets worse and I have to go to the doctor with him."

"Sure," I say flatly, thinking how easy it is for mothers to employ the verb *have*, like I *have* to leave work early to pick up Tyler's nut allergy results; I *have* to go get Tyler's organic baby puree before Whole Foods closes. I wonder what would ever happen if I said, "I *have* to meet Brie at happy hour or she's going to hook up with her ex-boyfriend who's just using her for sex."

"Better get that revise to me ASAP. You should be boning up on the latest in prenatal digestion anyway. The mother's *microbiome* has a significant effect." She eyes my stomach with a hint of suspicion.

"You know what all our moms say—I can eat whatever I want for the next five months."

"Watch out. I've seen people gain weight that never seems to come off with that attitude. It's just plain lazy."

Kicking away the piles of baby toys I've gathered over the years under my own desk, I start in on one of my August stories. This time it's on the benefits of unbleached cotton swaddling blankets costing upward of two hundred dollars, ethically sourced and "designed" in the USA by a cute couple in St. Louis who used to work in digital marketing in the city—perfectly punny adjectives about the benefits of organic cotton are coming easily ("Walk like an Egyptian"). Before I know it, it's 10 p.m. and the day, and night, are gone.

Wearily, I make my way to Alix's office to hand off the files for her top edit. An artful arrangement of lilies crowds the corner of her desk, an ever-present feature thanks to all the glowing coverage of advertisers. As I place the files on her desk, a few slide into her mouse and knock the screen alive. On it there's an email from Jeffry.

Locanda Verde. 8 p.m. reads the subject. Don't worry, it's all going to be okay. Wait a second. *That's odd. Why would they be going there?* It seems awfully intimate if it were for business purposes. Wait. Could they be having an affair? And she's using her "sick kid" as an excuse to cover for the fact that she didn't want to go on her own family vacation because her marriage is on the rocks? I snort to myself, that would be the kicker, now, wouldn't it.

Somehow I manage to make it to Friday—a few pints of vegan cashew may have helped—and just as I've shored myself up to face the day with the help of pure, delicious caffeine, I see Alix has made her way to my desk. She hands back a bunch of copy so covered in red it looks like someone's been wiping up a crime scene with it.

"Cynthia emailed me to tell you that the piece on new secondary C-section alternatives went in the completely wrong direction," Alix says. "You're going to have to research it more. The trends you found were lame," says Alix, dropping the story on my desk.

"But I also noted in the original proposal that there was nothing new out there. I did the research. That's what happens when the top editors come up with the headlines before the stories are actually written." It's another trait, along with all the made-up quotes, Alix seems to have brought with her from her old magazine.

"Well, do you want me to tell Cynthia that?" Alix looks peeved.

"Just tell her the truth—there aren't any real ways to make a C-section scar any smaller or minimize the pain. I found those acupuncture treatments in Chinatown and I thought they sounded promising."

"You know the issue." Alix's not conceding an inch. "Not mainstream enough. What soccer mom in Darien or Evanston is going to creep into some sketchy alterna-practice for strange herbs and needles? Back to the drawing board."

"But they do for fertility treatments. What's the difference?" I'm mad now so I don't care that Alix is giving me the death stare. "You *know* that's a different story."

Alix sniffs. "You do seem to find all the problems and never the solutions."

"Okay, I'll keep researching," I mutter, and take the copy out of her hands. Jules is nowhere to be seen for a postmortem bitch session. Now I'm going to be spending the weekend making up fake C-section alternatives, instead of meeting up with Addison and Brie tonight as I'd hoped.

My phone chimes loudly on the desk. I see that it's my mom. I have to answer this time.

"Just checking in to make sure you're still alive. I got your email last weekend about Paris. I'm sorry, Lizzie. I know how much that trip meant to you."

"Thanks, Mom. Yeah, it was pretty disappointing." Ever since her cancer's gone into remission, even though it all turned out fine, an odd thing has happened. I've been avoiding her calls. I think it's because I can't bear to feel it. That I could have lost her. And that I let her down. Which makes it even worse.

"I know you'll get there someday. You just have to be patient," she says, transferring over my pain, as always. "Well, I wanted to check in with you about Margaret's son's best friend. Did you see my email about that?"

My mom never interfered in my dating life before, but now grandchild envy has hit. All my friends from home have been moving back to the suburbs to be closer to their parents, and my mom is feeling left out. "Mom. I'm super busy with an article now."

"Too busy to make a two-minute phone call?"

"Sorry," I say, biting my lip, immediately feeling guilty—and mad—that my job doesn't often let me break focus for even a few minutes during the day to check in.

"So, what should I tell Margaret? Can you just give me a yes or no?"

"Thanks, Mom, but I'm not feeling the setup dates at the moment."

"You don't have to go to dinner. Just coffee," she urges.

"Mom, seriously, coffee's worse," I say, thinking that at least with dinner you can drink alcohol. I've attempted a few of these setups. They usually turn out to be the kind of guys who speak Klingon for fun.

"Okay, bye, sweetie. I'll just tell Margaret 'possible yes'—love you."

"Love you, too, Mom," I say, throwing my phone onto my desk in frustration.

At thirty-one, so far not one PH has come along. Since JR broke up with me five months ago I've gone on exactly two actual dates: Amir, the thirty-nine-year-old douchey divorced hedge-funder, who called me "too Catholic" because I wouldn't give him a blow job on the first date; and Taylor, the "internet entrepreneur" (really an unemployed web programmer)—the twenty-seven-year-old emotionally unstable crazy pants who told me he liked me because he "was into curvy girls who could pay for their own drinks." I'd deleted his contact from my phone immediately and canceled my subscription to OkCupid.

As I'm contemplating how cynical I've turned these days, Ryan's Facebook profile somehow magically opens on my desktop.

"Hey, looking for Europa League Finals tickets. Message me if you've got a hookup."

Yep, still cute, still "single," and no new lame flirty girl posts to his wall since I'd last checked (this morning). Then an email pops into my inbox reminding me Cynthia will be back on Monday. The tiger moms/French moms story must be in Final by Monday, which means another late night finishing up Alix's edits after she skips out at five unless I want to spend even more time working this weekend.

I elbow my iced coffee, spilling it all over. *Shit.* I grab for a twenty-dollar organic paper diaper we've been lauding when my phone starts buzzing itself off the desk.

Ryan reads the screen. My cheeks warm. I clear my throat and pick up the vibrating phone.

"Hey there, Ryan," I say, trying to sound casual.

"Deputy Editor Liz," chimes Ryan.

I chuckle. "I told you that's not my title."

"I don't know, there's just a ring to it," he chides. "Anyway, I thought I'd call to check in about our upcoming calendar and see if there were any more synergies. Sales was pleased with 'Mega-Multiples'—it brought in a boatload of new ad dollars."

"That's because I know what I'm doing," I say in a flirtatious tone.

"You sure do," says Ryan, not wasting a second.

Just then, I see an email from Jeffry:

RE: FMLA: Need back now!

I open the email and the contents make me cough.

Liz, if you don't return FMLA paperwork asap, you're at risk of termination once you go on maternity leave. You must sign by 3 p.m. I sit up in my chair.

"Liz? You still there?" asks Ryan.

"Yes, I'm here. Sorry. I just got an urgent email. I should probably go."

"Okay, no worries, but one more thing. I was wondering if we could set up a meeting at the *Paddy Cakes* office in the next couple of weeks. I'll bring our fall lineup, and you, Alix and I can go over the magazine plans to see if there are any more partnership opportunities. What do you say?"

Out of the corner of my eye, I see Jeffry walking down our floor right toward my cubicle with paperwork in his hands.

"Sounds good." My eyes dart back toward Jeffry. "Hmm, I'm a little busy next week—we're crashing a last-minute story. How about next Friday?"

Jeffry is coming toward my desk. I make a motion that I'm on the phone.

"Okay, Buckley, pencil me in," says Ryan.

I have to start sporting a bump next week, but I can't think of what to say. I'm thrown off guard reading the lines from FMLA paperwork: "...perjury will result in immediate termination and possible prosecution."

"Okay, we'll figure it out. Thanks for calling. I have to go now. Bye."

"Buh—" Ryan starts before I hang up.

"Bye!" I click down the receiver just as Jeffry reaches my desk.

"Liz, I need this paperwork signed. Now."

I look around toward Jules, who just gives me a scolding look. She knows I'm committing serious career suicide. But if I don't sign, I'll be fired. Besides, I'm not the only one who's not telling the truth around here, I think, as I imagine Alix sidling up with Jeffry in a dimly lit Locanda Verde corner booth. I take the pen and paperwork out of Jeffry's hands and sign *Elizabeth Joy Buckley.* In one sharp move the act is done. And, possibly, so am I.

Five

PUSH! ☺ Notification! Week 18: You've got backaches and swelling? You're growing a baby! Suck it up! Lol, j.k. But yeah, there's this really annoying thing called edema, or water retention, that can create some serious cankle action. Seriously, it's gross. Baby Smiles: 17!

When you find yourself on the verge of a major life transition, like walking across the Grand Canyon on a tightrope, the only way to get through it is to stay focused on one small detail. For me, today, the middle of my second official trimester when I'm about to "show," the detail at hand happens to be sliding a pair of too-small "Spawn-x" around my now-artificially-fattened frame.

This baby is finally going to get some use, I think, as I try with all my might to coax on the offending article of shapewear I'd bought for my friend Katie's wedding in the Hamptons two years ago. I was a bridesmaid and needed all the help I could get for her sky-blue Vera Wang silk shantung shift. Little could I predict it would be used for an entirely different purpose a few years down the road.

First, I pull out Hudson's bump with straps that go around my back. I slip it over my head. Then, I struggle to slide up the waist-reducing undergarments over it. Thank God my air-conditioning works, I think, remembering the record extreme summer heat Al Roker has predicted for this summer. Finally I put on the Lycra slip Hudson gave me to smooth the whole thing out. I take a deep breath and let it all out as the tiny bulge settles in place on my abdomen.

Taken all in, I barely recognize myself in the mirror.

Do I really have to do this today? I think, staring at my reflection.

Yes, I tell myself firmly. I have to start showing or else the timing of my plan—the October date I'd given Cynthia and Jeffry—won't work. And I figure if I don't go through with it, I never will. Just a few more weeks. A month, tops. Enough time to get some freelance assignments. Little pangs of terror shoot through my spine as I look in the mirror at myself almost five months pregnant.

Not bad, I think at first. I turn to each side, gazing at my profile to make sure no seams are showing. The cute mini-bump looks like a cross between those side view "before" shots of women in the diet pill ads intentionally sticking out their stomachs and the underweight pregnant models at five months we tend to use in *Paddy Cakes*—prenatal perfection.

At first I feel good, great even. But then I turn around and face the mirror head-on. A mental deadline barrels to the front of my brain. "Have a baby by thirty." I feel a small wave of sadness. How many chances have I let slip away because of the decision to prioritize work—or more accurately, allow work fear to overwhelm my life?

I get my bearings as I climb down the stairs of my apartment to the street. Not too different, I decide, as I walk down Columbus Avenue toward the subway. I decide to test the waters by heading into my local café on the corner. Waiting in line behind five others, people brush against me to get to yogurt parfaits in the refrigerator case. *Hey, watch it, I'm a pregnant woman!* I think as I nervously giggle to myself. My favorite barista takes my order, as I try to make a show of my bump beneath the Pea in the Pod green dress Addison sent me from her shoot and hope he'll notice. Although I practically rest my wallet on the top of my bump as I rifle through my change purse, he doesn't seem to notice anything different about me. I pay, give him a friendly smile and grab my cold brew.

A little deflated, I head out, sticking in my earbuds, and continue down the avenue toward the subway. For the first time I am one of the many pregnant women I see on the Upper West Side. It really is New York's maternity row. A funny feeling stirs inside me. Jealousy. Not for the babies in their bassinets, exactly, but for their accessories. First it's the strollers—I find myself wanting the blue one with the orange racing stripe—and then the clothes. I see a woman with a draped bohemian caftan over her bump, then another with a chic blue-and-white-striped Parisian-style top and leggings. They look so cute as they're rushing their children off to school. All of a sudden, out of the corner of my eye, I see my friend Elyse from college waiting for a cab. I cross over to the other side of the street like a madwoman, almost getting myself hit by traffic. At the other side, I look back. A cab has pulled over, but her eyes catch mine and she calls, "Liz!" I motion that I'll call her later.

Ugh. How am I going to avoid running into people?

Finally, I arrive at work. As I type in the code to open the glass doors to our office, an electric charge zaps me, like a reminder of the cruel reality I've created for myself.

Now or never.

I spot Alix over in the corner, hands full of proofs.

It's go time.

Life seems to pass in slow motion as I unfurl my gypsy scarf from my neck until my belly is fully revealed. I smooth down my jersey dress over it.

She's seen me.

Noticing, she walks over calmly, holding the folders that have come back from Cynthia.

"Hey, Alix, how's it going?" I ask with as big a smile as I can muster as she reaches my cube. "Ooh, my back hurts." I am rubbing my back and my belly simultaneously for full effect. Oh wait, *shoot*! That's in the third trimester.

"Uh, how are you feeling, Liz?" I can tell Alix has no idea what to say.

"Great!" My tone is overeager. I try to cover my nerves and am surprised at my extreme guilt. *Am I really doing this?*

"Good." She hands me a folder without making eye contact. "Can you do more research on this story about alternative baby bassinets? I can't find anything on Japanese wall-hanging cuddle caves. Have you seen the fall line yet?"

"Not yet, but I'll check with the PR contact." As I meet her eyes, I feel the heavy weight of the lie for the first time. I push my anxiety away. I have no choice.

"And can you pull some more quotes from celebs who've struggled with postpartum depression from LexisNexis, too? The ones we have aren't working." She continues to look me up and down until she seems satisfied with something.

"Not a problem, Alix." I'm glad for the distraction.

"So, I've been meaning to ask…" She shifts her weight. "Is, there…a…father in the picture?" I begin to sweat, feeling the panic rising.

"I'm not really ready to discuss that right now."

"As for your birth plan, you're not thinking of doing any type of crazy natural home birth, are you?"

"Uh, I'm really not sure yet," I sputter.

"Have you arranged a plan for child care going forward?"

I take a second, then realize, for once, I don't always have to jump for this woman. "Yes, I'll be happy to fill you and Jeffry in later on," I say coolly.

"Well, we're going to have to discuss it at some point soon since there will be two other women out when you're gone, and once you're back we'll need to plan for coverage." *Oh.* She only cares about whether I'll still be able to clock late hours. *Well, let her have fun sorting it out.* It feels good to take charge of my own destiny for once. "Also, Cynthia was pretty underwhelmed with your October 'First Steps' lineup…it needs to be redone."

When she leaves the cube, I remember back to when Alix first started working here. Her role was to bring in more up-market fashion designers to the feature articles in order to draw in more high-end advertisers like Chanel and Louis Vuitton.

She did what they asked. But the air in the office shifted. Beyond making us change quotes, she was always yelling at assistants, making people do her work for her, and finding ways to assert her cool presence in all the meetings with our executive editor and Cynthia.

Her life seems so easy with her Upper East Side town house and cottage on the bay in South Hampton, perfect banker husband and toddler Tyler, who's been dressed in couture since birth. I get the sense that it wasn't her talent or skill that got her to this position at *Paddy Cakes*, but her family connections. I hate to feel like I have a chip on my shoulder— my father's daughter in that regard. But I see Alix throw her monogrammed Goyard tote over her shoulder and ease her way toward the doors to go down to the café, as she texts on her phone—probably giving the nanny instructions—I can't help thinking some people are just born lucky.

By Thursday, I've pulled it off. Four full days of bumpage— no sign of being caught. Blousy tops thanks to a shipment of maternity gear from Addison's shoots help hide my faux belly from the rest of the staff, who sadly, must think I've just put on the pounds.

Before I even start working on a story, another email lands in my inbox.

See me. It's from Cynthia.

Ugh…here it is. The big reveal.

I'll make an appointment for this afternoon, I respond.

No, now, comes back instantly.

I summon my courage and try to remember my spiel about my "pregnancy."

This is it. I walk over to her glass office and tap meekly on her door. She motions to come in. Before I even have a chance to sit down, she begins the inquisition.

"Elizabeth, when I replaced Patricia last year, I knew it would be a rough transition for the staff as I raised the tone and direction of the magazine to higher standards."

I have no idea where this is going. I thought we were going to discuss my pregnancy, but maybe not.

Cynthia stares me straight in the eye. "Some of the staff seemed to get it instantly, like Alix. *Others* have had a bit of a rocky start."

I just nod, trying to stay two steps ahead with a response to what she might say.

"As you know, our newsstand sales have been on the de-cline for a few years now. It's been my job to bring the num-bers back up."

It was true. When *Paddy Cakes*, geared toward Brooklyn's Park Slope–style mommies in 2000, launched at the beginning of the millennium, we'd had early success. With the dot-com boom, "bourgeois-bohemian" maternity items were the perfect place for people to spend their extra income.

But when mommy websites launched, like *The Bump* and *Babble*, we saw the first slump in sales. Then about three years ago, we saw a huge drop, as more advertising dollars were leaving our pages to go to independent parenting websites like *Angry Mommy* and creative lifestyle bloggers with kids.

Since I wasn't responsible for that part of the business, I never really thought too much about it. But our editor, Patricia Holden, always did. She'd been asked to launch *Paddy Cakes* after making her mark as editor in chief at *Women's Health*. Earlier in her career, she'd won awards for her investigative features at *Vanity Fair* and *Rolling Stone*. I really liked her a lot and felt as though she had an unusual realness and warmth. I learned a lot from her careful edits, which helped me to add more layers of emotion in my narratives. Even though the promotions weren't huge ones, she was the one who decided to move me up from assistant editor to associate and then to articles editor. While the paychecks never really caught up, I held out hope something bigger and better would come.

Then she got fired. It was a Monday, and we were having our typical production meeting, but instead of Patricia coming in, our publisher entered the room. He quickly informed us that the magazine would now be heading in a slightly different direction, and that Patricia had chosen to move on to pursue other opportunities.

We learned that Cynthia Blackwell, who'd headed up British *Glitter*, would be replacing her. We all knew exactly who Blackwell was; the fifty-five-year-old ice queen had taken *Glitter* successfully from a regular to a rack-size magazine to a smaller handheld "subway-size" and subsequently doubled newsstand sales. She'd be making some changes at *Paddy Cakes*, he'd said. We all gasped at the thought, worrying about our job security, then lamenting that Patricia had been ousted because of factors in the marketplace out of her control.

We'd all heard tales of Cynthia's hard-line, take-no-prisoners approach to magazine editing. But we had no idea what to expect or whether or not our jobs would be saved. Initially, only a handful of changes had taken place.

The magazine has gotten a lot more glossy and celebrity-driven. Cynthia became obsessed with finding younger, hotter, cooler celeb moms and airbrushing the crap out of them on the cover. She was always harping on us to get more sensational stories to generate more buzz instead of doing the advice-driven stories we had been known for. But aside from the constant fear that a story would be cut at the last minute, which left one having to research and write a replacement until all hours to make the shipping deadline, nothing much changed.

When she'd hired Jeffry, his hard-nosed ways instilled more fear. But I just went along with the changes, too swamped with work to question things. Now, though, I was beginning to realize a focus on higher-end advertisers was probably just the tip of the iceberg.

"You remember the most important rule here at *Paddy Cakes*?" asks Cynthia, ratcheting me back to the present.

"Sell more copies?" I reply.

"Exactly," says Cynthia. "So you can imagine my surprise when I was reading your story ideas for October and saw that you'd pitched exactly the same kind of slush-driven muck that made this magazine tank 20 percent on the newsstand before I got here. I'm going to be blunt, Elizabeth. Your lineup was complete crap."

"I, uh…" I stammer, not knowing what to say, Okay, yes, I mean I *had* kind of called it in but still, I didn't think it was *terrible.*

"For example," Cynthia continues. "'This Sucks: Getting Your Baby to Learn to Latch'—this could go in any magazine. *Kiddos* even," naming our more accessible mass-market competitor.

"Right, but I downloaded the notes from this year's American College of Pediatricians conference. It was about a groundbreaking study with new techniques. It's a good chance to report on the news…" I say my case.

"Sod reporting the news," says Cynthia in total disgust, "I want to *make* news."

"I totally see what you're saying." I gulp in air. "I'll submit a new lineup by tomorrow." *There is no way I'm going to win this one.*

"Make it good," she says, turning away from me toward her computer. "I'm doing a bit of a rethink in terms of staffing over the next few months. Things may be changing. And while someone in your circumstances may have a little more…*leeway*…it's not a get-out-of-jail-free card."

"Yes," I say, quivering. "No problem." I get up and walk quickly back to my cube. Jules is there, tapping away on her keyboard, but when she sees the look on my face, she immediately turns to talk me down off the ledge.

I pick up my iced "decaf" and start sucking it furiously. "Cynthia finally brought it up."

"Seriously! What happened?" says Jules, turning her chair completely toward me as a sign of sympathy.

"Yep. On top of that, she just told me my October lineup was crap, and hinted she may fire me anyway."

"Eek," says Jules.

"It's so unfair. She comes in here, rips up all our stories, leaves us scrambling to write new ones in the time we're supposed to use for researching new stories, then expects the lineups we pull together in a few minutes to be perfect."

"It sucks, Liz. I'm sorry. I know she's come down way harder on features than health."

"No, not true. Your stories fly through with her. It's like everyone here seems to get it but me. Write stupid listicles about how you're lactating wrong and be done with it."

Jules puts her hand on my arm consolingly. "What are you going to do? Our paychecks have to come from somewhere."

"I guess I take it personally. I mean, moms out there don't want to read about the stuff they can't afford, right? They want real news about baby trends and advice to use in their own lives. That's what would sell our magazine, right?"

"Maybe, but people seem to like reading the stuff we've been doing lately. Like how celebs take off baby weight in two weeks or speed through African adoption agencies. It's not all bad."

Jules has a point, but Cynthia's comments have struck a nerve.

"And she barely mentioned me being pregnant. It's like she doesn't even care at this point. Maybe she's planning on firing me anyway and is just trying to work it out through HR!" I feel tears welling up out of pure frustration.

"Well, you can either get a new job and quit, or, learn to stop taking it personally, just get it done and go home, which is what I do."

"Hrumph," I spout, still wanting to sulk. "Okay, fine, if she wants stories like organic peanut butters that will get your kid into Princeton I will give it to her—founded or not," I say. I type the idea into a fresh text file I have open on my screen, pounding the keys for dramatic effect.

If my work doesn't improve and Cynthia has a vendetta against me, my fake pregnancy might be the only thing keeping me from getting fired. My chest starts to tighten and a lump forms in my throat. Getting fired would leave me with no options whatsoever.

Finally, the cover story comes back and thankfully, it has me so busy, I can barely register what happened, addressing emails with last-minute questions about the cover story and my other pages that are about to ship to the printer. Another email tings my inbox. From Mom, reads the subject line—she has never realized that people can see where it's from without writing it in the message heading as if it were a telegraph.

Hi, sweetie. Was thinking, you don't have to come home for my birthday if you don't want to. I know you're always busy with work and your friends. I'd just like some flowers. And a Lancôme lotion—if you can find it with a free gift with purchase. Love you, Mom xoxo.

Of course I'm coming home, Mom. Can't wait to see you, I email back. I have a five days to get the gifts. I log on to 1-800-Flowers.com, pick out a nice tulips arrangement and use a 20-percent-off code from an email promotion I received. Now I'll just have to get the Lancôme stuff and a few other things later. I am a good daughter, I tell myself, wringing my hands as I do. I remember the radiation days, when I had to pick and choose being there with her in the hospital over waiting around for copy to come back late on Fridays. Pressing Click, I add more to my credit card balance. She *deserves* it.

Then, another call sounds from my phone. I know the

caller ID number. It's Ryan. I pick up and try to clear all the lingering hostility from my throat.

"Hey, Deputy Editor Liz, sorry about being MIA—was crazy busy prepping for 100-pound-tumor man shoot. I wanted to tell you about it. Are we still on for our meeting tomorrow?"

Shoot, that's right. Tomorrow's Friday. "Hey, Ryan, I'm so sorry, but something's come up and I can't make the office meeting tomorrow." I'm secretly bummed, thinking how it *would* be nice to see him again. He takes it in with a pause.

"Okay, how about next week?"

I sigh, worried. There's no way he can come to the office now. If he did, he'd see me in full expectant-mother glory. "Ryan, I'm so sorry, but things have unexpectedly gotten much, uh, busier here during the day."

"Oh." He pauses. "Ditching me for karaoke lessons," he deadpans. "I understand."

I can hear the laugh in his voice.

"Okay, I have an idea. How about drinks?"

"Really?" I'm taken aback.

"Yeah, sure. What about McGann's on Eighth?" I know McGann's well. Ford and I used to sneak there for postwork bitch sessions.

"Okay, that could work."

"How about tonight? Seven thirty?" Ryan jets back.

"I'd love to," I say without thinking.

He says "great" and we click off. I notice that, for once in a long time, I am actually excited. The sensation, though foreign, reminds me almost of how it was in high school or college, when liking a guy was all about the feeling it gave you—not some inherent marriage potential—the "PH." I decide not to check his Facebook profile or status all day so I won't have his life fresh in my memory bank as he's telling it to me—not that I haven't already memorized his date of birth (February 15) and favorite movies (*Shawshank Redemption* and *Rudy*). I power through the rest of the day, and for some reason, the C-section rewrite pours out effortlessly.

Six

McGann's, a prototypical Irish pub in Hell's Kitchen, sits just far enough away from both Ryan's office in Times Square and mine. It's an easy choice and I love that Ryan picked a casual Irish pub over a fancy lounge-type place, which can often set a too-formal tone. I hope he's there before I am so I won't have to sit at the pub's bar alone, baby bump in my purse.

All my worries go away when I see him, already perched on a bar stool, with a worn paperback and a shot of Jameson in front of him. The glowing fire in the middle of the room relieves the chill in my bones from the rain outside. Paintings, European football memorabilia and old-fashioned Guinness ads line the cream walls. Tiffany lamp sconces give the whole bar a glow. I've forgotten how much I like this place.

"Buckley!" he says enthusiastically as he gets up.

"Hey there, Mr. Murphy," I say, trying to cover up my nerves with as much confidence as I can muster. He leans in to kiss my cheek while I reach out to shake his hand. We laugh at the mix-up and I try to babble on through it. "Starting strong, I see," I tell him, nodding at the Jameson. His warm smile makes me a little less anxious.

"Oh, that's not for me. That's for you," he says drily, dropping the amber drink in front of me on the bar. "I figured I'd try to get you all liquored up so I can steal *Paddy Cakes*' fall lineup," he says, taking my coat and finding a spot for it under the bar.

He pulls out the bar stool from beneath the rough-hewn counter, and I try to hop onto it with as much ladylike grace as one can have in big rubber boots and a dress. I take a sip of the whiskey, while I face toward the bar and start to fiddle with the bar menu, trying not to let on that I'm worrying if someone I know will stop by and catch me here, drinking.

"So, I don't know if you caught our 'Mega-Multiples' show the other night, but people have been saying it's Emmy worthy," says Ryan, dusting his shoulders off for effect.

"Yeah," I respond. "Not too bad. Pretty good for a novice. You, *you know*, didn't catch all the nuances of our article. How long have you been at the network again?"

"You're right," he says finally, returning the joke. "It didn't do *Paddy Cakes*' Pulitzer-winning prose justice."

I roll my eyes—we *both* know that's not the case.

"So, I bet you're going to be taking over Alix's job in a year's time," he says, mocking my seriousness a bit.

"Probably," I say with false smugness. "And what about you—this Emmy should seal your career trajectory, too. Have you picked out your corner office yet?"

Ryan takes a big sip of his whiskey. "Already got one," he says, flashing a grin.

"Corner office?"

"Emmy." He looks down offering only a bashful, yet sly look. Out of the corner of my eye, Seamus, barman with white hair and a bit of a belly beneath his black vest, is wiping down the bar and gives a nod.

Holding back how impressed I am, I reply, "Good. Be-cause I only associate with smart, successful people."

"Bet you do," he teases.

"So I bet you must love all the parenting stuff you're doing," I say sarcastically, filled with weariness from the past week. "If someone says the words *baby*, *bun*, *bump* or *bundle*, I think I'm going to shoot myself."

Ryan seems to get my meaning, yet he clears his throat. "Well, it's not all bad—some of the moms are smokin' hot," he says with a cheeky smile. "Anyway, I'm done with the parenting stuff for the next month or so. I'm probably going to be going on the 100-pound-tumor man shoot in the Amazon pretty soon."

"Ah, more Emmy-caliber stuff," I chide.

"You're just jealous," he says, flashing a hot grin.

"I am," I tell him solemnly, and from the electric flash of his eyes, he seems to understand.

We chitchat more about the "Mega-Multiple" show, and he asks if I liked the way it turned out; I let him know that in all honesty, I did. I tell him more about my job at *Paddy Cakes*, revealing a bit about Cynthia and Alix. It's nice to be able to talk shop to someone fresh about all this media stuff. From the slight bags under his blue eyes, and shaggy brown hair two weeks overdue for a cut, I can tell he seems to understand where I'm coming from. After we've made our way through our first drinks, our guards start to drop a bit. Should I see if we want another drink? "Seamus, another drink, please?" he says, drumming the bar with his fingers.

Seamus comes over to us. "Yer usual, mate?"

"You got it. It's a perfect night for it."

"What?" I ask.

"Rusty nail. Seamus makes some of the best in the city.

Or are you a lavender martini type of girl?" He looks at the back of the bar, and for a second his focus seems elsewhere.

"Um, no, I will have you know that I've had my fair share of rusty nails over the years." When I speak the words, he turns back to me with a smirk.

"Well, I'm glad, or I'd have to kick you out of the bar," he says, signaling the bartender to make it two. "And you know," he says, "I only associate with total boozehounds."

"Ha. But it's been a while. Can you remind me what's in them again?"

"Equal parts whiskey and Drambuie with an orange twist."

"Interesting. How'd you get into them?"

He pauses. "It was my dad's drink and I guess I picked it up from him."

Seamus hands us two yellowish-brown cocktails. The taste burns a bit, but it's sweet. "Mmm," I say. "I could get used to this." I look down.

"That's the plan," says Ryan, catching my eye.

As we're rounding out drink number two, we fall into a flirtatious rhythm, but his jokes are all tinged with trepidation, like he's being careful not to cross the professional line. The topics fall into the safe categories: sports teams (he's Phillies, I'm Mets) and my affinity for the geeky History Channel shows about Nostradamus, his for geeky man shows like *Top Gear*, though he does keep high-fiving me when we share a common viewpoint. I notice how easy it is to talk with Ryan.

"Sure you can handle it, Buckley?" he says, placing a hand on my back jokingly as Seamus puts the third rusty nail down on the counter for us.

"Oh, I can handle it," I reply, gaining a little more confidence.

"All right, I'll give you the third one, but only if you'll

tell me a secret," he says, pretending to hold the tumbler from me.

Maybe it's the alcohol, because all of a sudden, I feel myself getting a little brazen. I lower my head flirtatiously and look him directly in the eye, giving him the too-long stare, a move I'd perfected in my early twenties. "Like *what*?"

"Well, it doesn't exactly seem like *Paddy Cakes* is your end-all-be-all career choice. Say the magazine folded tomorrow, and you could do anything you wanted—a secret dream—what would it be?"

I immediately blush thinking, *if you only knew.*

"Waiting, Buckley."

I take another second. Up until this point, with everything meternity-related, I hadn't actually taken much time to ponder what I really want, only what would keep me from getting fired. But to my surprise, the answer comes to me quickly. "Easy. Quit my job. Travel the world and write about it." My shoulders drop in relief.

He immediately smiles and softens his eyes. "So underneath that gorgeous magazine editor exterior, you're really just a frustrated travel writer. I knew it." His compliment makes my cheeks warm, and I look away. When I return, I notice he's looking at me, staring.

"It would be amazing if one day my blog *MoveableFeast* would somehow get picked up and turned into a book like one of Bill Bryson's travelogues or Orwell's *Down and Out in Paris and London.*" I'm not sure what makes me reveal this, but for some reason I feel like it will intrigue him. "But, I haven't really been keeping it up. I've been so busy. And it's not really that good."

"You really know how to sell yourself, Buckley."

"Huh," I say, only now recognizing he's right.

"I can tell you've got a book in you. You know, a secret

adventurous side." He winks, and his compliment makes me blush outwardly and gulp inwardly. This time I smile, feeling a little more courage.

"Okay, I'll send you my next travel story tomorrow and you can tell me what you think," I tell him.

"I'd love to read anything you've written," he says, returning a more earnest expression, then smiling, as if he's thinking about something.

"Okay, so what's yours, Mr. Rising Star? Take over the network by bringing all of *Paddy Cakes'* best stories to life?"

He scrunches his nose, as if to say "not even close." He looks down for a few seconds. "Okay, don't make fun of me, Buckley, but I've got a secret plan, too. After a few things fall into place, I'm going to quit Discovery," he says, clearing his throat, "then once I raise funding, I'm going to produce and direct my own environmental documentary." He pauses, interested in my reaction.

I can't help but smile widely and there's a look in his eye— one of hopefulness.

Then he gets suddenly quiet. "Did you know that there are actually about thirty-one forms of electromagnetic energy that are self-reproducing and completely sustainable? Companies are doing this right now, and if we were to switch over from petroleum and natural gas, we could power the world's energy three times over."

This sudden revelation of a geeky side makes my heart warm. "I thought it was just wind power and solar power."

"Yes, there's that, but there's also this type of magnetic force field called a toroidal field. There's a company out in Palo Alto working on it. I saw them give a TED talk last year and have been in touch with them since."

"Really?"

"I pitched it to Discovery, but they turned me down. The

huge oil companies are some of our biggest advertisers," he says with a letdown look in his eye. "But don't worry, I'll get it out there—one of my buddies is a lawyer and is looking into coproducing with me, and our friend in finance is already helping us set up meetings with angel investors." His passion incites something in me. Something I haven't felt in a long time. Maybe not since my first big feature came out.

He seems to notice my pensiveness. "I'm not worried about you, either, Deputy Buckley. You're just resting up before your training day comes," he says with a soft wink, which gives me little tingles.

Then, he holds a finger up. "Sorry, gotta check this." He takes his phone from out of his pocket and scrolls through email, punching a short reply into the pad with his fingers. A wince forms across his features. "Sorry, I, ugh, have to go."

"Work?" I say, looking at him as he's fumbling in his pockets for cash to pay the bill. I offer to pay, but he gives me a look that says "no way."

"Yeah, ugh, okay, sure," he says, taking a second to consider something. Then he gives me a strange exaggerated eye roll.

I sigh and try to cover up my disappointment with a huge smile. I plop my drink down, and we both get up and put our coats on.

"Well, uh, thank you for the drinks," I say nervously, fidgeting with my coat as we wait for the bartender to come back.

"Yeah, we'll do it again soon. Don't forget to send me the blog link tomorrow!" says Ryan with a confident, eager grin, although behind it he seems a little worried. He flags the bartender down to pay. We walk out of the pub onto the rush of Eighth Avenue, and in two seconds he's hailed me a cab. Once I get in, I look out and see he's hailing one for himself. That's weird; his work is only five blocks away.

Great, maybe the work drama was just a cover. Maybe he has a girlfriend. This *was* just work drinks.

But still, for five quick seconds, I allow myself a daydream. One that has me by Ryan's side on a film set and jetting around the world with him to interview people who are trying to make a difference. How sexy it all seems. It doesn't feel like it has the weight of finding a PH. It feels like pure fun. I fish into my purse to check my phone, and there it sits. My second trimester. *Shut the fantasy down, Buckley. Shut it down.*

The next day at work, with thoughts of Ryan pushed far out of my brain, the realization of my impending doomed career, love life and incomprehensibly terrible baby scheme leave me with only one option: enter a state of total denial. Instead of using the rest of the afternoon to perfect my October lineup, then research new jobs, I spend the time reading a self-help galley that came to my inbox this morning: *The New Super Mom: How to Effectively Balance Work Life and Home Life.* Then, with about half an hour left before the end of the day, I brainstorm all new Shocking! Exciting! Glossy! stories, including an inspired "22 Ways to 'Fake' a Work-Home Balance," then turn in my revised lineup with my fingers crossed.

I knew if I were Jules, I would have taken Cynthia's feedback differently, making an Action Plan and plowing through it with complete aplomb. But I can't motivate myself to do anything no matter how hard I try. My brain feels like a murky swamp. My nerves jangle left and right as reality starts to set it in. I know what to do. Putting aside the pileup for once, I head out the office door toward home, texting A and B.

Seven

Friday night, 7:30 p.m. A perfect mix of crowded, but not too crowded, sixty–forty ratio men to women fill out the space at our go-to gastropub, Sparrow and Crow. Cellar-like and glowing, it's full of wooden farmhouse tables and candlesticks with wax dripping down the sides onto black wrought iron casters. Unfortunately the favorable conditions do nothing to help me push my current situation out of my mind.

As I enter the crowded bar, I see that Addison and Brie have already arrived and are already claiming their space in the spot we've deemed the "vortex," thanks to its ability to bring in men from three different angles—the back table, the side closest to the door, and the way to the bathrooms. As we sidle up to the bar, the barman notices us and takes our drink orders.

Never one to miss an opportunity to show off her toned arms, Addison has shown up in her usual tight-black-cropped tank, skinny jeans, heels combo. Brie favors low-cut, feminine, belted dresses that reveal her killer cleavage and tiny waist. Tonight's no different. We've all developed a formula for what works postthirty. Me, a loose, bohemian-style "with child" ready ensemble in case anyone I know should arrive.

Drinks in hand, Addison and Brie eye the room for possible prospects, goal-oriented and ready. So different from our midtwenties when these nights were just about having fun. I see Addison eyeing a cute group of youngish guys. Brie clicks into flirt mode, flicking her head back and running a few fingers through her hair, that is, when she's not checking her phone.

Lately, I've noticed that most of our conversations center around assuring one another that we're smart, beautiful and are going to be "okay." It goes on and on until we've reached a fever pitch of feeling hot, smiling around the bar widely. Not a soul seems to notice.

"So, what happened with Brady?" I ask Addison. She's eyeing the twentyish group of guys who seem to be playing fantasy football on their phones from their sporadic cheers and table slapping.

"Ooh, yes, the venture capitalist who met us out at karaoke?" asks Brie, intermittently checking her phone.

"How old is he again?" I ask, the only one fully attentive.

"Thirty. But it ended last night when I told him I needed more attention and he told me he needed a twenty-two-year-old," she says. "I told him he'd never find one as good as me in bed, but he was welcome to try."

"Aww, no. I'm sorry, that sucks," I tell her.

"It's okay. It's his loss. I've decided I'm just going to have as much fun as possible this summer. What else can you do?"

"Well, plan Secret-4-the-One isn't going as well as I'd hoped, either," says Brie, shoulders scrunched.

"What happened?" I ask, worried.

"So as soon as I launched into online dating full throttle, I met this guy at a *bookstore*—can you believe it? It was like straight out of a '90s rom-com. He's been traveling around the world *for years* after getting laid off on Wall Street. *Totally* my type."

"So? How did it go?"

"Okay," she says, smoothing her hair behind her ears. "Until I decided to go back home with him, and discovered that he had a hoof hanging above his bed."

"Seriously?"

"Oh, yeah. A hoof. Not even a dream catcher—I would have given him a pass on that one, but yeah, a hoof. He said it was considered a good luck charm to increase male virility. He said a town elder gave it to him in Burma." She turns up her nose.

"So no date number two?"

"Uh, yeah, ya think?" she says, smiling. "It's okay. The right one is out there, I know. I just have to clear a few more blockages in my love corner."

I consider keeping my crush on Ryan under wraps. Once it's out there, I know my friends will pick apart every detail, or "pinball" it. Brie and I've coined the term denoting the way in which your well-meaning friends can inadvertently send a nascent relationship straight into the gutter by commenting on each individual interaction and text too soon, before the blastocyst has fully implanted. One psychologically projected comment from Add or Brie, and I know I'll be swayed to start thinking the worst about the whole Ryan situation.

"So remember the guy I worked with on the mega-multiples story? Ryan Murphy? I went out with him last night. Well, it wasn't a date really. More of a work thing." My face warms as I say it out loud, even though I'd just decided not to.

"The cute Gap Jeans Guy from karaoke?" My two friends

stop staring around the room. I've now got their full attention. "Wait, you didn't even text me?" says Brie.

"Yeah, way to bury the lede," shoots Addison.

"It kinda happened last minute. I couldn't have him come to the office, so he asked me to go to drinks instead."

"And?" pushes Addison.

"It was fun. I don't know if it was a date per se. Well, maybe it was—I think he was flirting with me." I timidly tell them about the back-and-forth banter. "He wants to produce an environmental documentary and I think he's pretty legit about it." I look down for some reason, shy to reveal these details. "It's actually kind of awesome." I feel nervous all of a sudden. "Do you guys want another round?"

"I'm technically on a cleanse," says Brie, "I probably shouldn't. Well, okay."

"So did he make a move?" demands Addison.

"No. Right at the end he got a text, and he said he had to go suddenly." Both girls take a second to think about it.

"He probably just had a work thing. I'm sure it's no big deal," says Brie. "This is exciting."

I look over at Addison, whom I can typically count on to be more of a realist. "Yeah, I'm sure it's fine," she says with a look of reassurance. "Anyway, even if it is another girl, there's no reason why he wouldn't be totally into you, hot stuff."

I cringe a little at the compliment, which feels slightly untrue. "Well, even though it was super fun, I'm sure he's still in Peter Pan phase. I mean, he's thirty-seven, hot, works at a television network and lives in the East Village—that's basically like twenty-one in Manhattan guy years," I say, folding my arms over my chest.

"Liz, you can't think like that," says Addison. Brie waits carefully.

"Like what?" I'm a little peeved.

"Defeated."

"What? I'm just realistic. There are no real men in this city—only man-children who want mother-wives to be by their side and cook dinner for them. All I'm saying is that the chances are slim someone who is such a catch would be into me." I take a large sip of my drink.

"Enough!" says Addison. "I am not buying in to this internalized powerlessness. We're quality catches. Any guy would be thrilled to have us."

"It's not us. It's them." I wave over to the "brahs" who are now flinging chicken wing bones at one another, three-point-field-goal-style. "Things have changed so much in the past four years. Texting and Tinder culture has made life too easy for them. They think they can just Amazon.com a model girlfriend."

"Seriously," Brie says. "The only one with the power is the owner of those three evil black dots!"

"Liz, it's all about taking back the power and portraying confidence," says Addison. "Watch me."

Addison squares her shoulders, runs a hand through her curls, then walks right over to the boys in the corner, who, to her credit, light up as she starts talking to them. The next thing we know she's brought them over.

"I just asked these nice gentlemen if they could settle an argument we were having about what guys are really looking for in a woman." The guys look at Addison stupidly with their hands in their pockets like she's a cut of prime rib.

"When you're looking at girls online, what's the most important thing? Hotness or confidence?" The guys look at one another as if there's a *right* answer and a *real* answer. Still, Addison pushes.

"Confidence—she has to look like she doesn't give a shit," ventures one.

Addison beams. "See!" she says. "These guys get it."

"Like she's too good for you," adds the other.

"Exactly," confirms Addison. "A girl who knows her value."

"Like she knows how to take care of herself," interjects the first. "Hot."

"You guys get it," says Addison, resolute. "A girl who puts herself *first*."

"And tits out to here," interjects a third, now more relaxed. Addison crooks her brow.

"Like Kate Upton," says the second, slapping the first guy five.

"Yeah, and Jennifer Lawrence."

"Mixed with Mila Kunis."

"Exactly—total MILF, but young!" They look like wolves, salivating at the thought of prime MILF flesh.

"Thank you, boys, that will be enough."

They turn on their heels just as they start launching into another brotastic tirade. Not wanting to continue the conversation any further, I turn to the bar to gather a new round of drinks. "Two vodka sodas, splash of cran, and um, one rusty nail," I tell the barman, not sure what makes me do it.

As I wait for the drink order to come up, I think about my friends' theories. I know the real reason why we each haven't found our own PH—one who is smart, successful, kind and ready for a commitment. It's not because we live in a city where there are too many smart, single, professional women to men. Or don't practice enough "self-love."

It's that as we've followed our hearts, our passions and career prospects, guys have shrunk back, intimidated, and the power balance has shifted. Ever since the economic recession hit in 2008, all my friends have gotten really serious about their careers. When I look around at all my married friends, the wives have all become the breadwinners. The husbands, many of whom were handed pink slips, are the new lost boys.

Maybe it also has something to do with social media, I think, as Brie and Addison now stare into their phones like the great white light is calling them home. It's like the new fertile crescent—where all powerful ideas are exchanged— the Mediterranean of the Crusade times. Every woman I know is on it every single day, exchanging information— every single moment really.

"*This* is how you use apple cider vinegar nine ways."

"*This* is how you make Chia pudding in a mason jar."

"*This* is why the mommy wars are still raging."

"*This* is why we can't put up with fat shaming any longer."

"*This* is what's happening to young sex slaves in Mumbai."

"*This* is the real reason you can't lose those last ten pounds."

Thanks to our Pinterest, Twitter, Facebook and Instagram passwords, women now hold the keys to all the information, while men play "Grand Theft Auto." It's changed everything, I think, and relationships haven't caught up. No wonder Brady wanted a twenty-two-year-old—she's probably his intellectual equal. All of a sudden thirty-six-year-old Amal Alamuddin going for fifty-two-year-old George Clooney adds up.

"Liz, you know what the problem is. It's you," Brie says. "You've always been holding out until something perfect arrives. Waiting for a unicorn—they don't exist."

"That's not true. JR was no unicorn, trust me. But why should we be putting up with these douche bags with hoofs above their beds, or telling us to our faces that we're not twenty-two-year-olds, or leaving without reason after a perfectly nice night out? Why do we have to settle for that?

"You can make affirmations or target your prey all you want, but I'm facing facts. There are no more smart, successful, interesting men in this city. Only narcissist-psychopath finance guys who mentally give us their 'valuation' based on the sum of our body parts. Or developmentally arrested geeky tech guys who play video games all day, who lunge at you mad-eyed for a kiss on your awkward, conversationally challenged second date. Or, second-wave hipsters with dirty beards and 'I am a chef *and* a musician' tattoos who are looking for twenties twee bar-maidens. That's it. I'm not looking for a unicorn. There are no unicorns. We need to face it. We've missed the boat by being stuck in the wrong long-term relationships in our twenties. All the relatively stable types with short, nonimpulsive alleles have already married off with basic-bitch-type college girlfriends and live in Westport and are on to leading their gapster lives, sipping craft beer and pumpkin spiced lattes while they take pictures of their babies at the apple-picking orchard.

"All that's left are an emotionally stunted crop of underemployed, scruffy, pasty boy-men who are following the Don Draper path of transactional fucking, or are angrily divorced, or might have plans to commit to their bourbon collections—but not us—ever. The most we can expect is some last-minute, late-night outside-of-the-spoon cuddling. Definitely no PHs.

"If we're lucky, we'll meet transient drunken Australians who still have some masculine qualities left. That's our only hope..." I trail off, hit hard by the rusty nail that has snuck up on me. My friends look around, shell-shocked and hoping no one's heard.

"Hmm. Thaaaat's interesting."

All of a sudden, I twirl around to find this supremely hot, sandy-haired man—who has an Aussie accent. "Hello, I'm Gavin, from Melbourne. And you, my lady with the extremely acid tongue are..."

"Liz. Liz Buckley."

"Good to meet you, Liz. Love those theories. You're completely wrong about them, though. I can help you with that. Here's my number. Give me a call up sometime." With that, he knocks back what's left of his red wine, drops it on the bar and takes off toward the door as he gives me a wink.

I stand, red-faced, eating my words, holding his card, which says, "Gavin Bettencourt, executive importer/exporter. Barossa Distribution Co."

"It's the vortex. Works every time," says Addison.

"Every time." Brie nods.

At that, we're done for the night. I tell the girls I'll meet them for brunch that weekend, making sure they get in a cab. I hail one of my own, riding up Eighth Avenue toward midtown, noticing offhandedly all the restaurants lining the blocks, the same ones I've seen the past ten years.

I pull out my phone and casually scroll through the addresses, whiskey coursing through my veins in a way that doesn't make me feel drunk—more like high. I pop Gavin's number into my contacts—you never know—and then Ryan Murphy pops up at *R*.

Good 2 c u last night. I had fun. Let's do it again soon! I type out. For two seconds I question the second part, but part of me thinks we've gotten to that place in our friendship; the other part—the sober part—tells me it would be safer not to send this. But what the hell, Addison is right—why am I being so low-self-esteemy these days? I'm not. The old Liz wouldn't have cared. My finger hovers over the send key. Click.

The next morning at 11:14 a.m., with a dull ache in my left temple, I realize I'm late to my friend's baby shower in Westchester after the auto-reminder appears on my phone. I can't tell what I'm most queasy about—last night's pub out-ing or texting Ryan at 2:03 a.m. on a Friday night. Total rookie move.

Sitting on the train from Grand Central Station and looking out at the beautiful presummer blossoming of the trees along the Hudson River, my thinking softens toward what the girls were telling me last night. Even if Ryan is in his prime Peter Pan years, still, he's turning older and could change his agenda if the right girl came along.

When I get to my friend Katie's house, I have to admit, it's adorable. My old friend from high school must have gotten some help from her parents on the down payment. The three-bedroom Tudor-style home is on a quiet street in the same town the Clintons live, and orange marigolds are peeking their heads out from the ground in front of perfectly landscaped shrubbery. Taken altogether it feels, unlike me, very grown-up. Then again, my wants are more simple. I'd be really happy if I could find my soul mate and a life that didn't involve a long daily commute to the Bird Cage. I don't need West Elm, a grown-up couch or a Vitamix.

As I walk in, all of Katie's suburban friends are doing the "sit around a circle opening gifts, oohing and ahhing." I wonder if they know that to a trained baby-specialist like me, they look as though they are just going through the motions, or whether they are actually getting some joy out of staring at the same Baby Boppy they've seen at every other baby shower they've been to. Even the clothes from Baby Gap are starting to all look the same.

I amble in, and in one quick motion, Katie's sisters take my gift and hand me a mimosa. Everyone's staring at the mom-to-be as one of Katie's blonde sorority friends whispers a comment to her cohort decked out in Lilly Pulitzer. They look just about my age, but seem older, or at least more mature than I, and they size me up and down. My black stretchy material dress, whose empire waist gives me room for my post-night-out bloat, is probably not so baby-shower appropriate, but still very comfy.

As I look for an empty seat, I say a silent prayer that the women in the room with babies will not ask me to hold them. When I pick up one of my friend's babies my first thought is never, *Isn't she adorable?* It's usually, *How long do I have to hold her and smile before I pass her on to the next friend?* Not because I don't love babies—I do. It's because I find myself going into a thought sequence of the worst possible scenario—not holding her head correctly so her neck falls back, turning her into a paraplegic for life.

Thankfully there are no longing-to-be-held babies in sight, so I take a seat in the back to watch the gift opening. I realize the women are gossiping about my lateness when one says, "She probably got her the baby bib—women without kids always get *clothes*."

Ha! Wrong! I turn and stare at them with a self-satisfied grin. They don't realize I work at *Paddy Cakes* and may have been, oh, an hour late, but have stealthily arrived with the best gift ever: the Breast-a-nator 2000, the ultimate antimicrobial milking machine that's like a lactating spa in a box, and makes breastfeeding easy and comfortable.

Katie's just about opened every gift piled sky-high in her family room—which I am envying, especially the cool velveteen sectional from Crate and Barrel, when I see her sisters handing her mine. I start to smile with pride.

"Oh, my God! This is, like, two hundred dollars! Thank you so, so much, Liz. I didn't even register for it because I heard they were back-ordered in the States!" Katie exclaims, as she rips off the fancy embossed wrapping paper from my office's crafts closet.

"I had my press contact call in the newest model from Denmark," I say, beaming.

"How'd she know about *that*?" asks the blonde.

"I don't know," responds Lilly, "I didn't even hear about it until last summer, when one of my nipples was about to come off."

I decide to let everyone in the room in on my secret: "It won *Paddy Cakes'* Top 10 Best of Babies last year. It stimulates milk while simultaneously applying a blend of aloe vera, vitamin E and shea butter to the affected area. The suction is centrifugal, mimicking conditions in space, so the areola gets darker and more supple," I intone.

All Katie's friends are in shock and don't say another word. Her sisters just shoot over a good-for-you look.

"So, are *you* married?" says the blonde, turning to me while Katie and her sisters are putting away gifts. *Darn*, I think, *I almost got out of here scot-free.*

"Nope," I reply calmly. I've learned the best tactic to take in these situations is to play it cautiously optimistic.

"It's okay. You're what, twenty-nine? You still have plenty of time," says Lilly P. Wannabe.

"I'm thirty-one, actually," I say, "But it's okay, I'm not worried."

"Sure," she says, looking aghast and making no attempt to hide it. I know exactly what she's thinking from hearing it from all my friends who've made the exodus out of Manhattan. In suburban years, thirty-one is practically thirty-seven. "You'll be fine. You're cute, and I'm sure you get invited to all the fanciest magazine parties." I can tell her reassurance is fake.

"Yeah, it's fine. At this point I'm just waiting for the right guy to come along," I say. Then things start to turn in a way I'm not expecting.

"You shouldn't be in such a rush," says Blondie, now softening in an almost creepy, conspiratorial way. "I mean, I love my Madison, but sometimes I wish I'd waited a few years. And even now, I find myself looking at the sippy cup, wondering if anyone would know if I spiked it with a little of my Chardonnay to get her to go nappy for the afternoon."

"Yeah, I mean, my doctor's like, 'Whoa, hold up with the Xanax prescriptions for like a month,' heh," says Lilly, tittering nervously.

As the designated no-right-to-judge single girl, I feel like I've just been shanghaied into some strange mommy confessional. They're both looking at me pleadingly as if I have the answers for their postpartum ennui. At this point I need an exit strategy ASAP.

"Okay, well, I'm so hungover I could really use some McDonald's. Nice talking to you, ladies! Byeee!" I quickly say my goodbyes to Katie and her family and walk as fast as I can to the train station.

Why am I in such a fluster? I wonder as I'm waiting for the 3:47 Metro North. I mean, is it really so bad to be thirty-one and not chained down to some six-month-old who forces me not to eat, shower or go to the bathroom. Despite all my sad single life observations, I'm not really in the same mad dash to settle down that seems to plague all my still-single friends. The mythical biological clock doesn't seem to be ticking yet for me.

I see women pushing baby strollers and feel a twinge of guilt (maybe that's not quite the right emotion—sadness, dread?) that I don't want that. At least not yet. I know I want it in the future—in two or three years maybe (which is what I've been saying for the past five years, now that I'm thinking about it), but in any case, not right now. Not when I could be texting my best friends last minute to meet up for dinner, drinking one too many carafes of the house red and seeing where the night takes me. Impractical maybe since, as my mom reminds me constantly, my eggs are almost ready for their *AARP* subscription. But I can't help the way I feel.

The thing is, there's something about it that just feels so *prescribed*. It's not that I don't want to be a mom. Of course I do. I just want to choose it for myself. Not just go through the motions, managed and marketed to me by a tsunami of Buy Buy Baby, Paperless Post and Pinterest so that after all the dust has settled, it's just a series of Venmo transactions and I barely feel it.

When I get back to my apartment, it's almost five o'clock. Nothing from Ryan. I'm a little sad that I've apparently been cast aside by a PH yet again. I decide to do what single girls everywhere do in their most desperate states: get dressed up, call their friends and go out. With the hope that at least there could be a possibility of Ryan texting late at night. But after showering, squeezing myself into some nonmaternity jeans (thank you very much), and sending out what's-going-on-tonight? texts, things are looking down.

Ad and Brie aren't free—Brie is still tired from last night, and Addison's ex-boyfriend is in town. She would never admit it, but I bet Brady's actions have left her reeling, too, so she's probably decided to meet up for dinner and try to initiate some postdinner booty action. It looks like I am stuck hanging out by myself on a Saturday night.

I decide to make the best of it over a scrumptious pint of vegan cashew mint chip and an episode of a British reality show about young twentysomethings in Essex, England, I find on Hulu. The half-hour show is a series of vignettes of flirting, coffee dates, gossiping among the girls, feats of buffoonery among the guys, all building to a themed night out where the catfights finally combust to catharsis. They seem to be having so much *fun*, I think to myself, not overthinking everything. I decide to use the night to make a life list all of my own of the things I will do once I go on meternity leave (I include a few that I have already done for positive reinforcement):

Things to do before I'm ~~30~~ 35
1. ~~Live in New York.~~
2. ~~Become an editor at a magazine.~~
3. ~~Learn to speak French.~~
4. Have a French love affair.
5. Eat pasta in Italy.
6. Run a marathon.
7. Haggle with a salesperson at the bazaar in Marrakech.
8. Learn meditation from a yogi in India.
9. Sail to at least seven of the islands in Greece.
10. Walk the Great Wall of China.
11. Go diving in the Great Barrier Reef in Australia.
12. Spend a week doing nothing at all in Bali, Tahiti or other remote island destination.
13. Have an Anthony Bourdain–style eating adventure with Southeast Asia's street food vendors.
14. Get this close to an elephant in Kenya.
15. See the pyramids.
16. Hike to Machu Picchu.
17. Get paid to travel around the world for a living.
18. Write a bestselling women's travel memoir à la Elizabeth Gilbert.
19. Fall in love with someone who shares my dreams.
20. Have a kid or two.

Looking at the list, I'm suddenly filled with hope and optimism about my situation. Why hadn't I thought of faking pregnancy and quitting before? There is so much that I want to accomplish I need to start now, or else it will never happen. What if I did (metaphorically) take this pregnancy to full term? What if I did take my own meternity leave?

Fantasies of a three-month break start to flood my brain. I will take a few days to recover, then go off on the adventure of a lifetime. I don't know why, but it feels fated that I met Ryan. No expectations or anything, but by then I am sure I will have figured this whole thing out. He will have realized that I am not just a work colleague, have fallen madly in love with me, quit his job, too, and we will be on our way to leading an international life of magic and mystery (definition of what that actually means to be decided at a later date, but most likely akin to the lives lead by the Jolie-Pitts).

I'm so full of pride I decide to start another blog post: "Top 10 Trips of a Lifetime." For the image, I use a sunny one of me tanned in the Bahamas from three years ago, cropping out JR and Photoshopping my tummy and thigh areas ever so slightly. I check once more—no texts from Ryan. I have to decide where I will go first. As a French major in college, I've always dreamed of going to Morocco, and ever since I saw *Casablanca*, I've thought that there could be nothing sexier than the idea of getting lost among the bazaars, drinking Pernod, smoking a hookah on some café terrace and riding camels into the sunset, sharing my saddle with a charming man. That's it. I will go to Casablanca first. I find the movie in my Amazon library, and begin falling asleep. Mmm, that Humphrey Bogart is so sexy. Why can't there be any guys like that anymore...

Sunday morning I awake to find that there's a text waiting for me: Looking good, Buckley. I'd go with ya! PS Thanks for the booty-text:-) It's Ryan.

Eight

On the following Wednesday, it's time to get the October lineups back. There's only one feeling running through my bones: pure all-consuming terror.

"Edits are back, you sexy bitches," trills Caitlyn to just me and Jules, making us LOL. I know my revised lineup is in the pile and that in a few minutes, my fate (at least at the magazine) will be sealed.

Alix breezes toward our cube, cashmere duster trailing in the air behind her, rectangular tortoise-shell frames perched on her nose, reading through everything as she's walking. The suspense is killing me. She finally reaches our cube bank.

"Looks like she loved your October piece on antivaxxer measles hotbeds, Jules," she says, handing back her copy.

"And here's your stuff back, Liz," she says, handing me the pile of copy without a drop of emotion.

I sort through the pile to my lineup. There's only one word at the top: *Fine*. Odd.

Cynthia's large signature stares back at me in red ink at the top of the page, meaning it's approved.

I email Ford to see if he wants to do lunch, and luckily

he's up for it. I find him already in the café perched over a big salad. He pulls out his earbuds the second he sees me.

"Hey, Lizzie, you okay. How's it all going so far?" he greets me with a concerned look as he eyes my bump.

I guess my state of self-torture is starting to show.

"I'm fine. What's up with you? Anything good on the giveaway table today?" I say, trying to keep things positive.

"Just a few guides on Scotch, skull and crossbones cuff-links, patterned socks. The usual. What's up? You seem sad."

At his prompting, I totally lose it.

"I'm fine, I'm fine. It's just that my editor has deemed me an untouchable and is playing mind games with me. My crush is dangling crumbs of the start of something, and I'm subsisting on them as if I'm some witless lab rat. And I have no fucking clue where my life is headed, and I have no idea what to do about it. You know, the usual."

Ford just gives the pouty face and leans in for a big hug. "It's okay, Lizzie, we all go through these growing pains from time to time. It's how life works. The trick is to make a plan and take it step-by-step. That's all we can do. And eat Honey Cups, lots and lots of Honey Cups. Hey, let's go somewhere else for lunch today. This salad isn't doing it for me."

More than thankful for his suggestion, we head out for a hit of pure sugar at the nearest Honey Cup bakery. Things are looking brighter as we head back to the office, and while I'm grabbing a cold brew at the place across the street, I'm even inspired to do exactly what everyone keeps telling me to do—form an action plan—albeit one born out of delerium. I take out a fresh notepad with the *Paddy Cakes* rainbow balloon illustration at the top. (I love using fresh notepads: it always makes me feel like I can start over and change things.) "Action Plan," I write in medium black Sharpie as I begin another list.

1. Go get the rest of Hudson's creations.
2. Hit up Macy's for larger maternity Spawn-x.
3. Try on outfits to make sure they look real.
4. Wear form-fitting outfits so bump is in full view and realistic to staff.
5. Tell the staff that you've had unprotected sex, resulting in an unplanned pregnancy, that you are going to keep the baby at the expense of US taxpayers and contribute to the current single mother statistics on the rise in our society.
6. Discuss requisite 12-week maternity leave with Cynthia.
7. Go through with it, making sure bump expands week by week.
8. Plan "labor."
9. Leave for Morocco to start around-the-world travel adventure.

Okay, I'm an idiot.

When I get back from lunch, I roll my chair out from under the desk and the pile of books stacked on it makes me feel instantly guilty: *Beyond Expecting, La Leche League, Dr. Spock.* All contain Post-its about the first and second trimesters. There's even a stack of ultrasounds at twenty weeks, downloaded from the internet with a note from Jules on top, "Well, if you're going to do it, you better do it right." In a risky move, I tape the pictures to the left-hand corner of my cube. Thank God for Jules.

As Alix is making the usual afternoon rounds with copy. She nears my cube, but instead of her usual sneer, she looks suspicious. "Looks like Cynthia bought your revised ideas about the C-section alternatives, after all. Move ahead with it, I guess."

"Okay, great," I say. I don't quite know what to make of it as I read her comments and start in on the edits to the story.

I'm Googling for more on Chinese herbs when I see that I've already got a text. Could it be?

Good blog post this weekend, Buckley.

It's from Ryan.

Thanks!

A response comes back fast. You've gotta learn how to market yourself, Buckley—that's all part of the game… I could teach you a few pointers if you'd like. What are you doing Saturday? *Ahh.*

I think I could make myself available.

Good, come watch soccer with me at the 11th Street Bar. You know, soccer is a great metaphor for business dynamics.

I thought it was about grown men basing their lives on a small inanimate object.

Well, that's only to help us win over the small, animate ones. :)

You'll have to bribe me with rusty nails, I text back without thinking.

My face flushes red at the thought of hanging out with him. As much as I cared about JR, it never felt like this— jokey-flirty banter on top of so much chemical attraction.

I remember JR had made all the "right" moves at the start of our relationship. We'd met at a press event for a Procter

& Gamble product launch when I was twenty-six; he was a sales associate and twenty-nine at the time. When he took my number, something about him put me off a little—he had sort of an annoying habit of checking in at all the "hot" Meatpacking restaurants on Fridays and Saturdays, then spending the rest of the night on his phone seeing who'd liked his status updates. And constantly telling me to "just chill, babe," even while my mom was finishing up the last of her treatments. And I suspected toward the end he was texting his cute media coordinator more than me. But early on, he'd surprised me with his sweetness and genuine interest, and after a fun summer fling, I found myself smack in the middle of my first real, grown-up relationship.

We'd find the latest '60s *nouvelle vague* film (my favorite) playing down in the Village or the latest action movies (his), then get cake balls at Milk Bar. He'd let me pick out tiny little places I'd read about in *NY Mag* for romantic dinners, but after one too many vodka martinis, we'd often scream about stupid little things to avoid dealing with the real issue—that maybe we weren't right for one another.

So when he broke up with me, though it was a shock, it wasn't all bad. I was a little scared to launch into a whole other decade—the scary decade—with no prospects on the horizon. But at the same time, it felt like a relief. It's not as if I were waking up terrified every day, but the signs were beginning. Those mornings, after a shared bottle of Pinot Noir with Addison and Brie, it was a little strange to see the fine creases along the ridges of my forehead. Then one depressing afternoon this past fall, the sunlight streamed through the bathroom windows at full strength and seemed to shine directly on a patch of gray hair on the top of my head. Was this just a harbinger of the thirties death spiral? Would I be just another embittered single woman sharing '90s nostalgia on Facebook instead of pics of my kids at the pumpkin patch?

But today, with this recent round of texting, things are looking up. In a spurt of total impulsiveness, I decide to share a meme of a very happy-looking French bulldog wearing a paper crown and his tongue hanging out on Instagram. Me, this weekend. In the span of a few hours, I notice I have a new follower. It's Ryan. And he's "liked" it.

On Friday, after a day of relative calm, I'm so preoccupied that when Alix comes over and asks how I'm coming with "the finishing touches on" (read: "another complete rewrite") the best colleges piece for August because she has to catch an early flight to Bar Harbor to visit her in-laws this weekend, I say yes without thinking about it. Damn! I start to cringe, thinking that she's probably leaving for a weekend getaway with Jeffry.

A Facebook message appears from Ryan, almost as if in response. Around for the long weekend? Ready to come out and play with me tomorrow AM? ;) Here's a link to the fan page so you can bone up. I feel a tap on my shoulder. It's Alix.

"Ryan Murphy is messaging you on Facebook?" she says bemusedly.

"Yes, we met up last week to go over our new lineup and see if there were any future partnership opportunities coming up. I told him I'd email him something." I try to say it as though it's purely professional, but we both know it could signify something more. Alix waits a second, as if she's recalling some specific memory, then looks down at my bump.

"Hmm. Okay." She seems tentative. "You know we used to run around in the same social circles in my single days at *Vogue* when he was at HBO."

"What are you saying?"

"If I remember correctly, he had a reputation for being a total player. One of those guys who's out with the group, but that you always see texting for late-night plans kind of thing. I don't think I ever saw him with a girlfriend the entire time our groups were mixing."

I scrunch my face trying to connect this with the totally nice, down-to-earth, seemingly sensitive version I experienced at McGann's.

"Yeah, he was pretty hard-core. I remember there was a period of time when it got really bad." She rolls her eyes upward into the air, putting a finger to her nose, as if to mean he does a lot of coke.

"Oh. Really?"

"He's just one of those guys who works hard and plays harder. He's a fun guy if you're single, but I'd steer clear of someone like him for a person in *your shoes*." Alix folds her arms after putting down a story.

Ryan, a cokehead? This new piece of information makes me a little queasy, though it really doesn't seem like his personality. I try to find some way to reconcile the prospect of dating him, even though, generally, this would be a huge deal breaker.

I immerse myself in the copy and the day goes by rapidly. The next morning, though, Alix is at it again. "So, did you get me the postpartum depression research I asked for yet?" she says, interrupting my morning news catch-up.

"No, sorry, I was working on the multiracial stuff, the C-section revise and my October stories. I was going to do it by Monday."

"Liz, you really have to get more organized with this stuff. I was planning on working on it this weekend. Tyler's with Trevor and my mother-in-law."

"I thought you were going to Maine?"

"I've decided to stay after all. You've left me too much to do. Trevor's mother never gets to see her grandson, sooo…" Her tone seems tense, as if to cover up the fact she's probably secretly happy about this, since it leaves her time to hook up with Jeffry.

"Sorry to ruin your plans."

"When you're a mother, you'll understand the importance of planning and prioritization." With this, she tightens the belt on her long black cardigan and walks off without letting me respond.

Nine

Little nervous tingles wash over me as I pay the cabbie with my credit card, which thankfully does not come back declined. Though it's Saturday, I should be planning my exit strategy and rehearsing my conversation with Cynthia. Instead, I'm going to go hang out with a bunch of drunk men watching soccer in the East Village—and secretly, though I really shouldn't be here, I couldn't be happier.

Walking toward the dive bar filled with neon signs for European beers, I think to myself, *This must be a date, right?* It has to be. I smooth out my sweater, a French-style black-and-white-striped boat-neck top, hoping the effect, paired with jeans and black ballet flats, reads cute, cool and casual. Praying to God that none of our office underlings are doing the walk of shame this morning in the Village, I head toward the door. I'm expecting a sparse crowd this early in the morning, but it's the exact opposite. As soon as the heavy doors heave open, I feel the swell of heat and sweat mixed with the scent of spilled Heineken. A sea of men wearing red soccer jerseys are sloshing around, chanting drinking songs as they wait for the game to start.

"Buckley! You made it!" I hear a voice calling me from the middle of the room, then see Ryan's hand raised, holding a Guinness, waving me toward him. The men of all ages, and clearly a heavy mix of guys from the UK and other countries, part ways and allow me back as they look me up and down with a smile.

"Of course I made it!" I say as Ryan bumps into me, causing us to crash into one another and spill a bit of his beer on me.

"Very cool," he says, his huge smile wide. "Want one of these?" He motions down at his brown frothy drink. "Or were you expecting mimosas," he teases. I fake punch him in the ribs, and he nods at the barman, whom he clearly knows well, for a round of two more. *Great*, I think, he's perfect in every way, but of course, a partier.

As the game starts, the crowd of supporters sings and cheers so loud I can hardly hear Ryan as he attempts to explain how the season has gone, but pretty soon, the game's started and the crowd turns silent. Ryan jumps and hollers with each false call. His enthusiasm is sexy and when Liverpool scores its first goal right before the first half finishes, he grabs me by the shoulders into a tight hug. "Buckley, did you see that goal?"

Eventually as Liverpool wins 2–1 against Arsenal, the crowd, happy, now turns their attention away from the TV and in one collective swoop immediately starts ordering drinks.

"So what'd you think of the game? Not bad, right?" Ryan hands me my drink from the bar.

"Pretty good," I say, smiling and thinking, *is it bad that I'm the kind of girl who could spend her Saturday mornings in a bar full of sweaty drunken men, perfectly happy?* More than a few guys are aiming to get even more hammered, and they start crashing into me, spilling drops of beer. Ryan notices, steering me out of the way toward the front of the bar near the windows.

"It's more than good. We won! We're now number one in the Premiere League with just two more games to go! It's incredible!"

"Fine, congrats, then! Maybe not a metaphor for life, but slightly impressive." I wink.

"Are you kidding? They're like Zen warriors."

"I just saw a bunch of hot guys with neck tattoos and man buns running around a field."

"It's more than that," he says, getting all strangely serious and making a wiping motion near his eye, which he tries to hide. "We'll make a fan out of you someday. What do you say we get out of here?"

"Sure," I reply, a little tipsy.

"How about we get out of this neighborhood. I'm always here. Wanna hit the Standard Biergarten for some grub?"

I nod silently, just smiling, as he takes my hand to lead me outside toward a cab. I can swear that on his way out, some of his friends give him a look of approval and he nods one right back.

In the cab, I survey our body language: he's turned toward me, legs splayed and shoulders relaxed. It's a good sign, I think. I hear my phone buzz.

Ryan notices. "Work calls?"

"Yes, unfortunately." I roll my eyes as I reply to a text from Alix about her Facebook PTSD story if you haven't lost the baby weight fast enough.

"Wow. You're a busy woman," says Ryan, teasing, trying to get the phone out of my hands as it starts buzzing again.

"Usually I'm not," I say, finding myself reminded of JR and feeling a little irked by the charge. So what if I were?

Looking at the kindness in his eyes as he says it, I decide to leave it.

At the upscale beer garden, over beer steins and Wiener schnitzel, Ryan tells me he got his love of soccer from his dad, whose grandfather was from Cork, but had moved to Liverpool to work before finally immigrating to the States. As he's telling me the story, I can tell there's a bit of sadness in his eyes. When we finish up, it's only 1 p.m. and I can't be sure, but all signs point toward a perfect day as he leads me out.

"Want to take a walk along the High Line?" Ryan's eyes get glinty in the warm springtime sun. "I'll tell you about its construction. My buddy's firm worked on it."

"Sure!" I can't remember when I've ever been on a date like this before.

As we walk up, it's pretty much perfect. He highlights the fun factoids he knows about the shrubbery's eco-consciousness ("it's all weeds that were originally on the old railroad tracks") and how the wood has all been reclaimed. I can tell this is what lights him up, his passion. It's exciting.

At the north end, he pulls me to the edge where we gaze at the undulating curves of the Frank Gehry–designed building standing out along the West Side Highway. He reaches for my hand; once we're there, we linger a bit. All of a sudden, strangely nervous about where this could lead, I drop it quickly.

Ryan doesn't seem to let it bother him. "So, did you have fun today?" His blue eyes sparkle in the warm sun.

"Yes, actually. It's nice to not have to think about work on the weekends for once." But as if on cue, my phone chimes again, this time from Alix asking about another research detail on yoga breathing for toddlers. I quickly answer, typing away a response for a minute or so, and hit Send, letting out a tired sigh along with it.

"Ah, I get it," says Ryan.

"What?" I say, strangely nervous.

"You're a classic overachiever."

"You say that like it's a bad thing."

"Well, inherently, it isn't." He pauses for a second. "If you're doing it for yourself."

"Of course I am." Now I'm feeling defensive.

"Okay, then tell me how many emails you've answered so far this weekend on—" he takes a look at his watch "—Saturday at 1:30 p.m."

I give him a guilty look. "Only a couple."

"And how many new blog posts have you written?"

"Exactly zero," I say, suddenly getting his point. "But when your bosses pile work on you it's not always easy to just say no."

"I know, I know, you're destined for greatness," he says, seeming to sense my reaction. "All I'm saying is that you can't live for anyone else, Liz. You just have to live for yourself."

"That's easy for you to say," I say quickly, letting out a loud sigh. *I wasn't the one partying in a coke-filled haze in my twenties.*

"No, seriously, you've gotta stop trying to control everything."

"But, that's the only way to beat the competition."

"Not always," says Ryan, looking down. "Did you see how Liverpool played today? They were playing their own game. That's how you win."

I know he's probably right, but he still has no idea what I'm up against. I turn away and cross my arms, looking at the Hoboken side of the Hudson.

"Fine. Maybe you're not ready to hear it…but I'm around to help, anytime you need me." He punches my arm teasingly, which makes me smile a little. We stand in silence for a few moments, he pulls me back into a bear hug. It's nice. And feels important. Like he's getting as much from it as I am. Then, he says, "You've got choices, Buckley." He pulls me around toward downtown where the Freedom Tower faces us. "See that? It's a symbol. You can always rebuild after nothing. Remember that."

Then, out of the corner of my eye, I glimpse her—Cynthia—walking out of the Gehry building that sits facing the Hudson on the West Side Highway. She's probably waiting for a car—I forgot that she lives down there.

All of a sudden, I see her head turn in my direction, and I say, "I, uh, have to go now."

"What's wrong?"

I can't chance being spotted. "See you later, Ryan. I had fun."

"You don't seem like you did."

"No, I did!" I tell him, as he's staring at me with a dumbfounded expression.

The abruptness stirs up a feeling in his eyes, though I can't trace it. "Okay. I have some work ideas to talk to you about. Wanna set up a meeting this coming Friday?"

"Sure, just email me," I reply, thinking maybe this really is about work, after all. I turn in the exact opposite direction from Cynthia and hightail it to the traffic lights to hail a cab.

He looks at me blankly as the cab rolls away.

Ten

After yesterday's emotional roller coaster, I'm glad to be heading to the suburbs for my mom's birthday for the rest of the long Memorial Day weekend. Another night of boozing it up (and the potential of sending out hormone- and alcohol-fueled texts to Ryan) is not what my tender psyche needs right now.

A few new Dunkin' Donuts have moved into where some of the old diners used to be. But the ice cream shop where I worked summers as a teen is still there on Main Street. The bus pulls into a street behind a strip mall, heading toward my mom's apartment complex. After renting for about five years after the divorce, she was finally able to buy this past year. She swears she's much happier here in the small one-bedroom apartment "than living with your father" in our old house. But I wonder.

"Hi, sweetie," she says, embracing me with a huge hug, and at once I feel the two grapefruits that have replaced the softness. "Look at me! Fake boobs!" she proclaims, showing them off through her polyester cardigan sweater.

She's always "understood," giving me the easy pass about

not coming home for every treatment and the reconstructive surgery. But she didn't really. And I didn't really. I was there for the big events. The posttests, postdiagnosis. Chemo. Radiation. Hair. Mastectomies. But I can count, painfully, the moments I wasn't. I could have come home to stay with her throughout recovery. I could have held her hand during all the appointments. My aunt Judy was there. And her best friend Ellen from school. But not me. Not always. And the fact that she lets it slide haunts me. Shames me. For this. What? A job where I am faking a baby?

"A sixty-year-old with thirty-year-old boobs!" She laughs.

"No, they're great!"

"Well, anyway, how are you? Did they reschedule Paris, or is it done?"

"Done, but that's okay, they have me pretty busy now, so too much to do anyway."

"Have you heard anything from your father recently?"

"No," I say quickly.

"Lizzie, you really should get in touch with him. I know he'd like to hear from you."

"I will, Mom. I've just been busy at work."

She pauses a little stiffly. "Well, I finally boxed up all your old things, so you'll have to take a look through and decide what you eventually want to take back to the city with you, and what you want to throw away," she says. Though her place is small, she's decorated it with cute odds and ends she's found at HomeGoods.

"Mom, you know I have no space for anything in my apartment."

"Well, then, you'll have to part with it all, I guess. Now that I've downsized, there's no room, Lizzie... So tell me. Anything new happening at work these days? Any promotions?" she asks, taking a seat on the beige sectional, while I sit down in the slipcovered recliner.

"No, you know, the same," I say, trying to figure out what to tell her. "I told you how I almost got to interview Marigold Matthews, right?"

"Yes, sweetie, I love her on *Crime Theory*! And how about your dating life? Anything happening there? Are you sure you don't want me to set you up with Margaret's son's best friend?" she pushes.

"Mom, I'm fine. It's okay, really," I say, looking down.

"Probably better, Lizzie. If there's one thing that I've learned, it's that you can't depend on a man for happiness." Unable to voice my thoughts, I look down, which my mom notices quickly, giving me a soft look. "Have you heard from JR at all?" Something about him my mom had never liked.

"No," I say quietly.

"Don't worry, Lizzie, I know something good will happen soon."

I take a deep breath. "I just don't feel it yet and I'm thirty-one."

My mom gets up and pours us both a cup of chamomile.

"I never told you this, but your father and I tried for a long time to get pregnant. We were younger, but it took me almost two years to conceive," she says. "At that time infertility treatments didn't exist. Just judgmental friends and relatives and doctors telling me there was nothing I could do. Did I ever tell you that your father's mother told me that maybe God was punishing me because I had been on birth control for the first few years I was married?" She lets out a snuffle.

"Seriously?" I say, awestruck. "Granny Buckley said that? That's so awful."

"I'm sure that's where your father gets his stubbornness. Anyway, I'd always felt the same way you do. During my twenties, everyone told me I should be having children, but I kept putting it off. Then all of a sudden my biological clock started ticking and I just knew."

"Really?" I say hopefully. I readjust myself on the couch, tucking one leg under my bum. "I mean, I just haven't felt that yet."

"Yes, but times were different. Women didn't really have many other options. I enjoyed working in the school system—but motherhood was the norm. That's something I've always admired about you, how hard you've worked and how far you've come," she says, taking a slow sip of her tea. "Becoming a magazine editor is not something just anyone can do… I can't wait to see where you'll go next." She pauses. "I'm very proud of you, Lizzie."

I bury my nose in the tea and avert eye contact, which my mom notices.

"Don't worry, Lizzie. The time will come."

We spend the rest of the day hanging out, and after dinner, I go through my old journals and scrapbook albums that my mom has boxed up. She put them in my new room, which has a small daybed and also functions as a den and office.

At first it's fun to look at all the old pictures. But then I see a few from my junior and senior year of high school. Even though I'd always had a close circle of friends, I'd always felt like an outsider among most of my classmates whose fathers worked at the investment banks and who would talk of going to St. Bart's or on safari in Africa for spring break, while we were taking staycations before anyone knew what that meant.

My hands land on a scrapbook page from the junior year winter formal. There I'm posing with my friends. I remember my dad and mom were fighting a lot then—usually about money.

Toward the end of the year, he'd started going to Atlantic City on his days off without my mom. She tried to keep the peace, but then the attacks on the towers happened the first week I started my senior year. My dad wasn't working his usual shift at the airport that day, thank God. Looking back, the year seemed to fade into a blur completely.

Then, later in the year around the holidays, Dad was laid off for saying something to one of his superiors, and he started going to AC for a week at a time. She tried to keep the peace, but to no avail. Finally, my parents told me that they were getting divorced and selling our house—the one my mom's mother had grown up in—so they could afford my college tuition. He'd begun seeing another woman, a divorcée he'd met in a bar playing Keno. I could tell my mom was devastated, but she simply packed us up and we moved on. She found a small rental on the outskirts of our town.

Then, my sophomore year of college, my mother was diagnosed with a difficult to locate stage 3 breast cancer that kept threatening to metastasize. It had taken almost eight years in total to beat it—a toll that had devastated the both of us and one we faced alone.

My mom knocks at the door. "Lizzie, are you almost done? There's something I found the other day that I wanted to show you."

She comes in, sits on my bed and hands me a scrapbook. "This is one thing I'd never throw away." She pats a space next to her and I go sit down beside her. I open it to find articles, newspaper clippings and pictures—my entire life's accomplishments—including the letter announcing I'd been accepted into the prestigious Paris Sciences Po program for my junior year abroad. I'd turned it down—it would have been too expensive, and I'd needed to be at home anyway.

She wipes something out of the corner of her eye and

lets out a little laugh. "You didn't know I was keeping this. You've always amazed me, Lizzie, with your determination. You set out to do something and you always do it."

Eleven

Coming to work Tuesday morning after the long weekend, now almost a month in—the date I was supposed to be out of *Paddy Cakes* for good, I feel as if I am standing on the highway median strip in that old video game "Frogger." I know I'm going to get smacked no matter which way I head, so I stand still for just a little bit longer.

Before I can even settle in to "The Best Colleges for Toddlers" revise, I get an email notice from Caitlyn.

Everyone to the conference room, it reads.

I glance at Jules with an expression that says "think we should be worried?" We all look a little confused as we head over. By the scared-bunny looks on people's faces, I think we're all remembering what happened last time with the Cynthia announcement.

But once we see that there are ample Honey Cups and Diet Cokes, our chests give a collective sigh. Everyone takes a seat and Cynthia comes in, wearing a particularly expensive-looking structured black dress with nude heels, her cheeks frosty with luminating powder.

"I'd like to make an announcement," she says, peering

around the room. "As you know, starting July 1 Pamela will be going on maternity leave, and I'm sorry to say, she has decided to stay home."

We all look over at Pam, our executive editor, who's glowing. She's not even pretending she'll miss *Paddy Cakes*. She's been around for twelve years, is forty-two, married and is one of those superstars that rose to the position of executive editor at thirty. "We are very sad to see Pam leave," says Cynthia, trying to sound warm. "But this also gives us an exciting opportunity to rethink staffing. I have not decided yet whether we will be replacing her or reorganizing and promoting from within." Editors fidget in their seats.

"Show me your best and maybe you will see a change in title," says Cynthia, pausing for full dramatic effect, after panning her eyes around the room.

Just as she's about to leave, she lands on me and then looks down to my tiny bump, seeming to calculate something. All of a sudden it comes.

"And, I almost forgot! We have some other *wonderful* news. Liz will also be going on maternity leave this fall."

Thirty shocked faces turn and stare at me. I have absolutely no idea what to say. I take such a huge sip of my Diet Coke it makes me choke.

"Ha-ha, yes, it's really true," I giggle, wide-eyed as if I'm some deranged elf. Alix shoots me an icy look. I instinctively place my hands on my stomach in a protective fashion.

"It was sort of a surprise. Ha. But, well, I'm in my thirties, and after seeing everyone else go through it, I've realized that this is something I want for myself." I am trying hard not to allow my voice to crack. "I'm not getting any younger, and it happened, er, unexpectedly…"

I start to trail off as everyone's faces register emotions ranging from plain shocked to all kinds of horrified. Yes, everyone gets pregnant at *Paddy Cakes*, but no one does it unplanned without a rich husband to support her.

After a few seconds, everyone starts to congratulate me.

"Welcome to the club, new mama! I'm so happy for you!" says Chloe. "I'm putting together a whole basket of stuff for you. You're gonna need it. The hormones bring out the melasma. But I'll give you the *medical grade* stuff I keep in the secret part of the closet," she says, lowering her eyes.

"Want to come to lunch with us sometime?" says Patty. "We've got a regular table every Friday? Talk about mom stuff?"

"Whatever you read, do *not* go natural," says Deb, our health director. "Take the *drugs*, do you hear me."

I smile and nod to put people at ease, and then Jules and I hurry back to our seats.

All I can say is, you better hold on tight, because this is about to be a bump-y ride… Jules GChats. Did you see my email about the new bump tracker? Better check to see what size you should be this week before everyone starts asking!

Thanks. What about what happened with Pam? You know Alix is ready to pounce all over that. Think she's pissed she wasn't named executive editor? I reply.

Seriously. I bet Alix's already got the job, but Cynthia decided to use the opportunity to get us to work harder. This summer's gonna suck. I can forget about the road trip Henry and I were planning.

Sorry, Jules. I'll help you plan your staycation, I message back.

It's just—we're actually, well, thinking about moving.

What? I write back, shocked by this news. My office BFF could be leaving?

Can't talk now—more later.

Just then Cynthia slams her office door so loudly it cuts through the air of the entire floor. We all look up to see what's happening. Is Alix getting reprimanded?

"I told you—more humanity. I want to hear her inner dialogue. I want to hear how she hated her child when he first came out of the womb. Not disliked, not detested, but *hated* him. Couldn't *stand* the little brat's face," says Cynthia to Alix, who's trailing behind her like a lost puppy.

"But that's not how witnesses said Princess Diana was around little William—she loved him. I thought these never-before-seen pictures would be enough…" Alix is painfully trying to salvage the discussion, but clearly pissed at the inanity.

"That's not going to sell magazines, now is it," says Cynthia, with a sneer. Then, from out of nowhere, she calls my name wearily. "Elizabeth. Come over here." I wonder if Cynthia ever bothered to ask anyone if I'd rather be called Liz, or just read the staff list once and it stuck. "What are the trends in postpartum depression? Anything new out?"

I take a second to think. "Umm, nothing really new. But I could repackage the piece as a roundup about famous women who've had PPD. Use pull-quotes and beautiful black-and-white photography and call it, 'The PPD Spectrum No One's Talking About.'" Then, just for fun, I decide to out Alix. "We could use the Lexis search on quotes Alix asked me to pull for her last weekend."

"Perfect," Cynthia says. "Solutions, Alix. That's what sells magazines."

"Well, I could have come up with that," says Alix under her breath.

"What was that, Alix?" Cynthia asks.

"Nothing," she says.

Then Cynthia adds, "Okay, Elizabeth, have it to me by this afternoon. I have to leave early to go see my boyfriend's daughter's play. Five thousand dollars for acting lessons and she can't even pronounce 'Othello.' The girl's five already. I just don't understand it."

"No problem," I reply.

"Make sure to interview the top gynecologists for the story. Maybe we should use yours. Who's your ob-gyn?" The question catches me off guard completely.

I search for the first name that comes to my head, looking at the only thing in sight—the cupcake sitting on the desk in my cube. "Dr....Honey...cut."

Alix looks at me funny. "Dr. Honeycut? Never heard of him. What hospital is he affiliated with?" I start to sweat, racking my brain to guess which makes sense.

"I found him doing the high-def sonogram story," Jules says from her seat. She must have overheard my quivering tone. *Thank God for Jules.* "He's the best."

"Yep, the best," I say, nodding my head. *And I am the worst.*

The next day at work, I decide if I'm going to do this, I have to do it right. What does James Lipton always say to fledgling actors on *Inside the Actors Studio*? "To be a great actor, you must make a choice and commit." The bump firmly in place, I make my first choice: a form-fitting out-fit. As I walk into the office at 9:15 on the dot, Alix looks over. She's taking in my outfit, a tight white button-down tucked into a black pencil skirt with a red belt. It's a little provocative and not something I would normally ever wear, but it shows off the bump in all its glory. Everyone seems to be looking at me. I think I'm actually glowing.

"Hey, Liz, showing off the gams while preggers. Good for you," says Jeffry. If I don't have morning sickness, at least I have Jeffry to make me vomit. I smile, then walk toward my cube.

I have to present my August story proposals at a 9:30 a.m. editorial meeting, while Cynthia approves, rejects or alters them. I sense everyone's a little on edge today.

"Okay," says Cynthia, "who's ready to wow me for August? Think breast-feeding shame, think stroller shame, think C-section shame. What will disrupt pregnancy like Uber disrupted cabs? Ideas, people. Chop-chop!"

"I had an idea," says Lexi, an associate editor. "What if we highlight a few cool couples with toddlers who've ditched their careers in the city for the rustic bohemian life?"

"Boring! Not trendy enough. What's happening next year, not last year."

I give Jules a silent *eek* look at that one.

"Well, what about a story on improving baby selfies for social media? The latest fun filters, that kind of thing," Caitlyn spurts out.

"Did it. Last year. Read the goddamm magazine before you get here, Braylin…"

"It's Caitlyn."

"What the fuck ever! Ideas! I want ideas that will sell the bloody magazine!"

"What about algorithmic parenting—you know, using Facebook and Google insights to be a better parent?" calls out Charlie, our new web editor fresh from Harvard business school, hardly looking up from her laptop.

"Could be okay. There doesn't seem to be a lot of heart in it," says Cynthia. "Anyone else?"

Sitting up in my chair, I chime in. "Well, I was thinking, we've kind of done the whole mommy wars thing, and now the tiger Mom-French Mom thing. I was reading *Goop* the other day and thinking that maybe the newest 'mommy war' is the one we're having with ourselves." I hesitate, but to my surprise, everyone's still listening.

"Go on," says Cynthia.

"Facebook makes it seem as if everyone else has the perfect pumpkin-picking portraits, Pinterest makes it seem like everyone else has the mason-jar crafting lifestyle, while Gwyneth is telling us it's totally possible to have the tummy we had when we're nineteen."

"It's not. It's *so* not," says Deb, rolling her eyes.

"And let's not get started with the whole CrossFit/Paleo mom movement." Everyone nods. I start to pick up on the energy.

"No wonder women in their thirties and forties are experiencing more autoimmune diseases like irritable bowel syndrome and Hashimoto's thyroiditis—we literally can't stop attacking ourselves."

Cynthia looks at me now in a way I've never seen. "Good. So, what's the positive spin. The *solution*."

I start to get anxious waves. Not now. *Fight for it, Buckley.* I can do this. I take a big breath in, then try to relax. "*Meternity*. Maybe *that's* the new idea."

There's a glimmer of recognition in Cynthia's eyes.

"Before getting all stressed and helicoptery, or adhering to some rigid cultural system like tiger moms, or cadre like the French, or getting all obsessed with the social media movement du jour, which are all *external* systems, you check in with yourself first and do what makes the most sense for you, not, you know, the hypervigilance of free-range, but *real*.

Breathe, don't get all caught up. Give yourself a reality check and trust yourself. British reality show–style parenting!"

There's a quiet around the room. I worry that I've said something totally stupid.

"But American...our own version."

"Meaning?"

I grasp around. "Slightly more earnest?" Cynthia ponders it.

"And fat!"

"Ah," everyone says, nodding with total recognition.

"Instead of letting motherhood be coopted by brands, blogs and social media, it's time to take our power back. We're moms. We're better than this. A return to sanity. Not so much overthinking. Parenting can be...*fun*." With the *f* word tossed into it, most of the room looks at me as if I'm from Mars, but not Cynthia, who seems to get what I'm saying.

"*Meternity,*" says Cynthia, with a rare ease in her voice. "Love it. The new cure for modern American motherhood. We've tried the whole self-love thing before but no one's buying it—too self-helpy. This removes the 'I'm okay, you're okay' sentiment. Let's go with it. Make it big—an end of year story. *So* millennial. Our advertisers will eat it up." She's smiling now, widely, so I can feel it. Everyone is except Alix, who's looking down at her loafers.

Then, Cynthia looks directly at Alix and says, "Meternity. Now *that's* a big idea, everyone."

I smile, surprised by the newfound praise. "Elizabeth. Stay for a second after the meeting," says Cynthia.

This is it, I think. We're finally going to discuss things. But then Cynthia launches into something I'm not expecting.

"You know, I never really thought you'd amount to very much here. Your ideas are passable, and you are always here late at night, lurking around the office, but I don't know. Nothing about you really stood out."

Great, I think, *I am about to get fired.*

"But recently I've noticed a change. You seem to be working extra hard. Burning the midnight oil. Coming up with ideas that will take our brand to the next level. Keep up the good work." Though the comments are positive, her eyes retain a cautious look. I half grin, then stare down at my bump and quickly put my hands over it. A wider smile forms in the creases of my mouth. I nod silently as I turn to leave her office.

"She totally bought it!" I tell Jules over lunch in our cube area. I'd say this bump is giving me extra confidence. "Thank you, Little B," I say, staring down, directly talking to it. I'm on a high.

"Well, I thought the whole plan was to find a new job and get out of here after a month. On Friday, you'll be at twenty weeks. Everyone's going to be asking you to feel the baby," says Jules.

"I'll just tell them I'm one of those moms who doesn't like it when people touch her stomach."

"Fine, if you think you can get away with it," snaps Jules, turning away. "Sorry, have to work now."

I look at the pictures lining Jules's side of our cube.

"So you're thinking of moving?" I nudge.

Jules immediately launches in. "Well, Henry didn't take the GMATs seriously, and it's making me think we've gotta consider plan Bs," she says in a matter-of-fact way.

"Where would you go?"

"Maybe Raleigh-Durham or Charlotte, or even back to Hotlanta. Henry could still do graphic design and I could get a teaching fellowship. The cost of living is just so much cheaper, and we'd be closer to our parents if...when...we conceive."

"Wow," I say, taking it all in. "Have you started *trying*?" I ask tentatively. This is a surprise; I thought I had at least another year with childless Jules.

"God, no," she says. Her eyes dart away, looking to see if anyone's overheard.

"When would you move?" I ask.

"Henry gets his scores back soon. They'll pretty much determine his chances of getting into NYU or Columbia."

"Does he really want to be in business? I thought he liked his job."

"He does, but not enough to give up a future family."

I don't quite know what to say. A graphic designer at an ad agency in the city, Henry's always been more of the caretaker than the ambitious, career-driven one in the relationship—that's Jules. It's who he is. Her current push to get him to go to business school seems like forcing a square peg into a round hole.

For some reason, it feels like crossing a line to tell her that Henry's lack of business drive isn't going to change anytime soon—and maybe that's not such a bad thing. Maybe she should be the one applying to business school. I decide, instead, to table it until later, and revert to making light of things by forwarding her a cute "Cats Who Just Can't Handle It Right Now" listicle on BuzzFeed.

The next morning, Cynthia calls me back into her office. I keep repeating the details of week twenty from *What to Expect* as I walk in, on edge.

"Elizabeth, I'm having a bit of a problem with one of the September well stories now in manuscript—the yearly update on foreign adoption and surrogacy agencies. You've read it?"

"Uh, yes, Alix asked me to help her out on that one."

"It feels outdated—it's just about South America, Korea

and Africa. We should be reporting on the news in India and Mongolia, too. Include some analysis. As is, there's no substance to it." She sets the folder down on her desk and removes her reading glasses.

I think about how Alix had asked me to research the subjects. She said the only requisite for the women featured was they be pretty, young, somewhat diverse and upper-middle-class to "reflect our reader," as she put it. I thought some of the women weren't quite right—they hadn't even come back with children—but the focus was on appearance.

"Yes, you know, I thought so, too."

"Well, why didn't you say anything?" asks Cynthia quickly.

"Well, it was technically Alix's story, so…"

"Well, it's yours now. See if you can fix it by focusing more on the women's emotional experience. Go back to them for more narrative. Change the subjects and open it up to every country if you have to—just make sure to approve them through me first. You did do a good job on those tiger/French mom write-ups—I *think* you can manage this." She says this last part as if she's asking herself the question.

"I'll give it my best."

"You'd better."

I immediately get to work scheduling interviews with the original five women. If I can salvage their stories, I will. If not I'll try to track down other ones.

A few get back to me right away, excited to be profiled in *Paddy Cakes.* Later in the afternoon I'm able to speak with the first subject, Mary-Ellen Thomkins, a thirty-six-year-old painter from Vermont. I ask her to describe each detail of her story—the hardships of infertility and the difficulties she and her husband faced navigating a very foreign system—until she finally came home with a baby in her arms. She tells me that, actually, changing political systems and regulations have made it increasingly harder to adopt babies internationally in the past five years, and that I should investigate India.

After a bit of internet research, I learn that surrogacy *has* become big business in India, and because of increased demand from western couples—in particular, gay couples and straight couples looking for more affordable options—a great deal of it unregulated. Increasingly, highly paid agents are luring in young women to live in hospitals for nine months while their baby gestates for a few thousand rupees, then as soon as they go through labor, they're back on the streets.

Then, I happen upon a VICE video online that makes my stomach churn. Because the stakes are so high to provide a paying couple with a baby at the end of the nine months, some back-alley clinics are pumping women with more than one embryo. And these "extra babies" born of this process are being sold on the black market.

Wow, I think, as I sift through all the details. *This is a story that needs to be told.*

After talking to one of the women who went through the surrogacy process in Anand, a region in India where it is highly regulated, I realize that this is going to take days, if not all next week to get right. A feeling enters my stomach—not the dread I usually get before writing up a piece on the latest strollers or a manufactured mommy war. Instead it's like going to a new yoga class where I'll have to stretch a muscle that I haven't used in a while. This feels, well, *exciting.*

June

Twelve

PUSH! ☺ Notification! Week 20: Extra Snaps, anyone?! Now that you're over the hump of your second trimester you're fiiiiinally feeling the urge to return to your daily scheduled selfies—your nails are stronger and your hair is thicker and fuller than usual because of some cuhraaaazy pregnancy hormones! Baby Smiles: 35!

My September stories sail through fact-checking, and now, on Friday, as I put the finishing touches on the adoption and surrogacy story I feel happy with the progress I'm making at work, so much so that I haven't really taken the time to look outside the office. It's already almost time for the next bump size. The early June air is slightly warm, but luckily not making me sweat too badly. Addison Messengered me a magenta Grecian-inspired maternity dress earlier in the week and I've paired it with some black leggings and gold sandals. Who knew I'd find my fashion footing thanks to maternity clothes?

But the moment I set foot in the office, Jeffry catches

up with me. "What are your official maternity leave dates again?" he asks before I've even put down my bag.

"I'm still due October 20," I say nervously.

"Yes, I know. But are you going to leave a week earlier? You, know, just in case you pop sooner than expected?"

"No, I'd prefer to work right up until my due date," I say. "I'll let you know if that plan changes."

"Will you be staying out the full six weeks plus vacation?" he asks, his eyes narrowing, as I play with my hair.

"Yep! Going to take full advantage of that! Ha!"

Looking satisfied, he nods thanks, writes down the answers in his paper, then begins to walk away. But he stops.

"Liz, do you know what you're going to do after you give birth—in terms of child care?"

I splatter my drink, not expecting this at all. "I, uh."

"Babies are expensive," he quips. "Maybe you should be thinking about a plan."

"My mother is going to help out during the week," I answer quickly, finding confidence. "The rest, I'm still working out." He seems to take my answer at face value.

Alix comes up to us and notices my pink dress accentuating my bump.

"How are we doing today?" she says. "All good, I see."

"Hey, I have a doctor's appointment at noon," I say. "Would you cover for me in the cover lines meeting with Deb? I *have* to get some tests done."

"Sure. Okay," she says, almost warmly. "You probably *should* start thinking about child care—this city's best day cares have a mile-long waiting list." Was it me, or was she trying to be helpful just now?

At noon on the dot, I dart off to my "doctor's appointment"—the mani-pedi place across town. It's been years since I've had time during the week to get my nails done and it feels like Christmas. Why didn't I think of this plan before?

For the first time in a long time, I ditch boring light pink Ballet Slipper and choose a bold color that I imagine will somehow conjure up luck and love. Sexy Divide, a deep purple with gold specks from Essie's eco-friendly line, is calling my name. As the manicurist finishes up, I find myself filled with positivity. It feels good to take action—albeit slightly crazy action—and I feel alive. It's the first time I've taken time out of the office in years.

As the technician ushers me to the drying station, I think about the office reaction to my pregnancy.

Pam actually told me she was proud of what I was doing, and that at forty-two, she'd undergone three rounds of IVF to conceive. "I wish I'd known how hard it would be when I was younger," she'd said. "If you can conceive naturally, more power to you."

The younger assistants had halfheartedly congratulated me, but had mostly stayed away. On their 35K-a-year salaries, the idea of single motherhood was probably their worst nightmare. All except for Caitlyn, who actually asked me if she could take me to lunch to find out "more deets," most likely sensing the bump's positive effect on my career trajectory.

While I'm thinking about more ways to set aside time for "doctor's visits," I see the ash-blond "lob" or long, angled bob, reflected in the window and an immediate shiver runs down my spine. *Shit!* It's Cynthia. What would she be doing at the cheapo nail place? I turn around to face the wall as my nails dry under the ultraviolet lights. Does she know about my supposed doctor's appointment? "Elizabeth?"

I turn around slowly, shoulders braced, hoping for the best.

"Cynthia, uh, hi!"

She looks at me for a second, then cracks a microscopically small smile. "This place is cheap but good, isn't it? They do it so quickly you can just hop in and out," she starts.

"You're not overly concerned with the 'toxins' in the lacquer. *American neuroticism.*" Not knowing how to respond, I shrug.

"What color did you choose today?" I say as I walk over and show her the bottle of Sexy Divide.

"I think I'll do my usual—Wicked. See you back in the office." Her tone is totally indiscernible. Maybe she didn't know about my appointment. Phew. It's weird to see Cynthia in a nonwork environment. It's as if she's actually a real person.

Moments later, I recount the episode to Jules over a quick sushi-sashimi combo from the café's sushi bar, which Jules sternly reminds me is a no-no when expecting—*oops.* She seems shocked that Cynthia would be going to the nail place across the street, too, and not to some fancy spa in Soho. At about 2 p.m., as I am settling in to research on some story ideas, my auto cal reminder pops up: Ryan meeting.

Shit! I totally forgot that he's coming here to the offices, where my bump will be in plain view! I can't let him. Praying he hasn't yet left his office, I email him. Hey Ryan, unfortunately we have to crash a story by the end of the day so I have to cancel all my meetings for the rest of the day. Let's reschedule. I can come to your offices next week.

I get a message back within thirty seconds.

I'll believe your excuse this time, but you better make it up to me. What about drinks tonight…or are you jetting off to some unknown destination this weekend?

I know I shouldn't accept his invitation—that this will only lead to more complication—but I reply anyway that I think I can find room in my schedule.

Okay, McGann's it is. See you there at 5:30. Will be good to see you, Buckley.

At five thirty, I walk into a full-on Friday night after-work happy-hour crowd at the bar, bump safely in my bag. I'm not expecting it to be this packed. As I wade through all the men waiting for their 6 p.m. trains at Penn Station and hitting on girls way too young, I look around for Ryan. He doesn't seem to be here yet, so I order myself a vodka soda and wait it out, staring up at the TV playing baseball on ESPN.

A few seconds later, a sketchy older dude comes up to me. An accountant or salesman, I'm guessing, too lazy to even hide his ring finger, which does indeed have a gold band. "Has anyone ever told you how pretty your eyes are," he says, his white shirt wet with perspiration under the pits and his breath already gross and hoppy from his one-dollar Bud draft.

I smile politely, not sure how to handle it. "No, um, maybe, well, I think…" It only fans the flames.

"My name's Bob," he says, proffering a wet hand from the sweating beer. "What's yours?" I lightly shake the tips of his fingers as he gets pushed into me by the crowd. Just as I'm grasping for a way to end this conversation—

"Thanks for keeping my lady company, dude," I hear as Ryan pushes his way toward me. He wraps his arm around me and the guy slinks away. The warmth of his arms feels so wonderful that I have a minor brain freeze, and then Ryan pulls away.

"Sorry I said that. I just wanted to get that guy away from you."

"Not a problem," I say as I contort myself toward him.

"And sorry I'm late, Liz," he says as we both try to figure out whether a hug hello is now necessary. "My boss had me doing a ton of research today. I could use a real drink. And you're having one with me," he says, pulling my vodka soda out of my hand and signaling Seamus for two rusty nails.

We take the drinks, and then he leads me to a table close to the back of the bar where we can sit. It's noisy at first, so we just end up repeating ourselves a million times. But it does give us a good excuse to sit closely, whispering the answers into each other's ears. Then, after about an hour passes, the bridge-and-tunnel crowd thins out.

The conversation moves to where we went to college, and I tell him about my years in upstate New York, he tells me he went to USC for film. Then we talk about our similar upbringings. I find out that he grew up outside Pittsburgh, and that both our families are Irish Catholic, though his is bigger with a bunch of siblings and cousins always around, mine a little smaller and more of the silent, brooding variety.

By ten thirty or so, I can feel him opening up more, so I let my own guard down. He shares that his father was a fireman and passed away in a five-alarm house fire when he was a senior in college. He's the oldest in his family of four brothers and one sister, and he feels he's not sure he's doing the best job being a replacement father figure, spending most of his days working and nights watching soccer at East Village dive bars. It's a heartfelt revelation. His natural-sounding tone tells me that he seems to have made peace with his circumstances, which makes me respect him even more.

I debate whether to tell him about my parents' divorce and my mom's illness. Sometimes at the magazine I've had to keep up a protective front about my modest background, as if growing up near strip malls and the Jersey turnpike would somehow detract from my talents. Something pushes me to go for it, and I tell him the truth. "I'm really close with my mom, but my relationship with my father hasn't been the best since their divorce." I take a gulp of air. "He cheated on my mom." Ryan gives me an understanding look and gazes at me silently for a second.

"I get it. I really do, Liz. My only piece of advice would be not to hold on to the anger for too long. You'll wish you had that time back." His earnestness touches me.

At this point, Seamus has sent over a round on the house. Ryan gives a cheesy smile, changing the tone. "I've known Seamus from way back. Right, my mate?"

Seamus gives a nod. "Yer man's the finest in NYC. Hold on to this one, miss," he calls out.

Ryan gives me a self-confident smile.

"So," I begin, "what were you like in high school?"

"Very sneaky, Buckley, but that info doesn't come for free. You tell me first."

"Umm…" I say, debating exactly how to answer. Luckily Ryan takes a stab before I can respond.

"Bet you were the smart girl who never realized all the guys were secretly in love with her." His voice carries a more intentionally coy tone now, and I can tell he's flirting. But still, I find it hard to fully accept. If any guys were secretly in love with me, I was unaware. Ryan takes my drink and sets it down, grabbing my stool to move it one inch closer toward himself.

"It's possible," I say, letting him think it even if it isn't at all true. To my surprise, this admission makes his eyes widen in a little boy kind of way. It's different from their usual confident steadiness. He notices my glass has been emptied, finishes his own in one gulp and raises it toward the bartender for another round.

"Bet *you* had all the girls following you around," I joke back.

He looks sheepish. "Ha, yeah, the ladies loved me. You are right. About. That." I could swear he's saying it slowly, as if he doesn't quite believe it. I'm shocked—this guy is so good-looking. Could this be the goldmine that A and B and I always joke about, a hot guy who doesn't know how hot he is? Of course not. Not after what Alix told me.

"Well, it doesn't seem like it's that way for you now," I say, emboldened.

"Sorta," he admits. "It must be easy for you, though, Liz."

I wince, thinking, not exactly.

We stop and just look at each other for a moment. He places his hand on my knee.

Maybe it's the drinks—we've each had way more than we probably should—but he says something almost to himself so I can barely hear.

"I can tell you're special, Liz. You're your own person. Real."

I give him a ponderous look. "What do you mean?"

"I've seen you at Sing Sing, remember—Alanis Morissette?" My face gets hotter than I thought possible and I must look like a tomato.

"It didn't totally scare you?"

"It was *hot*," he says, bashfully. "I could see all the emotion you were bottling up. All that stuff. It's real. You got lost in it and didn't care how you looked. You weren't mugging for all the attention like other girls would be. Snapping selfies while they sing and just caught up in superficial, mundane crap like finding a rich banker. The potential husband hunters, I call them."

I give him a coy smile. "You mean you don't have a trust fund? Damn. Goodbye." I pretend to get up. He laughs.

"No, I mean, it's true, though, isn't it? Girls can be pretty cold in this city."

"That's not all true," I say. "I think most of us have just been burned too many times."

"So what are you looking for?" he asks.

I pause for a second to think about it, noticing that I never really have before.

"You know in the *Peanuts* cartoons, where Charlie Brown is always asking Lucy to hold the football? Whenever he goes to kick, she always pulls it away?"

"Yes." He looks at me curiously.

"I guess I'm just looking for a guy who won't pull the football away."

He takes a second to ponder it. "You don't want a Lucy," says Ryan finally.

"Exactly," I say. "Someone who won't run away when I let my guard down and be myself. And, of course, someone who'll go to Paris with me." I add half-jokingly as an afterthought, which makes him smile.

"One waits for the girl who loves Paris. They're smart, yet have romance in their heart."

"Who was that? Oscar Wilde?"

"Nope." A big, proud smile forms on his face. "Me." He slips his hand lightly around my midsection and pulls me closer to him. Then he scoots in so that our legs are completely touching. He looks over at me. It's *the* moment, the turning point when a guy signals that he likes you, at least for the moment, and that you know he wants to kiss you and that it can happen if you want it to.

He glances down at his phone. "It's 11:11, Buckley. Make a wish."

The childlike way he says it makes me smile. I close my

eyes, and then, for once in my life, say exactly what I'm thinking. "That you'll kiss me right now."

Pretty soon our heads come closer, our lips meet. His have an electric force behind them, but I can't quite make out the intent. Is it a fun thing to do in the moment? Does he want to come home with me? Is it a show of true feelings?

"You know what, Liz. You're beautiful," he murmurs, as if he is really seeing me for the first time.

He gently touches the sides of my face and pulls me in for a long kiss. Behind it is a weight and emotion I've never experienced. Like a hot shower melting the chill away from my bones after a day in the frigid ocean. I can tell on the spot that this is it. I will completely fall for Ryan Murphy if I let myself. We sit, kissing for a good minute or so, then break away, realizing that the bar might not be the best place to do this.

"Come with me," he says with a little grin.

He grabs my hand to pull me up. Before I really realize what's happening, he's helping me with my coat and we're out of the pub and hailing a cab together.

"Where are we going?"

"I want to show you something. Sir, can you take us to Thirty-Ninth and Seventh, please?" he tells the cabbie. "Is that okay?" he asks me. I nod. He places his hand on my knee and we sit in silence for a bit as the bright lights of Times Square flood in through the windows.

"What is it?"

"You'll see," says Ryan. We get out of the cab and then he leads me into the nondescript office building, signing in and nodding at the security guard who seems to know him. We enter the elevator, and he pushes the button for the seventh floor. Before we know it, the doors open to a very upscale editing suite. There's a full kitchen, fitted with stainless steel appliances and a fully stocked coffee and snack bar. He leads me past a row of plush red couches to one of the rooms in the back, flicking on the lights.

"I want to show you what I've been working on with my buddies." He turns on the setup and begins to load his files. All of a sudden it comes on the big screen as well as the smaller screens. His face stares back at us on-screen with the sound up full blast. We both laugh as he turns it down.

"This is the documentary I was telling you about."

"I didn't realize you were starring in it, too," I say.

"What, you think I have a face for radio, you're saying?" he teases.

Umm, the total opposite, I think, unable to stop staring at the screen.

"So basically, I'll be explaining the backstory behind this company we've found out in Palo Alto." We watch the minute of footage, and I'm honestly floored. He's got such a solid presence I can't stop staring. I find myself wanting more.

Once the file ends, I look at him and am shocked to find him with his head down, fidgeting a bit with his fingers. "Well? Whadja think?" He pushes some hair behind his ear.

"Honestly," I say simply. "It's awesome." He brightens, so I continue. "From what I can tell so far, it's going to be really, really good."

"Really? Aw, thanks, Liz. I mean, I could probably cut a bit from the first ten seconds. I don't know if everyone needs to see my mug for so long, but otherwise, yeah, I think it's going pretty well. I just need to find more time after work to work on it. I don't know when I'm going to have time. I think we're heading to Southeast Asia in a few weeks, actually."

"I know you'll figure it out," I say, sure that he will. He takes my compliment with a proud smile, then gives me a long, hard kiss.

"Thanks, Liz. Coming from you that means a lot."

His words warm my stomach.

He looks down. "You know I Googled you after the last time we hung out."

"You did? What did you find?" I smile.

"A helluva lot of baby articles," he jokes. "But I also found a profile you wrote three years ago about a single mother who'd made the choice to move forward with the pregnancy after she found out her daughter would have Down syndrome. You really captured the complexity of the situation. I really felt for her."

"It was one of the ones I was most proud of under our former editor, Patricia. I remember how it felt to see my first feature byline when I was twenty-eight." I loved working on that story.

Ryan seems to sense that I've gone somewhere. He swivels my chair toward him so our knees are touching and takes both of my hands, giving me a slow, soft kiss.

"Why don't you do more of that kind of stuff?"

I stop to think about it. "I don't know." An image of Alix comes up. "When I was twenty-eight, I remember feeling like I was on the right path, totally confident for once in my life. I was moving up in my career, taking chances and getting noticed. But just after that Cynthia and Alix came on board. I felt a shift. Like now, my ideas were too far out there or too risky. I don't know exactly. My stories don't always start with a point. They're kind of rambling and tangential, but they always make their way there. Patricia always got it, but with Cynthia and Alix, I just feel this contempt in their eyes every time I open my mouth in meetings. So I stopped. I guess I started playing smaller and smaller. I can't really blame Alix or the shift in the magazine industry. I did this to myself." I look down, balling my legs up beneath my arms, huddling on the chair.

"Do the stories end with something meaningful?"

"Yes, actually."

He thinks about it for a second. "You're an Irish storyteller. That's all. Yeats, Wilde, Joyce. Come on. All the greats were like that. There's nothing wrong with the way you write— you just do it differently."

Immediately an image comes to mind of my dad telling these long-winded stories when I was little. He'd tell us about what it was like to step up after his father died of a heart attack in the '50s when he was only sixteen, and how he took on work after school delivering meat from the Meatpacking District out to New Jersey for extra money. How my granny Buckley would make him save plastic Baggies and wash them out because of how little she had during the Depression. How the landlord would always be on the verge of sending them packing for being late with the rent, but he'd somehow strike a barter deal that would get them through to the next month.

There'd be one detail here and then, the story would go in an entirely different direction. I always remember wondering how things were going to come out at the end, yet loving the way he told it, always with a gleam in his eye as he looked up to some special place in the sky—the place where all these stories were held. When he finally came to the conclusion, everything would seem to magically fall into place. It was one of the only times I remember my mom smiling at him admiringly and my dad looking genuinely proud.

Ryan looks me straight in the eyes. "Liz, just because you do it differently doesn't mean you're doing it wrong. In the end, it's probably going to be your biggest strength."

"That's not what the internet wants right now."

"Longform's coming back. You're ahead of the curve. You might need some video along with it, though," he says with a smile.

I laugh and then he brings his hand to my knee. "You've got greatness in you. I know it." To my surprise, his comment brings a tiny tear to my eye. Something opens up in my chest and I feel a flutter.

"Sometimes I just feel lost," I admit.

He sighs, looking deeply into my eyes. "I know how that feels. You know what helps? Ever since I was a little kid, I'd do this thing called pathfinding. Whenever I'm unsure of what to do next, I just let my body lead the way. Literally. Like, I go out on the street and just starting walking. You'd be surprised where it takes you."

I shiver. "Actually, I think I know what you mean. I've been doing that, too."

"After my dad died, I'd wander the city. And the next thing I knew, I was filming everything left and right." He starts looking away. "I ended up making a little documentary about firefighters' lives after September 11th. Their home lives—after they took off their uniforms. It got some recognition and led to my first job in television production at HBO. Though it messed me up pretty bad for a while."

"The Emmy," I say softly, feeling my breath almost slip away. Ryan barely acknowledges the yes.

"Come on, Charlie Brown. I want to show you something else." He grabs my hand and leads me out to the main area, grabs a bottle of sparkling wine from the wine fridge, and finds two glasses, and puts them in my hands. "Let's go up to the roof."

"Okay," I tell him, excited at the idea. I feel around my bag for my phone, making a conscious effort to avoid the bump. It's 1:30 a.m. I should go home soon, but I want to keep this feeling going. We find the door to the rooftop out in the hallway and as we climb the stairs, I find myself looking at Ryan's butt. It looks so good I can't help but smack it.

"Hey," he teases back, "hands off the goods. Until we make it to the roof at least."

I laugh, and finally we head outside, making sure to place a brick in the door so we can get back in.

There's a hot tub. Ryan sees me eyeing it. I shoot him a mischievous grin. "We should go in!"

"Want to? Really?" He looks like a little boy at Christmas.

"Nah, we shouldn't," I say, coming to my senses. But in a split second, he's already stripped to his boxers and is dipping a foot in.

"No time like the present," he urges. I find myself nodding and following suit until we're both down to our underwear, which makes me blush. I notice he has an FDNY crest tattooed on his bicep.

"Come on, Liz," he says, not hiding the fact at all that he's stealing a look while drawing me toward the tub. We hop in, and I press the button to turn the bubbles on. Ryan pops the Prosecco and pours us each a glass, and immediately starts kissing the side of my neck. He looks at me for another second. He brushes the rest of my hair from my face, then slowly brings one arm down around my waist, pulling me into a straddle position on his lap and looking into my eyes, letting our foreheads touch for a few seconds before continuing to kiss me. His arms wrap around me in a way that feels foreign. Close. No agenda. I'm amazed at how hot my belly feels. Not in that sexy way that can happen with any random hookup, but true warmth—an opening up feeling.

His hands move all over my legs and I give in to the feeling. In my mind, I bargain with all the ways I can be honest and tell him about the bump. Then I think about everything he's told me—the importance he places on his personal integrity. No, I realize in no uncertain terms, I need to get out of *Paddy Cakes*, a new job at least. So this relationship can have *any* small possibility of working out. But right now, I need to be smart. Things can't escalate. "Liz?" Ryan asks. He puts his hands on both sides of my face. "Be here with me, Liz."

"Ryan," I start. "I can't. I've got to…" The words don't follow.

He kisses me again, which only makes it harder. And then on my collarbone. He unhooks my bra and slides it off and kisses the top of one of my breasts. He moves it away to kiss my stomach, and then the next thing I know, he's sliding me up onto the hot tub deck. There's a softness and a carefulness to all of his gestures that make me feel there's a true intention there. But if I allow him to continue, I'm going to get attached. Or worse, needy.

He seems to notice my hesitation. "Just lean back and relax, Liz. I'm really good at this." He winks. *Oooh.*

As I feel the amazing sensations of his mouth all over me, I stare up at the stars in the sky, my back cold against the Formica tub, my legs dangling in the bubbling hot waters, Ryan grabbing on to the backs of my thighs; for once, my mind goes totally quiet. I'm feeling the sensation rising up.

With JR, I used to get close, then lose it right before the end, falling back into my head, making some excuse, or worse, pretending. Now, here with Ryan, I can feel myself there. Almost. And again, back in my head, worried again about what all of this is about. My lower body slackens. Ryan seems to notice, coming up, kissing me all over my face, before whispering into my ears, a soft, "You are so sexy, Liz. I want to taste. Every. Single. Bit of you." There's a softness to his movements. *He cares.*

He pushes my thighs apart a little wider. *That does it.* A

low, full orgasm overtakes me without warning. I let it wash over me and he lies next to me as we look up at the stars together.

"See?" he says after a while. "Told you." His cheeky confidence brimming, as he comes out of the tub, grabs his jeans and pulls me off to lean against the side.

"You were right," I say, pulling on his button-down. "You are very talented. And dedicated."

"I try." He puts my hand in his and starts drawing little circles around it.

"What time is it?" I ask.

He checks his watch. "Almost 4:30 a.m. It's almost time for sunrise." He wraps an arm around my shoulder and we slink down and stare out at the waxing moon. "Might as well make it an all-nighter."

"I would go, but just your luck, I happen to be a sunrise connoisseur." I give him my best cheeky expression.

"Why's that?" returns Ryan.

"Each one is totally different. It can never be re-created again because the time and place won't be the same. In part, the reason why they're so sweet is because they're perfectly ephemeral."

My brain disarmed, I continue. "My dad taught me about watching the sky. When I was little, he'd often wake me up to go see the sunrise at the hill in our town whenever it was a particularly clear morning. 'The best things in life are free,' he'd tell me. I guess I never realized how much I missed seeing the sunrise, living here in the city."

"He must be proud of you."

"Not exactly. After my parents got a divorce, we kind of had a falling-out."

Ryan takes my hand and squeezes it, then starts to rub my

knee. We both look up at the deep inky blue sky now covered with nighttime clouds.

It's his turn to pause for a bit. "Well, if there's one thing I know, it's that nothing's worth holding a grudge over when it comes to family. I made that mistake before my dad died and I don't think I'll ever stop wishing I could have done things differently." He looks straight up to the sky.

"What happened?" I ask, putting my hand on his thigh.

He takes a deep breath before beginning. "Well, before my dad passed away, my brother was in a bad place. He got into the party scene through work. He'd be out all hours, hooking up with sleazy girls in bars, doing tons of coke. Finally it got so bad he couldn't pay his debts with his dealer." He looks at me now, pensively. It seems as if he's bracing for judgment. "It really wrecked my dad. He couldn't understand how it could have happened. I couldn't, either, to be totally honest. We were a really solid family growing up. I think the city just took its toll on him. My dad never said it outright, but I knew he felt as though it was up to me to straighten him out. I tried to do everything I could, but in the end, he wouldn't listen. I even offered to pay for him to go into rehabilitation, but he wouldn't accept. My brother and I got into a huge fight about it, and he chewed out my dad, too."

He looks away. It's as if this part really hurts him. His eyes hollow out in a way I haven't seen yet. "Then, one day there was a—a five-alarm fire, and it ended up taking my dad's life. Just like that. The next day Dad was gone."

Ryan turns away as if trying to hold something back. I try to offer my hand, rubbing his arm. He takes another deep breath and lets out a loud sigh. "He died with one son not speaking to him and the other one letting him down. He didn't deserve that." He twitches his nose a bit. "After that,

I made a promise I'd do whatever it took to get my brother straightened out. I finally got him into rehab and he got mostly sober with the hard drugs, but he's still drinking. I moved in with him to keep an eye on him."

His brow creases and I can feel the guilt is weighing on him.

"You can't beat yourself up," I say, trying to figure out a way to help him see that none of this is his fault. "Ryan, you can't save people until they want to be saved. Sometimes you have to let them make mistakes and walk away for a while."

"That's bullshit, Liz. Cowardly."

I maneuver myself so I'm facing him. The sun is now starting to come up.

"You can't always force people to do what they don't want to do."

"No, but you can keep showing up for them."

"Sometimes people don't deserve it."

"Everyone deserves a second chance."

"Not everyone."

I find myself getting annoyed. Ryan looks uncomfortable, too. We both sit, staring at the horizon over the East River. The sun's first rays turn the lower horizon a hazy purple.

"Yes, they do. If they're family."

"Ryan, my dad cheated on my mom, okay. And then abandoned her when she was going through cancer. It doesn't exactly make me want to forgive him." Ryan goes silent for a second.

"Well, sometimes we don't know how to handle the hardest stuff and we deal with it in stupid ways. But, that's in the past. Why can't you forgive him and let it go?"

"Ryan, you have no idea what you're talking about." We don't look at one another. I wrap my arms around myself, trying to warm up. He lets out a loud sigh. There's a silence between us for the first time.

"Look, there's the sunrise," Ryan says finally. Now the salmon-pink gassy layer rises above the buildings to the east. I want to go backward and redo what just happened. But I can't get what he said out of my head. *My dad hasn't called me for months—he's the one who left me and my mom. I should give him a second chance? Hardly. I'm no coward.*

"Where'd you go?" Ryan is now bristling. "You have to talk to me."

No, I don't, I find myself thinking reflexively. I check my phone. It's now almost five thirty and reality is starting to set in. Even though it's Saturday, I'd still planned to do a ton of research on the surrogacy story and I'm going to be tired all day. I'm getting stressed. Ugh. I stand up, smoothing out my clothes.

"I've had a nice time, Ryan, thanks. But I have to go now."

He pauses for a second as if trying to figure out what to say, then lets down his shoulders. "Okay, Liz. I understand. I'm just a piece of meat, here purely for your entertainment," he says, attempting a light joke, but for some reason it has the opposite effect on me this time. I wrap my arms around my shoulders protectively. He seems to revert back to work colleague mode, clapping his hands together.

"It's okay, Buckley, I have to go, too. This has been fun. Seriously. We'll hang out again?" His usual calm demeanor turns cooler.

"Sure, okay," I say, noticing he just said "hang out," instead of "see you." With my best attempt to appear cool again, we walk toward the door. Inside, I feel a weird mix of emotions—sad, searching for any way I can make this work in my favor. But my brain, foggy with so many drinks and no sleep, comes up with nothing.

"I'll call you," he says, picking up the glasses and then kissing me on the lips again as we find the inside door, and we walk through the editing suite. He looks around. "Actually, I have to turn off everything and save the latest versions of the files. You go on ahead," he tells me. I smile and say goodbye, walking toward the elevators, head full of static.

Thirteen

Saturday morning, an uncertain mania overtakes me. As I do errands, I replay details from last night in my head while sucking away at my cold brew, bump attached. And by midafternoon, with no new calls or texts from Ryan, I am feeling weird. Really weird. I try to put it out of my head all afternoon, but now Brie's birthday at the Wythe Hotel in Williamsburg is tonight, and all I can think of is that it would be great to bring him. Why hasn't he texted?

Heading to Williamsburg I'm still hopeful. Maybe something came up. Making sure my trench is belted tightly, in case anyone I know should spot me, I walk into the dimly lit hotel lobby, searching for Brie's party. The swanky hotel hosts celebrities, but Addison was able to pull off a free party space because of her connections in the fashion world.

I walk through the first-floor restaurant Reynard to the outdoor space in the back, lit up with Edison-style lights. The industrial-chic block is open and airy—different from all the standard hotels in Manhattan Addison, Brie and I have cut our teeth on in our twenties. Spirit lifting, I think. New. My friends greet me with a big hug as I set down Brie's gift—a bottle of her favorite perfume.

"Aw, thank you, sweetie. Thirty-one is already looking up!" says Brie brightly.

"How was your b-day so far, beauty?" I ask.

"Great! I did a little morning meditation, and then collected on that Tibetan foot massage *Lifehacker* coupon you sent me—thanks, Lizzie."

"No problem," I say, giving her a wink.

"Though, I have to say, I'm a little bit bummed. This guy from the *Bhagavad Gita* reading was supposed to come by tonight, but he texted that he's abstaining from alcohol this week and it would be too tempting to come out to a party." Brie's usual upbeat expression shifts a bit. "Honestly, I kinda hope Baxter shows up."

"But what about plan Secret-4-the-One?"

Brie just looks down. "It got tiring."

A few hours later, Baxter does arrive, with him a bunch of guys that are keeping Addison, and thankfully Brie, busy, while I hang out on the couch, looking longingly at my phone.

"How are we doing now?" Addison plops down in the space next to me. I know she means "Anything from Ryan?"

"Already over it," I say. The girls know that if Ryan texted, I'd tell them. But they also know the rules—they can't bring it up until I do.

"Liz, he'll text. You've just put up a few walls and he's trying to figure out how not to screw it up. That's what guys do."

"You think I put up walls?"

Brie nods emphatically.

"You've seen what I deal with on Tinder."

"I get it, but all those walls are keeping out the good stuff, too."

At about 2 a.m. with still nothing from Ryan, I am feeling irked.

Addison grabs the fourth drink from my hands, Brie's signature drink of the night: "healthtinis," supposedly filled with antioxidants, and containing a mix of gin, lavender liqueur, rosemary bitters and "ancient grain" alcohol—which happens to be overproof.

"Lizzie, maybe it's time to move to water." I grab it back as I start scrolling through my phone. I decide to text Ryan—I probably shouldn't. But I really want to. Maybe I can undo the weirdness between us. I text, What are you up to tonight? and then secretly I find the bartender for one last healthtini.

By 3:30 a.m. he still hasn't responded, and I can feel a darkness setting in through the cloud of the fermented ancient grains. I was wrong. He *is* just another Lucy.

Instead of retreating, though, this time I attempt the opposite, gaining the confidence to look out across the room. A cute, tall, blond guy seems to spot me out of nowhere, walks over and gives me a huge hug and smack kiss on the cheek and immediately, a fun and distracting back-and-forth banter begins to flow. Amazingly it's Gavin, from that night at Sparrow and Crow. The bartender calls last call, and then through the haze of the healthtinis, I feel him smushing his hand in mine while leading me out toward a cab to share a ride back into the city. The last thing I remember is his mouth on mine.

The alarm clock on my phone, which I always forget to turn off on the weekends, bores a hole in my head. It's 8 a.m.

"Owww!" I say, my head pounding.

"You could say that again," says someone from the other side of my bed. The sound is not Ryan's voice.

"Shit," I say in terror.

I look down to find all of my clothes still on. My down comforter and sheets pool around me as I lean over the left side of my bed to look for my purse, tightening into a cocoon. I fall off the bed onto the floor. "Ah!"

It's nowhere to be seen, but I do spot a pair of Rag and Bone jeans and a blue-checked shirt looking like it came from Brooks Brothers. I turn cold as I look to my right.

Right there on the bed is this supremely tanned, sandy-haired guy with his arms crossed behind his head. He's staring up at me with a bemused grin on his face. With stirring green eyes he looks a little bit like my favorite Australian actor crush, Chris Hemsworth.

"Who are you?" I ask, barely able to really look at him through my puffy, swelled-up eyes.

"Gavin," he starts, with his lips curling up into a devilish grin, clearly unworried. "You don't *remembah*?" he says, smiling up at me. Still, I'm surprised by how good-looking he is. "I gave you my number a few weeks ago at Sparrow and Crow?"

Oh, yeah, I think, *that* night I was talking to the Aussie guy.

"You texted me last night, and I happened to be out in Williamsburg, and well, one thing led to another." *Omigod, I must have tried to text Ryan. Damn you, cracked iPhone!*

"Sorry, I totally forgot you were in my phone!"

I grab my phone to confirm the mix-up.

Heysexywhat u up 2? I read, and the lame attempt makes me cringe—damn Brie and her healthtinis!

"I actually didn't mean to text you," I explain.

"Well, I think it turned out okay," he says.

"It did?" I ask meekly.

"I don't mind being a male escort, Liz, but we never settled our rates," he says impishly. "So this is the kind of apartment fancy magazine editors have these days, is it?" he says, scanning my diminutive studio. I'm a little embarrassed about the accumulation of clothing, books and other random assorted crap—including an old vision board Brie suggested I make, and a few pairs of unsexy undies—scattered in no particular order around the room.

Thank God I keep all the "bumps" in my closet. He leans over the other side of the bed to grab his clothes and the muscles on his back ripple. Oh, God. He is seriously hot. *But Ryan*, I think to myself, strangely guilty for a relationship that doesn't even exist.

"It's all I can afford since I'm pretty selective with my escorts and it eats into the bank account," I return playfully. He smiles at that. I scan my brain for any recollections of conversation from last night, but nothing immediately pops up.

"Well, I'd better be off," he says and pulls on his clothes and is out the door.

I hop out of bed on the other side and step on his money clip on my floor. He'll be calling to get it. *Perfect.* This is going to be another hungover Sunday.

Later in the day, Ford comes by for some take-out Thai and TV watching. In our early twenties, this used to be our weekly tradition. Luckily Ford still has no problem with British reality shows.

He tells me that he went out last night, too, with his friends from the gay men's hockey league to the bars in the West Village and, as has been the case for the past month, ended up texting Hudson late at night after too many manhattans. Hudson let him come over at 4 a.m. finally, but kicked him out early before going to brunch. Ford swears he knows it's a going-nowhere relationship, but I can tell from the sadness in his eyes as he's recounting the play-by-play, his heart's hooked and he can't stop himself.

I can't stop thinking about Ryan. Did he go out last night? When will he text me again? Despite the ending, I thought what we did meant something? Could I get away with setting up a totally work-related follow-up meeting? But all told, maybe it's for the best he didn't text.

Another wave of nausea strikes, causing me to heave up the *pad see ew* into the toilet (more like "pad see *eeeeew*," *ha! I'm too old for this*). I think about crawling back under my duvet. Ford must be telepathic, or having a bad hangover, too, because he looks at me and nods silently in agreement.

Just then I feel my phone buzzing. Aussie pops up on the phone, revealing a text.

Thanks for last night. Fun times. I think I left a few of my credit cards there, which is problematic since I'm on my way to the airport for a business trip. Had my passport and Australian cards at home, but would love to pick them up when I get back in a few weeks. Cheers.

I text back, Will have it waiting when you get back. Have a good trip.

"Eek!"

Ford notices my text frenzy. "If it weren't crazy, I'd say that bump is giving you major cred."

"I know. It's like I didn't exist at work before because I didn't have mommy-track status. I've spent the last ten years on the work, work, drink, work, sleep and more work track, and it's left me, well, like a woman without a passport. This whole meternity thing is finally making me feel like I fit in in some weird way—like I have a purpose."

"I hear you," says Ford. "Everyone wants to put me in this stereotypical role of the single gay man—I don't really like hanging out in most of the gay bars in Chelsea and am over my years of random hookups with strangers. I want a husband and a kid."

I frown solemnly. "Oh, God. You, too, now?"

"Yes! That is why I continue to do what I do...get intoxicated at press events, hook up with cute young things, and hope my farmers' market eggs *en casserole* brunch will woo them into a cohabitation arrangement akin to Cam, Mitchell and Lily on *Modern Family*." He winks.

I let out a huge belly laugh.

"The strange thing is, I want it, too. I mean, someday I want a kid. But I'm not willing to give up hope of finding the right guy."

"You will, Lizzie. I know it."

"You will, too, Ford. I know it."

"Now, the fun part," says Ford, thankfully changing the subject, "the part that makes all of us want to be moms and dads in the first place..."

"The clothes?"

"Nope...the names!" He pulls up the *Baby Name Wizard* book app and rattles through the "greatest hits" of the '80s, '90s and now. "How 'bout these 'rising stars'—'Allegra, Aura, Bai, Cocoa, Hyacinth, Jumbe, King,' which happens to be the fastest rising baby name for American boys."

"Nooo..." I hold back a laugh.

"Seriously. That's what it says!

"What about a new hipster 'normcore' name. 'Gene, Frank, Bob, Gary...'"

I turn my nose up, pulling up the app. "How about a '90s 'Throwback Must-See Thursday TV' name, 'Cody, Brandon, JR'?"

"Oh, God…" says Ford.

"That's another one."

"What?"

"God!" I giggle.

"Oh, Jesus."

"Yep, and that, too!" I find more, cackling out loud at the ridiculousness. "Listen to these—'Momo, Lindberg, Lucie—' with an *e* '—Montague, Spirit, Symphony, Schmoopie…' That's it," I whisper.

"What? Edith? Gertrude? Alice? Your favorite writers from Paris in the 1920s?"

"No, but you've got excellent taste." I give Ford a nod.

"Well, what then?"

"Lucie. Lucie Rose," I say quietly, brushing a hair out of my eye.

"I've been thinking about it," I admit out loud. "When I was younger, I had this camp counselor named Lucy. She was British and I always wanted to be like her. She'd tell us stories of all the men she'd dated in the south of France and Greece. I always thought she was so cool. I'd love to have a daughter just like her. With the French *e*. And Rose is my maternal grandmother's name. I'd like to give her a family name." From out of nowhere, my eyes well up.

"Uh, here. You're tearing up," says Ford, handing me a random napkin from Starbucks.

"Ford, what if I have missed my window? What if this never happens for me? And instead of pushing a Bugaboo, I'm stuck writing about them forever?"

"Well, you could always pull an Angelina," replies Ford, trying his best to cheer me up. "And look at those women on your cover of *Paddy Cakes*. You mean to tell me that a forty-five-year-old woman got pregnant *naturally*? Really? I don't think so. If they could get 'pregnant,' I'm sure by the time you're pushing forty they'll have invented some sper-minator cocktail so potent it'll make that healthtini you were drinking last night look like a Shirley Temple. Women will be having babies into their eighties in ten years. Just wait. If all of the business around babies keeps happening, Pfizer has to keep following, right? Right?"

"Yeah, I guess," I say, cheering up a bit. Thankful for Ford's comedic interventions, I click the "Baby Wizard" app closed. "I'd better go. I have to figure out what I'm going to wear tomorrow with the bump." But after Ford leaves, I pass out like a puppy dog.

Somehow I allow the weekend's indiscretions to evaporate and by Monday morning, on the way down Columbus Avenue toward the subway, I regain focus. I realize how many baby stores there are in my neighborhood. There's one called Kidville that seems to be selling trendy rocker baby gear and Columbus Toys boasts all-organic wooden furniture. Another has a sign for Sophie the Giraffe, a toy we've featured a million times at *Paddy Cakes*. It's been around for a century, is made from all natural materials, and the soft sponginess seems to soothe babies in an uncanny way. I smile. It would be the first thing I buy for little...*Lucie Rose*. The name I've secretly "chosen" for my own TBD baby pops into focus. *Well, at this point, why the eff not?*

Once at work, Alix passes back her edits as per usual, but instead of reacting, I just let her talk. Life is much easier when you stay focused on the task at hand.

All of a sudden, I see a photo text flash on my phone out of the corner of my eye. Could it be? I open it to find a gorgeous image of the sun just lighting up the sky, set behind a line of peaceful orange-robed monks taking alms.

The sunrise in Laos...for your collection, Charlie Brown. It's from Ryan. And sorry I couldn't text you earlier—they bumped the shoot up and I had to take off straightaway.

The hot orange sun in the expansive sky makes me sigh. Though my heart feels light as a feather, the bump beneath it feels like lead.

Fourteen

PUSH! ☺ Notification! Week 22: Uh-oh. Get ready for some pretty gross vaginal discharge! We're talking egg-white city! Baby Smiles: 5! [Eggs. Scared face. Rainy day. Baby bottle. Poop emojis.]

About a week goes by with nothing from Ryan. By the next Tuesday morning, I've given up, only to arrive early at work to find Jules hanging up the phone at her desk, her face blotchy with tears. "Jules," I ask, "what happened?"

"I just heard from my gynecologist," she says, her eyes stabbed with pain. "My AMH hormone is shockingly low and my progesterone levels are negligible. She says I have the eggs of a forty-three-year-old, which means very few and they're most likely of poor quality."

"What does that mean?"

"Liz, you *know* what that means."

"That's not what I—I..." I backtrack. "I mean, what does that mean for *you*."

"It means I'm going to have a harder time getting pregnant than most women my age. So, I have to decide if I want to start trying, like, now. Maybe even go through a round of IVF. The thing is—we really can't afford it."

"What are you going to do?" I say.

"Stick with the plan—have Henry get into business school—which will make me feel better about our financial future—and we'll start trying after that. But he has to get in. I can't afford to have a child and live here with Henry making his current salary. It's not happening."

"Ugh," I say lamely. Part of me understands what she's saying, but the other part worries about how much pressure she's putting on the situation. I stretch up, my bump inadvertently literally in her face.

"Liz." She straightens up before launching in. "At first I thought you were just kidding around with this whole meternity, but well, for the past few weeks, it's almost seemed as though you're deluded into thinking some magical baby will be appearing once this is all over."

"Yes. Lucie Rose." I nod, yawning.

"Liz!" She stands, grabbing my arms. "Snap out of it. This is not really happening. The whole plan was for you to get out of here within a month." She has the look on her face of someone trying to coax a schizophrenic into a mental institution. "I wasn't going to say anything, but I've looked into Halpren-Davies' policy on fraudulent health-care claims. Basically it says on-the-spot termination and they'll sue you for the amount of salary you're requesting."

I'm not expecting the Inquisition this early in the morning, but it immediately fires me up.

"Yeah, well, what if I decide to countersue, for, for discrimination! These past few weeks, I've basically been put on a pedestal, and it's all because of this bump!" I say, slapping myself in the stomach. "It's like being pregnant gives women this get-out-of-jail-free pass. Like, oooh, no one can get mad at Pippa for not catching that extra *z* on the word *lamaze* in my story on better birthing techniques."

"Wasn't that *your* mistake?" says Jules.

"No matter how much of their weight we've pulled when they're out, we never seem to get promoted, or even get a raise, or any notice," I say. "At least fifteen years ago we'd have gotten their job when they left the workplace to raise their children, but now, no way would HR allow it. You just have to smile when they return and start leaving early while we're here all hours of the night as if our lives aren't important. Doesn't it make you mad, too?"

"You know it has, but, well, when you start thinking about having a family, your feelings change. I *want* what all the moms on staff have, but with the way things are, I can't afford to have a baby. This *effing* industry," says Jules quietly. She's absolutely right. "I don't know what you plan to do, Liz, but you'd better think of something soon. Maybe you might want to put aside the hookups for a while to think of a plan."

I continue on to my desk. Jules is right. I really only have a few months to find a new job, or at least save enough money so I can quit, and all I've been doing is worrying about my dating life.

Enough, I tell myself. I make a decision then and there to become a sober monk. For the next few days, I plan to schedule "doctor's appointments" to start pitching travel stories—for real this time.

Propelled by the onslaught of nerves, I pen a quick list of travel story ideas: to be fully researched and fleshed out into full pitches later.

Romantic Dream Escapes
The Newest Secret Beaches
Hotel Hideaways Only Locals Know

Dream Destinations on a Budget
Island Getaways Only Hours Away

This isn't *so* hard, I think. Now I just need to find a few good examples of these places, write up pitches and send them out to editors. I quickly scan through my file for PR contacts and send out a few emails asking for leads on new destinations.

New career will commence with plenty of time before Lucie Rose is due. Boys, schmoys! This summer I vow to become a travel-writing machine. But first I check Ryan's Facebook status update one last time. In Laos for work. Fun times.

Finally, I put aside my freelance story ideas and work on my draft of my feature story for *Paddy Cakes*. I name it "Special Report: New Foreign Surrogacy Options," after I realize that there is big and timely news with nations such as Laos and Cambodia in Southeast Asia poised to become the next big options for safe, regulated surrogacy and adoptions.

As I put the finishing touches on each one of the five women's stories, sidebars and suggested caption copy, I realize it's more than 2,500 words. Longer than any other piece I've ever written in my life, and for the first time ever at *Paddy Cakes*, a feeling of pride surges through me. Checking the story into our copy management system, I feel a sense of lightness. I reflexively look down to my notepad to see what's next. Everything's been checked off. I can go home at 6 p.m. tonight.

Sun. Caffeine. A successful career. As I walk into the Bird Cage on Thursday, my mood could not be any better. The first email staring at me when I get in is from Ryan.

Hey, back from Laos—up to anything tonight? We're doing a story I wanted to tell you about. I open the attachment to see a picture of him standing there with five American-looking women, each holding a little baby in their arms. He looks so cute.

After not hearing from him this entire week, I'd all but lost hope. Okay if we stick around my neighborhood? I ask, so I can go home and change quickly after work.

Sure. Want to do dinner at Yangtze? he emails back quickly.

I would have guessed the bar of choice would begin with a *Mc* or *O* in the name.

Sure, I think I know it. I shoot back. I am surprised—and impressed. See you at 8. I sense a smile curving on my lips. I'm psyched to see him.

The day goes by uneventfully. Jules thankfully isn't still on my case. But my good mood quickly ends when I get an email from Cynthia at the end of the day.

At 6 p.m. on a Thursday this can't be good. I stand up, smooth out my bump under my dress and walk over to her glass office. I double tap meekly while I wait for the signal, which never arrives, so I walk in without it. Cynthia slowly rolls her chair around to face me head-on.

"At first I thought there must be some mistake," says Cynthia, her odd calm making my neck hair raise even more. "But I double-checked the name on the file. Elizabeth *Buck*-ley." She says each syllable slowly, her North London accent making her sound extra mean and indifferent.

"I couldn't believe it when I started reading about the mum going through misery in Cambodia, trying to get her baby, only to come back empty-handed and scammed out of thousands of dollars. The details were exquisite. Draining, sad, suspenseful. But then, I had to do a double take at the end of the story. The woman came back EMPTY-BLOODY-HANDED."

"I thought that's what *we* wanted," I finally finish.

"Did you approve the subjects through me first?"

"Of course," I stutter, forcing myself to think double hard. "I'm sure I can, uh, track down the paper with your signature," I say, voice all shaky.

"Oh, sod it. I don't need to see it. All I need to know is why you'd ever think I'd run something this bloody negative. No one wants to read about a woman who comes back without a *goddamned baby.*"

"Well, I, er, thought it would be useful to know what to watch out for," I say.

"Well, I can't run it. Find me a new mum," Cynthia says, turning away. "By end of day."

"Sure thing," I add chirpily. This means I have to cancel with Ryan. This is going to take all night, I think. I head back to my desk, sorting through my notes, hoping to find somewhere I previously overlooked. Nada. *Shit.* Staring up at the ceiling, I think to myself, *WWTMD.* What would a tiger mom do?

Then, I get an idea. I blast our "infertility support" Facebook group an update that we're looking for a mom on her way to Southeast Asia who is looking to adopt or work with a surrogate, and maybe there will be a chance that someone will respond with a lead. With just a few hours left in the day, chances are slim.

So many women unable to get pregnant, I think, feeling a twinge of guilt.

After ten minutes of posting, I'm still holding out hope that a woman will materialize out of thin air. A few good leads pop up, but by six thirty, no one cute, young or with exactly the right story, so I decide to text Ryan about canceling our plans.

Hey, I need to stay late tonight, so unfortunately have to cancel. Unless you know of anyone who may be looking to adopt or find a surrogate from your travels. Sorry.

Five seconds later, he texts back. Actually, we're doing a story on a group of women who went to Laos. That's what I wanted to talk to you about. I can get you one. When do you need her?

:) Like, two minutes?

Sure! I'll have her call you.

The phone rings, just as promised, and I'm able to get a perfect, heart-wrenching, beautifully drawn story from a woman named Kristy Nelson, who is thirty-eight and living in Columbus, Ohio. She's a single "choice mom" who decided to use a surrogate after failing to get pregnant on her own with donor sperm. I feel happy to tell this woman's story. And from her Facebook page, I can tell that she's cute and thin, thank God. And no sooner has this novel expression crept there than I feel my phone buzz hard against the desk.

How about that drink now?

It's Ryan.

It's nearly ten o'clock.

Meet me at my apartment for a rusty nail? I write, texting him the details.

See you there in 10 min. And I'm not rusty, trust me. ;)

I bound down the escalator steps out of my building and into a cab, removing the bump and stuffing it into my gym bag.

I head into my apartment to hide all forms of baby bumpage and then reapply my makeup, then check my phone. It's already 11 p.m. He said he'd be here thirty minutes ago.

Fifteen more minutes go by. Nothing.

Finally, the broken buzzer rings. I head down to let him in, but when I see him through the glass door, something's off.

"Sorry for keeping you waiting, Liz," he says, greeting me with a sloppy kiss, glassy eyes and smiling bigger than I've ever seen.

"That's okay, I guess. Were you at drinks?"

"Well, yeah, just my coworker Kendall." He goes to rest his arm against the doorway for support, but misses. He's wasted. "Can we go upstairs?" He tries to press against me, his breath boozy. This is not romantic—or even sexy. Am I just a hookup?

"How was Laos? I'm guessing you had fun," I say, an edge to my voice I'm not expecting.

Ryan looks totally taken aback. "Look, I'm really into you, Liz. Let's just go upstairs." He smells like that Sarah Jessica Parker perfume. I'm not twenty-four. I don't want to. Not like this.

"Listen, I'm not trying to be controlling, but what, I mean, what is your goal with all of this? You know, us, hooking up?"

"My *goal*? What are you talking about? I don't have any goal."

"It's just last time was—it was romantic. This is just—gross."

Maybe I can salvage the night, but then the words start bubbling out and I can't stop them. "It's a little ironic that you think all girls in NYC are controlling, but you can't be straight with me, either." *Shit, why am I saying this?*

His eyes look like a mix of crestfallen and angry. "Look, Liz. I never said that I think all the girls in New York are controlling. I said some of them are just hoping to lock down a husband without even knowing anything about them. That it can be creepy. I'm not sure why you're so upset. Let's just go upstairs, you're acting a little crazy."

Crazy, the default insult guys use when they have no other defense. The first time, he had to leave McGann's without telling me why. Then, he never called me after our big hookup, and now, he didn't even think enough of me to not make me wait tonight and shows up shit-faced. I'm not crazy, and for some reason, I can't let it go.

"I'm being *crazy*?" My tone takes a sharper edge.

"Well, *now* you are," he says.

"I'm not crazy, Ryan. You're just no different than every other guy in this city. All you want is some easy, uncomplicated girl to text and hook up with only when you feel like it."

With that, his eyes grow angry. "Liz, have you ever thought you might be making some pretty big assumptions here?"

"Look. I can't be hooking up with someone I can't trust, Ryan. Sorry."

"Okay, wow. That's all this was, then. Hmm. I guess I'll go, then." His tone comes out annoyed and angry, as if he can't wait to get out of here. He takes my face in his hands, gives me a hard kiss on the lips, looks straight into my eyes, then turns around and leaves without saying a word.

Fifteen

PUSH! ☺ Notification! Week 22: This week, your baby weighs in at a whopping pound, about the size of a small doll! Just like with your very first American Girl doll, you'll probably wanna bond. Yep, this is tooootally happening. Can you believe it?! WTF?! Lol. Baby Smiles: 7!

The next morning I can barely face myself, especially with a bump attached to my abdomen, so I decide, for once, to see if I can work from home. I should be more on edge about work, but I can't seem to summon the feelings to care after what happened last night. I write an email to Jeffry, telling him that I have a half-day doctor's appointment for tests and will be spending the rest of the day researching an organic baby food story we have coming up.

To my surprise, he gets right back to me. You're all caught up, so go ahead.

The early summer day is warm with crisp blue skies, and it lifts my mood a little once I walk out the door. I can't remember the last time I wasn't stuck in an office building on a day like this. I decide to wear the bump, just in case I run into anyone from work, and venture out for the day, armed with my phone and laptop, to install myself at City Bakery to write travel pitches.

Hopping off the subway, I make my way to the Union Square Greenmarket with all sorts of vegetables, breads and organic meats for sale. The flowers hit me first, their smell and glossy rainbow hues fresh with water from the hose. All around the market I see women toting canvas sacks, many with BabyBjörns and newborn slings. It's a new scene, and one totally different from the women surrounding me in bars, double-fisting Belvedere sodas and bucket bags.

"How many weeks?" asks a pregnant woman standing next to me at the peach stand. I go about my business, not realizing she's talking to me.

"How many weeks," she repeats, smiling. Out of habit, I start my lie. "Oh, almost six months." I can tell from her slightly quizzical expression that she's wondering the exact week, not the month. "Oh, almost twenty-three weeks," I blurt.

"Has she been moving up a storm?"

"Yes!" My hands feel wet with moisture as I face her questions.

"Do you know the sex?" she asks eagerly.

"Uh, yes, it's a little girl." I can feel myself almost tear up as I say it. I find it embarrassing how much I'm enjoying soaking up the attention.

"Little boys love their mamas. I shouldn't say this really, because I have two boys, but my third child, Sophie, is just the best. You're going to love having a little girl."

I smile, genuinely, rubbing my stomach. "I know. I was thrilled when I found out. So was my husband." Where this comes from, I have absolutely no idea. I swallow hard as a thought of Ryan briefly passes through my mind. Then, the line of questioning changes.

"So, where are you having her? I deliver at St. Luke's."

"I'm not sure yet." At that, her eyes gain a dimness.

"At six months? Eek. Well which hospital is your OB affiliated with?"

"Uh." I stammer. Damn, I knew there was something I forgot to prep. The birth plan. How dumb am I? She's now looking at me with a perplexed expression and one of concern.

"You don't know?"

"Oh, you know. Ha. Free-range parenting and all that! Feeling my way through…" I toss off airily. *Shit*. She's now staring at my left-hand ring finger.

"You've had all your ultrasounds?"

"Actually, it's…uh…right now!" I say quickly "Can't be late for an ultrasound! Baby hates it! Better go."

"I can give you the name of my doctor if you want," she calls out after me.

"That's okay! Thanks anyway, she's kicking hard!" I nervously titter as I run off toward the edge of the farmers' market. Once I'm out of sight, I duck into a Starbucks to pull out the bump immediately. Oh, Lord.

At City Bakery, a relaxing cappuccino and massive chocolate chip cookie later, I've sent off five query letters. I've got the genius idea of pitching a story about baby-friendly travel destinations to my favorite magazines: *Spa Finder*, *T+L*, *Destinations* and *Caribbean Living*, mentioning my *Paddy Cakes'* credentials as proof of my authority on the subject.

I immediately get a few bites back! The *Spa Finder* editor says they're planning their upcoming lineup and will "get back to me," and another from an interesting-looking publication called *Meetings and Conventions Bulletin* that Jules clued me in to. They say I can write anything I want for their blog—for free. But still, *progress*, I think, enthused.

By midafternoon, I've finished researching the upcoming baby food story—a profile on mompreneur organic home-made baby-food tycoons living in Irvington on the Hudson. *This working-from-home thing has its benefits.* I feel so much more productive. Staring around at the warm bakery, I feel younger, like my college days when I got work done at my own pace. *I could get used to this*, thinking how refreshing it is to work outside the walls of the Bird Cage. It's almost enough to distract me from the one thought that lingers—Will Ryan text to apologize for showing up drunk? Or am I supposed to apologize for making a big deal of it? I try to push away the thoughts of caring when all day long he does not.

Fueled by a productive day, I see if Addison and Brie will meet me downtown at The Smith for dinner.

As I walk in, the tables of the trendy eatery are already filling up. It's a little risky to be here—the type of place my coworkers might choose for dinner. So I've asked the hostess to seat us in the banquette section so we aren't in plain view.

I slip into the restroom to readjust myself and wait for a table at the bar next to a group of hopped-up twentysome-things, talking and texting loudly as I wait for my friends.

"Oh my God, best thing I ever did. *Best*," says a blonde, wearing a smartly cut management consultingesque pantsuit. Her two young friends look at her expectantly. I decide to listen in, wondering what they're saying. I'm sure it will be something like, breaking up with her boyfriend, or quitting her job to take a gap year. Secretly, it'll be nice to hear the kind of carefree talk you can only have in your twenties.

"I can't believe you did that," says her friend, equally b-school-alum looking.

"I just figured, I don't want to stress out about it and end up some thirtysomething wishing I'd frozen my eggs earlier."

Huh?

"But it's like fifteen thousand dollars. How did you afford it?"

"Graduation present." Early twentysomething smiles triumphantly. "Now, I can, like, date any guy I want, and not have to worry. So smart, right?"

"Sooooo smart," agree her two friends.

I wave down the bartender immediately and ask for a carafe of rosé. Oh, God, I think, texting Addison and Brie to get here ASAP. 21-year-olds are now freezing their eggs! I haven't even had my fake baby! The world is coming to an end!!! They both say that they'll be here in five.

"Should we be legitimately worried about this?" I ask my friends, still a bit in shock from the whole thing as we make our way to our booth.

"It might not be the *worst* idea ever. I've been looking into it actual—" says Addison.

"Wait, you have?" demands Brie. "Me, TOO!"

"Well...I have no idea where this business is headed and it's taking all my time, so I have to have a plan B, right?" says Addison, launching into the whole thing.

"You guys have both been researching this?" I look at Brie, then back at Addison, pleadingly.

"Doesn't everyone? I was going to set up some appointments in the fall if nothing pans out before that. I watched that TED talk you sent me on taking back our reproductive choice—"

"Wait," I say, disbelieving what I'm hearing. "Have you both been talking about babies behind my back?"

"We didn't want to worry you, honey. It's not a big deal.

You've got time," says Brie, although there's a note in her tone that doesn't believe it.

"Look, Lizzie, first things first. Figure out how you're getting out of *Paddy Cakes*. Then, we'll talk eggs."

Heads down, we silently scan our menus, as I begin to wonder whether everyone in New York is worried about fertility except me—the baby magazine editor. I feel so stupid. What have I been thinking? How fresh *are* my eggs? In a split second, I text Jules to find out the name of her new high-powered ob-gyn. Over dinner, our conversation, which normally flows as freely as our carafe of wine, is stilted. A powerlessness seems to sweep us all out to sea.

"Soooo, how is plan Secret-4-the-One going," I say, a little too eagerly, hoping not to have to discuss the Ryan situation quite yet, all the while feeling bad about the other night, and on alert for any Ryan texts.

Brie sets down her phone. "Not well. Five dates, five duds and I think I burned the whole Baxter thing into the ground."

"Really?" I ask. "You didn't tell me that."

"Yeah. I actually met up with him on Tuesday," says Brie, bashful.

"What happened?" Addison looks like she's already heard the story.

"Well…" Brie looks down. "We went through two bottles of malbec, he came back with me to my place. I totally thought we'd just hook up, but then we got to talking, and he proceeded to break down about his feelings about his ex-wife."

"You know that's your crack," I intone.

"Total wounded bird syndrome," chimes in Addison.

"Yep. So, I began to feel close to him—which made me

want to jump his bones. Of course, then I proceeded to go crazy when he didn't make a move."

We both give her a look, like we know what's coming next.

"I'm like, what's the matter? You don't want any of this? Why are you in my apartment?" Brie pretends to shake her boobs. "And he had no answer, so I kept drinking and continued on until I passed out on my couch. The next morning he was nowhere to be found. What the eff?"

"I just think this city makes guys totally fucked up," says Addison. "Member that investor guy I was talking to at Brie's party? Afterward we went back to my place, but in midmakeout, he took out his phone and actually answered a call from his girlfriend. I was like, are you kidding me?"

I sigh. "They probably smell baby fever. And now girls in their twenties are freezing their eggs, so there's that..." The girls barely register the joke.

"That reminds me. Have you heard from Ryan?" Addison looks around impatiently. "Why are they taking so long to refill our carafe?"

"Nope. I totally screwed it up—I think," I tell the girls, recounting the whole story from last night, as I battle the urge to check my phone.

"It's okay, sweetie," says Brie. "Our PH's are out there."

I cringe thinking about what Ryan said. "I'm not just looking for a PH, Brie."

"What I mean is, if Ryan doesn't come around, another one will." Brie looks down at my stomach.

"I know. And I actually don't know what I want at this point. I thought it was to be a travel writer. But now, I've really been enjoying writing these longer features. I feel like, maybe this is what I'm *supposed* to be doing with my life." I hunch my shoulders in defeat. "What am I going to do?"

"Look," Addison says, "when I was going back and forth on whether I should quit magazines, my dad asked me, 'Are you running away from something you don't want, or running toward something you do?'"

"How did you know what you wanted?" I ask.

"I just knew I wanted a bigger future for myself, and I knew that was never going to happen polishing someone else's copy. So I trusted my gut. And then I went for it."

"My gut seems to be getting bigger and bigger," I sniff to no one's amusement. Looking around the table, everyone looks tired. Still, I don't want to face my thoughts tonight so I ask if anyone wants to continue at the bar next door.

Addison yawns. "I would, but I have to work tomorrow. Halpren-Davies actually called me in for a meeting on Monday, so I want to prepare. I have no idea what they want—there's no way I'm going back on staff—or just hand over the *Couture Collective* blogger arsenal for some nominal fee to gain access to their *platform*."

Brie suddenly looks as if she's just thought of something, rubbing her hands together. "Will you come with me to this weekend intensive at the Life-Wise Institute tomorrow?" Brie asks me. "I'm supposed to bring a guest."

"I don't know, Brie. I'm not really into that stuff. Plus, I've got a lot going on if I'm going to start pitching articles."

"Come on, Lizzie, it will be good for you. You'll get a lot out of it."

"Okay, fine. Text me the address."

Brie gives me a big hug and then we wait until she gets in a cab. I decide to walk to save some money, and, as I do, I feel my phone ting. I see who it is. Ryan.

Hey Liz, guess what? Liverpool won the championship!

WTF?! I think. That's it? It's like he's completely erased what happened last night. And didn't think to ask me to the last game?! I reread the message, and in one quick second, I hit Delete.

Sixteen

PUSH! ☺ Notification! Week 22: Forgetting everything from your phone to your Gmail password? "Pregnancy brain" hormones are actually shrinking and changing your brain to prepare for motherhood—how creepy is that?! But don't worry, it's totally normal, and is happening to help you stay focused on the task at hand—i.e. not killing your kid. Baby Smiles: 1!

On Saturday morning, I meet Brie down on Twenty-Third and Park at a surprisingly normal-looking office tower. Still, I'm suspicious.

"Okay, don't look at me like that. It's going to be *fun*," she says. "You're going to break through all the barriers that have been holding you back. Green smoothie before we go in?"

"I don't know, Brie. With everything going on, I don't know if it's wise to try to break through any more barriers."

"I get it, sweetie. But, just keep an open mind."

My feisty friend and I take the elevator up to the eighteenth floor, where there are about thirty chairs lined up toward a front projector in a big open loft area. "That's for the group interactive sessions," says Brie, pointing toward six long conference-room-style tables at the other end.

To my surprise, very upwardly mobile-looking professional men and women file in, and for the next few hours we listen to a talk from the well-put-together leader. It's on living from the heart versus living from the head and finding your purpose and fulfilling your passion. All pretty interesting. I start actually thinking that Brie's right. After years in an industry obsessed with the latest trends, greatest idea, I have only been driven by living from my caffeine-fueled frontal lobe. *Maybe that's why it's been so hard to know what I really want.*

After lunch, we gather into smaller groups around the metal tables. Brie is placed with me. A woman with an uncontained mass of half curly, half wavy brown hair and bright red reading glasses that she keeps placing on and off the bridge of her nose, then the top of her head, seeming to forget the exact coordinates at both turns, introduces herself ominously as "Heidi, a reformed 'pleaser-avoider.'" She asks us to introduce ourselves, tell each other one life goal and one thing that we feel has been holding us back. *Hmm,* I think, *a job where I'm rewarded for commoditizing motherhood, an evil boss who loves to torture me, or my own twenty-two-week lie? Hard to choose.*

As we go around the table, I'm surprised to hear a variety of stories to which I can strangely relate. A well-heeled businesswoman in her early forties talks about how unfulfilled she is after giving up the chance to have a child with her husband for fear her business would suffer. An Indian man in his late twenties confesses that he's made millions on his tech start-ups, but he's never spoken to a woman outside his offices and stays home playing "World of Warcraft" most nights. Brie shares that she may be using her hookup situation to receive male affirmation that she's attractive because she's worried about growing older. Everyone nods understandingly. The emotion feels very raw and exposed for having just met these people.

But still, it's sad. And opens a vein.

"Hello, everyone. I'm Liz. I'm a thirty-one-year-old magazine editor." I hesitate for a second, then go for it. "I have a life goal of quitting my job to become a freelance writer," I say nervously.

"Wonderful," purrs Heidi. "What's one thing holding you back?"

"I don't know. Money. Some unfair circumstances at work, some people I've been in conflict with...general frustrations—"

"You're an easy one. An 'angry glosser,'" she says, cutting me off. "You've never been allowed to express your negative emotions, so you end up glossing over them with happier stories..." She smiles. I smile back. She totally gets it. Then she frowns, adding "...that unfortunately aren't your truth."

"Okay," I allow. "I'm...a bit...peeved."

A man in his late twenties with a what must be ironic SpongeBob SquarePants tattoo on his bicep nods in solemn agreement.

"Liz, the word I used was *angry*. So, what's that about, d'you think?" asks Heidi.

I think about it. "It's not about one thing, exactly. I have this little ball of fiery anger in my belly. It's just a collective anger. Anger for women in general. We're told to be everything and do everything and when we eff up in one little, tiny way, we're picked apart for it." The room seems appreciative, so I continue. "I'm angry that it's happening and I'm angry at the people who seem to be causing it."

"So, who's the cause of this collective anger?" she asks.

"Men?" I grasp.

"Really? You think it's men?" Clearly Heidi does not.

"*The* man?" I say in question form, though from Heidi's expression, I can tell that's not right, either.

"I know!" I say, getting an idea. "Other women?" I ask. "Mean, bitchy, controlling women who try to fake what they imagine men do to exert power. But actually men don't do that." SpongeBob is again nodding. He totally gets it. Everyone else, including Brie, looks a bit horrified.

"And how does it make you feel?"

"I feel like I want to rage. Or at least sing some Alanis Morissette." Brie can't hold back a snicker on that one.

"I guess I just feel like life has become untenable for women. We're told that if we'd just wake up an hour earlier to get to PowerCycle, and devote our waking lives to eating 'clean,' we'd be happy. But really, that just means you spend all day tracking down lean protein and vegetables with your time, which isn't easy, so that's all you think about. Power-Cycle and lean protein. PowerCycle and lean protein. As if that's the answer. And it's never an hour earlier than 8 a.m. It just gets earlier and earlier. Until the only time you can find another hour earlier is the middle of the night."

"I wake up at 3 a.m.," says the tired investment banker woman. Heads around the room nod in recognition.

"Why are we fucking killing ourselves? Right, ladies? So our yoga pants don't rupture a seam? For our husbands?"

"Screw 'em!" says the investment banker.

"Screw 'em," shouts another tired-looking woman in her thirties.

"Screw the man!" shouts SpongeBob. Everyone's nodding in appreciation.

But Uncontained Hair Heidi has a different look on her face. "Interesting. Very interesting."

I thought it would be embarrassing to admit to all these feelings, but instead I feel heard. I file my worksheets together and wait for her to move on to the next person. But instead she stays with me.

"And now try turning that last sentence around."

"What do you mean?"

"Well, here at Life-Wise we say that there are no victims. Only vanquishers. When we fall victim, we are powerless to change things. Do you want to be a victim to your circumstances, Liz? Or a divine creator?"

Suddenly, I realize this is not what I was expecting. Brie looks at me, poised for some apparent breakthrough that everyone else can see coming, but me.

"Uh, a divine creator?"

"Can you turn your sentence around to show how *you* created the events that have made you angry." *I didn't create them.* I hesitate. *Alix did.* "I'll help you. Would you say that maybe you've been the bitchy, controlling woman trying to fake being something that you're not?"

"Uh. No. Not really." Brie's eyes fall. "America and the media are making it like this—not me," I say, grasping and now embarrassed. "Like us children of the '70s feel like we have be '80s power women *and* '50s housewives because of Pinterest *and* '60s waifs *and* '90s supermodels. AmIright?" Now, SpongeBob looks away.

The leader looks as though she's reevaluating her approach.

"Liz, it's a difficult concept to get, but the purpose isn't to keep passing blame but taking responsibility for your actions," Brie says. "Here, have a green juice."

"No, thanks."

"Lizzie, take the green juice."

I shake Brie away. "No, thanks. Excuse me. I've got to go to the bathroom."

She follows after me, coming into the washroom behind me. "Brie, I don't want the goddamn green juice!"

She looks taken aback. "Lizzie, I know that was rough, but do you know how huge that was? You did some major internal work today. That's how it all starts. You're having the breakthrough," she says, a bit too wide-eyed for my liking.

"Brie, this isn't green juice. It's Kool-Aid. You guys are all on crack. Life just happens. That's it. As much as we'd all like to go around being 'creators,' we can't control everything that happens to us. Some things are destined to be, whether we like them or not."

"Lizzie, that's not how I see it anymore. This stuff works for me. It's about letting go of all our bullshit stories and designing our lives."

"Brie, it's all a marketing scam—a pyramid scheme to get vulnerable people to shell out money to start hawking this stuff to even bigger fools."

Brie looks hurt. A rare flash of anger passes through her usually warm brown eyes. I immediately feel bad. "Brie, I'm sorry. I didn't mean that. I guess I see it differently. We don't have control over everything that happens to us. Fate takes its course—and doesn't always end in our favor."

"That's not true," she says. "We do have a choice in what happens to us."

"Well, then, I guess you think I brought all of this on myself."

Brie looks at me differently...not the usual supportive friend I've known for forever. "If we're being honest, Lizzie. Yes. Yes, I do."

It's not what I want, expect or need to hear. A moment of blind, dark rage overcomes me. "You have no fucking clue what it's like to do the right thing for ten fucking years, and have nothing pan out like you thought it would. A job where they treat you like a subhuman because you haven't reproduced, a lonely, empty apartment to come home to at night, and friends who talk about freezing their eggs behind your back and pass a shitload of judgment to your face!"

"Liz, do you know how ungrateful you sound right now? Do you have any idea how much you've been given? The gifts you have? Rather than cursing the universe you should be shaking your hands up saying how thankful you are, you ungrateful, whiny bitch."

We both look taken aback.

"I have to get back in there." She's the first one to speak.

"Okay." I wait a few minutes, throw my juice in the trash and head out.

As the elevator descends, I glance at my phone and see another text.

Buckley, what's up? You aren't returning my texts now—that's cold. Hope u are well J. It's another one from Ryan.

Want to know what's cold? Pulling the football away like Lucy. Angrily, I delete his texts, then in a strange fit—most likely induced by sounds of the group huffing and chanting in a weird tribal way—most likely thanks to green juice and the collective anger of wounded women everywhere—I delete Ryan from my Facebook friends.

July

Seventeen

PUSH! ☺ Notification! Week 24: You may wanna queue up some sad 'flix...pregnancy hormones can affect tear production, causing waterworks...invest in some waterproof mascara, like this one from our friends at Bourjois-Jolie. Baby Smiles: 5!

Days go by in a blur. I busy myself with work, getting home at a decent hour and sending out travel pitches and résumés to potential job leads as my "pregnancy advances," through month six, and I even start writing my blog again.

Spaces in between are all Ryan. But what can I do? He seemed to take this seriously, then super not seriously, then never apologized or followed up in any real way. And it doesn't help that every single Instagram iced coffee post I've put up, he's hearted. Every single one.

By July 1, I decide enough is enough. Time to forget about him and get serious. Clean the slate. I bust out a new gerbera-pink maternity sheath, complete with jewels at the neckline, from Barneys' in-house line. *Thanks, Addison*, I think, as I pull on the pretty dress. She's been getting a load of new sponsorships—and I've been benefitting.

Later in the day, Jeffry pulls me to the side. "Liz, I need to talk to you. You're still coming back, right?"

"Yes, of course," I say.

"Cynthia asked me to check in with you about it."

"Oh, okay, cool," I answer.

"Yeah, and uh, it looks like the pregnancy is treating you well."

"Thanks, Jeffry," I say quickly and jet out. Just then I see Alix waiting for me back at my cube. She looks pissed.

"So we got back the final layout of 'Postpartum Depression'—looks like Cynthia was pleased."

"Good," I say tentatively.

"But she did have one last question about homeopathic remedies that might be helpful," she says, showing me the red line on the layout. "I thought we could reach out to your doctor for a quote—you know, Dr. Honeycut."

I try to hide a gasp. Could she have found out?

"And did you?" I ask.

"I asked Jules for the contact info; she said she'd email it. In the meantime I Googled him, but couldn't find him anywhere. Can you send his info to me?"

"He's actually away this week," I say quickly. "I'll get you a better source ASAP."

"Okay, better be in by first thing tomorrow," she says.

I dig around for replacement physicians, then head home at about 6 p.m. and begin to do my now nightly rubdown of my chafed midsection. If I really were pregnant, my books tell me I'd probably be dealing with indigestion, night sweats and insomnia. Maybe the pregnant women in the office don't have it as easy as I'd thought. As I'm contemplating the unfairness of it all, I hear my phone chime.

Aussie, reads the phone's caller ID.

Ah, it's Gavin! It's been almost a month—surely he couldn't

be asking about his wallet now, after all this time. A thought of Ryan blows through my brain. But, Gavin is also good-looking, employed and seemingly not a serial killer. "Hey there," I say.

"Hey there yourself. How'r'ya going?" His tone is chipper and warm.

"Uh, good, fine. How are you going yourself?" *Damn, why did I just pretend to have an Aussie accent myself? Now he thinks I'm making fun of him.*

"Just fine, thanks," he says, a little swayed. "Heya, sorry for taking so long to call you. I was out of the country on business. You still have my billfold, do ya?"

"Let me just check to make sure I have yours. You know, lots of men park their wallets under my bed," I say, unable to help myself.

"Ha. Mine's the black one."

I open the worn-in Louis Vuitton billfold. "Gavin Bettencourt, thirty-nine, Manhattan, New York. You're a blood donor, a member of the Printing House Squash Club, like carrying twenties, though aren't obsessive about keeping them all in order, and you have, let's see here…a *purple* Amex card."

"Hey, yeah, and if you're done rifling through the contents of my wallet, I'll be needing that purple Amex."

"Not if I don't use it for my own purposes first," I jet back.

"And what purposes would those be?" His tone quiets.

"You know, trip to France, new summer wardrobe, upgraded membership to my male escort service…"

He starts to laugh. "I'd give you a discount rate—you just have to ask nicely."

Hmm.

"Well, I'm here if you'd like to stop by and pick it up. Do you, uh, live in the area?"

"No, I live downtown, in the West Village. Jane Street."

"Ooh, I love Jane Street! I used to live downtown, too, and spent hours in the Paris Commune. My friends would make fun of me because I'd pretend I was Ernest Hemingway. I'd order an espresso and nurse it for hours, reading and writing my 'deep thoughts.' How and *why* am I talking about this?"

"Er, sounds fun..." he says, snapping me back to the present.

"Yeah, it was," I say wistfully. "Well, guess my bestselling novel has yet to materialize. I work for a baby magazine now."

"Oh, do you? Right. That would explain it!"

"What?"

"Those baby books and magazines under your bed!"

"Oh, no, no, no, no, no, no, no! Yeah, no, I'm totally *not* pregnant."

"Those are mutually exclusive, yeah?" he teases.

"In my case they are."

"Can I get my wallet cards tomorrow, then? Is it okay to drop by your apartment around eight? I'll take you to my favorite wine bar in your neighborhood for a proper thank-you drink for keeping them safe for me."

Without thinking, I reply, "Yes, uh, sure. See you then."

"Yep," says Gavin, clicking the phone off.

I take a deep breath in. Running off to Australia is a neat solution I hadn't thought of yet, albeit completely insane.

The next night, I'm attempting to reposition my bump in the bathroom before heading home for my date, when all of a sudden Cynthia walks in. I try to remain still and quiet, hoping she won't notice me bent over, but she comes right up to me. As I flip back up, blood rushes to my face. "Elizabeth, Liz, I've been waiting until some things worked out in HR before officially talking to you. I'll put it bluntly. I really like the work you've been doing lately. 'Fair-Trade Families' was absolutely *spot-on* in the end—just the right make-them-sit-up-and-give-us-their-full-attention story I've been hoping for. How'd you like to try writing features in the well on a more regular basis?"

"Uh. Sure. That'd be great," I stammer, thinking about that news headline—*oof.*

"Now, as for your pregnancy… I can see that you've been filling out a little through the face and thighs—"

"Um, yes, the pregnancy is going well. Everything is on track. My due date is still October 20."

"I'm now going to tell you something I've never told anyone at this magazine. I'm not sure why, but you seem like the kind of girl who can keep a secret."

I cringe at the thought of this.

"I'd just made editor in chief at Italian *Bella.* I was having an affair with the publisher at the time. *Married.*" I look down for a brief second. "Oh, don't look at me like that," scoffs Cynthia, folding her arms. "American puritanism. Anyway, one night after we got the numbers back on a record-breaking March issue, we went out to celebrate and got a little careless." Cynthia says with an air of vulnerability I've never before seen.

"A few weeks later, I was forced to make, well, a life-changing decision. Let's just say we made a deal. If I did something about my situation, and brought sales up by 25 percent in a year, he'd double my salary and make sure I was well regarded in the company. I was single at the time, and the thought of a whole other life to take care of…" Cynthia stiffens up a bit. "Let's just say I held my end up of the deal and he held his. I was just about your age and I was not about to give up a career I'd fought so hard for to be a, well, single mum," she says disdainfully. "People might think differently now, I suppose. I might have certain, *er*, regrets myself," she says, her eyes narrowing. "But it was the best decision for me at the time. I can count on you not to reveal this to anyone on staff," she says, eyes lowering.

"Of course," I say. For once, I know I won't tell anyone, not even Jules.

"Now you tell me," she says, eyes. "Whose little bump is this?" she asks, moving her hands to her hips.

"It's not someone you know. Just like you, I didn't exactly know what I was going to do myself. I wanted to make sure it was kept quiet until I did." My face warms at the lie. I don't know where I'm coming up with this, but it seems to be believable.

My knees shake, but Cynthia's expression softens into genuine concern. "I won't pry any further, Elizabeth, but I wanted to mention I loved what you did with 'Best Colleges for Toddlers,' 'The New PPD Spectrum' and 'The Surrogacy Report.' Let's just say as long as you keep pumping out these five-star features, you'll be taken care of during your maternity leave and we'll be sure to discuss your growing future at *Paddy Cakes* when you return," she says, a hint of a smile on her lips. But like lightning, her expression changes. "You *are* returning, right?" Her face hardens ever so slightly.

"Yes, of course," I hear myself saying quickly, completely perplexed by this new turn of events. "I wouldn't dream of leaving," I say. Could it be that being pregnant is like rocket fuel for my career? Did I just commit to coming *back* after maternity leave?

I make it home with barely enough time to pull out my bump, throw on a loose purple silk tank dress and attempt a few comb-throughs of my hair. I hear the buzzer ring, and do a quick scan of the apartment in the very unlikely case that there is some post-wine-bar action later. No bump, no baby books, no maternity materials or mommy blogs open on my computer. *Zzzzzzz* chimes the buzzer.

"Hey, all ready up they-ah," says Gavin into the speakerphone.

"Be down in a saay-c!" I sing back in an Australian accent. *Wait, why am I still talking in an Australian accent?*

I see him turn around as I come outside my building. Gavin's green eyes are sparkling and his outfit is perfectly casual-cool: a green plaid button-down rolled up around his wrists, the kind of well-fitting jeans only select few men know how to find, a brown belt sitting just right above his cute butt and Brooklyn-style brown suede Hush Puppies.

"Hello, gorgeous." Gavin gives me a distinct, *not bad* look. I may be paranoid, but I think I also catch him quickly checking my belly for signs of life, because he then seems to look relieved. Despite my attempts not to feel anything— nervous, excited, shaky—an instant surge of chemical attraction runs through my lower half.

I hand him his wallet. "The purple Amex is still there. You can check."

"If you bought that dress with it, I approve."

We head a little ways down Columbus Avenue to Bin 71, a small wine bar with fewer than twenty seats and dim lighting, which I reason will be good for my skin as well as remaining incognito.

For a few fun hours Gavin tells me about where he's from in the Barossa Valley, and that his family owns some of the top vineyards in Southern Australia. His parents never pressured him to take over, encouraging him to go to business school in the States. But he can see himself going back one day to continue building the company with his brother's family.

Wine is in his blood. He traveled the world as a backpacker after uni, and now does it for his own wine importing business. He's out of town for weeks at a time, which has been rough on past relationships. It might be the fifteen-dollar-glasses of "Cab Sav," as he calls it, but envisioning him in the world's wine regions—France, Italy, South America—is pretty sexy, admittedly. I soak up his stories like a sponge. I am truly interested. Though, I'm also careful to remain pulled back a bit. He seems to sense it—like a tiger ready to pounce.

"So, now you've gone and got me all vulnerable, Liz. Totally unfair on a first date. You know they're supposed to be all about footsie under the table." He gives me a wide, playful grin. "It's only fair that you share your secret vulnerability. I know you've got one. Spill it."

Ha, if you only knew, I think, but the wine has emboldened me.

"This is my card of choice," I say, reaching into my bag and pulling out my passport. I once read in *Sex and the Single Girl* that Helen Gurley Brown always kept hers on her in case she was ever offered a last-minute trip across the world.

He seems interested, so I keep going. "Much to my mother's delight, I inherited her love of all things French. I was going to study in Paris for my junior year abroad."

"Let me take a look at that." I hand over the stiff book. "There aren't any stamps? So wait, you didn't go to Paris?"

"Not exactly."

"Why's that?"

"I had to turn it down. Made more sense for me to stay home."

He gives me a ponderous look. "For a girl who's all about

travel, you should really think about setting foot on a plane, now, shouldn't ya?"

"I'm working on it," I say. I wonder what he would think if I told him about my secret pregnancy scheme. Something tells me he's also had a mischievous past and wouldn't totally judge me.

"But you're in your thirties now, aren't cha. Isn't it time to start thinking about settling down?" What? His question seems far from fair on a first date—and one I'm not prepared to answer.

"Can't you do both? Travel and have a family?"

"No, not at the beginning," he says plainly.

"Well, I will. I absolutely don't see why it's not possible," I say, a little aggressively, which seems to have the opposite effect than I'm expecting.

"I like this fiery side of you, Liz. Even if you're wrong." He signals the bartender. "Sir, give us your 1999 Chateau Estephe Grand Cru," Gavin says, making it a point to show us both the line on the menu: $150.

The waiter returns, pouring the burgundy liquid into Gavin's glass. "I think you'll like this one, Liz. It's earthy, full-bodied, complex." Then, winking at the waiter, "I like my wine like I like my women."

"The lady would like to try?"

I take a sip, not indulging him. "Not bad."

"Not bad. It's the best out there. One of my first major buys here in New York."

"Not bad." I hold firm.

Gavin takes the wine out of my hands. "Okay, I've heard enough, love. Shut up and let me kiss you," he says, grabbing the back of my head to move in for a kiss. His eyes close to soft slits, but mine remain wide-open. As much as I think he's probably the hottest man I've ever dated, and as much as his facial angularity is doing mighty strange things to my lower abdominal region, my heart's just not in it. I pull away.

"I've had a great time, Gavin," I tell him quickly. "Thank you for the drinks, but I've got to make it an early night. Big day at work tomorrow."

A little surprised, he starts to backtrack, reaching toward my hand with his. "You don't want to go back to your apartment, love? I could open a bottle I just got today, and we could drink it and talk more about your passport. Or, you know, other things." Eek.

I stand up and gather my coat and bag. "Well, thank you for a lovely evening. I'm sure you're glad to have all your cards back."

"Yes, sure, Lizzie," he says, changing clip. "I'll call you to see if you're around for group drinks sometime with your girlfriends. Would you like that?"

"Sure," I say coolly. "You have my number."

"Great. Want me to get you a taxi, love?"

"No, that's okay. It's just a few blocks up," I counter, thinking he'll probably stand up to get me one anyway. As I near the door, I look back and see that he's already looking down at his phone.

I enter my dark apartment and plop down my bag, fall into bed and stare off into space, my little metal Eiffel Tower statue on my bedside table taunting me. "Australian-dangling-his-global-travels-in-my-face-player douche bag—*argh!*" I scream out loud to no one in particular. *I don't need a man to take me to Paris. I will get there on my own. Someday soon.* I pull my covers around me tight, a fit of resolution covering up the tempestuous sea beneath.

Eighteen

The pastel pink, yellow, green and blue–bedecked convention hall is everything I'm expecting and more as I arrive at the Javits Center with Ford for "The Ultimate Baby Shower" event, my six-month bump firmly in place. The "New York Fashion Week of Maternal Couture" showcases all the latest baby products coming out next year, available now for viewing by wholesalers, big-box retailers, smaller baby stores around the country and the press—and this year it seems bigger than ever. There's even a catwalk. Deep down, I'm excited.

"You can thank Kate Middleton and Kim Kardashian for all this," says Ford, as we make our way through the main entrance. "They've really done an amazing job codifying the original biblical archetypes for women," says Ford. We come up to a collection of rather scary, completely customizable life-size dolls meant to overtake American Girl mania, thanks to what looks like pure extra-terrestrial-like size and abnormally small waists even for "pweens" as we've started calling pretweens of the very specific age of ten.

"Think about it. Kate is the virginal mother, Kim, the

vampy Mary Magdalene. Women define themselves by which camp they're currently siding with. Do you put your son-king first? Or, do you choose to hold on to your own sexy image above all else?"

"What if you side with both?" I say, pawing "Jessica's" creepy doll hair.

"Look at this collection of dolls. Perfectly diverse, with one African-American girl, two Hispanic girls, one Asian, one Indian, one Native American and five Caucasian girls with different hair colors and eye shapes. You choose the exact combination of facial features that looks like you. Easy. There's an algorithm to life now. All of our choices are being dictated by Google. You better get used to it."

"That's just if you live in your head," I say, thinking of the Life-Wise intensive with Brie, wistfully. "I think we have a greater choice, and I'm choosing to live from my heart from now on."

"Ah, I've given up on that a *looongg* time ago. Too painful."

We find the VIP beauty lounge at the back of the hall. Trying all the creams, elixers, serums, it's like I've hit the jackpot. An assistant offers to give me the third-trimester makeover. She says in the end, the trick to looking awake and alive in the throws of new momdom—and as you age in general—is all about the brows, which no one ever realizes.

I admit that I've never even given my brows a second thought. The lady pulls out a beige-colored wand, running through my thin, yet unruly brows, smoothing them into a shape worthy of Brooke Shields herself. I look focused. Clear. A woman with intention. Staring back at me is no longer Liz, girl about town. No, instead it's something completely different... I'm a woman. A woman who could be mistaken for a mother.

Even Ford notices. "Well, hello, Kate Middleton."

I tousle my hair over one eye and pout my lips into the biggest duck face I can muster. "With a little Kim K. thrown in for good measure?" I joke.

"Yes, exactly, with all the 'cosmetic enhancements' you're wearing these days."

"Evil," I say, playfully punching his arm. We do one more lap around the event, and by 4 p.m. we're both wiped. I say my goodbyes to Ford and then tell him I'll text him before getting in the cab. Back at home, I take out another pad, this time Moleskine I've been saving for a special occasion, thinking that's it. I'm going to be a "divine creator" as Brie's intensive suggested.

Things I've Been Putting Off for "The Future"
- Owning a car
- Going to Target to buy household items at cheaper costs instead of purchasing things like toilet paper at the last possible second (i.e. after take-out napkins have run out)
- Buying "adult" furniture from places like One Kings Lane and Joss & Main
- Hosting dinner parties
- Going on a vacation I've planned for months rather than going on a last-minute closeout deal on Travelzoo that's cheap and not really where I want to go (like Fort Lauderdale)
- Having friends "around" and "just to drop in"
- Following a real exercise plan
- Cooking healthy dinners instead of eating out of cartons (see: hummus and vegan cashew ice cream)
- Crafting (i.e. printing out photos from the internet and framing them)

- Having a "kitchen" with a "dishwasher" and "laundry room" with "washer and dryer" (not likely anytime soon)
- Getting married
- Having a baby

All of a sudden, looking at this list, I realize at thirty-one I've been living life like a college student. Even though it's 11:59 p.m. I text Ford.

Why have we been putting off real lives? Living half lives on an "Island of Lost Children" that keeps us in perennial college state?

I get a quick reply back. Too many manhattans. :) Literally, I think. *Manhattan has fogged up our brains. Cupcakes and caffeine and cocktails to keep us from moving on with our lives.*
Seriously, though. Why do we do it? I text back.

Seriously? I think it's given us a creative outlet. We're building up material like an arrow drawing back in a bow. All this struggle will make for a great book one day.

Or movie, I think, if I could ever write it.
Should we leave and move to Portland? I write.

Maine or Oregon?

Either?

But would they be as exciting?

Probably not, but would we care if we had real lives? If we were actually happy?

Yeah. Dunno. Probably.

:).

Can I bring Hudson? :)

I pull the covers around me. I'm proud of my newfound maturity and my newfound eyebrows, I think, as I doze off to the opening monologue of *Saturday Night Live,* wearing my bump to bed because, despite all evidence to the contrary, it's what feels good.

Sunday's a different story, though. It's a beautiful July Fourth weekend, the kind that taunts you for not having a boyfriend to hang out with in Central Park, picnicking and throwing the Frisbee around. Twilight sets in during my run in the park, and dark thoughts that have begun to haunt me on Sunday evenings return. I've basically been doing the same routine now for eight years—longer than I have at any other point in my life—but it's all of a sudden starting to feel very, very old. Every Sunday I finish up an overdue story for work while watching bad TV and call it a night, usually by myself. Even when I was with JR, as I would lie there waiting to fall asleep, I still felt alone.

These past few Sundays, though, have felt especially tinged with sadness. I think back to Ryan. I am pretty positive now that I missed my chance with him by baring my soul too early, and well, probably opening up physically too soon, too. Nice, well-educated, funny guys with jobs tend to hold out until the last possible minute, capitalizing on this city's endless supply of hot women, then end up with emotionally stable, little-blonde-girl wives—like his coworker Kendall.

Still, what burns me is that I thought Ryan was one of the good ones—the ones that don't really know how great they are. I find myself replaying every detail of our first date, searching for clues or signs that he might have secretly really liked me. It's a pathetic time-waster, I know, because deep down, if he really did, he'd be here. The rejection doesn't feel as bad as it used to in a hard-edged dramatic sense—just low-level sad. After years of dating, I've come to realize that not everyone's right for each other, even if each has the perfect résumé so to speak. But with Ryan, I felt a genuine connection. Something real. And I am starting to worry that in my thirties, it will just become more and more rare as guys see me as only an equation—my age, plus my hotness, minus my apparent craziness and urge to race down the aisle. Is this really going to be my reality from this point forward—a romantic algorithm? Will my dating life consist of me trying to cover up my secret insecurity about my age and biological clock, things I have absolutely no control over? Is this really my only choice? I run hard, trying to outrace the tears spilling down my cheeks.

Back in my apartment, I take a long, hot, shower, then check my phone, hoping for some sort of miracle—some text from Ryan saying he wants to really talk. Instead I see a Facebook alert. I grow cold. Unbeknownst to me, Alix has tagged me, even though I thought I'd made sure to block the whole *Paddy Cakes* staff—damn you, cracked iPhone 4! There, plain as day, for my entire list of three hundred contacts to see, including my mother, father, cousins and even my granny Buckley, is a picture of the entire staff, taken at the most recent meeting—my bump in full glory, captioned, You looked so pretty this week—thought you might like to share, lovely mother-to-be! x-Alix.

Within the span of thirty seconds, my wall is flooded with countless messages. Congrats!

I didn't even know!

Woo-hoo! Who's the lucky dad? say my college friends, old work colleagues and my cousins in Trenton.

I'm waiting for the one I know will be coming very shortly. My mom. I decide to preempt it. I have to come clean.

"Mom," I say meekly, when she picks up on the first ring.

"Lizzie, what in God's good grace is going on? You're not pregnant, are you? I saw you on Face-Space."

Confused, I take a good hard swallow, a big deep breath, but before I can explain, my mom jumps in.

"Is it JR's?"

"God, no, NO!" I say, not knowing where I'm even going with this. "It was an accident—something happened at work. I was going to tell you—"

"Oh. Oh—" she interjects. The phone drops down to the floor. Finally I hear my mom again. And she's *cheering*.

"I get to be a GRANDMOTHER!" She yells it over and over. It's as if she's doing her own senior-ladies-Zumba-inspired version of the happy dance on the other end of the phone. I can feel a glee in my mom that I haven't seen since before the divorce, before she got sick. It feels so nice. I almost can't say anything back. I don't want to take this away from her yet. "Lizzie, I didn't want to tell you, but I've been stocking up, secretly, on little baby clothes, hoping this day would come!"

"Wait. So you're not…disappointed?"

"Well, you're thirty-one. And this is the new millennium. It's okay these days to have children out of wedlock—I mean, on your own. Look at that Angelina Jolie…I love her for standing up to cancer, but she was a home-wrecker and a single mom and it all seemed to work out for her!"

"Really?" I say, shocked.

"You've made me the happiest woman on the planet today. Thank you."

"Of course, Mom," I find myself saying. We go over almost every detail. The sex, how far along I am, ideas for names—she tears up at the middle name Rose, after my grandmother—birth plan ideas ("You're not doing any of those crazy natural birthing tubs, are you?") and child care plans. She says she can come into the city three days a week, "Mondays, Tuesdays and Thursdays—Zumba is on Fridays." When I hang up, I realize it's as if I've finally done something truly right in her eyes for once. Then guilt floods in and is enormous. I can't imagine taking this away from her right now. Plus, I realize, if I have a shower, I'm going to need her to think I'm pregnant. She has to be there. And she has to believe it. There's no way I can tell her. At least not right now.

Then I see a text from Addison. ???!!!

That was unplanned! I text back.

You like it unplanned, don't you :), she shoots back.

Brie texts, too. Well, at least you can stop worrying about how you were going to make it Facebook official! It's the first I've heard from her since our fight in the bathroom. Is she making up? I'm feeling too guilty right now to find out.

I spend the rest of the night letting calls from friends and family go straight to voice mail. I take a harder look at my other friends' Facebook pages, filled with pics of babies in cute Fourth of July outfits. Babies at the beach, babies at the park, babies playing golf with their dads. It's as if this has become the summer of babies for all my old college and high-school friends, everyone, it seems besides Addison, Brie and me. Well, not me. *Wait a second.* Why don't more people care about my baby! Lucie Rose is just as important as

Elyse's baby, Callie! Just because we don't live in fancy *West-port* leading pumpkin-patch-visiting, artisanal-ale-sipping gapster lives! I find myself thinking strangely. All of a sudden, I've become my dad.

And then I see it, a call registers his number. Dad, reads the Jersey area code. Not ready to face this, I find myself sending the call straight to voice mail. Later on, I listen, dulled by a pint of Ciao Bella hazelnut gelato—not even vegan cashew.

"Lizziebee," he calls me, his nickname for me since I was four, "it's Dad. I just heard from your uncle Louie that you're, you're pregnant? He said he saw it online. Is it true? Call me please, if you have a chance. It's been a while. Yep, yep. Dad."

His tone feels far away, unsure. I click the phone off, feeling a torrent of pain sweep through my side. I can't call him. Not yet. Not right now. If I did, I know everything would start to unravel.

Nineteen

After a few weeks of planning, it's finally here—my baby shower. In the end, Ford, Addison, Brie and Jules went in together to help plan my party at Alice's Tea Cup, a cute, *Alice in Wonderland*–themed teahouse on the Upper East Side.

Getting ready this morning, I pull on my outfit over my month-seven bump, a neon floral print Lilly Pulitzer–style maternity sheath with a pink cardigan that might seem a little over-the-top, but I know full well everyone will be eyeing my stomach today. *I really have to figure this out. This was not the plan*, I think, scanning myself anxiously in the mirror for any sign of seam.

In the taxi on the way through the park, I hit Delete on the latest message from my mom, feeling incredibly guilty that she's called eight times since the Facebook post went up.

After Jules had sent the Paperless Post invitation out, I'd

squeezed my eyes shut for a second. As RSVPs trickled in, I was surprised to find that everyone was strangely blasé about it, not even really mentioning it to me. Maybe in this day and age getting pregnant semi—on purpose, without a mate, is not all that crazy.

Getting out of the cab at Alice's, I find myself tearing up a little as I walk in. The room—a small space on the second floor of the whimsically painted town house—is decorated with hot pink and navy blue place settings. No storks, balloons or pastel colors are anywhere to be seen. If a baby shower could feel trendy and cool, this is it. Totally my style.

Glancing around the stunning display, I see that pretty much all of my coworkers are here, even the moms with kids, digging into triple-stacked towers of yummy-looking tea sandwiches. There's even a perfectly styled pile of beautifully wrapped gifts. I feel bad for fooling everyone but also strangely happy. And then, as I turn the corner into the room, I snap to another sensation: ultimate, stomach-clenching guilt. My mom. I steel myself to start pretending to be "pregnant," in front of the one woman who, at the core of her DNA, has been watching my weight fluctuations since birth.

I consider turning around and hightailing it out of there. I could send Jules a text saying I'm sick. They'd have to believe me, right? Then, as I walk two more steps into the room, the whole crowd notices me, starts to clap and cheer, and my mom spots me. I know there's no going back.

I smile warmly and immediately beeline it to her, pulling her into a close hug while she stares at me in total shock. Tearing up, she looks at me and my bump under, in her eyes, the perfect, Reagan-era maternity shift dress. It's as if the image she's guarded closely in the base of her heart has finally come true. "You look beautiful, sweetie," she whispers. Then her face turns from one of pride to concern in the flash of a second.

"Lizzie, didn't you get my voice mails? I know how busy you are at work, but there's a *lot* we still have to discuss. Have you been going to the doctor? Is everything all right? Healthy? I'm your mother—I worry," she whispers into my ear. As we pull away, I see a large white box resting in her hands, and as she hands it to Jules, I see she's wearing her favorite pastel pink suit, complete with peony corsage.

How am I going to pull this off? Thankfully Ford swaggers over, already a little tipsy from one too many "preglinis." Which funnily enough, contain the exact same contents as Brie's healthtinis. "Thank you for coming, Mrs. Buckley. Isn't she just glowing," he says. I eye him hard.

"I'll keep her away from the *Paddy Cakes* staff," he whispers to me as a bit of syrupy cocktail splashes out from his glass onto my bump.

"Thanks!" I whisper back.

"Time to open the gifts," Jules announces. I can see in her eyes that she's worried for me.

Let's make this quick, I think. I try to act like all the other expectant mothers I've seen recently. What do they do again? Rub their stomachs and look like they're in some hormonal foggy daze? I attempt my best *fog*.

"Thank you all so much for coming. I never thought I'd see this day," I remark.

"Neither did I," I overhear Alix snickering to Tamara.

"Well, I think it's great," says Charlie, our web director, and the only other single person nearing thirty on staff, as if to say "finally, us matrimonially challenged girls finally get some attention, too."

"But now that it's here, and even though my circumstances are a little *unusual* for *Paddy Cakes*, I appreciate all of your support in these past months. I hope that I can come to you for all your secrets and advice. I know I will need it."

"What she needs is a baby daddy," Ford drunkenly jokes. No one looks amused.

"Okay, this first gift is from...hmm..." I read the card, "Nellie." I tear off the paper from a huge box. It's a Stokke 6500 high chair. "Thank you so much! How thoughtful."

"I called it in," she says, meaning as a product editor she didn't have to pay for it.

Jules hands me the next one, a smaller box wrapped in unbleached brown paper with a pastel plaid bow, signed by my former editor in chief. "This one's from Patricia."

"She couldn't be here," says Jules, with what only I can detect is a slight eye roll, "but she wanted me to tell you she's so happy for you." I untie the wrapping to reveal the contents, as well as the attached card.

"A *Pat the Bunny* book," I say. "Some things never go out of style," it reads.

A collective *aww* comes from everyone around the room.

"This one's from Alix," I say, managing to avoid direct eye contact. "Ooh, it's a cashmere nursing blanket from Teddy Bar!" Teddy Bar is the pricey organic baby boutique and lactation lounge. Again, *oohs* and *ahs* around the room, as Alix gives a tight-lipped grin. "And this one's from..." I say, looking at the card "... Mom!" I look over at my mom. I carefully open the thick, embossed white wrapping paper. On top is a baby book including a few photos from when I was little and underneath is a blanket made of various patchwork quilts.

I immediately start tearing up. I look at my mother, whose eyes are welling up, too, with tissues in hand, proud, but a little embarrassed by all the attention.

"I've been working on it for years, waiting until this day to give it to you. It has pieces of quilts from when you were a baby, my baby quilt, my mother's and her mother's. I hope you'll love it just as much as I did when I wrapped you up tight, my little bundle of joy." Sighs at the gift's thoughtfulness echo around the room.

"Of course, Mom, thank you. It means so much." I suck. My mom has clearly put so much time and effort into this quilt, and it was meant for my baby. A real baby.

"Well, thank you so much, everyone," I say with an undercurrent of anxiety, hoping to wrap up things quickly. There's a warmth around the room that all feels familiar— the general sense of approbation and anticipation that groups of women seem to extend collectively when their friends are nearing the end of pregnancy. After a delicious cake with lemon curd in the center is cut and passed around, I start to signal the end. I can't stand looking at people in the eye anymore and lying to them.

Everyone chitchats for a while as we finish the cake. "Yes, thank you. You can go now!" says Ford hastily to the crowd. "Now, who's ready for happy hour across the street!" He's had way too many at this point. I give my thank-yous to all of my coworkers as they shuffle out of the restaurant, resting my hand on my bump lovingly for full effect.

My mom waits patiently as I say my goodbyes to the staff, then comes over when it's just Jules and me. "Lizzie, don't take this the wrong way, but you seem—nervous. Is everything okay with the baby?"

"Yes. I promise I'll explain later."

Her brow furrows with concern, but she seems to accept my response as I lead her out and put her in a cab to Port Authority. Jules graciously volunteers to help me clean up. I've decided I'm going to send all of the gifts to Kristy, the contact Ryan gave me for my surrogacy story, for her new little daughter, Emerson. As I pile stuff into bags, Jules and I start talking.

"You know, I think when I saw this day in my head, I envisioned my cute husband bringing the car around," I say wryly.

"You mean BabyBjorn dad," says Jules, referring to our running joke about the solid, strong man many of our mutual friends were married to—the kind who watches the game, but also does the laundry. He cleans the dishes after she cooks, and is there to push the stroller around the park while training for a triathlon.

"Remember last year, Elyse just had to telepath that it was the end of the shower, and her husband, Chris, was right there with the Forester."

"Well, I hate to tell you but you know what baby daddies hate more than anything?"

"When you forget to DVR *Real Housewives*?"

"Well, that, but also when their wife has faked a pregnancy and is now virtually unemployable—you know how they like double incomes," chides Jules.

"Well, the way Cynthia's been loving my stories lately, I think my future is assured at *Paddy Cakes*."

"Yes, Cynthia's loving on you now, but you realize babies aren't exactly a verboten topic of conversation around the office. The vultures will ask you everything from the moment little 'Lucie Rose' is born."

As she says this, I actually catch myself looking lovingly down at my bump.

"First it'll be which day care she's going to, or whether you'll be hiring a nanny...then where she'll be enrolling in pre-K," says Jules, furthering the line of questioning.

"I've already thought of that," I say, thanking myself for a recent stroll around the Upper West Side for more in-depth "research."

"She's going to the Le Jardin Française preschool," I go on, now looking off into the distance. "She's going to be bi-lingual, and we're going to speak French at the dinner table, and when she's old enough to go to preschool, she'll have an automatic in at the Lycée Français," I say brightly, referring to the prestigious French high school where students not only have to take the SATs, but also prepare for the baccalaureate.

Jules isn't having any of it. "And how are you going to afford that? You know an editor's salary at *Paddy Cakes* isn't even enough for Pampers!"

"I haven't quite worked out all the details, but I think these hormones are affecting my brain in some weird way. I've never felt more relaxed. It's like everything will just work out okay."

"Hold up, Teen Mom! These 'hormones' aren't really there." Jules stops bagging gifts for a second.

"What the fuck? Why have you been so cranky recently? At least you're married. That's the hard part, remember? Finding the love of your life. Maybe you should realize how good you have it? You and Henry have the perfect relation-ship, you live the high life without kids, and you're able to do all the fun stuff you want. You went to China *and* Chile last year! Your Facebook pictures are amazing."

Jules just gives a half smile.

"What?" I ask, perturbed.

"Nothing's perfect. You know that, Liz." Jules looks down.

I can tell I've triggered something, so I reply, "I know, I'm sorry. What's up?"

"What do you think, Liz, people just snap their fingers and things work out like they're magically supposed to all the time? It's not always that easy. Henry's GMATs suck. He's not going to get in anywhere."

"You know what, Jules? I think you're wrong. It can be. I know things haven't been working out for you lately, but I think there's another option you're not realizing."

"What do you mean?"

"Out of you and Henry, do you know who should be applying to business schools?"

Jules looks taken aback.

"You practically quote Sheryl Sandberg every day, Jules. You're organized, methodical, smart and entrepreneurial."

"You're saying I should be going to b-school. Huh. Huh. Oh." She scratches her head as if the thought never occurred to her—the Bird Cage strikes again.

In the cab ride home, I look down at the blanket my mom gave me, the one thing I'm not going to be giving away. I wonder what it'd be like to be using this stuff for real with my very own little baby, rocking her gently to sleep, then going to bed with my husband. An image of Ryan pops into my brain.

Back at my apartment, I take off the bump and slide into the tub, rubbing my achy muscles. I have to give it to pregnant women—after a day of standing around in heels, my back is killing me. The ache then shifts from my lower body upward to my head and now that I'm alone, I feel an intense migraine coming on. I'm now an "expecting mother" with only a few months to go and reality starts to sink in. I need to come up with a plan to not only carry myself through the pregnancy, but to take care of myself afterward for the rest of my life.

Will I officially take maternity leave? Quit my job and reveal the truth? That would undoubtedly mean that I could never work in magazines again. But what's the other option? Pretend to have a baby and keep working at *Paddy Cakes*? No way could I keep up the ruse with thirty very nosy women. And if I try to get a job at another magazine, the industry is pretty small and people will talk. Having a bump is one thing, but pretending to have a living, breathing child is a different thing altogether.

What about my romantic life? How would I be able to keep up this secret double life if a guy were in the picture? And what if this fake bump prevents me from having a real baby of my own one day? I can feel the proverbial clock begin to tick and I realize that's what's been waking me up so early in the mornings—my own heart, starting to beat faster for something I haven't even realized I've wanted until just now—though still far off, a vision starts to paint a shadowy outline—of a real-life Lucie Rose. The reality of all of this sends me into a panic. I start to breathe quicker and my chest tightens. *I have made the stupidest mistake of my life.*

I get out of the tub and dry off, but I can't stop thinking about what a fool I am. I get into bed, but toss and turn the whole night. I contemplate the most ridiculous solutions, like telling everyone it was all just water weight after a dieting backslide and that I was just too embarrassed to admit it.

Deep into the night, a dark thought strikes me. I could feign a miscarriage. But there's just something so karmically wrong about it, I immediately shrug it off. Then, I think, I could just quit. If I get out now, maybe I can still save myself, if not my career.

I wake up the next morning groggy and tired, and realize that I'm going to have to tell everyone what I've done. Own up to my mistakes and end this once and for all. It might get me fired, but it's the right thing to do.

Twenty

PUSH! ☺ Notification! Week 27: Is Red Bull, like, your new BFF? Well, you probably shouldn't be drinking Red Bull, but whatevs. Welcome to the (sleepless) world of preg-somnia! Heartburn, leg cramps, bathroom runs are just some of the fun! Baby Smiles: 9!

The gray skies start to open halfway on my walk to work, and even though I remembered to bring my umbrella, my flip-flopped feet slip and slide atop the damp pavement. I'm so early to work that it looks as though I'm the only one who's come in yet. I turn on my computer and check my email. The first message is from Cynthia. "See me as soon as you get in. Urgent matters to discuss."

Okay, perfect. I will tell her everything. My chest is pounding and I feel light-headed. All the blood in my body feels like it's rushing to my face.

Walking over to her office, I see Cynthia through the glass, turned toward her computer, ever-present macchiato on her desk. *This should be easy.* I tap lightly.

Cynthia turns toward me, nodding me in.

I pad over to the chair, feeling as though I might faint, grabbing on to the sides of my stomach for balance.

"So. I've been thinking about your *situation*," starts Cynthia.

"Yes," I say. "Me, too. There's actually something I need to tell you." I can barely get the words out, but now that I've said them, there's no going back.

"Well, I'll go first. I know that as a single working woman, your budget's going to be...*tight*." Her sharp features soften ever so slightly. "I want you to know that I recognize that you haven't received more than our usual standard of living increase in salary in the ten years that you've been here. We're in budget talks at the moment and Jeffry mentioned that you've been taking on many of the senior editor's assignments. I've decided to continue monitoring your performance these next few months. If you continue with your current progress, once the baby arrives, I'll raise your salary to one hundred thousand and offer you a title change to deputy editor. I'll be expecting even more of you, but this new increase in salary should help at least a little more with child care. Oh, and the expenses for a new mobile will also be covered. You can pick one up downstairs in IT today. Can't have you missing important messages with...that beleaguered contraption."

The news is so unbelievable I don't know what to say. My whole life I'd been scrounging and saving just to afford my tiny studio on my salary. I can't even fathom what that amount of money would mean—and it's the title I've been coveting. My mom will be so proud to hear the news. My mind goes blank as I hear myself saying, "Thank you for this opportunity, Cynthia. Of course I'll work as hard as I can."

Friday, I'm finishing up a bunch of late finals when I get a random 5:45 p.m. incoming text from Gavin. Hello dear Elizabeth. If you haven't skipped town for Timbuktu yet, I was wondering if you'd like to join me and some mates at the Mondrian Rooftop tonight for a media party. The GM passed on some VIP passes to the celebrity function since one of my importers is sponsoring it. The lovely Addison and Brie are invited, too. Just let me know and I'll put your names on the list. Cheers, love.

Clicking off the phone, I wonder why he invited me. I know he's not interested in me as a girlfriend, and yet I made it clear enough that I wasn't looking for a hookup-only situation.

Excited anyway about the night's possibilities, Addison, Brie and I meet up for drinks at a wine bar in the West Village before the party. For once, we're all in the exact same place—single, but feeling strangely confident. After each going through a bad run of going-nowhere guys this spring, it feels like there's a change in the midsummer night air.

"Maybe he really likes you, Liz," says Brie, after I've re-reminded her of all the facts from date one with Gavin. "It's not totally out of the question. Plus, you're looking hot these days. All the bump-wearing is paying off!"

"Aw, thanks, B," I say, looking down at my figure sheepishly. I guess I have shrunken in size a bit—maybe from carrying a fifteen-pound orb ten hours a day? I feel a slight wave of worry and glance around the trendy bar for coworkers. It's a risk to be out without my bump, but it's so hot tonight I couldn't bear it. I've brought it in a big carryall tote just in case.

"Maybe he realizes what he's missing out on," Addison says, giving me a suggestive wink. "But really, even if he does turn out to be a total player, what do you have to lose by hanging out with him and his friends? They're all cute. Try not to think so hard and just have fun."

"Besides, after your meternity leave, you'll be off traveling," she says jokily. "We better take advantage of any cute guy connections while we've got 'em!" Addison straightens up a bit to arrange herself, dabbing on some coral lip gloss.

Maybe the girls are right—thirty-one isn't old, I think, looking around at our glowing faces. It's been a record twenty-one straight days of Brie not texting Baxter, and a slew of new, not horrible online dates, and I can see the change in her face—she's happy, her phone no longer a third appendage. And I think we're past our fight. Think—or hope.

Addison's just back from a Hamptons weekend, where she's managed to get in some sun between signing two new lucrative deals. The glow of success is showing up on her face. We finish up our bottle of rosé, settle the tab and then head across town to the Mondrian Hotel.

Inside, the bar upstairs is packed. I immediately recognize the corporate signage on the walls. It's a Discovery Channel party? Oh, no! I can't believe it! Will Ryan be here?

I'm shocked at how loud the music is in the all-glass space. We head over to the bar area already jammed with tons of crop-top-bedecked LBGs vying for shrub n' sodas, the summer's new classed-up vodka sodas. I see Gavin talking with some of the same friends we met that first night. One has a British-celeb-chef look, complete with dyed-green steampunk-style hair. There's a tall, blond, clean-cut-looking guy, and a slightly older, aging-rock-star type. I'm still slightly nervous about seeing Ryan, but he's nowhere in sight. I smile at Gavin's navy cotton blazer and jeans mixed with his soccer sneakers.

"Why hello, gorgeous," says Gavin, giving me a kiss on the cheek. "Good to see you again. And hello, Addison, Brie. It's been too long."

Gavin's friend Doug, also tall and blond, gets us drinks.

The DJ spins get louder and louder, so we swap chatting for dancing. *Eek, this is going to be one of those nights.* When Gavin finds me dancing with Addison he has to shout in my ear, "Addison's looking sexy, isn't she? Bet she'll have her pick of the men tonight."

Smiling back, I realize, *ah yes*, maybe he's into *her.* I shrug it off, knowing it doesn't matter anyway. I've already made my decision about him.

I walk over to Brie and Doug since Gavin and Addison have gone back to dancing, but the music's too loud to break into their conversation. Doug puts a big arm around Brie and they start to dance. Then Gavin comes over to me and spins me around again, swooping in to give me a peck on the cheek. "Mmm, you smell nice, Liz," he says. "What is it? Vanilla?" I give him a playful punch in the stomach and a look that says, "What exactly are you up to tonight?"

The music finally dies down, and Doug offers us all another shot. As he turns toward the bar, Gavin now has his arm around Brie.

"You're so cool."

"Foreign men always have better taste," Brie says back flirtatiously.

"I love this girl," Gavin says to me in front of Brie and Doug. "Brie, you are the marrying kind, you know that," to which Brie lights up. *Humph, am I not the marrying kind?* I think.

Just then, out of the corner of my eye, I spot him—Ryan. He's with a twentysomething, heavily highlighted "bouncy" girl if there ever was one. I try to turn and face the other way, but it's too late. He notices me, too, and does a double take.

"Hey, Liz!" he says, walking over as the blonde girl trails behind.

"Hi," I respond meekly. His energy makes my stomach flip-flop as it always does.

He goes in for a big hug, and I end up spilling a little bit of champagne on his shirt, which he brushes off good-naturedly. His open smile makes it seem like he's genuinely happy to see me. "You look *good*. So you managed to get in, huh?"

"I, uh," I stammer. Even with a few drinks in me, I feel myself blushing. Despite what happened between us, the butterflies are still there. "I'm here with a group of friends," nodding at my clearly drunken compatriots clowning around on the dance floor. Doug looks as though he's attempting the running man to impress Brie with ironic goofiness. "You?"

"Discovery thought it'd be a good idea to launch the new season of *Top Gear* here. I asked Kendall to put your name on the media list and was hoping you'd make it."

"Really? I didn't get the invite."

"That's strange…" starts Ryan. Just then, the blonde catches up next to Ryan and slides an arm through his elbow, wearing some sort of off-the-shoulder, barely-covering-her-butt "festival" dress. Her whole aura reads "uncomplicated."

"Hi there," she smiles, eyeing me up and down.

"Hi."

"Kendall, this is Liz Buckley—you remember, we worked on the mega-multiples and Laos stories with her at *Paddy Cakes*?" He gives me a warm smile.

"Liz, this is Kendall—she's my coworker at Discovery."

"Nice to meet you," I say. This is who he was probably going shot for shot with the night of our falling-out. She's definitely still a good two to three years away from the big 3-0. I find myself looking off toward my group of friends as a protective measure so Ryan won't see the disappointment in my face.

"Hey, good to meet you," she says, smiling. Her eyes dart back and forth between Ryan and me.

"Liz's name was on the list, right, K?"

"I'm sure I put it on," she says with nothing but a courteous smile. Feeling a sudden urge to leave, I quickly say, "Nice to meet you, Kendall. Talk to you later, Ryan." And turn smack into Gavin, who wraps both hands around my waist sloppily.

"Who's this, Lizzie?" says Gavin, looking Kendall up and down.

"Oh, these are my friends from Discovery Channel."

"Good to meet you, mates," says Gavin. He tightens his grip around my waist, then drunkenly nuzzles into my neck.

Ryan gives me a perplexed look. "Good seeing you, Liz. Let's talk soon about our upcoming lineup."

"Sure," I say as Ryan walks away. Gavin swoops in for a kiss. Before I can push him away, his pillowy lips press against my face with force behind them. He bites my lower lip teasingly and pulls back with a dirty look.

I back away slightly. "Hmm, why not go for Addison? You seemed to be having a good time with her earlier," I say, not knowing why I'm pushing my friend on my crush.

He looks a little confused, and then gives me a wink. "That's why I like you, my dear. You're funny," he says, kissing me again on my cheek.

I glance back, and to my dismay, I see that Ryan's caught the whole thing.

We continue dancing, and all of a sudden it's 3:45 a.m. I hit the bathroom, then meander toward the coat check, broken apart from my friends by the sea of revelers.

As I'm nearing the front of the line, I'm lost in my own head, attempting to make sense of my emotions. Am I willing to go home with Gavin tonight? Fumbling for a few dollars from my little purse, I see someone hand money to the coat-check girl, then take my tote with the bump in it and hand it to me. It's Ryan. I look at him, confused.

"I've got it," he says.

"Thanks, you don't have to..."

He cuts me off, leaning down toward my ear. "Good seeing you tonight, Buckley. Get home safe." And then as an afterthought, he adds, "You might want to be careful with that guy."

"I'm sure I will," I say.

But he's already steadying Kendall as she changes from heels into Grecian sandal flats.

In the VIP room, the night begins to blur into colors only, and after one more round, everyone's dispersing. Gavin has grabbed us a cab back to my apartment. But on the way toward the Upper West Side, while we're nearing Jane Street, something tells me to say something to the cab driver.

"Two stops, please."

"C'mon, Liz, what are you doing? Don't you want me to come over?"

The whole Ryan spotting has me thrown. "No, sorry, Gavin. Not tonight."

I scroll through my phone to the one single message I'd saved. Charlie Brown, we won! I'm noticing there are now three red hearts showing up I've never noticed before... emojis—they're now finally coming through on my phone.

Gavin, sensing that I'm serious, makes an exasperated sigh. He's probably hoping some last-ditch effort will make me give in. We say nothing, and when the cab gets to his apartment, he throws me a five-dollar bill. "Night, Liz."

August

Twenty-One

This week, all the cards seem to be stacked against me. "Oh, my GOD!" I scream to no one in particular while performing my familiar morning routine. Normally it's easy to squeeze the bump into place and secure it with model tape, snap on the Spawn-x slip and slide a cute maternity dress over everything. But in the dead heat of early August, my dress gets stuck on my bump and starts twisting and bunching up around my head like, ironically, *a used condom.*

A heavy wave of emotion hits me. *What in the hell am I doing?* Only a few months ago, everything was fine. I was going through life without all these unnecessary complications. Now, I'm completely stuck.

At the office, I haven't even set my coffee down when Alix comes over to my cube.

"I never got to tell you, I simply adorrred your shower,"

she purrs. "It was so homey, not like mine at the St. Regis. You only need so many Tiffany rattles, right?"

"Right," I deadpan, trying to keep focused.

"Oh, and I forgot to tell you," she says, rifling through the pile of papers back from Cynthia. "You know the feature on family-friendly travel destinations you pitched? Cynthia thinks it would be popular with advertisers, so it's going in as a late add to the November issue. Since you're pregnant, they're sending you to Newport to stay at Vanderbilt Spa and Suites to try out their prenatal spa services and family-friendly amenities. They've just opened."

I'm too dumbfounded for words—the travel features are usually written by Pam. It's the cushiest assignment on staff, since you basically get to go to a five-star resort for free and write about it. I can't believe my luck.

I check out the hotel online—it looks incredible. The property is divided into about forty-five newly redesigned suites, an infinity pool overlooking the sea, a "sea-to-table" restaurant and a full-service spa with coastally inspired treatments. I'll get to sit by the pool, drink "virgin" cocktails, and explore the waterfront area, all while technically "working." I immediately text Addison and Brie to see if they want to try to get in on it with me and take advantage of the free accommodations.

To my surprise, they both pass. I can't take any time off because of Fashion Week, but have a blast, Addison texts back.

My September weekends are already booked—Doug already asked me to a wedding in Philly! says Brie. Wow. Our night out at the Mondrian materialized into something with potential. Undeterred, I start to plan the story, and feel a familiar tingle of anticipation. I want to find sites off the beaten path to add to my story. I might even pitch the story to other travel publications. Then, I see a link on TripAdvisor to surf camps in Rhode Island just a thirty-minute drive from where I'll be staying. I click through and find a boho-looking beachside resort started by a couple from the Rhode Island School of Design. It looks inexpensive, and I make a mental note to spend a day there, too. I'll keep it to myself—surfing doesn't exactly jibe for a woman who's more than thirty-weeks pregnant.

I look down at my bump. "Lucie, are you ready for your first big trip?" I can swear I feel some strange movement coming from deep inside my stomach—maybe it's just my digestive system, or maybe my little baby will be a world traveler just like her mommy. Oh, jeez, I'm losing it.

I attempt to pull together thoughts for a think piece on latchkey GenX parents and the resulting spate of attachment parenting apps, when I see Jules is back from a lunchtime press event, beaming. "Check your email," she says excitedly. I log in and see it.

FW: Top Editor, Well-Heeled Traveler.
Available immediately. Well-Heeled Traveler, the premier trade magazine for the luxury travel gear market seeks an experienced top editor to write and polish copy to a gleam. Must have knowledge of the fashion market. Must be able to travel for conferences. Experience at a major national magazine a bonus.

Jules has sent me the perfect job posting.

"I know the managing editor. I've already put in a good word for you. Plus, I was getting tired of being the only one who's stressed about you not actually having a baby," she quips at a whisper, turning back in her chair.

It's not freelancing, but it is a way out of this mess. I send off my résumé, hoping that in a few short weeks I will be finally relieved of the bump.

★ ★ ★

Later in the week, Addison invites Brie and I over to her place to show us its new "look," which some of her design friends helped her with. Her oversize West Village one-bedroom with terrace now looks like a beautiful high-end French manor home with all different sorts of "griege" items she's sourced from ABC Carpet and Home—not even Joss & Main.

"It's the color of the year!" she says triumphantly. I'm scared to sit on—or ask the price of—the faux reclaimed vintage armchairs and bed linens and accessories. She must be doing *well*.

I suggest heading to Sparrow and Crow, but Addison is reticent. "I don't know, Lizzie, the only guys that seem interested in me lately are fiftysomething businessmen or twenty-eight-year-old boy toys. Every guy in his thirties seems threatened when I start talking about my job."

"Go for the boy toys," I tell her.

"I know, but I've been feeling so bodycon lately. I mean, how can I compete with these early twentysomethings?"

"Are you kidding me?" I scoff. "I'm the one who should be bodycon."

Brie reaches out to touch Addison's arm. "Addison, I was right where you were earlier this summer, but things can change when you least expect it. Doug is great. Even though I am a little worried I'm still acting out my mild clinginess/abandonment pattern..."

"Brie, have you ever thought it might be his mild douche pattern?"

"Addison," Brie intones.

"Argh! Maybe I should just accept that I'm going to be alone if I want to be successful in my career. Fuck it. Hear that, Universe!" She takes a huge sip of her rosé.

At that, Brie looks like she's swallowed a bird and takes it as a cue to beg off for Doug's. Addison reluctantly agrees to come out with me to Sparrow and Crow. When we arrive, the crowd is indeed heavy with the twentysomething men that Addison is so weary of. Still, after a few vodka sodas, a cute, compact-looking guy with a deep tan and warm brown eyes starts chatting her up. I tell her that I'm going to head out, and she responds with a hopeful glint.

The next morning I see a text from A: His name is Jacques. 28. Works for LMVH and is here on business from Paris. Went all the way...ooh la la.

I laugh to myself. The law of attraction, Addison-style: act like you're ready to give up and score a hot, young French dude.

Around eleven, I head out to do laundry and run twin Bugaboo stroller into granny cart into my friend Elyse. "Aaaah!" I feel terrible I didn't reach out when I saw her commenting all over my Facebook, but with the new baby, I'm sure she was busy anyway. Be-bumped and Facebook official, I can no longer hide. I start to sweat.

"Lizzie, Lizzie! I thought that was you...it's been, what, four months, and I saw you're pregnant?" She looks worried, careful not to offend me. "Why didn't you call me?"

"I, uh, well, it was unplanned," I say, hanging my head down in shame. I'm sweating all over now. Elyse doesn't quite know how to take it, either.

"I was wondering why you didn't return my calls. I've been worried about you."

"I was trying to figure out what I was going to do for a while." Oh God, I think, wringing my hands. I've just pretended I was thinking about not going through with the pregnancy. *I'm a monster.*

"I wouldn't have judged you...trust me," she says with a

look like, *she knows*. "Well, you look great. Not a bloated appendage in sight." She burps one of her beautiful red-headed twin girls while pushing the stroller with the other back and forth...

"Thanks," I say, pushing off the compliment. "Callie and Ro are so cute!"

"Live up the pre-baby life while you can. Once your little one comes, all of a sudden you'll be thankful for your single days," says Elyse, brushing at a spot of spit-up on her polo shirt with ferociousness before throwing her hand up as Callie starts to fuss.

Maybe I don't really want to "live it up" anymore, I think to myself. I pick up the other sleep-deprived baby, cooing into her ear, making the five *s*'s, the old trick we've lauded countless times at *Paddy Cakes*. When that doesn't work, I pull out a tissue and gently swipe it over her forehead again and again and that does it. She's out cold. My friend looks at me, shocked. "I read it on PaddyCakes.com," I say. *Oh I want this*, I think, holding Callie in my arms. *I really want this.*

Elyse catches me, and then her smile changes. "I caught Chris on Tinder."

"What!" Coffee comes out of my nose. Elyse and Chris have been together since college.

"Yep, he said he just got 'bored,' and decided to download it one day."

"Wait—how did you catch him?"

She immediately looks guilty. "Well, I was on it, too."

Wait—what!

"Lizzie, we've been together since freshman year. He was the first and only guy I've ever slept with—things happen. You'll see when you're married..." She trails off like it's a given that events like finding your spouse on a dating app will just "happen"—and worse, that it's actually no big deal.

"Elyse, I'm so sorry." Then I add meekly, "What are you going to do?"

"Well, at first I considered divorce, of course. But then I started looking at real estate—and realized pretty quickly *that* wasn't going to happen. So instead I got real and said, 'Okay, you get a profile, I get a profile. One week. And then we're moving to Westport. I had some fun chatting with all these random guys actually! But now I realize how hard you have it. I would *not* want to be single. Do you know who kept Messaging me? The married guys! And Chris, actually. It was kind of cute." She actually looks at his profile pic of himself lovingly. "Look, he's Messaging me now about meeting up for a martini later on when his mom gets into town—it's actually kind of hot."

At that, Callie starts projectile vomiting. I look at her and think, *You and me both, kid.*

Back home, I check in with Addison for details on last night. She's still at his place, which she conveys in the form of a French-flag emoji–filled text.

He's 28! But soooo hot. *Eek!* Still here. Call later!

Brie is free to talk. When I tell her about my motherhood realization, I expect her to be surprised, but she's not.

"Why is it weird that you want a baby, sweetie?"

"I don't know, surprised."

"I'm going to tell you something shocking," says Brie, quieting her tone. "I honestly don't worry if Doug starts off, you know, with no condom on."

"Really?" I ask. Of the three of us, I'd always been the freak about birth control, but Brie has been religious about condom use. Addison not so much.

"We had the whole health, monogamy talks, and we both ultimately want a family, so I just keep thinking, if it happened it really wouldn't be so bad." She sighs. "Strange, right?"

"How were things last night?"

"Fine. I told Doug I was worried I was being too clingy and he told me point-blank that he secretly likes how affectionate I am. We made a pact to be honest with each other."

"How adult."

"I know, right? Funny how easy life can get when you just tell the truth."

That's it. Brie is done; Doug is her person. I tell her I'm thrilled for her—well, not the unprotected sex part, but the rest of it. Pretty soon it will just be down to me and Addison in the Last Girl Standing category.

Twenty-Two

PUSH! ☺ Notification! Week 31: Dayum, those are some sex hormones! A surge during your third trimester may have you feeling super sexual—and then at times, totally not. We suggest just going with it, because once this baby comes...well, you won't be thinking about sex. Baby Smiles: 50!

The mid-August heat wave is making me feel...frisky. I look it up. Yep. Right on schedule, I have the last-eight-week lusties.

I look at the latest text from Gavin again. We're just friends now; I think I've made that clear. It would be nice to talk. I ask him how his travels have been going. He responds almost immediately, suggesting dinner downtown to "catch up," and I respond yes.

My face feels flush as I fight back a little smile. Jules notices from the other side of the cube. She's tapping her watch to signal it's time for her first appointment with Dr. Lakshmi the "power-fertility" doctor she told me about. She's asked me to join her since Henry can't make it.

At lunchtime, we hop in the cab and go across town. I can tell Jules is nervous. I clutch her hand.

"What if she tells me I can't have kids?" says Jules, her Mach-10 anxiety beginning to set in as she sinks down into her seat. My normally assertive friend now looks small. I pull her into a huge hug.

"I have a good feeling that's not the case. Trust me. They say pregnant women are psychic," I respond, putting my arm around her in a distinctly (new) maternal way (for me.)

We walk into the office reception area decorated all in white. The desk is lit by pink and blue neon under the cabinets. Not a baby picture in sight. But a huge pic of Dr. Lakshmi, a beautiful Indian woman, wearing the requisite white doctor's coat and huge diamond-encrusted Chanel earrings, smiles confidently. We both give each other strange looks, and Jules shrugs. "Impressive, right?"

"I guess," I say as Jules checks in. After a fifteen-minute wait in an examining room, Dr. Lakshmi enters and tells Jules loudly that all her blood work has come back perfect. She says she's had excellent success with hormone therapy and will give Jules supplemental progesterone to get her ovulation cycle back on track. Worst case, they can think about IUI or IVF, but not until they've exhausted rounds of her most recent "cutting-edge" drugs, which makes Jules smile triumphantly. I can tell her stress has lowered—at least for now.

Then, Dr. Lakshmi turns her attention to me. "And how far along are you?" The question, totally out of context and in context at once, obviously flusters me. Feeling like I'm at confession, I decide to come clean. "Oh, this bump isn't mine—it's for a story. I'm not pregnant, actually, but would, you know, like to be one day. Maybe in three to five years, or sooner! Ha!" I add nervously. Her eyes narrow, seeming as if she's looking at the lines in my forehead suspiciously.

"You're over thirty, correct?"

"Yes," I squeak out.

"That's all well and good that you think you'd like to have a baby in three to five years, but life doesn't always work out the way we hope. Planning is key. Have you had your FSH or LH levels checked?"

"Not exactly?" It comes out as a question, rather than a response.

"Wait, you mean to tell me that you work at a baby magazine, you're over thirty and you've never had your FSH levels checked? I assume you've thought about freezing your eggs."

"Not yet, no. I thought I had some time," I tell her.

"She thought she had *time*," she remarks to Jules snarkily.

"I was in a relationship. Then it ended. I'm figuring out my options. That's why I'm here now."

"She was in a relationship," once again Dr. Lakshmi tells Jules.

I cower in the chair like a six-year-old. Ahhh. I don't need this stress!

"Look. I'm going to be honest with you. Too many women of your generation go around thinking they've got all the time in the world to have children. That they can wait until they're forty, then start trying because they see Halle Berry having kids at forty-six. Do you know whose eggs she used?"

Jules and I look at each other like we've been caught jumping on the bed.

"Fertility isn't something you play around with," says Dr. Lakshmi. "If you want a baby, you've got to work for it," she says, slapping her clipboard against the cold metal table. "It takes planning. Quick. Give me your gynecologist's name. I can look up your most recent labs if you want me to. I've created a database in the cloud and many of the more cutting-edge doctors in the city have partnered with me."

"Okay, I guess."

She shakes her head as I hand over my information. "Ah, yes, your doctor's registered with us. Electronic signature, please?" I use the stylus to sign yes on her tablet.

The page finally loads, and Dr. Lakshmi does not look happy. "I see here that while everything checked out, your thyroid hormones were all off at your last appointment. You did nothing about them?"

"No," I say, now scared, which she notices. "My doctor didn't mention it."

"We have to be our own fertility advocates!" she says sharply, sending a flood of tears to my eyes, which finally softens her.

"Woah…your progesterone is basically at zero. Wait a minute. Your cortisol, too, totally depleted." She looks at my cheeks and my upper arms. "Do you have a lot of stress in your life?"

Ugh… I don't even speak before she starts again.

"I've been seeing this a lot. Professional women, totally burned out by thirty. Have you had your adrenals checked? Any traumas in the past ten years?" I list them laundry-style: divorce, cancer, financial stress, potential firing, onslaught of double workload brought on by intentionally clueless, rich dinosaur, young mom.

"Wow. With that list, I'm surprised you haven't had a psychotic breakdown."

Hmm.

"Listen, there are things you can do to improve the matter. As a start, many of our women have had success removing gluten, sugar and caffeine from their diets."

"What if she's heavily reliant on gluten, sugar and caffeine in her diet to make it through every day?" quips Jules. Dr. Lakshmi doesn't look amused.

"Have you thought about a meditation practice. Stress is really the biggest factor. Most likely, you've got some adrenal fatigue issues due to job stress. I'm working on an entire longitudinal study on Generation X versus Millennial attitudes toward stress, resilience and fertility. You could learn a thing or two from twentysomething millennials who are now thinking about their fertility just as they would with a 401K."

Have you ever thought that you might be the ones causing said stress? Just saying.

"Well, at the very least try to cut back on alcohol. Get outside. Maybe think about starting a window garden." Jules and I just look at each other in misery. "And a gratitude journal." The final swing. I can't help hide a snicker.

"Look." She's noticed. "I'm not going to play any more games with you two, hold your hands or sing you through this. You've got to want this. If you don't, I don't want to see your faces in my office. Think of me like your fertility boot-camp officer. I don't waste time with lazy-ass women. This is New York City. You want drugs, I'll get you drugs. You want the best acupuncturist in this city? You're in. You want cysto-blast technology that would make eugenicists blush, I've got it. You want designer sperm so hot *Paddy Cakes* would kill to put that baby on the cover, it's yours. But I do not suffer fools. Especially ones who can't get their carbohydrate addictions under control. Now out! I don't want to see you until you've lost five pounds and wiped those precious smirks off your faces!" Jules and I both scamper to our feet.

"I like her," says Jules.

"Me, too," I say, as we run out of the doors back toward the Bird Cage.

★ ★ ★

Dr. Lakshmi's sobering words of advice make me wonder if I am wasting my time with Gavin. Thanks to this disclosure about my errant progesterone and possible adrenal burnout, my date is the last thing that's on my mind. Still, as I walk out of the doors of the Bird Cage, I think, *Stay in control and you'll be fine. Of course* I can stay in control. I am Liz Buckley, master of the universe.

Riding toward the West Village, the summer heat fills the cab and overwhelms the AC. This time of the year the air feels heavy before the late summer rain arrives. The hair on the back of my neck is hot and sweaty.

I swipe my ATM card to pay the fare, clenching at the thought of my ever-declining bank balance. I jump out and smooth the front of my dress on the street corner, then rifle through my overstuffed bag and pull up the Google Map directions. As I look up, I realize Gavin is staring at me from across the street, laughing.

"Looking good there, gorgeous," he says, crossing Waverley Place to meet me. He leans in and gives me a quick kiss on the lips, before I can realize it, and then a big smile.

"You know, Liz, I couldn't stop thinking about you these past few weeks," he says later, trying to hide a grin while reading his menu.

"Really?" I feel a surge of electricity rush in.

"Really," he says resolutely, coming in for a kiss on my cheek. I feel his warmth. *I may be succumbing. Just a little.*

At dinner, we proceed to get into an easy, fun expectationless rhythm, as we talk about the minutiae of our jobs and our friends; when I begin to let my guard down, he takes out his phone to show me pictures of his brother's family, who's in town for the next week. He's got dozens of pictures of his four-year-old niece, Dani, running through his family's vineyards from a recent trip back home. As he shows me, I can tell he's a bit lit up. Then, as the restaurant is closing, we settle up and head out toward the curb. At 10 p.m. it's still terribly hot out. He checks his phone again.

"Looks like Santo and crew are at the Pig. Want to go meet up with them?" A flash of excitement swells inside. The third floor of The Spotted Pig is the late-night meeting spot of all the celeb chefs in New York City. The thought of meeting foodie royalty like April Bloomfield is thrilling. How I wish I could interview her for my blog. Could it be that Gavin really has an in with them?

"Sure, of course," I try to say coolly.

In a few minutes, we're already out of a cab and walking up the steps to the notorious top floor of the gastropub on West Eleventh Street.

Inside, early '80s punk is playing and inked-up chefs are sitting around a crowded table, digging into bowls of pasta and drinking tumblers of wine. They give Gavin a nod when we walk in. I'm dying to Instagram this and tag Ford.

"What would you like to drink?" asks Gavin up at the bar area.

"You choose a wine," I say, taking in the scene around the room, as I notice some of the guys are chatting up younger, very thin, pretty girls who I'm guessing are either models or actresses in their twenties.

"So will it be this 2000 Barolo, or the usual Bogan stuff you're hawking, Gav," teases Johnny, who teaches at the New York Culinary Institute and who, from *Top Chef*, I know used to be the head pastry chef at Daniel. Gavin introduces me, and Johnny passes both of us half pours in tumblers.

"Oh, you know I've upped my ante these days," Gavin says, glancing at me. He pulls out his own bottle from his messenger bag and quickly pours us new glasses. "Try this.

It's young—Barossa Valley Raz, '13—but destined to be a classic."

Johnny sniffs and quickly swills it back. Then, lingering to let the aromas hit his palate, looks me up and down. "Not bad, Gav. You're doing better than I thought."

Gavin just gives a naughty look in return.

I take sips of both. "I think I like Johnny's better. It's more polished and refined."

"Don't fool yourself, love," jokes Gavin. "It's all marketing. Beyond that slick exterior, lies vulnerable and tempestuous little grapes that can turn." Johnny smirks. "Shiraz are more upfront grapes. What you see is what you get. That's something I value."

"Oh, what the fuck do you know? Liz, here's a man who's afraid of showing his vulnerability."

"Fuckin' bloody pretty boy chef," teases Gavin.

"Fuckin' Aussie wanker," Johnny fires back.

"Hey, hey now, there's room in the sandbox for both of you," I tease. They smile. While Gavin turns to chat up one of the Spotted Pig's wine buyers, Johnny continues.

"So what do you do, Liz?" he says, changing the subject.

"I'm a magazine editor."

"Nice." Johnny looks interested and impressed. Since chefs rely on good press, I can tell he's well aware of how my industry works, and that in his world at least, editors can be important people to know. "Where?"

"Paddy Cakes," I reply.

"Very cool. They just featured my buddy's new restaurant upstate on the Hudson, I think, on some family-friendly, farm-to-table roundup on foodie getaways for families. It helped get him more press."

I nod, smiling.

"So what's a beautiful magazine editor who's clearly got

her shit together doing hanging around with this wanker?" His flirtatiousness warms me up, and it's also just loud enough that Gavin seems to hear, and puts a hand on my knee.

"Oh, he's just someone I called in from a male escort service—he's cute, but bad taste in wine," I joke, and Gavin overhears, giving me a playful jab in my side.

In an hour, the tiny top-floor space is now filled with younger-looking chefs, more models and a few members of the cast of *Boardwalk Empire*. I'm getting tired, so I make a signal to Gavin that it might be time to leave. He turns and nods, and asks to stay just a minute.

"So I saw Elle the other day," a young chef quietly says to Gavin, though I'm able to overhear. "And Olivia was asking about you, too." The chef gives Gavin an unmistakably sly look, which makes Gavin squirm a bit. They could just be wine contacts, I think. We're having such a good night that I'm not going to spoil it with negative assumptions. Plus, we're not together, something I've made clear, so it shouldn't matter.

"Wanna get out of here, love?" asks Gavin finally, clapping his hands closed, then standing up, taking my hand. Gavin says his goodbyes and we make our way down the creaky darkened stairwell. Now is the moment, I tell myself. I'm ready for my first hookup since the Ryan debacle.

Once outside on the curb, he sweeps me into his arms and gives me a good, long, deep kiss, then, jolting me out of my reverie, says, "I had a great night, love. Don't worry, I'll put you in a cab."

In a blur, his arm is up and he's already hailed a cab. I get a quick peck, and then I'm somehow staring at him, a taxi window between us as he blows me a kiss. What the what?!

Twenty-Three

Saturday, I text Addison and Brie and suggest a '90s movie marathon night at my place. Addison texts back that her twenty-eight-year-old Frenchie is in town on business and has tickets for the Governers Ball on Randall's Island. Brie texts that she is heading to Doug's family's beach house in Amagansett for the weekend. I end up walking the whole Bridle Path on Saturday morning wearing the bump—it's become my new normal.

First thing Sunday morning, I have no shame in trying out Irving Farm, the new gapster coffee shop in my neighborhood in order to pen a blog post about it on *Moveable-Feast*. This time, I think about Alix's polish and conciseness in finalizing the copy rather than my typical verbal spew. I add an array of imagery to create a collage-like effect that I have to admit, makes it really pop. *This is the difference between a magazine editor and a blogger.* Moments after I set it live, Gavin's texting.

Hey, love, I know it's last-minute notice, but my brother and sister-in-law are in town. They've asked me to watch Dani and the baby for a few hours while they attend to some business. Care to help me? Something inside pulls at me.

I text him back, simply, Sure, and agree to meet at Belvedere Castle in the park. When I walk up over the hill toward the Sheep Meadow, I spot his sandy locks. He's dressed down in a faded blue V-neck T, khaki shorts, flip-flops—and he's holding the hand of a little girl wearing a handmade fairy princess dress. His back is turned, so I walk up to greet him, smacking his butt. He turns toward me, and I notice he's on the phone with someone. As he turns toward me, strapped to the front of him is a BabyBjorn.

"Lizzie! Glad you can make it!" A few beads of sweat drip down the sides of his face. Dani starts dancing on his toes and then hopping off. The baby starts shrieking wildly as he bends down to pick dandelions with Dani.

"Dandelions for the most beautiful *Dani*lion," he says, offering his niece a flower, lighting her up as he tries to calm the fussy baby. He looks different than I've ever seen him. Vulnerable. And nervous. Instantly, an instinct kicks in, and I begin taking charge.

"Dani, want to play follow the leader with me? Uncle Gavin's on the phone!"

"Sure," the curly haired little blonde girl says with the cutest lisp-tinged Australian accent. She grabs my hand, and I swing her around, then start skipping around the park with her while Gavin finishes his call. Finally, he comes to meet us. We each take one of her hands as we walk up the steps to the top of the castle. It feels, well, magical.

But Gavin's phone keeps going off, distracting him. I take Dani to the lookout point in the tower by myself. Pretty soon, I can feel her already warm personality softening even further as she asks me to pick her up.

"Lizzie, you're pretty," she says, pushing a wisp off my face as we stare out at the lawn in front of us.

"Thank you, Dani. You are, too."

"I know," she says, cutely, brushing her curls off my face. "Uncle Gavo tells me that I'm the prettiest of all his girls." I wince. Then Dani changes gears, calling for Gavin to come over. "I want ife cream!" Gavin clicks the phone shut and walks over to us now.

"It's eleven thirty in the morning, Dani. You can't have ife cream."

"I want ife cream"

"Me, too!" I say, siding with Dani.

"Do you really need ice cream, Lizzie, come on."

"Gavin, it's a thing," I reason. "All girls need ice cream on hot summer days."

"Yeah, Uncle Gavo, all girls need ice cream. It's a fing!" Dani nods in agreement.

"Okay, I'm just going to make one more call. Hold on." Gavin walks toward the stairs until he's out of eyesight.

"My uncle Gavin talks to girls a lot."

"He does?"

"Yes, but you're my favorite."

"Oh, why's that?"

"Because you like the same stuff I do. Like ife cream."

"How long has Uncle Gavo been talking to girls?"

Dani looks confused as she's thinking about it, then seems to lose focus as a golden Lab bounds up the stairs. "I don't know, doggie!"

"All right, my beauties, ready to go?" says Gavin, returning.

We walk down the steps toward the Belgian waffle food truck, and Gavin generously treats us to one waffle sundae each, and both Dani and I manage to get it all over our noses.

Afterward, the three of us walk toward the Bridle Path. From the look in Dani's eyes, she's clearly enamored with her uncle. As I see how he treats her—like a princess—I begin to think about possibilities, too. It's as if he's had practice at this. But how could that be? To my knowledge he's been traveling the world his whole adult life, hopping from port to port.

We find a patch in the grass near the rocky crag near Eighty-First Street, and Dani pulls a few books from the diaper bag, including *The Giving Tree*. We sit, me on one side, Dani in the middle, Gavin and the baby on the other, as he's actually feeding the baby with a bottle of breast milk.

I page through—about the boy swinging from her branches, and sleeping in her shade, and then over time cutting down her trunk and sailing away, then finally coming back. And all the while, the tree was happy. Dani looks on, rapt.

By the end of the story, wetness fills the corner of my eyes, and Gavin can tell.

"I don't get it. Why would he cut down the tree if he loved her?" Dani asks me, worried.

"It's about a mother's love," I tell her. "Moms do anything for their kids," I tell her solemnly. She still seems a bit worried.

"And they tickle them! Here…" I tickle her side. "And here!" I tickle her foot. I look at Gavin, and there's a softening. He gives me a half smile. Then, clears his throat. Dani's waving away the tiredness in her eyes already.

"Two o'clock, girls, time to get back."

"Noooooo, not yet, Uncle Gavo!"

"You, my little princess, need to get back home into bed for your beauty rest. And you my *big* princess do, too." Gavin gives me a devilish grin.

"I want to stay out with Lizzie!" cries Dani.

"Dani, you know Uncle Gavo would want nothing more

than to keep playing fairy princess with you, but we've got to get you home, honey. Maybe you can see Aunt Lizzie in the fall and come pumpkin picking with us!"

"Make a promise, Uncle Gavo."

"I promise, Dani. And good uncles don't break their promises." He winks at me, and in that moment, I feel a strange warmth. Could he be thinking about some potential future with me?

"Okay. Bye, Lizzie." She all of a sudden jams her head into my side, wrapping her arms around my legs in a tight hug. I kiss the top of her head.

"I'm just going to go drop her and the baby, Eloise, off. Will you be around later tonight? Maybe we can grab some dinner near you?"

"I can come with you, it's no problem. It's been forever since I've driven around in a car. It would be nice."

"No, that's okay," he says quickly. "I want to get in a little gym time. Come to my place around eight?"

I tell him sure, surprised, but happy to see this side of him, and later on in the evening, I walk out of the Fourteenth Street subway toward Jane Street.

When I finally arrive at his apartment, inside, it's exactly how I've pictured it. A triple-level in a townhome, with a loft bed on the second level and another downstairs. In the living room, there are book stacks as high as the ceiling, filled to the brim with hardbounds and softbounds. Leather club chairs frame the fireplace, almost as if it were some colonial expat trading post. Cardboard wine boxes are scattered everywhere. I check out some of the titles, and it's the usual traveler fare: Hemingway, Orwell, Bryson, Dalrymple, Hunter S. Thompson. The classics: *King Lear, Great Expectations, Moby Dick,* and then I smirk. There's an original softbound, heavily dog-eared, of *French Women Don't Get Fat.*

"So I'm glad you could come out today. Dani really liked you. I could tell."

"She's a cutie," I reply.

"I wanted to see you before my next business trip," says Gavin.

"Where are you heading to this time?" I question, fighting the feeling of nervous tingles in my stomach.

"This week we're jetting off to San Sebastian, in Spain, to check out a potential new winery source. Their wines are young and rustic, but show potential. I'll be back at the end of the week, though."

He leans across the table to give me a peck on the lips.

"Don't you like the older, mature wines, too?" I tease.

"Nah, they're overrated. Too expensive and high-maintenance. You've got to store 'em at just the right temperature, and looking for the perfect buyer's a pain."

"But older wines have a depth you just can't find in the young ones," I say, holding on.

"Eh, I'll take the young ones for now," he says, not even looking me in the eye.

I get up and push the chair in so forcefully it screeches across the floor. He notices my standoffishness.

"C'mon, love. What's the matter?"

"Oh, just work stuff," I say.

"Well, can I take your mind off it with another glass? There's a French spot on Perry that has my bottles. They've got those old, stuffy wines you like so much," he teases.

"Okay fine," I acquiesce, and we head over to the restaurant. Once we're seated, I mention my upcoming press trip to Newport. "I'm really excited to check out the surrounding towns…maybe seek out some clam stands to recommend," I say, taking a sip of my wine, as he gulps down the last of his.

"They're putting me up for free. I'm hoping this can lead to more travel assignments," I tell him.

"That's superb, love. I keep meaning to check out your blog."

"You should. It's pretty good stuff," I tell him cheekily.

"I bet it is," he tells me.

After another hour, our conversation shifts. His eyes seem to lower and are more open. And there's a focus there that I haven't seen yet. "You were great with Dani, today. Thanks."

"Of course. I had fun. She's a great little girl."

He acknowledges it. "So, Liz, I have to ask you something I've been wondering for a bit," he says. "Are you dating anyone else right now?"

"No, not currently," I say with apprehension. "Why?"

He looks strangely serious. "Well, er, I just like you, that's all. I have for a while. And want to make sure I'm prepared if I have to beat out any of the competition."

"Really?" As I ask, my stomach clenches. I'm not sure what the feeling means.

"Why not? I like you. You're sexy. And you don't take any of my shit, which I *really* like."

"I thought this was just for fun," I say demurely.

"Well, I'm not proposing marriage this second."

"Right. That's what I thought. Come on, I know it's not anything serious with you." I sit back in my chair.

"What if it is?" He reaches for my hand and pulls me in toward him, giving me a small kiss. I honestly am not expecting any of this.

"Well, you don't have to worry about that. I'm not really dating anyone right now. I'm too busy with work." A brief thought of Ryan passes through my mind, but I've realized he's not really part of the picture anymore.

"That's good," he says, and starts kissing me softly.

"So how do you feel about me? Any red flags?"

I think about this question for a second. While it has been fun hanging out with Gavin, I'm not expecting this at all. Not right now. Not with meternity looming. Still, what I saw today opened my eyes to a whole other side of him. Maybe I can let it go. Just a bit more. He's not proposing marriage, and I'm not accepting. "Well," I say, "purple Amexes aside, no red flags. *Yet.*"

"Good. I don't see any red flags, either."

He leans in and kisses me more deeply. "You're so sexy," he says, looking at my eyes, and then my nose, and then my lips. "Your lips are so juicy. I want to bite you."

We kiss, and for once, I get a sense of his vulnerability that he usually keeps so hidden. His eyes soften as he pulls away to look at me. His eyes seem different—open, as if he's really looking at me for once. "Maybe you'll be the girl who makes me give up my vagabond lifestyle."

I say nothing, trying to make sense of my feelings. But it's hard—hearing that he's placing me in his future hits a place I'd disconnected from entirely.

He touches my arm and brings his head toward mine.

"Good. Now that's settled. I've been invited to another *Top Chef* castoff's new restaurant project in Williamsburg. Wanna come with me? It's next weekend. You know, as my date? You can meet all my importer friends." He grins. I tell him sure, and we walk back to his apartment.

Once inside, he lifts me up and brings me over to his bed, where we continue to make out for quite a while. Gavin playfully pins my arms down, and then stares into my eyes. I feel him growing hard against me underneath his jeans. We start rocking together, slowly, and I'm amazed to find how connected we feel. He stops for an instant, and nuzzles into my neck. "Liz, I want you," he whispers.

· At once I feel a spectacular mix of emotions: lust, my heart opening, a tinge of sadness and then a swoop of fear. Adding a sincere love interest to the mix now is not what I need.

"Come on, Liz. Don't you want *me*?" I feel a sweetness in the way he says it. A vulnerability. Like it *matters* if I say yes. I nod back demurely. A second later, he grabs the top of my ankles in one hand, throws my legs over his shoulders and I feel him pushing into me over our clothes slowly again and again, which sends little fiery pulsing throughout my whole body. He moves his head down toward my waist and begins to unbutton my jeans. "You mean a lot to me, Liz. I just want to feel close to you."

"Are you, um, safe?"

"Tested last month. And I haven't been with anyone else since." He looks me directly in the eyes. "I wouldn't lie about that."

He moves his hand down and begins rubbing over my thong, finally sending me out of my head and in my body. Before I realize it, he's thrown off my shirt and jeans, moved my panties down and slipped inside of me a few times, and then I find a condom for him to put on. Considering I've been on birth control since I was sixteen because of an overly heavy period, I decide not to let it worry me.

For the next moments, he builds momentum on top, then repositions me so I'm on top of him, leaning back on his knees. He takes hold of my hips, guiding them as we keep rocking together back and forth. Though his moves feel honed to perfection, I also feel like we're also instinctively in tune, which finally makes me lose self-consciousness. "I've been waiting for this moment ever since I laid eyes on you that night at the pub," says Gavin, now going with my lead as I start swirling my hips around his, trying to find what feels good for me. He tells me to take my top off, then pulls off my bra, playing softly with my swelling breasts.

"Your body is amazing. You're such a…a woman."

With that, he grows super, super hard inside me, and after rocking for a while, all the sensation makes me orgasm so hard I can feel the aftershocks throughout my body for over a minute. In the moments after, he wraps his arms around me, and I feel a tension in his biceps, as if he's subconsciously protecting me. Half-asleep, he whispers something I'm not expecting to hear into my ear.

"You were really great with Dani today."

"Thanks. She's a great little girl."

Then, "Do you want to be a mum?" It's almost an after-thought.

Feeling completely open, I admit that, yes, I do. Very much. He pulls me around toward him to face him. "Can I tell you my little secret? You seem like a girl who can keep a secret."

Oh, God. Another secret.

He pulls his arms away from me to his sides.

"I have a child. Sam. He's seventeen as of October 20." His eyes hold a look of trepidation and bullishness, almost daring me to say what I think. I stay silent, letting him continue. He tells me it was an accident. When he was twenty-two. With a waitress at his family's vineyard. She was thirty-two, he says, and wanted to get herself knocked up most likely because she was struggling. His family made him give her parental rights, and they set up a trust fund. Gavin's seen his son a couple of times since, but hasn't formed any kind of bond. I ask him if he wants to. "I have a feeling he's better off without me at this point. Nope. My job is to send him money to make sure he's okay."

"But you have to have a relationship with him. I'm sure he'd rather know you than just receive a check every year."

"Lizzie, there are some things in life that don't work out as we'd hoped. You just have to live with it. When you're a parent, you'll understand," he says, almost drifting off. "Good-looking kid, though. His mother's Indonesian."

Gavin has a son? Born on Lucie Rose's birthday? I roll away from him, eyes wide-open, twisting the sheets along with me as I hear Gavin start to snore. A new sadness opens in me that I've never before felt. I may be stuck in a lie, but all of a sudden, I feel naive. The complexities of this world run deeper and more intertwined than I've ever before realized. But at the same time, I've never felt more alive.

Twenty-Four

The next morning I stir a bit, grabbing my phone to check the time—which causes him to wake. With the light of day flooding in through the curtains, Gavin immediately untangles himself from me. Before I've realized what's happened, he pops into the shower, calling out "Morning, love" behind him, the signs of his honest revelations erased with the daylight.

Once out of the shower, I take a gander at his toned, hairless chest. His six-pack is perfect.

"So, uh, I'm off to San Sebastian tonight, but I'm back Thursday. Dinner then?" He pulls some juice out of the fridge, takes a hefty swig and checks briefly to see if I want any, then claps his hands together and closes his eyes. He then takes a long centering breath and places his hands in a prayer stance, then into a karate chop. "What a great night last night, huh? I'm going to downward dog the *fuck* out of this class."

"Class?"

"I've got power yoga at nine. But feel free to stay here as long as you need, love. I've got an Amazon hookup on the TV so you can watch those British reality shows I know you like." He pulls on his shirt, grabs his keys and takes off, bang-ing the door loudly as he closes it without saying goodbye. I'm dumbfounded. I pull the covers back over my head and a rush of feeling comes haunting me. What am I doing? I'm not even supposed to like this guy!

I notice a framed photo in the corner of him with a little half-Asian boy of about six. And next to it: gratitude journal. I throw my pillow at it.

Emergency Text Summit, re: emotionally f****d status. Review/Insights.

Addison: WeWork Battery Park Plaza
The whole thing doesn't sound promising, but some guys are weird—you never know. His always going away for business makes it hard.

Brie: PowerCycle, Noho
Go for it, Liz. What do you have to lose? After what he told you at the restaurant, it sounds like he's turned a corner by revealing his intentions.

Liz: 86th and Columbus
But what about him leaving in the morning?

Brie: You aren't exactly Miss Open-and-Available yourself. Maybe he's picking up on the vibes that you can't really devote yourself to a relationship right now. Doug says Gavin's like a thoroughbred horse that spooks easily with any kind of controlling behavior. He's a good guy, but just has a bit of a hair trigger. [Horse emoji. Gun emoji.]

Liz: Maybe you're right. So, has the Frenchie guy Jacques been around lately? [French flag emoji.]

Addison: We went out twice after that first Saturday, and again yesterday. You know, I didn't think he was a real prospect, but I'm kinda really liking him a lot. He doesn't seem to be intimidated by my career—he says he loves that about me. I think it's his European mindset. Plus, honestly, guys, he's so, so amazing in bed. He's going to be my date to the VMAs on Thursday—but I mean, should I really be considering him as a prospect? He's only 28!

Liz: I think you're right about the European thing…don't rule things out.

Addison: I guess the age thing does weird me out a bit. I mean, you know how old my dad's new girlfriend is? 26. Yep. Creepy.

Brie: I don't know, hon, get it while the getting's good. Doug and I have been having a bit of miscommunication issues in the past few weeks. Nothing serious, but sometimes he'll get cranky when he's stressed about work and then our night's basically shot. And he always used to text me a million times a night. Now, he sometimes waits until the next morning if he's out with the guys.

Liz: That's not such a big deal.

Brie: That's always what happens when guys get comfortable. There's a little pull-back phase.

Addison: Listen, don't worry. Just go get some protein and caffeine and you'll be fine.

Brie: Urban Organic Juice Bar
Addison's right. Don't worry, it'll all be fine.

Liz: Momofuku Milk Bar.
I KNOOOOOWW.

There's another text interrupting our chat: Hey Miss Old Vines, want to meet me for dinner as soon as I'm back? I have a surprise for you. It's Gavin.

Liz: He has a surprise for me.

Brie: Ooh. You're on Lock Down, Liz.

Additon: Yep, it's the define the relationship moment!

Brie: Good luck!

Me: Ahhhhhh

Brie: You know what comes next... PH!!!

But do I want to be?

My newfound "locked down" relationship has me in such a daze that on Thursday morning, I barely freak out when I see a note from Cynthia asking me to come in to talk immediately. In her office, the air feels less chilly than usual. A big arrangement of purple and white lilies graces her desk, and with it a note apparently from our publisher. She eyes me checking out the card.

"July was our biggest seller yet," she says evenly. "Ten percent better than last year on the newsstand. I'm sure it was because of your handling of the last-minute tiger-French mom cover story. Here's to *happy accidents.*

"There have been a bunch of last-minute projects on

which you've really burned the midnight oil," she starts. "I know it's been tough, but I see you logging the time to get the details and quotes that make these stories stand out. It's a quality I look for in all my top editors. That's what sells magazines," says Cynthia with a smile that reaches her eyes. Her warmth feels genuine.

"Liz, I wanted you to be the first to know. Once you come back, I'm giving you the promotion and title change we spoke about. You'll be handling the news features entirely. Not just writing and editing, but top-editing junior staffers, as well. It would be in addition to the front-of-book pages you've already got, but I'll make sure some of Caitlyn's time is available to support you."

"Well, sure, of course. That sounds great," I stumble over my words a bit, for fear of making a misstep. "But doesn't Alix cover news features?"

"I told you, I've been rethinking things a bit around here." Her smile morphs into a conspiratorial grin. "She's a bit preoccupied at the moment," she says slowly. "I'd rather you take some of it off of her plate—officially. She'll now be working from home a day or two a week, so I think it's best if she handles some of the beauty and fashion features that don't need last-minute attention."

Wow. This is a huge political land mine. Alix is out and I am in. She has just gone from being one of Cynthia's right-hand editors to joining the women on staff with a "special deal."

Alix, for all her Hamptons and socialite references, has never ceded power. I respect that about her. So I'm afraid.

"Thank you. I appreciate your confidence in my abilities," I say to Cynthia.

"Right, keep up the good work." Cynthia's lips curl one millimeter, so I hop up and out of her office.

Just as I'm settling into my cubicle seat, Alix appears out

of nowhere, carrying her purse, along with another tote bag filled to the brim with products. She sets the bag down.

"Heard about your promotion. Congrats," she says stiffly. "You know, I was the one who suggested you get the job."

"Really?" I say.

"Those features are the toughest to report, and I knew your section was way too easy for anyone to spend more than a few days per month on, so I thought I'd hand it off to you."

"Thanks," I offer.

"You can thank me by not screwing it up," Alix says.

She picks up the enormous bag of products and storms off. I'm not quite sure what to make of all this.

Que pasa? Write Jules over Gmail.

Well, let's just say I can now afford Lucie Rose's day care, I say, recounting my conversation with Cynthia.

I'm expecting a "let's go to happy hour to celebrate," but instead, Jules just emails back a halfhearted ha. I take it as a sign to get back to work. Now that I'm becoming Cynthia's right hand, I need to get serious.

I hammer into the writing of innovations. While knee-deep in my story, my phone buzzes on my desk. It's a text from Gavin. Can't wait to see you tonight—I've got big news.

When I arrive, he's already sitting at the bar of The Waverly Inn (damn, I love his restaurant hookups) looking *dashing*. Even if that word is slightly outdated, it fits him, with his deep navy suit and white collared shirt unbuttoned. I bound down the stairs toward the front bar. The crowd is hopping in the dimly lit space. The dark painted walls are lined with various pieces of artwork, as are the rounded banquettes, filled with New York City's cultural elite.

"Hey, there," he says, as I make my way around a twentysomething girl squad by the front. He flashes me a sexy look for a split second, but then stiffens. "What's that?"

My eyes widen in horror. I was so shaken by the turn of events with Cynthia that I'd completely forgotten to take out the bump.

I panic, trying to muster any kind of excuse I can. "Oh, ha, yeah, we were doing an experiential piece today, and they wanted to shoot expectant mothers in the park. At the last minute they had me fill in, and test out the new line of belly bands—yep, they're comfy all right. But, yep, looking at my watch, it's been twelve hours, so I'm allowed to take it off now. Phew. Ha." I laugh nervously.

"Fine by me, *Mummy*." He gives a sudden eyebrow raise.

"Maybe it's this bump, but I'm starving." I finger the zipper on the side of my dress.

"Well, we've got the five-course prix fixe menu ready upstairs—I had them put the order in already because you were late."

"Sorry about that—I was caught up talking to my ed—"

"No worries." His expression's flat. "Just try not to do it again. What do you want to drink? Champers?"

I decide to keep my wits about me tonight... I'm just not feeling the booze as much these days. "Oh, just water for me, if that's okay." He turns up his nose at first, but then accepts my answer and I excuse myself to run to the bathroom to remove "the evidence." When I return, he's typing something into his phone. He stands to greet me. "After you, m'lady," he says, guiding me toward the back room.

At the table, Gavin keeps typing away. "Sorry, business."

"No worries," I say. "So what's the big news? Actually, I have some pretty big career news, too..."

"One second, love. Okay?" He continues typing, which is starting to irritate me, but before I can launch in, the waiter's come to take our drink orders and we move on to discussing the nutritional value and weather of the soil in Tuscany, which actually I find pretty interesting. It seems Gavin's glad to have found someone who actually does, too.

We get sidetracked into two hours of wonderfully flirty conversation, and I feel myself wondering—could he be serious about a future with me? Is it just that he had an anticommitment hair trigger and I've somehow inadvertently deactivated it?

As I'm going in for the last bite of sticky toffee pudding off of Gavin's plate, he gives me a soft smile. I decide to ask him about his plans for the fall.

The response isn't what I'm expecting.

"Ah, love, this is the big news I've been meaning to tell you about. I've been promoted to the lead distributor for our Europe territories. It means I'll be away again a few times on business in the fall, longish trips, actually—harvest season. I'll be back in town a few times, but not for very long. Isn't that wild? Have you made any travel plans besides Newport for the fall yet?" he says, genuinely interested but not seeming to realize that news of our impending hiatus is affecting me way more than him.

My throat feels like it's closing. All of a sudden my water glass is very heavy in my hand, so I rest it on the table. This wasn't lockdown. This was another romantic-comedy side plot I totally forgot about: "girl in every port."

"I should be back for Columbus Day," he continues. "Maybe we can take a trip to the North Fork for a long weekend. Would you like that? Think you can get vacation?" *Hmm, that's Lucie Rose's supposed due date*, I think to myself.

"Sure. I haven't taken a real vacation besides Newport for more than a year now, so they should let me." I start stuffing a spoonful of the cloying pudding into my mouth. "But what about pumpkin picking with Dani?"

Gavin looks away from me. "Not sure now. I'm sorry, love. I'm sure we'll figure out something."

I just sit there, not saying a word. Gavin senses the pause and starts again.

"Good, then we're settled. Until then, I'll set up Skype and we can have regular dates—topless of course," he says with a smirk.

"Mmm, very funny," I say, on the defensive for any more disappointing news.

"Maybe this will cheer you up," says Gavin, reaching under the table for something. "On my way through duty free in Paris, I picked up something that I thought you might like." I squinch my nose. Gavin pulls out a blood-orange-colored shopping bag.

He holds it out, logo not turned up. "Can you guess what it is?"

I know exactly what it is…a bag from Hermès. They fill up Alix's office regularly. That could mean hundreds of dollars. I don't dare guess.

"Go ahead, open it."

Inside is a square box, gleaming in gunmetal, covered with the characteristic equestrian print. I carefully open it. Out slides a white scarf, covered in a beautiful purple print of some sort. It's a slightly bohemian illustration, and on it is the classic Hermès logo, along with *Trésors Recouverts*. Rediscovered treasure.

"I thought you should own one if you should ever get to Paris," says Gavin, grinning.

The gesture is incredibly sweet. These cost hundreds of dollars. I've seen Alix sporting them under cardigans. Still, though, the scarf is beautiful, but it feels mature for my taste.

"I love it, Gavin. Thank you," I say simply.

"I also must admit I thought of you wearing it during our Skype sessions—with nothing else," he says with a dirty grin.

We continue our conversation, and a piece of me settles into the realization... Gavin isn't going to be The One. Not nearly. I get up to use the restroom, and while waiting for the loo, check my texts, of which there seem to be dozens.

There's one timed 9 p.m. It's from Brie: Doug told me he thinks I'm The One!

I text back: What!? in disbelief. I knew she'd been going out with Doug for a little more than a month now, but I didn't realize it'd become that serious. I start dialing immediately, and when she picks up, Brie launches straight in without even saying hello.

"So remember when we were going out that last time, and I told you he'd said he wanted to take me to his brother's engagement party?"

"Uh-huh!" I say enthusiastically, though it's only a vague memory.

"Well, that was last night and everything was going so great. He introduced me to everyone—his parents included—as his girlfriend! And then we went back to his place, and he looked at me and said, 'I love you, Brie. I see a future with you!' And I said it right back! I didn't even hesitate! It's amazing!"

"Oh, Brie. I'm so happy for you," I gush. And I am. I feel like a freak who will never find love *and* I'm so happy for her I could burst.

"I've got to go—we're about to go into the movie theater." She hangs up.

I text Addison next, unsure what to do, and she boils it down in one simple question, as per usual.

Addison: Does he make you feel thin or fat?

Liz: French moms don't get fat.

Addison: [Angry face emoji.] C'mon. Out with it. [Cookies, candies, pizza emojis.]

Liz: [Cookies, candies, pizza emojis.]

Addison: Then you know what to do.

When I return, he's already paid the check. "Wanna come back to my place for a bit? We can, you know, try on your scarf? See how it fits?" He casually leans over and starts kissing my neck slowly. The hairs begin to stand on end, tempting me. Maybe I'm being silly. Inventing drama in light of Brie's revelation.

"Yes, maybe. Okay," I respond. "You look a little tired. Did you get in this morning on the red-eye?"

"Uh, no, late last night, actually. I caught up with a mate in town from Dubai who was also jet-lagged. That's why I couldn't get back to you until this afternoon, Lizzie. Just a bit hungova," he says, giving me a kiss on the cheek. I decide to leave it. "So tell me about how your week was," he says, as we start walking on Waverly. It's as if he's not really listening but knows that it's the right thing to say.

"Actually, I want to talk to you about something."

"Oh, let's not get into anything too serious. Not sure I can take it tonight, Liz, just heard bad news about weather in southern Tuscany rotting half of our vineyards."

"No, it's not about work. I, er, just wanted to tell you about something that's been weighing on me lately, and see what you thought about it."

"Sure."

He seems fidgety, though, and keeps pulling out his phone every few minutes. I know he's got to answer emails on Australian time, but still, this distracted quality is really starting to irritate me.

"If you've got something you've got to do, I don't have to come back," I say, hoping he'll realize he's acting like a gnat and calm down. But just the opposite happens.

"Actually, my mate's just texting, and was hoping we'd meet up again tonight so I told him I'd try to catch him later for a drink," he says. "Everything okay, love?" he asks.

"Fine," I say coolly. His ADD quality is starting to irritate me. He pulls out his phone again, looks at it, and says, "My mate's calling me now. Do you mind if I take this?"

"Fine," I say, dumbfounded. Why in the world would he need to speak privately?

As he's walking around the corner with the phone up to his ear. I see him laugh and smile in a way that you usually don't when talking to your "mate."

I feel something in the pit of my stomach and I can't blame it on "Lucie Rose." I'm not the girl who will make him quit his vagabond lifestyle.

After about ten minutes of me standing on the street corner, he's back and all smiles until he sees my withered expression.

"I, uh, sorry," he says, looking guilty. "I have to cut the night short, love. What's your next weekend looking like? I want to see you again before I leave on my big trip," he throws in, but from his tone I can tell it's an empty invitation.

My tongue feels prickly all of a sudden. "You know, Gavin. I really like you. And I think what we've had has been fun. But in my experience, when a guy is ready for something real, he goes all in, and when he's not, well, that's what you're doing with me now." I can't stop. "I think we should be honest and let this thing go."

He looks surprised. "Whoa, Liz," he says defensively, "My business takes me away all the time. I've told you that it's hard for me to see someone frequently. I thought you were one of those girls who got it? At least for now."

"Sorry," I say. "I guess at this point I know what I want. And it's not this."

"So that's it, then?" he says quickly, glancing down at his phone that's begun to vibrate.

"Yeah, I guess. Glad to see you care."

"You know I care," he says. "I'm just not on the same speed as you."

"I'm not on any 'speed,'" I say.

"Well, I know how baby obsessed you are, especially with your job. That day with my niece, I could tell you had baby fever. I guess I'm not ready to be pressured into something serious right now because of your age."

"*My* age? You're thirty-nine!" My mouth hangs open. In the next second, I back away, looking around for any cabs, and then punching frantically in my phone for an Uber.

"Hold on now, love, why all the anger?"

"It's just that, well, I wasn't looking for a relationship, but then you brought me out with Dani, and then we hooked up, and you asked me to be exclusive, and I thought, well, you were serious."

He looks genuinely taken aback, then cagey. "Look, Lizzie, we're unconventional. We're travelers. Not people who want to be tied down. Boring, old bogans living in the suburbs..."

"I, uh..." In a way he's right—or used to be—but now, the feelings are all shifting inside of me, like loosening faults gearing up for an earthquake.

He reaches for my hand. "Are you sure you even want that for yourself right now? I mean...you do like your wine... that's not exactly motherhood material..."

I push it away, feeling like someone's just punched me in the gut. Then, a fierceness begins to form. The two sides coming together in the middle. It feels like…a sense of resolve I haven't experienced in a great while.

"Yes, I might like wine, and yes, I want a family, but I want to have a career and travel, too. My maternal longings don't have to put me into any kind of box just because your mind isn't big enough to wrap itself around a more expansive idea. And I refuse to be put in one." And with that my knight in shining Uber arrives. Paid for by me.

Back at home, I turn on the TV and surf through the channels, lingering on an old World War II documentary, the kind my dad always used to watch on Sundays on the "boob tube" in our den. As the bombers flying through the sky thunder in the background, I fall into my couch and find my now-bestie bump, slipping it on for comfort. My laptop sits next to me, open.

I've been purposely avoiding Facebook, having deactivated it after the whole Alix debacle, but I can no longer take it anymore. I quickly make sure that any pregnancy pics are still untagged, and that Ryan is still blocked from seeing my feed, then immediately check his status. As I'm scrolling through his profile, everything seems to be normal: a bunch of posts about work, the soccer league he's in, some photos of him biking upstate. Phew.

Then I spot it—a new photo album. I can't help myself as I look through what seems to be a twenty-seventh birthday in Nantucket—Kendall's—and in almost every single pic, Ryan's there, right next to her, arm wrapped around her tanned, Lilly Pulitzer halter–wearing shoulders.

I immediately slap the laptop closed. A little red alert on my phone signals an incoming text.

Addison: Guess what?! You're going to be an auntie!

Twenty-Five

PUSH! ☺ Notification! Week 33: Woo-hoo! Almost there! Your uterus is like, hello Braxton Hicks contractions. As you get closer to term, they'll get stronger and stronger—like you at Power-Cycle! Baby Smiles: 75!

The sky twinkles a sunny light blue as I make my way down to the office Monday morning, still reeling. "You've really popped, Liz," declares Alix the following Monday at work before I even have a chance to put down my "decaf" cold brew. This time, I barely acknowledge her.

In the span of twenty-four hours, virtually everything in my world has changed. Brie has found her soul mate and now Addison is going to be a mom. After seeing her text, I immediately called her back, to which she shocks me with one hundred percent total elation. "Lizzie, I can't believe it, but I'm so happy. I know it's only been a month, but it feels right," she says. "You have to meet Jacques—he's a really good guy—a man. He understands my commitment to my job and plans to move to New York so we can be together.

I know he's young, but he's nothing like the men here—he seems *evolved*."

"That's amazing," I tell her, withholding my anxiousness. If anyone can handle life as an evolved coparenting, coworking location-independent-living couple, it's Addison.

I start to focus on an edit when I see an email from Caitlyn: Everyone to the conference room immediately.

I head over with Jules, not saying a word. Could this mean layoffs? Everyone is looking around the room wondering. There are Diet Cokes and Honey Cups—but are they conciliatory?

Once everyone's taken their seats, Cynthia comes in and stands at the head of the conference room table. Everyone on staff is quiet. "I have some excellent news," she says, breaking into a cool smile. "We've just been told by the president of the company himself that we've won a Magazine Editors Association Award for general excellence in reporting!"

Everyone breathes a huge sigh of relief and starts to smile. People start grabbing Diet Cokes and Honey Cups, and relax in their seats.

"I'm also pleased to announce that we've been awarded best service feature for 'Fair-Trade Families' by our own Elizabeth."

Immediately I flush. Jules gives me a huge hug, and Cynthia beams. I can't believe it. An MEAA award is a mark of excellence. Receiving one is a career pinnacle. In the span of two seconds, I've become A-list all the way. Cynthia says nothing, but her warm, open smile conveys all I need to know. I'm not going anywhere.

In the flush of excitement, I ask Jules if she wants to come for drinks with me after work to celebrate. She says she's trying to take things low-key these days while trying. Brie is also busy, and Addison is going to dinner with Jacquès.

And then I think of Ryan. Before I know it, the cupcakes from the conference room party have made me text something that is probably *no bueno*: I have some good news. Even through a fizzy haze, I know this is a good idea for now, but a bad idea for my future. Beneath it, however, something tells me that Ryan won't mind.

A few seconds later, I get a response.

Buckley! Good 2 hear from u! What r u up 2?

I start typing back the response I've secretly been dreaming of for the past week. It would be great to see you.

Well, where you at later?

I can meet you at the Yards? The rooftop bar near the West Side Highway?

Perfect. At 7? Be there soon, Ms. Buckley. Will be good to see u!

After work, I take extra time to primp, then make my way over. As I enter the swanky loft space, I look around nervously. The brick walls are filled with various paintings from Chelsea's premier galleries. I find the elevator and ride to the top, texting Ryan that I'm going to be at the corner, overlooking the Hudson.

When he arrives, I feel it everywhere in my body. The warmth. His eyes find mine, and there's a softening.

"Hey, Liz, you look *good*!" says Ryan, coming right up and giving me a kiss on the cheek. I don't pull away. He's wearing a navy suit and sky-blue tie, not his typical jeans and statement T. Maybe it's just the August heat, but he's looking unusually hot tonight. Like a man.

Just for one quick moment I entertain the thought of what our babies might look like. He, just like me, has Irish-blue eyes and light brown hair, and his tall frame has just a hint of thirtysomething beer belly, but is mostly muscular. Strong arms. He definitely has good genes, I think, smiling to myself. He would look sooo good with a BabyBjorn strapped to the front of his chest.

"Thanks. So do you," I say, beaming through the champagne.

"What are you having?" He touches my drink.

"Another glass of this stuff, I guess," I say.

We raise our glasses and say "Cheers," glossing over the whole turn of events earlier in the spring, and catch up on work and recent life events. I find out he's recently been made head of the digital video department at Discovery. I recount my MEAA good news. He seems genuinely happy for me.

I'm feeling pleasantly drunk and after one more touch on the arm from Ryan, I'm willing to put my cards on the table.

"So I hope I didn't take you away from another happy hour out with Kendall."

He looks at me, confused.

"No. Why would you think that?"

"Isn't she your girlfriend?"

He gives me a questioning look, but doesn't say anything.

I look down, sheepishly. "I saw the pictures on Facebook."

"No," he says, mystified. "I thought I told you—she's my coworker. We've been working on a lot of projects recently—and I'm helping her transition to my old job. We've worked together forever and we're really good friends, but I think of her as a little sister."

My shoulders soften at his words, and he smiles.

All of a sudden Alanis starts playing. We both notice and Ryan shoots me a knowing smile.

We pause, listening silently to the tune for a few moments. Then, he touches my knee. "I tried reaching out to you three times, but you never called me back."

Hmm. He's right. He did. "I just thought, you know, you were one of those guys who wasn't looking for a real relationship. I was protecting myself."

"Why would you feel like you had to do that?"

"Well, you kept leaving quickly—and I thought our dates were all work-related, well except for that last one.

"And you never texted me after. I guess I thought you didn't like me," I respond.

He looks down as though he genuinely feels bad. "Well, I would have, but you're not exactly easy to read, Liz. I mean, you pushed my hand away that day at the Highline, got cold on me that night on the roof, canceled our meeting because of some random excuse about work, turned me away that night after you invited me to your apartment. I know your job is everything to you, so I didn't want to get in the way and take up too much of your time or distract you from your goals. I was playing it cool."

Huh, I guess I'd never really considered that I could have given off that impression.

"But you showed up at my apartment sloppy drunk?"

"I'm sorry Lizzie, that was totally rude of me. But hey, after I sent you that contact at six, you didn't text me back until ten. I sat in McGanns with Kendall waiting for you, trying to decipher it…and I had a few." He looks down, genuinely embarrassed. *Damn cracked iPhone!*

"I'm pretty sure I texted back, but I don't think it made it to you."

"Really," he says, his head rising. "I thought you weren't that into me."

"Really? I thought you weren't that into me."

"No, the opposite. I've always thought you're interesting, you're smart, you're funny, when you talk about your ideas, you get all cute and you're…sexy." I look down, realizing that his impression of me is ultimately how I'd like to see myself. "You've got dreams, Liz—real ones. Not like some girls who just care about copying and pasting a life off some Pinterest page."

"Board," I correct absentmindedly.

"And then you called me a player that day outside your apartment. That really hurt, Liz. Not all guys in this city are douche bags, you know. It was like nothing I'd done up until that point mattered to you and you'd already formed your opinions."

"I guess, I interpreted what you said about the potential husband stuff to mean that you weren't looking for anything serious."

"I can see how you'd think that. But no, it's just, well, a lot of girls don't see me—the whole person. To them, I'm just some guy with a job who'll take them out to expensive dinners. It could be me, or anyone. I'm looking for something real. A girl who can hang in an Irish pub, drink a rusty nail. Or two." I can't help a little grin from forming.

"Well, anyway, I moved to Brooklyn—Greenpoint—really cool neighborhood. My brother's doing really well, and got a place of his own. You should come out sometime. We've got better bars. And coffee shops where you can write."

Now I feel bad.

"I wanted to say something that night I saw you at the Mondrian, but then I saw you with that Australian dude. I thought you'd moved on and were doing well in your career so I didn't want to mess things up for you. Even though that guy seemed like a total tool."

"Trust me, Ryan, that wasn't anything."

"Really, don't lie to me, Liz, or you'll break my heart all over again."

I want to tell him the truth—I owe him that. "Look Ryan, I can see how you'd think I was flaky, but it's really not the case. I meant what I said—I really do want to travel around the world, like soon, while I still have the chance. And to that end I, well, I did something pretty bold—and stupid— several months ago…"

His face lights up, and he jumps in speaking over me, "I'm traveling all the time now, too, Liz."

"Really?"

"Yep. Now, what did you want to tell me?"

I chicken out. "I'm, uh, looking into other options for work, and thinking of going freelance in October. October 20 to be exact."

His smile brightens. "I'm going to quit my job at the end of the year and travel for six months to research the documentary before it starts filming." As much as I want to reveal my secret, I hold back. I know now exactly what I'm going to do. I'm going to quit my job on October 20 and not look back. I'll live my dream of writing and traveling the world. Ryan or no Ryan. Even if my bank account balance is zero. Negative zero. I'll make it work. Somehow.

"Hey, want to get out of here?" asks Ryan.

"Yes," I reply.

We wade through the crowd, taking the elevator down toward the street. Ryan hails a cab on the corner of Thirty-Fourth Street and Tenth, and, as we get in, I feel very adult. It's as if the cloudy haze of twentysomething confusion has all but burned away. What's there is the clear blue sky of clarity…would things have been this easy and direct had I just revealed what was in my heart long ago?

The Adele song "Hello" comes on and we find ourselves moving our heads in silence, at the very same time, which makes both of us smile.

"You never answered the question you asked me that time in McGann's. What is it you're looking for?"

He doesn't hesitate. "Easy, a big love." He falls silent. "You know, Humphrey Bogart and Ingrid Bergman–style."

"But they didn't end up on the plane together," I tease.

"Oh, if that was me, that would have *never* happened. I would have caught up with her eventually."

Riding all the way up Amsterdam, we're holding hands, catching up on the past few months. It's about midnight when we approach my apartment, and this time, I feel confident that I'm ready to be with Ryan. I've got a golden glow as he leans in to kiss me softly before we get out of the cab.

And then I see him, sitting on my stoop. *Oh, God.* It's Gavin. *He didn't go to Italy.*

When we get out of the cab, I can tell he's been drinking by the way he's kind of sprawled out, lounging on the steps leading up to my apartment building. He looks at me, then Ryan, then he starts talking.

"Oh, sorry. Did I interrupt something, Liz?"

I look over at Ryan. He looks shell-shocked.

"You certainly move fast, Liz. I guess I should have expected it." Gavin lights a cigarette. "Who's this dude?"

Ryan just gives me a look of stabbed pain. "You're serious right now, Liz?"

"Mate, time to leave," says Gavin somewhat aggressively. "We need to work some things out."

"Gavin, this isn't the time…it's over… You need to leave. Ryan, I can totally explai—"

"Liz, Doug told me about your situation," Gavin interrupts. Oh, no, could Brie have said something about my fake pregnancy? What could she have been thinking? I feel my limbs start to go numb. I have to stop him from saying anything in front of Ryan.

"Gavin, there is no situation. You have to go."

"I'm not going anywhere."

I turn to look at Ryan, inexplicably say the thing I don't want to. "Ryan, I'm so sorry. Can we get together tomorrow and I'll explain?"

Ryan looks at me, hurt in his eyes.

"Huh? Liz, why?" Ryan just looks at the Aussie, and then back at me with confusion.

I don't know how to respond, so I stand there with a pleading look.

"Liz, whatever it is, just tell me," demands Ryan. It seems like there's a hopeful look, like he'll believe what I say.

Gavin starts to get up, impatient. "Mate, like I said, get outta here." Ryan just looks at Gavin with disgust, trying to contemplate what's going on.

"Dude, hold up. Let Liz finish what she has to say."

"What are you—her rebound guy or something, mate? We've got some things to work out—I just found out that I'm going to be a father."

Ryan's eyes widen in disbelief, and for a few seconds he's completely white, taking it all in. I have no idea what Gavin is talking about.

"Is this true, Liz?"

I contemplate telling Gavin and Ryan the truth right here. A lump forms in my throat and I can't find the words, as a rush of adrenaline seems to lift me off of my feet. What would he think? My expression must seem like a look of guilt, because Ryan coldly says, "Guess you got your start traveling around the world a little bit sooner than I thought." With that, Ryan turns around, walks to the street corner and hails a cab. Before I can run after him, he's gone.

I turn around to face Gavin, seething. "What the *fuck* was that? You know I'm not pregnant."

"You're not?" Gavin looks amazed, then relieved.

"Of course not. Why would you think that?"

"I was out with Doug last night, I was asking about you and he said Brie said her best friend was pregnant..."

I let out a huge sigh. "Okay, this is going to sound completely nuts, but I have something to tell you," I say. "Let's go inside."

Once we get up to my apartment, he sits on my couch and seems to brace himself.

"First of all, Addison's the one who's pregnant. Not me."

"Oh, shit," says Gavin. His jaw drops to the floor.

"But there is something I need to get off my chest, too. You know how I always have baby books around and talk about how much I hate my job?"

"Uh-huh."

I move over to my hall closet and find all six bumps, loading them up in my arms, before slipping one over my hips and under my dress. I walk out into my living room. "I'm not pregnant. But I have been *pretending* to be."

Gavin's eyes grow wide in disbelief. "Lizzie, why on earth would you want to do that?"

Up until this point, I haven't been totally sure myself. "For a few reasons, actually." I take a deep breath, then look him in the eye. "But one being that I'm trying to prove a point—to myself really. That I've been overlooked where I work because I'm not a mom. And that pregnant women and women with kids get preferential treatment." He looks completely confused, then starts to laugh all of a sudden—hard.

"Good on ya, Liz. I didn't think you'd have it in ya, you little tart!"

The humor breaks the tension, and I can't contain myself. The next thing we know we're both laughing hysterically to the point of tears.

Once we've caught our breaths, Gavin continues, giving me a cheeky eye raise. "Go on. Explain yourself."

For the next five minutes I tell him the entire story: the day of Pippa's shower and canceling my Paris trip, Alix's affair, the cover story stand-down and finally deciding to go through with it. I tell him how differently I've been treated recently. To my total shock he seems to understand, giving me a huge kiss on my forehead.

"So you don't think I'm totally nuts?"

"Well, it's certainly bonkers. But as us Aussies say, YOLO—you only live once. Life isn't all about work, Lizzie."

"Really?" I wonder, feeling a relief that at least someone sees the nutty logic to all of this.

"Yes. And let me know if I can help—you know, with that." He winks at me, looking down at my stomach.

"I think we're better off as friends," I say, realizing that Gavin will always be a flirt if he has the chance. "Think you can handle that?"

"I do." He stiffens up a bit. "In all honesty, Lizzie, you're better off. I'm not good for any woman right now. Before I can be with someone, I've got to become the guy I want to be. Does that make sense?"

"Yep," I tell him. Finally, it does. "But why didn't you just tell me that?"

"You had all these expectations. I knew I'd just disappoint you."

"Gavin, I'm a thirtysomething single woman living in post–*Sex and the City,* Tinder-and-texting culture New York. I know how to handle disappointment."

He laughs hard. "Good on you. I guess you're right." He gives me a quick peck on my forehead. He looks again at me with his charming flirtatious look and swoops in for a kiss, but this time it's just on the cheek. "Bye, Lizzie. Good seeing you."

"Uh-huh," I say sarcastically as I open the door and push him toward it. "Bye!"

"I'll text you for drinks once I'm back in a month—with the girls?"

"Maybe. We'll see. Bye." I send him out with one more push, slamming the door shut with a loud thud.

The next morning I awake to check my phone, hoping for a reply from Ryan to my voice mails asking to explain. Nothing.

Heartbroken, I realize I'm going to be late to work. And with the late-August swamp, I know I'll be sweating all day. For a second I wonder how I will ever pull off month eight. That's why everyone must try to go for September conceptions, I realize, thinking of all of my friends from back home who'd gotten pregnant on their first tries just after Labor Day so they could be out on maternity leave for the three months of summer.

My basketball-size bump is calling. I pull on my sack dress, big space-age neoprene bump and maternity Spawn-x to smooth out all the panty lines. When doing my makeup, I add extra shine powder and lip venom to create that "glow."

But it's all for naught. My heart feels like it's ready to give in amidst the weight of the bump. Did last night really happen?

On the subway to work, I can't stop thinking about what happened with Ryan. I'm so lost in thought that I barely notice when I bump into someone very familiar just as I'm crossing the street at Twenty-Third.

"Well, hello there, miss. Long time no see." It's Seamus, the bartender from McGann's. And I'm wearing my neoprene love child. He looks down, mystified about how to respond.

"Oh, no. This—it's for a story. It's not real."

He looks strangely relieved. "You should stop by the pub.

We've started karaoke on Friday and Saturday nights. We need more ladies."

"Ha. I will," I tell him, cringing. "Thanks."

"Have a lovely day, miss. And you should think about one of those one day," he says, looking at my bump. "Suits you."

Later that morning, Jules peers intently at an article online. For as long as I've known her, she's read the big medical websites every morning and tends to forward me clips that contain potential story ideas, or just weird and ridiculous baby trends. Knowing not to bother her, I start to load my personal email, hoping for something, anything from Ryan. But instead, a different note is awaiting me. Hello from Well-Heeled Traveler. Sorry it's taken me so long to reply, but we've been on a hiring freeze for a bit. The position is now open again. Might you still be interested in the role?

Yay!

I resend my cover letter and résumé straightaway, and am shocked when I get a reply right away.

Thanks for your quick response. Your résumé looks impeccable and we loved your clips. We're a small staff, and are looking to fill the position immediately. How soon can you come in? replies the manager.

This afternoon? I write back immediately.

Perfect, see you at 3 p.m.

The afternoon comes quickly, and after spending the morning creating a book of clips, I feel more ready than ever. I walk out of the office, turn the corner to McDonald's, and make the switch into my regular clothes, then hail a taxi up to Madison in the East Forties. The managing editor said that Die Cast Publishing was on the sixth floor; as I hit the Garment District, I realize that it might be one of the smaller, less well-known companies. Halpren-Davies is one of the top five publishing companies, so this would be a bit of an adjustment. But still, writing about travel, any kind of travel, and rescuing myself from my current situation is top priority.

I get out of the taxi onto the crowded street around the corner from Grand Central Station. Small shops containing bright Indian saris fill both sides of the block. This can't be right, I think, realizing that it looks like the company is upstairs from one of these clothing shops. The dirty keypad shows Die Cast Publishing next to number six. I push the buzzer and am immediately let up.

The elevator doors part open on the sixth floor. "Hello, Liz!" booms a sweaty man in his fifties with with curly white hair as I walk off the elevator. "I'm Frank. Good to meet you," he says, leading me to his office. There's a fan in the window and it feels as though the AC isn't turned on.

"So, you heard about the position from Jules Keane, did you? We met at a conference a few years back when she was at *Parents*."

"Yes, she forwarded me the posting! Thanks for having me come in," I say with a hopeful glance as I look around the dim hallways. He guides me to his office where I take a seat.

"Yes, yes, of course. Now, let me take a look at your résumé." I hand him the freshly printed sheet.

"It looks as though you've been at *Paddy Cakes* mostly. Is that correct?"

"Yes, but I've held a variety of different positions. Look, I'll show you the stories I've worked on." I hand him my book of clips, showcasing "Fair-Trade Families." He flips through quickly.

"Very impressive!" he says with enthusiasm. "We could use someone of your talents here at *Well-Heeled Traveler*. *Paddy Cakes* is a national magazine with a very good reputation.

You realize that we don't have the same budget for photography or freelancers that they do, right?"

"Oh, not to worry," I say. "I'm looking to make a change to a smaller workplace where I can take on more responsibility. And travel has always been a passion of mine."

"Yes, well, the travel will mostly be to trade shows at conference centers around the country—Las Vegas, Atlanta, Orlando—that sort of thing," he says.

"That's, uh, perfect," I say, hiding my apprehension. He exhales, looking relieved.

"Well, Liz, usually I ask editors to take a test, but I can see from your copy that you'd be bringing a great deal of skill, talent and experience to *Well-Heeled Traveler*. I'd like to offer you the position on the spot. I'll email you an offer letter."

I'm taken aback. I had no idea things would happen this quickly. I take a look around the room. It's a little different from the glass offices and gourmet cafeteria I've been used to for the past eight years. But it would be a chance to make a fresh start, meet travel contacts in the industry and save me from my current conundrum.

"Can I take a few days to think about it?" I ask.

He looks a little uneasy. "Sure, I guess I can give you a few days. I understand it's a big decision." He hands me a few back issues. "Take a look. Think it over."

"Thanks," I say, standing up. "Good meeting you. I'll be in touch." Frank shakes my hand and leads me to the elevator where we awkwardly stand waiting without much to say. I notice old blown-up covers from the '80s on the walls. *Paddy Cakes* would never have an issue older than six months, let alone from twenty years ago. I will definitely have to check out the website before I give him my final answer.

"Call me as soon as you decide," says Frank urgently as the elevator doors close.

September

Twenty-Six

I gaze out the limo window thinking about all that's happened. When the offer letter finally came in from *Well-Heeled Traveler* on Wednesday, it turned out to be 35K. Less than I made *ten years ago*? No. To travel around the US attending conferences for the latest canvas carry-ons? No, no, no. Before I have a chance to rethink it, I send a polite response turning it down, as the concrete swiftly changes to quaint coastal houses while we make our way up I95.

We finally reach the destination and I check in. As I walk around the old mansion overlooking the bluff that has just been renovated to a modern take on stately nineteenth-century glory, complete with a brand-new sixteen-thousand-foot bilevel spa, opening to a saltwater pool overlooking the gray-blue Atlantic below, I can barely take it all in. It's breathtaking.

"Oh, sorry, miss. Ma'am. I didn't see that you are…" says a cute man dressed in a navy suit, with a blue-and-white-plaid shirt, and a cute bright orange tie, bumping—literally—right into my bump as he's doing the same. He seems to be in his early thirties, handsome with dark hair and a bit of stubble. Indian. He has an aristocratic roll to his r's.

"No worries. You didn't send me into premature labor," I say cheerily.

"Wouldn't want to do that. I'm no good at delivering babies, only researching them."

"Oh, are you a doctor?" I ask, brightening.

He looks at my unadorned ring finger and continues unfazed, taking the seat next to mine. "Yes, well, I am a fertility researcher during the week, but on the weekends, I'm a world-renowned surfer," he says, tugging open the top button of his shirt to reveal a surfer T. "Underneath this suit and tie beats the heart of Laird Hamilton."

We end up talking for almost an hour. He tells me that he's taking a quick break for the Labor Day weekend to do some surfing. I explain my assignment at *Paddy Cakes*. I keep my whole pregnancy lie going. We talk about our travels and I find out that he's launching a start-up with his friends from business school to help connect women to clinical trials, fertility being the biggest one. I smile at the irony. Then, I tell him about the surrogacy special and we discuss the need for greater regulation and transparency, protection for the surrogates and couples alike.

"That gives me an idea…" he says, his warm brown eyes now glistening. "What if we developed an app—almost like Tinder meets WhatsApp—where you could see the woman who is gestating your baby."

"Yes," I pick up, lighting up at the idea. "You can message with her, FaceTime with her—and only fully vetted programs through International Human Rights Campaign could take part?"

"Exactly."

"My boss is calling it 'Fair-Trade Families' as a dark, snarky joke, but maybe that could work."

His eyes light up as he pulls out a business card. "I don't believe we've officially introduced ourselves. I'm Ashwin. Ashwin Rajal."

A red string bracelet with a few gold beads on it catches my eye. I ask him if the symbol has any significance.

"It's called Rakhi. It was given to me from my older sister back in Delhi during a very spiritual religious holiday."

"What's that charm on it?" I say, noticing the multiple-limbed deity.

"It represents Shiva, the god of destruction—my namesake," says my new friend.

"That's a strange thing to be wearing," I say.

"Well," he says, "what comes after destruction is renewal?" He grins, then continues, "You can't start a new life without destroying the old one, can you?"

"Very true." My face reddens a bit.

As a bellhop arrives to bring him to his room, he gives me a little kiss on the cheek.

"Let me know if you want to get away from our fancy five-star digs and go get some real food."

"I will. And my name's Liz Buckley. Nice to meet you."

"Pleasure to meet you, Liz," he says, nodding.

Inside the room—an airy suite with a king-size canopy bed, flat-screen TV and shower with Jacuzzi—I see that the publicist left a note telling me she'd meet me for dinner at 8 p.m. Oddly, the room doesn't feel glamorous—it feels almost sterile—too perfect and commercial—covering up what was originally there with the same "modern luxury" as everyone else these days. Is this what I really want to do? Write about chain-style travel destinations? Is this the dream?

Setting aside a black cotton halter dress to change into, I

unpack my things into the beach-wood armoire. The halter covers my bump just perfectly, but the top shows a monstrous amount of cleavage. I dab a little perfume stolen from the beauty closet at work onto my collarbone.

I glance across the marble lobby, noticing its large crystal chandelier hanging down in the center. On the other side I spot the publicist. She's dressed cutely in a navy linen sheath dress and shoulder-length, bone-straight blond hair. She introduces herself as Paige, and tells me not to hesitate if there's anything she can do to make my stay more comfortable. Over dinner at the five-star Sand Dollar restaurant we chat about the hotel, then go straight to the topic of conversation that bonds every woman on the planet: men.

Paige is twenty-six and worried that her boyfriend of three years isn't going to propose anytime soon. I tell her, in the best motherly way I can muster, "You can't wait forever... we've all got a window, you see, and if he doesn't see what he has, then he's not good enough for you." She shakes her head in relief and resolve. And I mean it.

The next morning is filled with a breakfast of avocado toast (omega 3s, good for the microbiome and adrenals), then some lounging by the pool (overall reduction in stress good for hormonal levels). I survey the property, taking in all the key details for my impending story.

It's amazing how much time can go by with legs dangling in the water and staring up at the sky. How different from my life at the magazine, where every second seems to be filled with two actions, one I'm taking and one I should be taking.

The next thing I know it's almost twilight again. I decide to go back to the room to shower and change, then head over to the bar for a "virgin" cocktail (really a version of Brie's healthtinis). I take my drink and sit at the pool observing everyone's comings and goings. I feel more relaxed than I have been in a while. *Bringing Up Bébé* would surely approve.

The next morning at the spa, things are a bit more anxiety-provoking. While I'm signed up to try the prenatal massage, specifically, I know that I can't without the spa director knowing what's up. In a strange tug-of-war, I have to convince them that I *don't* want a ninety-minute, head-to-toe treatment with two therapists.

"Ma'am, we have you booked for the treatment. Our spa director made it especially for *you*."

"I'm so sorry," I start, trying to come up with any reason why I can't.

"We can't change it now."

"Can I come back later, then? I know *Paddy Cakes* would appreciate the courtesy," I say, invoking the brand, sending a guilty pang through my side.

The woman at the desk looks me up and down. It's unclear which way the situation will go. Then, inspired by the seashells dotting the table, I get an idea.

"I'm so sorry. I just can't have a massage right now... I think I had a bad oyster at dinner last night." I eye the therapist nervously hoping she'll get my meaning—and let me reschedule. She confers with another therapist. Then her face brightens. "We will be able to accommodate you with a signature facial instead, which is very good for aging skin."

I thank them for the kindness, then wait my turn, until a therapist brings me to the room, where I drift off to sleep as my face and shoulders are kneaded and pulled during the spa's signature ninety-minute facial and third-eye oil treatment poured from a seashell.

Halfway through, the massage therapist says, "You are lucky. Your feet are not swollen."

"Ha-ha, yes, lucky!" I say, rubbing the bump. We make

it through. I walk back to my room and I'm completely surprised to find a message waiting for me on voice mail.

It's from Ashwin, the guy I met in the lobby. What could he possibly want with a pregnant woman? It's amazing. The bump really is like a magnet beacon of femininity—could he actually be interested in me?

"Hey there, Liz. I thought you might like to meet me and a bunch of my new friends at a *real* fish shack down the coast a bit—I'll send a car if you're up for it." I call back and leave a message saying I'll be happy to join him. He was pretty cute, actually. I spend the next few hours by the pool, followed by a long outfit selection. In the end, I decide to go with a simple brown halter dress, turquoise-and-gold sandals, and my floppy hat. Perfectly loose so that my bump doesn't appear too large.

Getting there takes about fifteen minutes on the highway. I make sure the bump is secured firmly in place as I wander onto the sandy stone pathway toward a weatherworn beach shack. The rusted multicolored beach chairs circa 1979 are a far cry from the leather beach beds I've been reclining on all day.

As I walk under the thatched roof, I look over at a bunch of younger guys sitting and laughing at a plastic table twenty yards from the shoreline. They're each holding a can of PBR, and I suddenly feel a little out of place in my floppy hat. Even my turquoise-and-gold sandals feel a little too dressy for this place.

"Liz!" shouts an accented voice from behind the open-air bar to my right. "Glad you could make it."

Ashwin hands me a lemonade, and we go join the others who are discussing, of all things, border-crossing tactics in Central America. Turns out they're photojournalists up here to cover the lobster trawlers.

"Fly to Bocas Del Toro, then take the first bus to Cartagena."

"No way, dude, I almost got knifed in the chest by some guerrillas doing that, man. You've got to fly the inter-Panama airline."

Ashwin just gives me a look like, "isn't this great?"

Is the travel writer lifestyle really what I really want? I wonder, as I notice the guys grumbling over who bought the last dime bag of pot. Waiting to wash my clothes at a local laundromat every week? Carping over who paid five dollars for the round last night because my budget of fifteen dollars a day didn't allow being generous?

Around eleven Ashwin takes me in a cab back to the hotel. As he says good-night, he surprises me with a compliment.

"I understand. The Vanderbilt's more your style. A beautiful woman like you deserves nothing but the best. Good night, fair Elizabeth."

As the attendant opens the cab door under the portico back at the Vanderbilt, I think to myself, *maybe he's right*.

Before I can even process it, I enter my chilly hotel room and notice the red light blinking again on the room's phone. Odd. But when I hear the familiar low, pinched voice on the voice mail, I realize that I'm in trouble.

"Liz, where are you! We've been trying to get ahold of you all night! We've booked Marigold Matthews for November. Tamara's finally convinced her to talk. She's flying into Providence tomorrow for the shoot—and you're doing the interview!" It's from Alix.

I immediately check in on our internal email and in the span of a few hours, I see that she has emailed me multiple times, each with details about the shoot, notes from Cynthia about what she's looking for—buzz-worthy sound bites to get us press—as well as a breakdown for tomorrow. Philip's coming in with his camera crew, and since I'm pregnant, Cynthia thought it would be a great ploy to get Marigold to reveal all her secret pre- and postpregnancy dieting tricks… and worse, who the baby daddy is.

Alix has forwarded me a note Cynthia's written her.

Don't let Liz back in the building without a quote about something scandalous and diet-related. What pills was she taking when she was feigning exhaustion? Did she get the mummy tuck? What happened? If we don't get that we're screwed. No one will pick us up.

I notice that from the email thread below, Alix has had a little bit of back-and-forth.

Tamara, our celebrity booker, has weighed in, too. What if we get her to talk about what it's like as a single mom. It's a little softer, but Liz will be the perfect one to pull it out of her.

From Cynthia: That could work, but I still want the diet tricks, too. If we don't get them, I'll pull the interview.

From Alix: I'm sure we can do it.

I call Alix, and she gives me the scoop. I'm terrified. I've never done a celeb cover story before and I'm not sure I can handle getting Marigold to reveal what exactly happened when she feigned exhaustion, and about life as a single mom. The stress of writing the story is one thing. But 50 percent of our magazine sales rely on our cover celeb: this means it's up to me to sell this month's magazine.

I pull off the bump and get into the shower to calm my nerves. The water pours over me, and as I'm looking up into the stars, I can only hear one voice in my head. *Don't screw this up, Liz.*

★ ★ ★

The next morning, I head to the buffet breakfast bar early, armed with printouts from the business center of all of Marigold's recent interviews, questions Alix has pulled together and notes from Cynthia for a cram session before Philip gets here at eleven. No amount of strong New England coffee is helping. The whole morning, I can barely see straight. I'm not only figuring out what to ask, but I also have to pretend what it's like to be in my last trimester and make it seem real to a person who's just had a baby herself. What if she finds out? What if Philip does?

Finally, Philip arrives, two hours late because of train delays. Then, in what seems like an hour, Marigold's *Crime Theory* publicist shows up at the main restaurant area telling us she's ready to be shot and interviewed in her private cottage directly overlooking the ocean. We truck over and even though I've seen Tamara go through it a hundred times, I'm still a little starstruck when I finally see TV's biggest star.

She's eating a cheeseburger.

"Hey! How are you? I'm Marigold! Good to meet you!" says the six-foot golden blonde as she wipes a bit of ketchup from the corner of her mouth.

I'm a little shocked by the totally casual greeting. Could this be? Is she actually really nice? Her publicist seems relieved and then I sense something.

"When are you due? It can only be a couple of months now, right?" she says cheerily. *It's my bump! She wants to talk pregnancy.* Philip gives a resigned look since he's done this a hundred times and directs his assistant to start helping him set up on the beach. The publicist gives me a look that tells me to sit down. "You've got forty-five minutes, Liz. I'll be outside with the crew. Let me know if you need anything, Marigold."

Marigold just smiles and nods at the publicist as I set my tote bag full of papers and printouts next to me, nervously taking a seat at Marigold's table.

"It's way past lunchtime. You must be starving! When I was pregnant, I was always craving milk shakes, macaroni and cheese, and lemonade." Marigold passes me a menu to order something from room service. *So much for diet tricks.*

"I'm okay," I say, pushing the menu aside on the table. She looks genuinely sweet, happy and friendly. "I was hoping to ask you a few questions about life as a new mom and what it was like working while pregnant."

Marigold just nods and smiles, waiting for me to begin.

I turn on the tape recorder. "I'm going to record this."

"Yes, ha, I know," she says with a good-natured smile.

"So, are you enjoying motherhood so far?"

"Yes, very much!"

"How is Jacob doing?"

"He's doing well, but I prefer not to discuss him in too much detail. I can talk about life as a mom, but I like to keep that part of my life private." *Okay.*

"So, uh, are you breastfeeding?" *What a lame question.*

"Yes. But it wasn't easy at first. I'd get a lactation consultant if you're planning on it. Do you have a birth plan yet?"

"Uh, sort of." Nerves are getting to me now, and I decide to just come out with it. "So, did you, uh, find it difficult to lose the baby weight?"

"Actually, no. It just kind of slid right off with the breastfeeding. I didn't have to change my diet or do any special exercise." Her lips reveal a smidgen of tightness. *Right. Shit. Okay. Refocus.*

"So, you were not only shooting *Crime Theory* this past spring, but were also working on an independent film from your own production company, and in the last stages of pregnancy. What was that like?"

"Oh, you know," she says, waving at my bump like I should understand. "Not easy, but I managed." *This woman is going to give me nothing.*

What am I going to do? All of these answers are totally boring, and worst of all, I'm guessing they're completely true. I look down at my questions, trying to find anything that could lead to a sound bite, smiling as I'm biting my pen. I don't see anything. I'm screwed. All of a sudden, the papers get caught on my bump and all fall in a tumble toward the ground. As I'm awkwardly trying to pick them up with my bump blocking me, I look down at "Lucie Rose." I realize I have to do it. I have to use her. I wipe a bead of sweat from the side of my forehead.

"I'm about ready to burst right now, and I've got about two months to go. Working all day, it's so tiring. And the thought of being a single mom—I mean, it's pretty scary."

Marigold looks at me as if she's deciding what to reveal and how. *Could I have just made an inroad?*

"The father isn't going to be part of the baby's life?" She asks me carefully, with a look of understanding.

"No." This is it. I have to lie again to gain her sympathy. "We were just dating casually. When he found out, he didn't take it well and I decided it would be better for my child to only have people around who wanted to be there." Immediately a wave of extreme guilt overtakes me. I can't even look at Marigold, but then I go for it. "How did you decide to have the baby on your own?"

Now it's Marigold's turn to look a little uncomfortable. "Well, it wasn't easy, but you know, it's a lot easier with help. Do you have a good support system?"

"Yes, well, my mother…" I respond, and then I redirect

to an easier-to-answer question. "I'm really worried about how I'm going to fit everything in and not feel totally exhausted. How did you strike a balance between work life and home life?"

Marigold looks as if she's happy to answer this one. "As any woman knows, it's never easy to find a balance at work and in life. But my motto is Be Flexible. When people are too rigid about their perfect balance, setting parameters about how much they should be working each day, it's putting another set of limitations on you that can cause even more stress. I think the best thing is to go where curiosity strikes—even if it means a little bit more work on some days, resting on others," she says with a wink. Could she be referring to her "exhaustion episode"? I let her continue. "When you're passionate about something and you're living in the moment, oftentimes you're happier, and the rest falls into place. And it's my firm belief that happy moms equal happy babies."

"Totally…"

"You can't have it all if you try to do it on your own. For single moms, it's all about developing a crucial constellation of love and support. If you have that, yes, you've got a shot at having it all."

"That's exactly what I was telling my coworkers. It's all about *we*ternity."

"Yep, exactly…" She laughs.

It's the perfect quote. I smile up toward Marigold while I take notes.

"Do you want to see a picture of Jacob?"

"Yes! I'd love to." I exhale.

I'm relieved to find out I've somehow bonded with the star, and after looking at pictures for a few minutes, I finally get her to reveal something huge—why she decided to go ahead and become a single mom at age forty-one in the first place. She describes her feelings about her breakup with a popular Olympic triathlete a few years back, and how she realized her time was running out and that she didn't want to wait for the perfect man to come along. Finally, I get a great nugget that I can picture as the pull quote.

"True strength comes when you stop trying to control everything and accept that it's all happening exactly as it should."

I'm so in the moment that I find myself telling her that I felt exactly the same way. I tell her that now that my pregnancy is happening, I'm happy about it. She even reveals that the secret to losing the baby weight was going vegan. "Seitan burger," she says, nodding her head toward her plate. "Tastes totally real!" By the end of the forty-five minutes, we're chatting like old friends, and as I'm wrapping up, she tells me to put down the recorder.

"I'm going to tell you this, Liz, because you seem like a woman who can keep a secret. You know the 'exhaustion' that was being reported in the news? Well, let's just say it wasn't exactly exhaustion. It was in fact one of those times I was talking about—I needed to take some time off to relax and recharge. There are some very helpful doctors out there who know how to keep you looking your best. Let's just say hormone-therapy has come a *long* way. HGH is a *miracle*. I can give you their info, if you need it. Us 'choice' moms have to stick together." She winks.

I can't believe it. She's basically revealed that she visited a "mummy tummy clinic"—it's exactly what I needed. But it's off the record. I can't use it. Marigold winks at me, and the publicist comes in to let her know that Philip is ready.

We head outside, and my mind is abuzz. Even though I had to sell part of my soul, I just nailed the interview. Even without the last bit, I'll be totally fine. I revel in the sun while watching the shoot. Flaxen and cream-white couture caftans have been called in from Paris ateliers, and with the piles of chunky crystal quartz jewels amid the sparse, natural seascape, the effect is mesmerizing. The simplicity of the pale neutrals with the complexity of the lighting scape creates a never-been-done lunar eclipse effect that will look brilliant in the pages. Alix's visual asthetic is singular. *This is why I work at a magazine*, I think. Marigold looks amazing in her strappy silver bikini, almost like a Bond Girl, and I can see on Philip's laptop that the shots are stunning. After they've been shooting for a few hours, Marigold's publicist says, "It's a wrap." But before we leave, Philip calls me over.

"So, did we get everything we need?" I spot her. Alix is here. HERE!

"Yes, uh, I think you're going to be very happy. But you didn't have to come up—I had it all under control," I say, tittering.

"I wouldn't have, but we hadn't heard from you, and then it was too late to cancel. But that's okay, I needed a little break anyway." The moment of complicity isn't lost on me. I smile back, nervous. "So, I'll leave you two to finish up—find me at the pool bar." She starts taking off in the other direction, toward the main area.

"Liz, get in the water. We're going to take your photo now, so you can be listed in the contributing editor page," Philip says.

"Uh, no. Ha. That's okay." I giggle nervously.

"Get in the water."

"No."

"Liz, just do it," says Philip, resigned.

"NO!"

"Don't make me text Alix…"

"Fine." I edge in. "Just waist up, okay? I feel fat."

"You're glowing," Philip says with false enthusiasm as a dig. "But you're going to have to take off the caftan."

I nervously take it off. I have to do this or else he'll know. I get in the water up to my legs as Philip begins shooting, directing me to turn to the left and turn to the right.

After a few shots, I ask to check out what the photos look like, and there staring back is something I'm not expecting: Liz, completely, one hundred percent happy. I do look good. Beautiful even.

A little giddy, I return to the water and let a wave of emotion wash over me. Relief. Then freedom. I turn to face the shore head-on. "Okay, fine, Philip. Take your best shot."

Then, all of a sudden, a huge wave hits my back and knocks me over with a ferocious force. And Philip is still clicking away, capturing it all.

As I'm submerging, I feel the odd sensation of my bump filling up like a big, wet, bloated sponge. It's as if it's absorbed fifty pounds of water in the span of a second. Shit! I forgot the underside is not made of latex! I'm beneath the waves and can't get up. If I do, Philip will see it all leak out of my suit. What do I do? Philip's just standing there twenty feet away, camera in hand, looking perplexed and waiting for me to stand.

"What are you doing in there? If you're going to the bathroom, I don't want to know."

Then I get a thought. If I turn around, he won't see. I start to stand up, hoping with all my might that my trick works. But then, something really bad happens. As the water comes flooding back out down my legs, the bump starts to shrivel up like an oversize, strange, craggy raisin. I try maniacally to smooth it out, but to my horror, Philip's moved a bit to the right, and is in full view of my wringing-it-out trick, mouth agape. Luckily he's alone.

"Uh, Liz, what just happened?"

I let my shoulders unscrunch as I walk out of the water to him, and then launch into my story. He takes it all in, and then says the one thing I am scared to hear.

"Listen, Liz. I like you. I really do. You're cool. But I can't help you lie to cover this up. I'll stay silent, but if anything happens and I need to come clean about it, I'm gonna. This is too good a gig and I don't want to lose it."

I know I can't ask him to lie for me. "I understand, Philip. Do what you have to do."

He looks down, scrolling through his phone. "Alix just texted me asking me to email her the photos. I have to."

"Wait twenty minutes," I plead, in a panic, then immediately head to the ladies' room, dry out my bump under the hand dryer as best I can, then hightail it to the bar, where thankfully, Alix is already perched, drink in hand.

"Oh, there you are. How did it go? I asked Philip to send me the film." She's upending the contents of her makeshift skinny gin and tonic into her mouth.

"Yes, he's just doing an edit, then he'll send you the best."

"Oh, no need. I'll pick which one to go with," she says haughtily. "Don't worry, I won't pick anything that makes you look too fat."

"Bartender," I say, signaling, unsure what to do. "Could I please have a soda water, splash of cran."

Alix eyes me with a look of boredom. "Oh, Liz, that's hardly necessary."

"You can have one or two drinks at least when you're nearing the end of your pregnancy." There's a tone in her voice that sounds off. Like she's already had a few.

"Oh, ha, I shouldn't," I say nervously. Then, I get an idea. "Okay, maybe just one of their craft pilsners. It is pretty hot. I'm sure I'll sweat it all right out."

"Exactly," she affirms conspiratorially. "I drank pretty much all the way through with Tyler. He turned out fine." She sneers. "Though he is sort of a prissy mama's boy." She starts tapping her glass on the table. "Where is this film? Philip's usually quicker than this."

"Don't you need another G & T? I'm sure you do," I say, trying to distract her.

"Well, yes, always, but I shouldn't before we finish these selects…" She gives me a sideways glance, then eyes my re-plumped bump, then seems to make some sort of inner concession. "Oh, whatever… Bartender!" she says, motioning him over to our area of the sea-glass-tiled outdoor bar. "What in the way of special reserve Islays do you have?" *Whoa, she knows her stuff*, I think.

The bartender smiles, murmurs, "Of course, Miss Stephenson," and takes out a special key that seems to unlock a cabinet to the side of the main well. He proffers three separate crystal decanters. Alix takes one look, then says, "Oh, who cares. A finger of each."

And I have to do nothing else. Two hours later, she's slurring. Thankfully, Philip's held off. The Scotch has opened up a wellspring and pretty soon, we've bonded over all the signs, symptoms and annoyances of pregnancy…it's like, she trusts me.

"Have some. Come on. Just do it."

I pretend to take a sip to appease her. "Pretty bird. Pretty bird," she says at a wayward bird. I wave the seagull away. Now I'm feeling worried, but in the other direction. How am I going to make sure she gets back to her room? "Do you think you should slow down?"

"You'll see when you have a kid. You'll be guzzling the stuff." I start getting nervous that now I'm going to have to drag Alix to her room. "Having kids isn't all it's cracked up to be. Trust me. The iPad will be your *best* friend. Do yourself a favor and download 'Minecraft' *now*."

"Oh, I'm sure you're just kidding," I say, trying to stop this whole line of talk. "I'm excited to be a mom, actual—"

"You'll see," she interjects. "You'll be clamoring to come to work, too, after dealing with a needy, impatient, little being who only acts nice when he wants a tit. Not to mention your husband, or partner, who will have stopped caring about them entirely... Oh, sorry, Liz. I forgot. There's no partner in the picture, is there. I didn't mean to be rude about it. What was it? One-time thing? You can tell me..."

I feel like I have nothing to lose at this point, so I make up another lie that has been on my mind for a while. "Yes, Alix. It was. Well, a few-times thing. But nothing serious. I decided I couldn't not go through with it, though. Maybe I'll tell him...when the time is right." I strangely, offhandedly, think of Ryan. Alix, out of nowhere, puts a hand on my arm.

"Honestly, right before I met Trevor, I had a *situation* myself...ended in miscarriage early on, actually...but maybe I would have kept it, just like you're doing..." Alix, looks down, takes another sip. This is a different side to her. "I think it's admirable, actually...you're owning the *untidy* consequences of your actions. That's real life. Hard things happen. You've got to just live with them. Not taking the easy way out like all these candy-assed millennials." She throws a hand up in the air to underscore her point.

All of a sudden, Alix's face softens a notch. It's rare. And in that moment I actually consider liking her. "The magazine business has changed. You know, with all the perks, car service, clothing budget, et cetera. I'm making a quarter of what I used to at *Traveler's* Families offshoot." She lowers her eyes, as if to reveal something she's not sure she should.

"I knew it was unkind dumping the remainders on you

all the time, but I couldn't help it. It's been because of these last-minute ad buys. We're still working through our new strategy. Turns out people don't want salacious content as much as we thought. Research says they still want leading service features and gripping emotional essays like we used to do…comments have said 'more substance'—they can get salacious stuff online."

I look on, now understanding a greater truth. Alix has been shielding me from the dirtier side of the business— not, as I thought, just dumping work on me. She continues, looking sadder into her crystal shot glass. "These young girls on staff. They're such coddled, spoiled little brats. I want to just shout at them all the time. Stop being so ENTITLED and pull yourselves together. The world isn't set up to cater to every one of their snotty little faces, but that's what they expect now. That Caitlyn is going to amount to nothing! Nothing, you hear me! Now that you're going to be a mother, you'll understand what it's like to make hard choices for your family. You really have to grow up and accept that the world is not what you thought it was." Her faraway look tells me all I need to know. "Oh, the email from Philip finally came in!"

"Bartender! Another round, please," I call out, hoping for a miracle. Alix squints through a boozy haze. I place her drink squarely in front of her after it's poured.

"What are these? She says, looking closer. That's weird. Is there something wrong with the film? Your stomach—it looks fla—"

"Let me have a look?" I grab the phone away from Alix, pretending to look and handily delete all the dangerous ones I can find just as she's tossing back the next special reserve.

"Let me have it."

"No, I've got it."

"Liz, you're not good at this…lemme…"

"Bartender!" I call out, scared. "Oh, here's the best shot of me. Can we just go with this," I say, highlighting one of the first ones, and handing her another shot, which will hopefully blur her ability to see. She grabs the phone back, peering into the open image.

"That'll do. Not bad. We'll Photoshop that one for you. Us moms have to stick together, right?" *Ugh.*

"Yes, exactly," I say, finding one of the Scotch glasses, and emptying the contents into my mouth, drowning in the idea that now, on top of everything, Alix expects me to be her new best friend.

I head back to my room to finish both stories—Marigold and the travel feature—and send an immediate email to *Well-Heeled Traveler* asking for the job.

Twenty-Seven

PUSH! ☺ Notification! Week 34: KonMari Method-much? Get ready for some strange drives to declutter and organize as your nesting instinct starts to kick in. Baby Smiles: 65!

Tanned, but certainly not well rested, as I come home to my apartment, reality sets back in. The moment I step in something feels off to me.

Taking in a deep breath, I look around the room. The tattered tapestry from college I'm using as a tablecloth for my kitchen table doesn't look shabby chic anymore, just plain shabby. The crumbs from the morning's toast I had before I left still litter the counter and depress me, and my zebra-print duvet just feels postcollege twentysomething in a way that makes my skin crawl.

In the next few hours, I do a complete feng shui overhaul, rearranging all the furniture in my apartment. I "fold" all my sweaters facing up, align my closet so it's rising up to the right and touch each and every single item in my studio to see if it provides a spark of joy as per the most stringent acolyte of Marie Kondo. I even roll my socks up into sushi rolls and in the end, I've gotten rid of twenty-seven piles, which I proudly show off on Instagram in an almost-embarrassingly smug moment of gapsterdom. (Hoping Ryan will like it; he does not.)

As KonMari dictates, I leave the paperwork and bills to the end, only to find one from my building that I've neglected to open. With all the recent upgrades they've been making to the building, at the end of the year they'll be increasing the rent by six hundred dollars a month, to twenty-four hundred dollars! Twenty-four hundred dollars for a studio? I can never afford that! Even on my new salary. I start to sweat as panic reaches my chest. That's almost two-thirds of my take-home pay. What am I going to do? Damn you, Kondo! I've Kondo'd myself out of an apartment!

Then, I open my email only to find a note from *Well-Heeled Traveler.* Subject: Position. Thanks for reconsidering the offer, but unfortunately Well-Heeled Traveler will be closing imminently. I'm sorry, Liz, I know you were looking forward to taking the position. All the best, Frank.

Shit. I've Kondo'd myself out of a job, too.

I knock on the glass door, and Cynthia waves me in over her shoulder as she's responding to her own email.

"Hi," I say meekly.

"Hello." Moderate in tone, I think, not too terrible.

Cynthia wheels around, staring at me with a tight-lipped, eyeless smile. Then she erupts, "Very good. Very good work on the Marigold piece! Bravo!"

Phew. I guess I'm still safe for the moment.

"I asked for details about her diet, but it turned out even better than I expected. Good emotional writing, Buckley. It was almost perfect. I'm going to take one last look at the transcript before it ships to make sure we've got the juiciest stuff in there. And I never got to personally congratulate you on the 'Fair-Trade Families' piece. I never thought you'd pull it off, but you did. Impressive. That MEAA will do wonders for advertising."

"Thanks," I say tentatively, knowing a sucker punch could be right around the corner.

"So, I've spoken with Marketing, and we'd like to plan an event—a big one, timed for midfall sweeps—right before you leave for maternity leave."

"Oh," I say, brightening.

"Yes. In honor of the 'Fair-Trade Families' story coming out in the October issue. And we'd like to partner with the Discovery Channel on their show. In the end, we used the same subject, that Ohio woman Kristy Nelson, correct?"

"Yes, we did," I say. At the mention of Discovery, I feel as though someone's punching me in the stomach.

"I'll work with the publisher to give them a heads-up, but I'll be looking to you to work with PR to handle the coordination of our partnership announcement through various media. Reach out to make sure Discovery's on board."

"Will do," I say, trying to hide my apprehension.

I rush back to my desk, but Jules is nowhere to be found. I pull the fair-trade file, and stare at my contacts folder—Ryan's name is at the top. Do I contact him? Or one of his colleagues? This is certainly awkward. And if we do have the event together, he will most certainly see my bump. What am I going to do?

A few minutes later, I see a new email in my inbox with the subject "Fair-Trade Families."

But it's not from Ryan. It's from Kendall. I immediately click it open.

Dear Liz,

I just received an email from the Paddy Cakes marketing department, and read the great news—it looks as though we'll be planning an event together! Ryan's handed me the info on the piece, since he's now heading up the digital video department and isn't going to be able to help out or attend the event. Just let me know what you need, and I'll be happy to help you coordinate from this end.

Best,

Kendall Johnson

P.S. I'm really sorry about the mix-up at the Mondrian earlier this summer. We totally had you on the list. It must have been a miscommunication with the intern sending out the invites. I sincerely apologize for that.

Oof, Ryan wasn't lying.

The following Monday morning more press releases on baby gear continue to fill my inbox, prompting me to dive into story pitches for October—the month of my supposed due date. Even though I can afford to wait a few days on the pitches, something urges me to start them now. I'm able to come up with at least twenty great story ideas for the issue— "When the Helicopter Kid Crashes and Burns," "Should You Emoji with Your Preverbal Kid?" and "The Myth of the 'Warrior Birth'...5 Ex–Water Warriors Tell All."

Just then, Caitlyn breezes by, her hair in a perfect ballet bun, a clean white vest perfectly skims her black tank and black jeans, Rag and Bone booties clacking at double-time magazine editor pace—the cauldron has boiled her down, too. Millennial or not, she's made the *Devil Wears Prada* transformation we all do. I ask her to help, and she's more than happy to. "Whatever you need, Lizzie." Within an hour, she's

fleshed them all out. Looking around, I realize she's probably working twice as hard as the rest of the staff and not
sweating it for a second. Alix is wrong—Caitlyn is going to
be running this place someday.

Then I see Jeffry has emailed me: Subject: Tonight. You and
Alix will need to stay late tonight to make Cynthia's changes before it goes out the door at midnight. Sorry.

I open our copy management program to see that Cynthia has left notes throughout the file requesting last-minute
fixes to the Marigold story. They look pretty easy, except
for the last paragraph where it goes into all the details about
the cosmetic work that Marigold had done postpregnancy—
including the quote that was off-the-record. She must have
pulled it from the raw transcription.

I know *Access Hollywood* and all the gossip blogs will run it,
giving us an instant newsstand hit when it comes out, but we
need to take it out. I gear myself up for a fight, going through
my stance over and over in my head. Then I get up, smooth
out my belly once more, and walk over to Alix's office.

I can see she's reading through the file, too. She gives me
an eye roll through the glass, then nods me in.

"Have a seat. Have you read the notes yet?"

"Yes, I just did." I clear my throat. "I can make all the
fixes, but we need to cut the last paragraph and add in more
about her vegan diet. Maybe we can call Gwyneth's favorite
vegan chef for a recipe or two. We may need to get a stringer
to supply some more quotes from friends about how great
she looks now that she's gone vegan. But we can't use the
initial quote. She said it was off-the-record."

Alix gives me a dismissive look. "Leave your morals at the
door, Liz. We both know the quote's staying in."

"No. It isn't." I fold my arms across my chest.

"Liz, don't try to argue. Extra reporting will take all night.

And we both know the quote's too good to pass up. Plus, I'm not dealing with Cynthia." She heaves a huge sigh and rubs her face. I'm surprised that her tone isn't mean. It's tired.

"I'll do the reporting and tell Cynthia myself," I reply firmly.

"Liz, it's not worth…" The phone rings, and Alix checks the screen. She mouths, *It's Tyler.*

Her tone changes completely. "Hello, darling! How is your day?" Tyler must be answering because for a moment she's silent.

"Wait, Daddy's not there? Marisol is?" She seems confused. "Let me speak to her, then. I'll say good-night. Okay, darling?

"Claudia, what happened? Trevor's still not home? Did he tell you when he would be?" Her lips tighten. "Fine. Tell him I'll be home in an hour." Then Tyler must be back on. "I know, darling, Mommy misses you, too—so much. We'll go to the Children's Museum this weekend. Yes, I promise. Bye, darling, see you tomorrow. I know, darling, Mommy's sorry. I love you very much, too. Bye."

Alix perches the phone in its receiver. "Look, I don't really care what happens, Liz. Cut it if you want. Just make sure to tell Cynthia. I can stay for an hour to help you, but then I'm going home."

I nod silently and go back to my desk to call a stringer out in LA to get more details from Marigold's former costar about how great Marigold's looking these days. She even lets slide that she's happy to see her with a new beau, a Hollywood agent a few years older than she is, which is just as good of an exclusive as the tummy tuck.

Looking quickly into Alix's office once more, I wonder whether she's told her husband about Jeffry. I email Cynthia about the changes, remind her that the original quote was off-the-record, and that we can't run it at the risk of being sued. To my total shock, I receive an email back exactly four minutes later. Fine. Sounds good is all it says.

The next day around lunchtime, I notice Alix gathering her trench coat and bag. She comes over to my desk, her eyes wide with excitement.

"I have a press luncheon today for La Mer 'Les Stretch.' It's their new line for pregnancy-related stretch marks and you're coming with me!"

"I, uh, really should finish up my December story lineups."

"No buts, Liz. This stuff is not even available in the States until next summer and it's selling for three hundred dollars a tube on eBay. You can't pass up a free goody bag full of it. Especially if you're going to do the nude shoot next Monday."

"What nude shoot?"

"Cynthia didn't mention it yet? We're rounding up the top ten '90s mom trends and thought it would be cute to have you pose like Demi Moore on the cover of *Vanity Fair.*"

"What! No one told me that?" I gulp.

"No excuses. You're doing it and that's it. Your arms and legs are perfection. I can't see why you'd have any issue going in the buff. You should be proud of your body. Don't be such a shrinking violet."

"I'd rather not."

"Okay, well, we certainly can't *force* you…we'll talk about it more later this afternoon. It's not like we won't use Photoshop of course…"

She leads me downstairs to the car and in fifteen minutes we're downtown at Cafe Cluny for the private luncheon. As we walk into the restaurant I notice Claire Rodgers, a PR contact I've seen around for years, but for some reason can't place where I know her from originally.

"Liz! How are you!" She walks over toward me and Alix, eyes widening. Before I realize what's happening, her eyes are focused on my bump.

"Wow! I didn't realize you were married and pregnant! Congratulations." She beams, giving me a big hug.

I get an uncomfortable feeling, realizing I'm going to have to lie yet again. "Actually, well, not really the married part." I give an awkward smile, hoping she won't pry. "But thanks."

"So you're doing the single mom thing, that's great!" Her PR training and Botox hides any anxiousness at the thought. "And good for you for wanting to try to keep up the travel writing when you're going to be a mom! I got the questions you sent me about new resort openings in the Caribbean, but I'm so sorry I haven't had time to respond. They just moved me over to a major beauty account. But I read your travel blog—loved your stuff about Newport! Let me pass you on to my friend Linda who's handling our Caribbean destinations right now."

Alix looks confused, but says nothing.

"Uh, thanks, that would be great. Good seeing you again!"

Once she leaves, Alix pulls me to the side immediately.

"Liz, what is going on? Are you freelancing on top of everything?"

"No!"

Her face changes. "Something's up. What is it?"

I look back like a deer in headlights and try to figure out what to do. Should I come clean? A bead of sweat runs down the side of my face as I hope someone will intervene and save me. But staring at Alix's perfectly made-up face, cheeks pinched tight from fillers, all the anger from the past few months pools at my temples. I've made it this far.

"Look, Liz, I can tell you're lying. Just tell me. What is

going on with you? Is the baby…not healthy? Do you know who the father is? What is it?"

I feel like I'm about to pass out. The bump, now a good fifteen pounds in front of me, feels like it's sliding down my frame from sweating so much. Could Alix be on to me? Am I going to have to quit right here on the spot? Is it over? Then I get a brain wave.

"I was waiting to tell everyone this, but well, the truth is… I'm trying to work things out with the father. I decided to tell him, and now he wants to be a part of the baby's life."

"What?" Alix looks like she's just heard a bomb go off.

"Yes, he's dragging my character through the dirt to try to arrange joint-custody…"

"I know you've wanted to keep the paternity a secret, but you can tell me. I'll understand—trust me." Her look is still incredulous. I scan the room nervously, wishing desperately that I could get out of this somehow.

"I didn't want to tell anyone on staff, because, well, I was embarrassed."

For a few quick moments, Alix is silent, trying to work out how this could possibly be, and then she continues.

"There's nothing to be embarrassed about, Liz. It's commendable to go to court to fight for this. You should have said something." Her look turns haughty. She seems to be thinking about this new piece of information and how it could directly benefit her. Then I get another idea.

"That's why I don't want to do the pregnancy nude shoot. I can't be a part of anything that could be used against me."

"I can understand that."

"Please, Alix, you can't tell anyone—not Jeffry and not Cynthia."

"Of course not," says Alix with a look of protectiveness I've never seen before. Then, she looks as if she's trying to decide whether to tell me something else, then bites her lip. "So what are we going to substitute for nude moms?"

"Well," I say, trying to think of something off the top of my head. As I look around the room at my fellow magazine editors and PR managers, all totally overworked, I see them all sipping away on the daytime Chardonnays. Thinking about my cousin in the suburbs who constantly hosts bunco games where plenty of wine is poured during the afternoon, I have an idea.

"How about secret alcoholic moms! It's totally the top trend of the decade. We do something hard-hitting about a link between the stress of motherhood and alcoholism. It could work." I gulp, thinking it's certainly been true for me.

Alix looks circumspect. "It is a good idea, actually. Realistic."

I smile with relief.

She pauses momentarily, then gives me her answer. "Fine. I'll get Cynthia's approval. Let the art department know we're going in a different direction when we're back at the office."

Phew, I think. But now what am I going to do about my "negligent daddy" lie? It's getting way too complicated for me...

When I get back to work, Jules is smiling ear to ear.

"What's up?" I ask her suspiciously.

Even though she's sitting right beside me, she texts me and tells me to look at my phone. Right there waiting is a bottle emoji and a baby's head.

"A baby?"

She nods yes. "Can you believe it?"

"That Dr. Lakshmi's *good*!" I smile. The news sends shivers down my spine, I can barely contain my happiness for Jules. "When are you due?"

"February first—you'll be back from your 'maternity

leave.' Incredible, right?" We both give one another a sad smile. Things are changing, but happily for the better.

"I'm *so* planning your shower. What do you want? A ballet pink theme or teddy bears and ducks?" I joke to break the silence.

"If you so much as have one pink tutu I will never speak to you again. You know that."

"Ha. Promise. But you know there will be cupcakes."

"Oh, *that* I'm counting on."

Looking at my October calendar staring right in front of me, it hits me that I'm acting as though I'm pregnant, too, and, in a way, I've fooled myself into thinking I'm really going on maternity leave. But the truth is, I'm no longer craving the fast-paced life of adventure I so longed for. I start to feel a crazy mix of guilt and secret longing for this life of baby making. I'm happy at *Paddy Cakes* and wish my baby were the real thing.

Jules isn't the only one moving forward. Everyone's moving forward, and even though I am in denial about it, I am, too, whether I like it or not.

Just then, I see a call from Addison.

Liz, you're never going to believe what just happened!

Did you find out the sex? Is it a girl? My heart begins to swell.

Not yet, but call me.

I immediately dial her number and she answers on the first ring.

"Liz. Halpren-Davies just bought me out. Thirty FUCK-ING million."

★ ★ ★

Addison recounts all the amazing details. This news was a total shock. This now meant she could live anywhere in the world she wanted—and that probably meant spending a great deal of time abroad closer to Jacques's family in Paris.

"Want to meet up to celebrate?" I ask, completely giddy.

"Hon, I want to sign on the dotted line before the champagne—or in my case—the mocktails—are poured. Okay if we plan for Friday night?"

As I'm walking home in the crisp September night air, I contemplate the possibilities of all of my friends' developments and try woefully to push away my own. But in light of everyone's good fortune, I can't help but wonder what I will do now as my "constellation of support" is all but moving on. *Paddy Cakes* is all I really have. Without it, I won't be able to afford my apartment on a freelance salary, and studios are going for more than that, even in Bushwick.

Alix had seemed to believe the baby daddy lie. Could I really tell people that? Could I actually pull it off? Actually go away for "labor" and come back *sans* baby, but with a bellyful of deceit? Could I keep this lie going forever and get to keep the job I've grown to love? Staring at all the families with babies in strollers, all the thoughts come flooding down like a deluge.

Suddenly my phone starts ringing.

"Lizzie, it's Mom. There's been an accident with your father. You need to come home."

Twenty-Eight

I rush back to my apartment and stuff some clothes in my bag, then hop in a cab down to the Port Authority. Unexpectedly, when I email Alix my story, she tells me not to worry, she'll handle all the details on the story as well as the Discovery event. Luckily there's a 9 p.m. bus leaving in the next five minutes, and I'm able to get on. When I'm on the bus, my mom recounts the details over the phone.

My dad was in Atlantic City again today and had finally run up too much debt. Trying to pawn his watch on one of the seedier streets, he'd been beaten up and was now in the emergency room. He'd been hurt pretty badly, but the doctors say he is going to be fine. Still, insists my mom, I need to come home to see him.

As I get off the bus, her demeanor is noticeably different from all the other times I've seen her. I kiss her on the cheek, and then get into the car to silence.

After five minutes of driving, my mom speaks. "They had me still listed as his emergency contact on his insurance card. Lizzie, I know you and your dad haven't had the best relationship, but it's important that you see him."

"But…"

"No buts, Lizzie. There is nothing more important than family."

"And what about—" I look down at my bebumped stomach.

She doesn't even acknowledge it as we drive in silence the rest of the way to the hospital. I hadn't seen my dad in almost a year…since last Christmas. I'm not sure how I am going to react. A guilty pang surfaces: maybe hitting rock bottom like this will finally make him see how low he's sunk.

"He looks pretty bad, sweetie. Be prepared," my mom says, squeezing my arm.

As I walk into the brightly lit room, the TV blaring at the back for the other patient, I spot my dad. In his hospital gown with a bandaged face, he's not the imposing, angry man I remember. He seems old, sad and pitiful.

I have no idea what to say. I walk up to the bed, the cold hospital lights illuminate him, us, our life and our problems. I can't run away this time.

For a few seconds, we say nothing. We just look at one another, an odd role reversal—me standing there above his bed, parental, him lying there like a child. I feel nothing but resentment.

"I never wanted you to see me like this, Lizzie," says my dad, looking at me, with his fat lip throbbing.

Just then, a doctor who seems to be only a little bit older than me walks in and gives me a sympathetic look. "Other than a black eye and cracked ribs, there was nothing else too serious. It looks like he'll be just fine."

"Thank you. That's good to hear," I say, pressing my lips together into a weak smile.

The doctor leaves. I turn toward my dad and from out of

nowhere I feel a surge of anger. "What were you thinking?" I say, unable to hold back.

"Lizzie, I couldn't help it. I'm sorry. I was just trying to get back on my feet...it's been hard for me...since your mother left."

"Don't you understand, Dad, how this isn't going to help you? How leaving us was the wrong thing for you to do?"

"Leaving you? I don't understand, Lizzie." His eyes register an expression of true hurt.

"You always taught me to fight, but when it came time to fight for us, you bailed," I try to explain, the words getting stuck in a ball of glue in my throat.

He stares up at me, his eyes full of sorrow.

"Lizzie, I was doing it all *for* you. Don't you understand? I wanted a better life for you. It was the only way. I had to. I thought maybe if I could regain my footing a bit, your mom might, well, consider..." He trails off.

"So you had an affair and went to Atlantic City?"

He moves his gaze down toward his hands. My mom looks at us both, stoically. It's almost as if she were hoping for this to happen.

Then I see a look of fear in his eyes—like he's worried that he might lose me forever.

"I'm sorry I let you down, Lizzie. I really am," he says.

It's all a bit much for me to take, as I feel a flood of tears welling up. "Well, I'm glad that you're going to be okay," I say, not ready to fully accept what he's saying. Then, I think of Ryan. *This is the best he can do.* I see that now. "It's going to be okay. We'll get through this. I'll call to see how you're doing."

My mom understands immediately that it's time to leave. She tells my father that she's called my uncle and that he'll be there shortly with my cousins.

My dad may or may not get better. He may stop gambling or he may not. In a moment of clarity, I realize he's made his choices, and now I have to make mine.

On the way back in the car, my mom looks really concerned.

"Sweetie, you've always taken on this family's burdens, but you have to go live your life."

"Mom, you don't—"

"I'm alive. I have boobs of a thirty-year-old. What more do I need—other than a granddaughter—"

"Mom, pull over."

"What?"

"Just pull over." There, by the side of the highway I come clean. Everything pours out of me. The first day. Missing Paris. The bumps. The compounding lies. By the end, I'm terrified to look up and see the look in my mom's eyes. But instead of anger, there's a sadness. As if she's let *me* down.

"Lizzie, we talk a lot about the victim/martyr trope in the support group. Sometimes family members can keep us stuck in the past by maintaining hypervigilance and enabling our 'sick' identities forever. Yes, cancer was the biggest fight of our lives. But we made it. I'm okay now. I'm not a victim, and neither are you. I made every single choice with open eyes and I wouldn't take back one bit of it. Your generation is always overthinking everything. Life happens, you make the best decisions you can and then make the best of it. I love my new life—and my new boobs—and so does Harold…"

Who's Harold, now? I think.

"Maybe you should consider a lift…you're going to need it after you breastfeed Lucie Rose—" She laughs.

"Mom!"

"If your job is making you so unhappy, quit. Go get on

the first plane to Paris. We only have one life. And remember, you always have a place to come home to."

That night, I'm roused by a very, very strange dream. I'm in an all-white room, and at the far end, there's a woman sitting at a white CEO-style desk, her chair turned back to me. When I reach her, I see the placard says, "Founder/CEO Fit-Baby." It's the creator of the millennial app I've been checking all these months.

Sensing I've arrived, she turns back around to face me. She's wearing a white catsuit, and her hair is cut into a sleek bob. I ask the one question I've been wondering since this all began. "What is the secret Baby Smiles algorithm? What do the numbers mean?"

She chuckles. And then louder and louder until her cackles fill the entire room. She looks me dead in the eye.

"There is no algorithm. It's all random. We're just fucking with you. You pregnant women have gotten waaaay too neurotic."

I wake up in a pool of sweat.

October

Twenty-Nine

PUSH! ☺ Notification! Week 38: Get ready to get it, girl: Braxton Hicks contractions; water breaking and the loss of the mucus plug ("the cork" that seals the opening of your uterus). And finally, for the grand finale of gross—the "bloody show," or red or pink discharge from the broken capillaries that occur during dilation…enjoy! If any of these happen, labor could be very close. Baby Smiles: 20! [Babies emojis! Bottles emojis!]

The day of the event, I reach for my phone. There's an email from Cynthia: Subject: Mothers of Discovery Event. E—Hope you're prepared to say a few remarks—C.

The event starts at 6 p.m., at our office building's event space on the fortieth floor. Because of the "Mega-Multiples" story, "Fair-Trade Families" and our partnership with Discovery Channel, the spotlight will be on me. I would have killed for this opportunity a year ago, but now, I would kill to have Alix take my place. I spend the night before lying awake in bed, paralyzed by a bitter feeling of dread.

"Might as well go out with a bang," I say to myself early the next morning as I tug on a black V-neck dress I found in the *Naomi Marx* fashion closet earlier this summer in preparation for month nine (all the while hoping I wouldn't have to use it). It looks like something Elizabeth Taylor would have worn in *Cat on a Hot Tin Roof*—its sexy plunging neckline, three-quarter-inch sleeves and pencil skirt hug my curves.

I make a conscious effort to not think about the fact that Ryan won't be there tonight, as I ride the herky-jerky train to work. I take a deep breath, thinking, how many more chances with guys who could be potential husbands will I have left? My thirty-second birthday is approaching in a little more than two months, and who will want to date someone who'd faked her own pregnancy and been thrown into jail for fraud? More important, how will I get through these next few weeks, character intact?

In the next few hours, my whole life will change. My two choices are painfully staring at me in the face: the first one is my bag, packed with travel clothes and letter of resignation; the second one the month-nine bump, along with it a complicated story and a lie I'll be forced to tell for the next how many years.

What if ten years down the road I regret not taking my chances and doing what I'd always dreamed? Are we allowed to keep some dreams and throw away the others that no longer fit? Or will those dreams come back to haunt us later on when time has run out? I make one final list.

Things I'm Grateful For

Mom
Dad
Addison
Brie
Jules
Ford

Cynthia

Alix

My job

My health

Cold Brew

The chance to write stories that matter to women

A chance to know Ryan Murphy

A chance to dream about Lucie Rose

As I trudge down the bus steps and up to the office, *March of the Penguins*–style due to the heavy medicine-ball-like orb secured firmly to my midsection, I resign myself to just getting through the long day ahead.

Morning passes like lightning, as Cynthia's out for most of it getting hair and makeup done at her apartment downtown. Even Alix leaves at about 3 p.m. for the same reason, telling me she'll see me upstairs on the fortieth floor event space at 6 p.m. sharp. "Cynthia's expecting you to say a few words," she says as she's on her way out the door.

Jules, who's on the wait list, offers to help me come up with something to say, thankfully, and I let her write it out for me. In a mix of sheer exhaustion and panic, I notice it's five forty-five. As I do, a familiar name pops into my inbox.

Free tonight for dinner? reads the subject line. It's from Gavin. He must be back in town. The message reads, Hey love, want to grab a bite tonight? And maybe a little vino afterward?

I reply back, No, but I have a better idea. Do you have a tux cleaned and pressed? I need your services for a party tonight.

Just as I have a feeling he will, he responds, Why of course. I am always happy to be your escort, Liz Buckley.

I tell him to meet me in the next half hour or so, and give him the download on what he'll need to say. At least I'll have nice arm candy. I wonder if everyone will think he's the father. Ha. I laugh bitterly to myself.

Jules comes out of the bathroom in a green silk empire-waist dress, and her own bump is just now barely detectable. She hasn't told anyone yet. She gives me a big smile and hands me the cards on which my speech is written. "You should be all set. I just did the typical, 'thank you, ladies and gentleman, it was a huge pleasure working in partnership with Discovery,' blah, blah, blah."

"You're the best," I say.

"I know," she responds, squeezing my arm. "Well, come on. Time to finish what you started."

We walk through the doors to the elevator banks and press forty. As we hit the company's top floor where all the executives sit, there's a faint din of clinking glasses and laughter. Purple and blue lights illuminate various screens around the room, which are now playing images from our story. Discovery's version of "Fair-Trade Families," which includes images of Kristy and the other women, is looping over and over on the large screens. Despite the sense of impending doom, another feeling—pride—swells up inside me. I am proud to have made this happen.

A waiter walks by carrying a tray of drinks, and I grab a glass of champagne without thinking. Jules, eyeing my bump, removes it from my hand and sets it on the bar next to us, replacing it with sparkling water. "Watch it," she says, patting my stomach.

"Oh, yeah. Old habits…" I tell her. My eyes scan the room. I know I should be concentrating on a variety of things, including what I'm going to say, how to react if anyone mentions my impending pregnancy, or even keeping an eye on the door for Gavin, but I am having a hard time focusing. All I can think of is Ryan. Is there some small chance that he'll come? It's already six thirty now, and there's no sign of him. Even though Ryan seeing my bump could set a whole chain of events in motion that I am not ready for, deep down, I am still secretly hoping to see him.

Jules goes off to find the appetizer station, and suddenly I am left alone. I decide to go to the bathroom to check my bump one last time before I'm up in front of a hundred people. In the stall, I suddenly overhear someone's voice talking on a cell phone. It's Alix.

"So that's it, then," she says with a bitter tone.

"I'll pick up Tyler tonight, and then you can get your things this weekend." There's another brief pause.

"That's—that's not what we said. But fine. I'll have my lawyer talk to yours tomorrow. You don't have to make things this difficult. I told you—I want a clean break as long as Tyler gets to stay at the house in the city and go to his school."

It seems as though Alix's finalizing the terms of a divorce. Is it really happening? Is she really going to be with Jeffry? It must be why she's been a little calmer and nicer to me these past few weeks.

I hear her punch off the phone and walk out. I come out of the stall, and do one last check in the mirror, comb my fingers through my hair, adjust my top so just the right amount of cleavage is showing and walk out.

As I saunter out of the bathroom, I see Gavin's tuxedoed back. Even with his back to me, I can still tell how dapper he's looking tonight. I grab a martini from the bar to take to him, and as I reach him, I notice he's talking to Alix.

"Well hello, Liz. I didn't realize you'd be bringing such a handsome date tonight."

Gavin smiles his signature toothy grin, the one I remember

seeing at the bar the first night I met him. "Oh, I'm just arm candy, really. Hired out. Right, Liz," he says, winking at me.

"This is Gavin… Honeycut," I say, handing him my drink. "Gavin, this is Alix Stephenson."

"Liz is so close to popping, it's smart to have me around. I can take her to the hospital if need be," says Gavin. I squint my eyes at him as if to say, "thanks for doing this," as Alix looks around.

"Liz, you should have brought the doctor to the offices before," she says, clearly noticing Gavin's attractiveness while glancing down at his ring finger.

"She knew I'd be too much of a rascal around so many beautiful women. Couldn't trust me," Gavin replies.

"I can see that," says Alix, giving me a warm smile and walking off.

"That's Alix?" asks Gavin.

"Married with kid. Though, I think she's getting a divorce," I tell him.

"Best kind—no expectations," he says under his breath, lingering in his gaze at her.

"So, you'll take me to the hospital?" I tease, breaking the tension.

"Only if you let me name the baby… Ephraim Rutherford."

"Where'd you get that one?" I say, letting out a guffaw.

Gavin looks hurt. "That's my father's name, you doozler."

"Oops!" I give him a guilty look and clasp my hand over my mouth. I feel a tap on my left shoulder.

"Hello, Liz."

It's Ryan. *God.*

I cough as he catches me midbite, and as I'm choking on my mini shiitake mushroom quiche, Cynthia walks over.

"So, Liz, you've never introduced me to your counterpart

at Discovery. Or, your handsome date," she says, smiling in Gavin's direction.

I swallow hard and try to make the best of this situation. Gavin just gives me a look as if to say, "don't ask me."

Turning around, my bump now facing Ryan, I notice he is turning bright red. Still, he says nothing.

"Cynthia, this is…" I swallow "…Dr. Honeycut, my ob-gyn." Gavin smiles widely. I can't even bear to look at Ryan. "And this is Ryan. Ryan Murphy. He's the man responsible for bringing my story to life."

"Good to meet you, Cynthia," says Ryan, shaking her hand.

"Well, what do you think? Will you continue work-ing with our Elizabeth here? She'll be out for the next few months, but I'm sure once she's back, you'll have a lot to talk about."

My face turns red. No one says anything for what seems like a minute.

"I'm sure we will. She's been a pleasure to work with so far—a total pro," he says. "If you'll excuse me, I have to go make sure everything's set with the video." He seems to in-tentionally be avoiding my gaze as he walks off.

"Well, you're up first, Elizabeth. I'll introduce you, then you'll say your remarks, and we'll play the video. Got it?"

"Ready," I peep, giving the biggest smile I can muster, though my stomach is turning. The lights dim, and Cyn-thia takes her place at the podium. The spotlight shines on her as images from the magazine are displayed on the big screen behind her.

"In the past year, we've been privileged to work with many important partners on stories that have pushed the needle in the field of motherhood. It's not only been a critical success and a commercial success, but it's been personally rewarding to be able to 'birth,' so to speak, such moving, important stories of women who've overcome great odds to fulfill personal missions. I could go on about how grateful I am to have been able to help bring them to life in the magazine, but I would like you all now to hear from one of the people most responsible for one of these important stories—'Fair-Trade Families'—Elizabeth Buckley."

The crowd titters as a light applause ripples. I somehow make my way onstage into the white heat. My fingers clench the cards, but I can feel the wetness from my hands soaking them through. The spotlight shines so brightly on my face, I can barely make out the faces. But there is one, Ryan's, directly in front of me, looking expectantly. I stand at the podium and start to read from the cards Jules has prepared.

"It's my great honor to stand before you today to share the story of this special report on the latest *safe* surrogacy options." I look at the next sentence, and I see that my sweat has obscured Jules's penmanship. *Ugh.* I lose focus for a split second, and look around for help. Jules just looks at me, eyes wide. Then I see Ryan, and I think of his words that night at McGann's, *You're just waiting for your training day to come.* Training day's here. I take a deep breath, beginning again.

"I stand before you a changed woman," I say, waving a hand at my bump. The audience laughs a little as they realize my intended meaning. "If you'd have asked me a little more than nine months ago if I'd be speaking to you all here today, like this, I can guarantee you I would have told you no chance." The audience just hangs, waiting for what comes next. "But after working on bringing the stories of these amazing women, I've learned a lot. About motherhood. But more importantly about the special kind of strength women have—the enduring kind."

I pause for a second, looking around. I see Jules's face to

the right, urging me to continue. My nose begins to twitch, but I shake it off.

"Sometimes it's hard to know exactly what you want. But then there comes a point when you do. And when that day arrives, you go after it with all your heart. Women are amazing at this—you know—when they're on a mission," I say, stumbling.

Ryan seems to be waiting for what I'm going to say next. I continue. "Nothing will stop their maternal instinct. You can't change it. You can't fight it. It's there, no matter if the circumstances surrounding you aren't ideal. Or you don't have the right paperwork, or a body that will support it, or a partner to help you," I say, looking down. "But when it's your time, you know. Your priorities shift, and all of a sudden, what you thought was so important, well, it isn't anymore. All you can see before you is the choice you know you have to fight for. And when you do, your heart becomes wider than you could ever realize." My lip starts to quiver, and I feel like if I don't leave, I will break down. "Thank you, very much, for the opportunity to tell this great story. Thank you to these women for sharing it. And thank you to Discovery Channel for helping us find it," I say. As the crowd erupts into deep applause, I look directly into Ryan's perplexed eyes, and run quickly to the bathroom to compose myself.

After about five minutes, Jules comes to find me, and hands me a tissue from her purse as I'm wiping away the mascara beneath my eyes. "Well, that wasn't what I wrote," she says, smiling.

"Nope, I went off track," I respond with a sarcastic laugh. "It was awful, right?"

"Nope. It was better than anything I could have written," she says, giving me a hug.

We walk out of the bathroom, and as Jules heads into the room I see Ryan. He looks like he's about to jet off without saying a word, but then turns and walks right up and corners me.

"Buckley, can you just level with me? First you act as though you really like me, then you dump me on the street corner, then you never call me again. Then you tell me you want to go out with me, but it turns out you're dating some douche bag—who's your ob-gyn. Can you please just level with me? What is going on? Are you pregnant? Is that dude the father or something?"

"Ryan, I've wanted to tell you the whole time," I start, wanting to tell him the truth so badly it hurts. Even though I see my colleagues not far off, I start in with my story, but it doesn't come out how I'm hoping.

"You know how women at your work will go on maternity leave for months, dropping their workload onto your pile without a care..." This isn't coming out right. Ryan just looks at me, waiting for what I have to say.

"Well, I also wanted that, some time off. A break. To figure out what I really wanted. Then, late last spring, Alix and Jeffry wouldn't let me take my vacation to Paris, which forced me..."

"Forced you to what?"

"No. Well, sort of, I mean. Somehow they assumed I was pregnant. And I didn't deny it."

He just looks at me like I'm crazy.

"So you're pretending you're pregnant? Why exactly?"

"So that I can take three months off to travel and use the time to kick-start a freelance writing career—just like I told you." I look around hoping no one else has heard. Luckily the speeches are continuing behind us.

He stares at me, dumbfounded, trying to take it all in.

"So basically you're doing exactly what you despise the other women you work with for doing, but instead of actually having a baby—something worthwhile—you're using your company's money to go on vacation?"

I stare at him, helpless.

"Buckley, I'm sorry, but that's too screwed up, even for me," he says, starting to back away.

My voice grows louder, drawing the attention of the crowd. But I don't care. "Wait, I explained it all badly—I know it sounds wrong. I mean, you know how you were talking about your dream of directing your screenplay one day? That's how I feel."

"So you lied?" he says, now trying to understand.

I pause. "I never meant to… Well, yes, I did." My head falls.

"The sad thing is that I always thought you were different—better. I guess I always looked at you as that type of girl you don't find in this city, someone real. I didn't realize you're even more screwed up than all the others." He turns toward the door. At the same moment, Cynthia, Alix and Jeffry start heading toward us.

"But I'm not. I'm telling you the truth. If you'll just let me explain. Let's go to McGann's right now…" He cuts me off.

"I wish you'd just been honest with me from the beginning, Liz. Best of luck to you and your pal, Dr. Honeycut."

Two seconds later, Gavin appears. "Wait!" I call after Ryan, running after him as he rushes off through the hallway toward the elevators. All of a sudden, a waiter comes out of the service entrance, and I smash into him. The entire platter of rosé champagne flutes comes crashing into me, sending a splash of champagne high into the air, then down all over my bump. "Noooo!" I cry out.

"I'm so sorry, miss!" says the waiter, trying to clean up the mess and dry me off with his towel, but it's too late. All the champagne has gotten inside my clothing, sending the bump slipping to the floor just as Cynthia, Alix and Jeffry arrive.

I reach down to the floor, attempting to pick up the now-soggy bump, but I realize I've been caught red-handed—as everyone stares at me, trying to make sense of it all.

"Uh, love, will you be needing me to take you to the hospital now?" attempts Gavin.

"Huh?" says Jeffry. "You're not—"

"What?" says Alix. "I *knew* something strange was going on!"

"Interesting," says Cynthia, her gray eyes narrowing with an indiscernible look.

It's over. I've lost everything.

Crestfallen and shaky, I sink over my knees in agony. Jules and Gavin attempt to help me up, but my legs are like jelly.

Only Cynthia speaks now.

"Pull yourself together, then see me in my office."

Oy. This definitely wasn't in the birth plan.

Labor

Good luck and be well on this, the greatest journey of your life: your journey towards motherhood.

—*The Pregnancy Countdown Book*

Thirty

"Come in," says Cynthia. For the first time ever, I don't attempt to read her.

I shuffle in, close the door behind me and sit down, ready to lose my job, pack up my life in New York and move home to New Jersey.

"I'm sorry," I say, the words sounding hollow, even to me.

Just then, to my complete shock, there's Alix tapping on the door.

Cynthia looks over and waves her in impatiently. "What is it?"

"Before Liz starts in on the whole thing, I wanted to make sure I was here, too."

I just stare at her, dumbfounded. Really? Does she really have to be here during my final implosion to witness it all?

"Why is that?" asks Cynthia icily.

"Well, for one, it was my idea," Alix replies firmly.

I sit there in shock, not knowing what to say.

"When Liz and I were brainstorming a while back about ways to reinvigorate the magazine and bring back a succession of articles that would really sell, I thought, why not have her go undercover, writing about what it's really like to be pregnant in the workplace?"

Cynthia is now intrigued, and I'm too shocked to say anything.

"So we decided, uh, *together*, that Liz would fake a pregnancy. We wanted to make sure no one would know—not even you, Cynthia—to see how she would be treated. Does a pregnant worker get more, or less, rights as someone in the same place who's single and without kids? The whole workplace flexibility/*Lean In* stuff is very trendy right now. It's the last battleground for women."

Wait a second. This could actually work.

"Yes, I, uh, wanted to show how women are getting unfair treatment in some ways and boosted in others," I chime in. "And I had to be the one to do it, since I was the only person on staff with the seniority, but still single and without kids." Then, I get a brainstorm, adding, "We could even do a survey of a thousand women to find out the current state of prenatal rights in the workplace."

Cynthia takes about five seconds to digest it all. The room is completely silent, and I'm scared to breathe. She looks at me, narrowing her gaze, and then at Alix. My lungs feel trapped in my chest.

"Fabulous!" she erupts. "Excellent. Genius, even. Prenatal rights! Don't know why I didn't think of it. Experiential stories are perfect for viral traffic. This will boost metrics. Have you contacted web and PR yet?"

Alix and I are speechless—she bought it!

"Well, no, we wanted to see what you thought," says Alix, brightening immediately.

"I will right now!" I say, chiming in.

We rush out, taking two seconds to let what just happened

sink in. I walk to my cube slowly, and Alix follows me back. Then, I turn to her.

"Wh—"

"Shh," she says. "Just listen. You think it's so easy, Liz, being a mom? Well, imagine if your husband was never home, and you had a screaming sick kid to take care of trying to get diagnosed, all while trying to hold down a job and maintain this perfect image of Upper East Side wife and mother."

So that's why Alix was always having to leave all the time. I'm a horrible person.

"But why didn't you say anything?"

"I was embarrassed. Trevor and I have an iron-clad prenup…so I could lose the town house. Child support was negligible, but now it's looking like Tyler may need specialists, maybe even a special school. I needed Jeffry to help me make a case. Whatever the outcome, life as a single mom is not going to be easy, especially on an editor's salary. If I could take credit for the idea of the fake pregnancy, I'd be back in Cynthia's favor. And I guess I thought, well, neither of us are so different, here. Being a working mom is not all it's cracked up to be—you don't realize how good you have it, Liz. You're free to do whatever you want, whenever you want. I have responsibilities you could never imagine."

"I don't know what to say," I respond.

"Just do a good job on the article. It'll help us both."

I sit in my cube in silence and think about what just happened. I've still got a job. But, really, I'm in no better shape than I was six months ago.

Jules and Gavin both text me to see if I'm okay. I let them know I'll call them in a bit. I consider texting Addison and Brie. Ford also texts, but with news I'm not expecting. Portland! is all it reads.

Which one? I write back.

Not sure yet, but I just gave notice! We'll find out soon! :)

I slump back in my chair. That's it, then. The MEAA award glimmers in the corner, taunting me. Then, I think of my dad. *Fight for it, Lizzie.*

I know what to do.

I first run to the bathroom with a change of clothes—jeans and a gypsy top—and change out of my wet dress. I grab my coat and bag, then take the elevator down all the way to the first-floor lobby, walking outside into the brisk October air, letting it wash over my body—uncovered—for the first time in six months. I start walking up Seventh, all the way to Forty-Ninth Street, cutting over to Eighth, where I wait patiently for the traffic light to turn to green, then bound across into the familiar place. But Ryan is nowhere to be found.

Seamus is there, though, in his usual spot, wiping down the bar.

"Where is he?" I ask simply.

"Haven't seen him, tonight, Lizzie. I'm sorry."

"You know my name?"

"Ryan's told me about you a bit." He brings his head down. Then looks around. "I shouldn't be telling ye, but he took quite a shine to you in the end."

"But why didn't he just tell me that?" Again, Seamus looks down, as if trying to decide whether to tell me something.

"Lizzie, Ryan's been through a lot."

"What do you mean?" My stomach falls. He immediately grows silent.

"Did yer man ever tell you how his father died?"

My stomach lurches. "Yes, in a terrible fire about fifteen years ago." Seamus appears to steady himself.

"He did. There," he says simply. He points to a picture of the twin blue flames lighting up the night sky in place of them. My entire body convulses. All of a sudden it all makes sense. The seriousness. Why he could possibly be single, still. His insistence that I make things up with my father. The documentary about alternative energy sources. *He's a unicorn.*

Seamus acknowledges my understanding with a look of recognition. "Stephen Murphy was a member of New York City's finest and a regular here before he moved to Philadelphia with his family when he retired. When that sorry day happened, he got in his car to be with his old ladder just like many of the retired men did—and didn't make it out. He didn't have to be here." Tears roll down my cheeks. Why didn't Ryan tell me?

"I've known Stephen my whole life. Ryan comes here, I think, in part to hear me tell stories—I'm an Irish storyteller—you know. We can go on and on. I think he comes to keep his dad's memory alive. Ryan's really been the rock for the whole family. But he has no one to lean on himself. He's had a hard time letting people become close. The way he talked about you earlier this summer, I thought maybe he might finally have found his girl. He's been holding out for the right one for a long time." I quietly tear up as he tells me.

"Seamus, I've done something incredibly stupid—"

"I know, miss. I figured when I saw you that day. Just tell him the truth. If it's meant to be, it will be."

I heave a huge sigh. I have to make this right. Then, all of a sudden, in walks Ryan. His face looks crestfallen. His eyes, puffy and swollen. Then, when he sees me, there's a hint of anger. His eyes grow dark.

"What are you doing here?"

"Ryan, I need to explain something to you."

"I think I've heard enough."

"Please." My voice strengthens. Seamus walks away, letting us be.

"Ryan," I start. "I was telling the truth before. I was pretending to be pregnant at work."

"But why?" His eyes are searching.

"I don't know. I felt trapped and claustrophobic and it felt like I had no other choice. It was stupid. But I have learned a lot along the way. I don't regret it. Most importantly that I'm never going to put aside going after what I really want. I'm going to tell the truth from now on. And the truth is, I want you."

At the admission, Ryan puts his laptop bag down hard on the table. "You know, it's not that easy, Lizzie. You really hurt me. A lot. I want to trust you, but I just don't know if I can."

"I understand," I say simply. "But you know, you didn't tell me the whole truth, either."

He looks taken aback. "Seamus told me everything," I say, sending my eyes toward the poster. He flinches.

"Oh. I don't—" He takes a deep breath. "I don't really tell people about that."

"But why?"

"Lizzie, you'd never understand, but I don't want to see the look of pity. I can't see it anymore. I had enough of that. I just want to put it behind me." He looks down. I draw his head up. We both look at one another, taking it all in.

"I'm sorry. I guess, I thought that you were just too good. I could never tell you."

"I'm not that good, Lizzie, trust me. I was pretty messed up after it all happened. Seamus has had to pull me out of the toilet on occasion." He catches himself getting lost in the memory and then straightens up.

We both look down for a second, hands in our laps.

"Do you think you could forgive me? I'll be here. Anytime. Not pregnant. You know. Available."

"I just don't know." He looks off to the distance.

"Ryan, you once told me that everyone deserves a second chance. You don't have to give me one and I'll understand if you never want to talk to me again, but I don't want to make another stupid mistake that I'll regret, so I'm asking for your forgiveness if you'll give it to me." I sit still. I've got to take my licks.

Ryan stares only at his hands, ringing them together. I gaze back at him, realizing the mysteries that connect us and the ones that tie us together full-circle are deeper and more mysterious than we'll ever understand. Why the mommy wars? Why meternity? Why breast cancer? Why divorce? Why do we continue to hurt one another? Whatever the answers are, I vow in this moment to never lie to Ryan ever again, if given the chance to be with him. The awareness seems to click as he moves his eyes up from his hands to my own. Still, there's grief. Long buried and new, mixing together, still simmering.

Then, out of the corner of my eye, I see Seamus has been watching the whole thing.

And then, the lights go down. I can't believe it. Karaoke night is starting.

He nods. I know what I've got to do. I walk over to Seamus who is holding the songbook, then bring it back over.

"What song do you want? I'm singing."

"Liz, don't. Please don't," says Ryan.

"That's it. Here I go…" Alanis starts up, and the familiar tune plays.

"A traffic jam, when you're already late. A no-smoking

sign, on a cigarette break. It's like ten thousand spoons when all you need is a knife…"

Ryan shakes his head.

"I have to," I tell him.

"You can't."

"It's like meeting the man of your dreams…"

"Oh, God, Liz Buckley. I can't let you do this alone," butts in Ryan, grabbing the mike.

"And then meeting his beautiful wife…" he sings out, looking at me, and thankfully, we finish the song together.

"You know I never got that song," he says. "None of it's ironic."

"I think it's about life…all of it is…" I say, as Ryan pulls me in and kisses me hard on the lips. And this time, I know it's for real.

Thirty-One

The next day—Saturday—I come into the office, trying to finish up all my work and, honestly, trying to put it all out of my mind. While I'm researching the state of maternal rights in the workplace, an email from Cynthia pops into my inbox. It's 7:30 p.m. and no one else is in the office besides us.

"Come over."

I shoot right over, worried. And from the look on her face, Cynthia can tell.

"Close the door."

I do as she says and sit down. She stares at me for what feels like five minutes, silent. Then she starts.

"Elizabeth. Alix's story idea is great, but it's not the total truth, is it, now?"

I look down, unsure of how to respond.

"I'll answer that for you. No. As for the fake pregnancy, I've known all along. Do you think I'd be so stupid to believe that over the course of six months, your plumpness would never so much as extend beyond the beautiful perfectly round orb on your waist? And that contributing editor film from Newport—that was just too much."

My heart feels like it's about to stop.

"One question," says Cynthia in an uncharacteristically soft tone, which surprises me. I'd have thought the first words out of her mouth would be in the form of high-pitched shrieking.

"Why did you do it?"

I'm not expecting this question and have no answer to give. Instead of thinking into the future or past for an answer, measuring my sentences or trying to control the situation, I find myself spilling it, words coming out on their own.

"I don't know," I start. "I was just so sick of, of, trying so hard, and seeing everyone else get rewarded. Of not being noticed. And of thinking all my work would never be read or appreciated. Feeling like the only ideas that were getting accepted weren't ones that I believed in. I mean, who needs to pay a thousand dollars for a stroller, or teach their newborn Cantonese or get matching Barbour jackets that they're just going to grow out of in three months anyway?" I am panting, but continue.

"I wanted to travel the world and find my voice, and write deep, meaningful stories that matter to women. I'm so sick of overthinking everything and worrying about pleasing everyone but myself. I did it because I thought that Alix and Jeffry were having an affair—but, really, I think it was because I felt burned out, and that I didn't care what the consequences were. I just knew that I needed to unstick myself any way that I could. I just needed a 'meternity.'"

By the end, I am out of breath.

"Are you finished?" Cynthia asks. My eyes, wet with exhausted tears, were staring down this whole time, and as I was saying this I wasn't even looking up to see her expression.

"Yes," I say solemnly.

"Look, what is it that you want? What do you *really* want?" Cynthia says. Again I'm a little taken aback. "I know the articles about thousand-dollar strollers are ridiculous, but that's what drives numbers. I actually thought you were enjoying writing the features. You were doing a great job on them and winning the awards that keep us in business."

I don't know where she is going with this, so instead of speaking, I think it best to let her talk.

"Look, Liz, when I was your age, I felt exactly the same way you did. We didn't have as many choices then or, God, even fifteen years ago. We were told that hard work and a cutthroat spirit would get us where we wanted to go. It was sold to me, too, that getting to the next step in your career would make you happy. Well, luckily it has for me—in a way," she says, taking a deep, long breath. "But I know it's not that way for everyone. I thought long and hard about all the ways I could fire you last night, but then I realized, I'd just be doing the same exact thing that was done to me—leaving a smart woman with no options."

I can't believe what she is saying.

"You've heard me say it, time and time again—what is the one thing I'm most concerned about, Elizabeth?"

"Selling magazines," I quickly utter, not even thinking twice.

"Exactly," says Cynthia in a measured tone. "So I plan to propose a deal. Write the story you just lived for the past six months—your experiences posing as a pregnant woman in an office where maternity may be rewarded or viewed as a detriment. Make it insidery, investigative, buzzy and most importantly, *award winning*. And of course, make it sell my magazine. Do that and you will have a future here as a features writer. Your name will be on the masthead as editor-at-large, contracted to write twelve investigative pieces on the latest issues to position us as the thought-leader in the motherhood space."

I cannot believe what I am hearing. I am going to be contracted to write one story a month, and probably make double my salary. I've got a special deal.

"They must generate buzz, and I will not keep you on unless the stories make me, and the rest of the general public, weep their sodding eyes out. I do believe you have it in you, Buckley."

"Thank you, Cynthia. But I have to ask—why aren't you firing me?"

"I think I've explained myself well enough in these past months for you to know the true answer to that question," says Cynthia, looking at me pointedly, her expression loaded with all the sorrow, hard choices and maternal pride she'd never allowed herself to reveal to anyone, let alone me. I decide not to pry any further, knowing some things don't need to be said outright.

"Thank you, then. I won't let you down."

"Of course you won't, Buckley. And I've alerted Discovery Channel about it, your friend Ryan Murphy—told him it was top secret, so they weren't allowed to say a word until now. I think it will make a great story for air, don't you?"

"Yes, of course," I say, turning to walk out, a single tear streaking down my cheek.

"Don't forget to empty out your cube."

I walk over to my cubicle and on my desk are three things: a split of champagne, a single Honey Cup and an envelope. I tear it open. The note is on Cynthia's signature gold foil-embossed letterhead.

Keys to the house in Marrakech. Call Mohammed to let him know when you're coming. Enjoy your 'meternity.'
—xo, Cynthia

A New Life

You know more than you think you do... Better to relax and make a few mistakes than try too hard to be perfect.

—*Dr. Spock's Baby and Child Care: 9th Edition*

Epilogue

I was running late to the airport, but I wasn't worried. I wanted to get the latest issue of *Paddy Cakes* with my story in it. I'd gone back and forth with Alix for the past month, making sure I got all the gritty details of the life of a pregnant woman in the workplace pitch-perfect. "Meternity: The Secret Life of a Pregnant Magazine Editor" was the first story in the well, and the biggest line on the cover. It had already made a story on the *Today* show, where Cynthia went on to talk about how *Paddy Cakes* represented the changing face of maternity benefits in the workplace. It was excellent PR for the magazine, and for the company as a whole. There was talk of my story being submitted for the national magazine awards in December, but at that point, I'd be in Phuket, lounging on the beach and developing the Fair-Trade Families app.

My Ray-Bans perched on the top of my head, I looked at myself in the taxi window as I slammed the door shut, grabbed my single roller bag, liking the feeling of my new "work wear": a leather motorcycle jacket, gypsy scarf, jeans and Pumas. The lines in my forehead had seemed to vanish overnight, and the golden streaks in my hair had come out after a weekend trip to Miami to write at Cynthia's house on Star Island.

I smile, thinking that I never expected things, especially the guy waiting for me at the bag check-in spot, to turn out this way.

"Why, hello, Ms. Buckley."

"Why, hello, Mr. Murphy," I say, looking at how hot my fellow traveler looks standing there at the terminal with his own backpack.

"Of all the terminals in all the airports in this city, you had to show up here."

"You know, I think this is going to be the start of a beautiful friendship," I say back.

"I think you're right," Ryan says, leaning in for a kiss before taking my hand as we take our seats on the last Air France flight of the night. We'll be touching down in Marrakech, but not before a few nights' layover in Paris. I rifle through my bag, this time sure I'll make it through security, the only sign of maternity-related materials is a pregnancy test—yet to be taken.

I think back to my treasure map analogy I made so many months ago before all of this started. Maybe somewhere between PH algorithms, cat-cubicledom, tiger momism and French, there was one other option that many women often neglect to realize: *meternity*, where you birth the exact life you want according to your dreams. It might take a miracle, but if you just jump right in, and you're honest about your wishes, eventually things will work themselves out in ways that you never could have expected.

★ ★ ★ ★ ★

Acknowledgments

It takes a constellation of love and support to write a novel. These are superstars in my universe: Emma Parry for firmly (and quickly) believing in the idea, Kathy Sagan (for championing it from the *very* beginning), and both for offering so much wisdom, guidance and hand-holding through a very looong "pregnancy"; Nicole Brebner and Margaret Marbury for seeing its initial potential and advocating behind the scenes; Shara Alexander and the Harlequin/MIRA publicity and marketing team for their standout support; Jonathan Sirota for his legal wizardry; Kate Lewis, Meredith Rollins, Jill Herzig, Jennifer Barrett, Ann Shoket, Ellen Breslau, Jane Chesnutt, Stephanie Abarbanel, Kristin O'Brien, Alyssa Giaccobe, Emma Sussman, Star and Eliot Kaplan for giving me every opportunity and teaching me all I know; Meredith Bodgas, Kristine Brabson, Lauren Clifford Knudsen, Anna Davies, Ava Feuer, Brie Schwartz, Allison Berry, Tiffany Blackstone, Hannah Hickock, Marla Horenbeim, Sarah Smith, Jennifer Conrad, Cari Dineen, Jennifer Rainey Marquez, Harry Marquez, Robb Riedel, Greg Robertson, Kim Tranell, Liz Perle, Joanna Saltz, Elisa Benson, Neha Gandhi, Carissa Tozzi, Raymond Braun, Bernadette Anat, Kelli Acciardo, Dan Koday, Julie Pennell, Annemarie Conte and Robyn Moreno for representing an embarrassment of riches in the work wives and husbands department; Ali Body, Sophie Gilmour, Jen Schrader, Marie-Elena Martinez, Stephen Lee, Serena Jones and Kristen Harmel for so much help and encouragement all along the way; Nicola Kraus for eleventh-hour lifesaving, cutting conviction and spy-like book notes drop-offs; Deborah Burns and Francis Cholle for breaking the mold when it comes to mentorship; Mariola Zaremba and Carolyn Swift for seeing the greater possibilities before I could; my Lost Girls Jennifer Brennan, Courtney Dubin, Holly Corbett, Julie Hochheiser Ilkovitch, Amanda Kreuser and Sheree Almy for more love, support and late-night karaoke than a girl could ask for; my always comedic, enduring and steadfast Hamilton crew, Sarah Henry, Carroll Lang, and Weatherly Hammond who inspired the whole thing when she said, "You need a *me*-ternity leave"; Casey and Greg Bates, Kristina Davidson, Katie Lombardi, Sondra Berger, and Kerri and Joe Basile for a lifetime of unwavering friendship; Alanis Morissette for granting permission for the use of song lyrics to her seminal (and personally very meaningful to me) anthems "You Oughta Know" and "Ironic"; Erik Sharkey for believing in me from the beginning and, finally, Pamela Foye for embodying *Giving Tree*–level strength, wisdom and unconditional love and for being the perfect mix of tiger and French (and Daniel Foye from the ether).

METERNITY

MEGHANN FOYE

Reader's Guide

MIRA

Why did you want to write a book about a single woman who fakes being pregnant?

It was born out of simple frustration, jealousy and burnout. When my three closest friends announced they were pregnant and would be taking the summer off for maternity leave, it almost pushed me over the brink! I was newly 31, had been working like a dog for the past 8 years and wanted a maternity leave myself.

Do you feel there's some injustice in the workplace for post-30 single women right now? How so?

Without meaning it, having a child is really the only excuse a woman can use to get out of regular working hours or to leave early. Single women don't have the same luxury and therefore can become the office "secretaries," taking on the extra work and little cleanup projects and finishing up when the mothers on staff have a hard stop. No baby = no excuse not to work.

Why is this moment a particularly tough time for women in the workplace in general? Single women and mothers alike?

After 2008, at least in New York, many of the support headcount were lost in favor of tightening up the bottom line—at least in magazines in New York. We all had to become our own assistants at work, then go home and take care of all the traditional "womanly" roles, as well. It's become quite exhausting and a new balancing act that we've never experienced before. Technology is supposedly the savior and meant to pick up some of the slack, yet I think we're all still realizing that apps have their limits and won't tuck your kids into bed at night.

Has fervor over pregnancy, babies and new motherhood reached a peak? How so?

Yes. As an editor at RedbookMag.com, baby headlines dominate our newsfeeds each morning. Mommy wars are raging online as women redefine all the rules of parenting. I like to say we're in an era of #norulesmoms as we analyze the fallout of our own mothers' parenting styles and have technology and social media providing us with way too much data. Now, all the old dogma is up for reinterpretation. And it's making us all a little nutty.

How has technology and social media changed the experience of pregnancy?

We have waaaay too much information at our fingertips as Fitbits and social media show us all the various ways we could be doing things differently. Everywhere we look, we see images of "perfect" moms from perfect Kate Middleton to sexy Kim Kardashian to creative lifestyle bloggers whose curated LA homes, stunning boho style and corresponding baby on the hip make it all look like it's easy to be fashionable, well-slept and a perfect parent all at the same time. And with articles flying in our faces about how there are #noexcuses to lose the baby weight, it can make you feel as though you're failing in every way.

How has social media changed things if you're single, but hoping to find love and have a family?

Well, if you're single, and 31, there's a funny turning point where a succession of love, marriage and baby carriage moments are thrown at you each day, making you hyperaware of all that you're missing. It can make you desperate and grasping, even if the men in your life aren't Mr. Right.

How has the media (print, online, blogs, social media) changed expectations for single women and mothers?

It's added on this extra set of expectations that were never there before. Now your choices are on view for all to judge and condemn with each and every "like." It's the difference between analog and hi-def parenting. It's actually probably creating a new form of trauma that we'll only start to understand in years to come!

What does Meternity mean for you?

It means a moment of space and time to stop and take a look at all the choices you've made that have led you to your current life, then taking a bit of breathing room to discover what it is that you really want out of life, love and parenting, and a moment where you get to decide exactly which choices are right for you going forward. It's the necessary "gap" moment that our culture desperately needs before moving forward with adulthood and all its responsibilities, including motherhood.

Do all women need a break before they decide to go on to the next chapter of their lives? Why?

Yes, Gen X are now burned out at 40, Gen Y are burned out at 30 and millennials are burned out by the time they graduate college. We all desperately need an Elizabeth Gilbert, Cheryl Strayed-style heroine's journey where we rediscover ourselves so that we can become the best parents we can be and end the cycle of heaping those expectations and unmet needs onto the next generation of children, as many of our parents, though well meaning, did to us as they were just struggling to make it through, rather than thriving.

What are the particular challenges for all women right now in balancing life, love, careers and the choice to become a mom?

When and how you will become a mother is the biggest choice we face as women, yet at this particular moment, there is a tremendous amount of stress placed on us by expectations set on social media, clashing with economic and work-life realities. It's easy to want to overthink it, yet it's the only area of our lives that isn't necessarily under our control. That fact can create a tremendous amount of underlying stress for women 25–45.

1. Have you experienced the office politics that Liz faces at *Paddy Cakes*, in which colleagues with children are given more flexibility, better work hours or less workload? Does this policy breed resentment among coworkers? Should it?

2. Is the action that Liz takes—to turn a misunderstanding into a fake pregnancy—illegal or just highly risky? Would you be tempted to do the same under the circumstances?

3. Liz says she is going to use her newly found free time to pursue more meaningful work, but instead she seems to become enamored with the idea of being pregnant. Do you think her fantasy about how motherhood would change her life is realistic? Is having a baby or being a mother essential to having a full life?

4. In your experience, is it harder today than twenty years ago for women to achieve a healthy work, life and love balance? Why or why not?

5. Do you think Tinder has had an impact on the way people date? Has it changed the way men in particular, but

women as well, view commitment? How else has it affected relationships?

6. Liz has trouble financially making ends meet, but she also chooses to spend money on such experiences as drinking, dining and clubbing with her friends. At one point she judges her life by the things she has not yet acquired. Is she being fair to herself? Is this a valid way to look at life?

7. Why do you think Liz has had trouble finding the right partner in life? Is she too fussy? Not lucky enough? Do you think chance plays a role?

8. If you had a chance to have a "meternity" leave, how would you spend your time?